CW01457596

HARE-CURSED

Thou Shalt Not Suffer a Witch to Live

© T M Creedy 2020

This novel was written under 'lock down', during the Covid-19 Corona virus global pandemic of 2020.

It is dedicated to all the people who kept the world turning – the medical staff, care staff, cleaners, supermarket workers, delivery drivers, public transport workers, pharmacy staff and everyone else who selflessly kept on doing their jobs in such uncertain and dangerous times.

Thank you – all of you – you are true superheroes.

CHAPTER ONE

Leah

London 2019

They kept saying I was lucky.

'She's lucky she turned her face away...' This from the paramedics who first attended me when I was scrabbling blindly on the cold pavement outside the restaurant, surrounded by a circle of curious on-lookers all filming my screams on their phones.

'She's lucky she was wearing her hair down; her fringe covered her eyes and shielded them from the worst of it...' This from the A&E staff who were busy holding me down on the gurney while they cut my top from my body. My favourite red top. Clingy, sexy and just a hint of sparkle, it was my go-to top when I was feeling good and wanted the world to know. Now it was in shreds on a hospital floor.

'You're lucky Mrs Walsh didn't get a chance to get closer to you. Only some of the acid she had in that cup actually hit you. If she'd had a clearer shot it would have been so much worse...' This from the police officers who came to the hospital to take my statement in the days following the attack. 'If Mr Walsh hadn't stepped in and grabbed her arm, she would have hit you directly in the face.'

Oh, well done to you then, Liam. Well done for grabbing your psycho wife's arm when she was throwing sulfuric acid at my face. Your psycho PREGNANT wife whom I knew nothing about.

Lucky, lucky, lucky me.

Jennet's Story

Jersey 1603

And who are you, come here to this miserable place?

A nun? Soeur Marie-Thérése - a nun come to give comfort to the damned, and hear their confessions before the hangman's rope tightens like a lover's embrace around their scrawny necks.

I am sorry. Forgive me Sister, forgive me for laughing. You should know that I have only ever been to church twice in my whole life, and both times I was chased away. I have never confessed nor been given divine forgiveness so for you to offer me this now is a waste of your good time, Sister. In any case a confession is only the half of it. A confession tells you the what but it does not tell you the why. For you to hear my confession I must tell you my whole story.

You do? I beg your pardon, Sister, I do not mean to laugh at you again. You truly want to hear my whole story, here in this filthy pit where your fine grey robes will carry the stink of gaol back to the nunnery with you? Here, where death stalks the floor and carries one of us off to hell each night, cheating the hangman of his penny?

Ah, Sister Marie-Thérése, you surely must have heard of me already? Oh, you are newly arrived from France. Is this your Godly work then? Is this what God calls you to do? I think it only fair to tell you, your good works may be better served by talking with someone else. See, over there, against that wall? That is Frances. He is accused of stealing a pitcher of ale. He is but a boy, and he cries for his mother each night. He has the fever now, and

4

will not last long enough to fear his hanging, and that is his blessing. Mayhap he would be a better soul for you to save, for I tell you, Sister, I have no soul to save.

Why do I say that? Sister, don't you know? Ah, get comfortable, Sister; as comfortable as you can on this floor of rancid straw and human filth, for my story starts from my birth nearly fifteen years ago.

Does the word 'witch' bother you Sister?

Hey-la and there you have it. I am pronounced a witch. Condemned to burn without prayers or mercy, my ashes scattered to the four winds and never my name to be spoken again.

This was always going to be my fate, if those who have known me since I was born were to be believed. One look at my face was enough to tell them that I was cursed and, when combined with my mother's sorry tale, I was ever on the downward path to Hell as soon as I drew my first breath.

My mother's story is well-known; told and re-told at the hearths of young women about to marry or to those who are newly wed, as a warning against the sins of temptation and gluttony. One day when she was late into her pregnancy with me and my twin brother, my mother was walking the cliff path on the north coast in the hope of finding some early blackberries. This was a fair walk for someone who was so near her time, but the temptation of the sweet juicy berries on her tongue compelled her to walk the four miles there and back. She was thinking about those berries, she would say in each pious re-telling, thinking about how good they would taste, how they would help to slake her thirst, for the day was hot and the path was dusty.

As she plodded along slowly, enjoying the cooling sea breezes, she put her foot down without looking and it landed upon a small pile of loose stones. The stones caused her to skid, and with her being so ungainly she was obliged to clutch at the prickly growth of the furze bushes on the sides of the path, or else she would have skidded onto her arse and caused us both to jolt in her womb. As she righted herself, her palms pricked and bleeding like Christ's own head when he wore his crown of thorns, she made another step onto the path and, at that moment - probably scared out of concealment by the sudden assault on her hiding place - a large black hare ran out from under the bushes and darted under my mother's feet.

As the hare sprung across her path and disappeared into the cracks and crags in the scrubby cliff, my mother screamed and fell, right upon her swollen belly, where she lay stunned and winded for some time. As far as bad omens go, seeing a black hare whilst with child was one of the worst. Having a black hare cross your path while pregnant was worse by tenfold. Everyone knows that a hare is a witch in her daylight form and by running across your feet she had marked your baby for her own. The child inside you would be cursed, there was no hope for Christ's grace or mercy upon it.

As my mother lay face down in the dust, she began to have pains deep in her womb and in her back. Pains that told her the babies were coming for Mme Le Brun, the old woman who helped at birthings and laying-outs, had already told her there were two babes to bear. My mother was all alone on the path still, and she could not stand without aid as the weight of her stomach and the birthing pains kept dragging her down again and again so that she had no choice but to give birth there on the ground amid the stones and dirt.

My brother was born first. He had the most perfect face, she would say, like one of God's angels made into flesh and blood. It is hard for her to remember this part without the pain of it showing plain upon her face but tell it she does. It is the hardest lesson she has ever had to learn and it is her Christian duty to tell others so that they might learn from it also. My brother's perfect face was not enough to not notice the rest of him. He had no hands nor feet, just withered stumps which he waved feebly a few times before being still and silent in her arms. He did not draw breath and his eyes would never open. As he died, she held him close, her perfect-faced boy, with the wasted limbs and the fine, thick black hair which covered every inch of his body from neck to ruined leg. Within the half hour I would come out next, slithering on a path of mucus and blood, following my twin brother into the cruel daylight. I came out roaring, already crying out my disappointment in the world, but with the right number of hands and feet and as pink and healthy as any babe had ever been born before me. I had a caul covering my features which my mother scraped off with her fingernails only to wish she had left it alone and had never seen the truth of my face. The sighting of the black hare had caused me to have a large cleft in my lip, which twisted right up into my tiny nose, exposing a hole in the top of my mouth which would never close. The hare-witch had marked me for her own and given me the features of her own daytime form.

I was hare-cursed.

I also had a large port-wine stain over my left cheek, exactly in the shape of a blackberry. It was a mark that would forever taunt my mother - put there by the Devil to remind her of her sins, and that she was the cause of my curse.

My mother admits to thinking of leaving me there on the cliff. Alone and naked, exposed to the elements, I would surely not last a night and a pure death would be a blessing to my cursed form. As she sat pondering this with me on the grass beside her, for she could not bear to touch me again, the wife of the farmer who owned the adjacent land came upon her on the path. Seeing the pitiful, lifeless form of my brother, and noticing the pink healthiness of my own limbs, she gathered me up in her aprons, clucking and rocking me.

'Don't touch it. She's cursed,' my mother said bluntly.

'Ach, I can see,' the farmer's wife replied. 'Was it a hare?'

My mother nodded. The farmer's wife sighed.

'Like as not, she'll not live long anyhow. With a mouth like that she'll not be able to give suck. Mebbe best for her to have the peace of Christ upon her as she goes. Why not take her home and get the priest to bless her afore she perishes.'

The farmer's wife gathered up the body of my dead twin, noticing his perfect face for the first time. 'God's mercy on you, madame, for you will know the pain of loss twice over.' And with that she helped my mother to her feet and, still swaddling me to her own breast, she aided her across the field to her farmhouse.

I did not die, as predicted. I did not thrive either, but I survived. Driven to madness by the loss of her babies and the pain in her breasts, she devised a way for me to feed from her, involving a scrap of rag which she would drape onto my open lips. My desperate hungry cries caused her milk to flow unbidden and as the rag became wet with it, it would dribble down into my angry red mouth giving me a little sustenance. As I grew a little older, I did indeed learn to suck but by then my mother could not stomach looking down into the twisted maw of my face so she gave me a rag soaked in goats milk and left me lying on the floor of our cottage while she went about her daily work. When my first teeth grew in, she would give me a pap of bread and milk to chew on, turning her face away when a good deal of it *dribbled out of my mouth and down my chin. With my prominent front teeth, I looked even more like a hare and I quickly learned that I was both a curse and a burden on my poor mother. My father, a great pig of a man, tried to persuade her to drown me in the slop bucket and call it a natural death. No one expected me to live anyhow so it would not be a cause for gossip if I succumbed at any moment. But my mother couldn't do it. She was a devout Calvinist and it was her firm belief that I was sent to her as a punishment for wanting something she should have resisted the temptation of.*

And so, I lived. If you could call it living. Reviled, unwanted, greeted with slaps and kicks if I did not move fast enough. The good folk of this parish of Grouville treated me with equal amounts of fear and superstition. They would spit at me if I was within sight and cross their fingers in the sign of the blessed cross as if to ward off the Devil. The first words I ever remember hearing were the words "Hare-witch" and they were words which would follow me all of my short life.

CHAPTER TWO

Leah

It was going to be our third date. I was going to sleep with him that night for the first time. All those weeks of delicious teasing and testing, the flirty emails, the suggestive texts; I had decided that tonight would be the night. We'd had two dates since matching on Tinder when his profile had made me laugh out loud. He'd described himself as "an honest bad boy" and went on to list his positive attributes as "fun-loving, funny, fun to be around". He was looking for true love, he said. He was tired of meaningless hook-ups and random sex with strangers. It should have made me swipe him away. I wasn't interested in men who made no secret of how much they slept around, but something in his words struck a chord. It WAS all so meaningless, this internet dating lark. The chances of being matched with someone who shared your hopes and dreams and values were virtually nil. The chances of finding someone with decent morals were even less. So, we started chatting and he did make me laugh, I admit. He was single, he told me, definitely single - had been so for ages.

Our first tentative actual meeting in the real world took place in an anonymous Starbucks. I was a carefully choreographed five minutes late exactly. I opened the door and he was stood at the near end of the counter, just two feet away. I burst out laughing. He was wearing a red carnation in the buttonhole of his Paul Smith shirt.

'I wanted you to see me straight away, as soon as you came in,' he said with a grin. 'And I wanted you to have no chance of sneaking away when you did.'

In fact, I had no thoughts of sneaking away at all. His profile photo hadn't shown the whole package, and I had the fleeting thought that I was probably one of very few women who didn't immediately feel a sense of disappointment when meeting a blind date for the first time. Tall and broad-shouldered with short brown hair and blue eyes twinkling with mischief, he was - as my mother would have said - "very nicely made".

We got on famously, talking long into the late afternoon. We shared a love of bad horror movies and TV shows about ghost hunting. We both adored red wine and good pasta, and hated peas and people with bad manners. Sitting across from each other in a tiny corner table, we smiled happily and foolishly at ourselves, both knowing that this was the start of something. Something wonderful, something magical and most of all, something very, very physical. When we finally parted with a simple kiss on the cheek, we had already made plans to have lunch together in a few days' time. He asked me to choose the venue so we went to my favourite Italian place, where the red and white checked tablecloths were plastic and the walls were hung with dark and dingy prints of Italian landscapes, but where the food was to die for and the wine list very reasonably priced.

Our second date was a tense affair. Texts had been flying between us constantly since our Starbucks date. Testing each other, looking for boundaries, asking awkward questions.

'What is this? What are you looking for?' I would text.
'I don't want to be hurt again,' he would reply.
'I'm not after a casual fling,' I would throw out there.
'I want to see you again,' he would say.

We ate Tuscan porterhouse and rigatoni flavoured with vodka sauce, barely tasting the sublime flavours and subtle seasonings of herbs. We drank a decent bottle of Sangiovese, both of us drinking far more and far more quickly than we usually would in order to cover up the

11

sudden shyness which had sprung up between us. We touched often, our hands brushed each other gently, his fingers light upon my cheek as he smoothed a stray hair away. Our eyes locked and we stared at each other in wonder. 'You,' we both seemed to say. 'It's you.'

We kissed goodbye in the orange glare of the streetlight outside my flat. He had walked me home, our hands entwined, both of us strolling slowly so we could make our time together last just a little bit longer despite the steady fine drizzle that was falling into the night. At my door, he traced the curve of my cheek with his thumb and pressed a light kiss upon my lips. I leaned into his solidness and the kiss deepened. He moved so his arms were encircling my waist and pulled me into him, the kiss going on and on and on until we were both breathless and laughing. A few more kisses and plans made for dinner the next night, we finally said goodbye and I let myself into my cosy, homely flat, where I lay alone in my bed and smiled into the darkness at the thought of what was to come.

All that day I was on a high. It was going to be perfect; I would make it so. I cleaned my flat to within an inch of its life, and put out the special Jo Malone candles that I only lit on special occasions. I made up my bed with fresh linen and arranged pillows and throws in what I hoped was an inviting way. I bought good wine, and everything we would need for a luxurious breakfast the next morning - bacon, pastries, fresh orange juice. I hoped he would stay the night, I assumed that he would want to. Once I was satisfied that I could do no more to enhance the scene of the seduction, I turned to myself. I scrubbed, exfoliated, plucked, massaged and moisturised every part of my body until I was pink and glowing. I already knew that I would wear my favourite red top that night so I just had to choose between my black skinny satin trousers which made my legs look long and thin, or my black pencil skirt, which was a bit office-y, but had the advantage of being able to wear stockings underneath along with the highest of my high heels. The skirt won. I imagined Liam's delight as I ran a stockinged foot up his leg under the restaurant table and shivered with lust as I pictured his hand finding my warm flesh above the lacy stocking top.

I phoned for a taxi. No way was I going to walk. My shoes were absolutely car to bar only. As I sat in the back seat watching the streets pass I felt the absurd desire to giggle, to bounce up and down on the seat with glee and to tell the silent taxi driver that I was going on a DATE! that would definitely, definitely end in SEX! later tonight. The fizzing in my stomach sent pleasurable shocks to my groin which intensified as we got closer to the restaurant. Liam was waiting for me outside, leaning casually on the wall next door. I waved as the taxi drew up and he rushed to open my door and take my hand.

'Hi, you,' he grinned and leaned in to kiss me.

'Hi yourself.' I breathed him in, he smelled divine. We looked at each other and laughed. We both knew that this was to be our night, the beginning of everything.

'Liam!'

We didn't hear her voice at first, we were too busy grinning stupidly at each other.

'Liam bloody Walsh, you fucking cheating scumbag!' This time the name registered and we both turned, still holding hands, to see a small woman with scraped-back hair and a hugely pregnant belly waddling towards us. She had a snarl on her face and was holding a large take-out coffee cup in her hand.

'Liam?' I asked quietly. He dropped my hand and touched my shoulder reassuringly.

'Stay here,' he said.

'Liam!' The woman shouted, the name ending in a wail. 'Liammmm! Why? You promised! You said there would be no more!'

13

The woman was sobbing now, standing clumsily only a few feet away. Liam walked up to her and whispered some words. I couldn't make them out but it was obviously the wrong thing to say because the woman shouted 'NO!' and pulled away from him, lurching awkwardly towards me.

'And you! You bitch! I'm his wife! Do you know he's got two fucking kids at home as well as this one on the way?' She gestured to her bump under her ill-fitting coat. 'Do you know you're just the latest whore in a very, very long line of them? Where did you meet him, eh? Online? Tell you he was single, looking for love, afraid of being hurt?' She was waving the coffee cup around wildly but the plastic lid stopped any spillage. 'He does that. He has a system. Do you know how many women there have been, just this year alone?' she hissed at me. I couldn't answer, of course I couldn't. I had no idea. I turned to look at Liam. He was grabbing at the woman's other arm, trying to pull her away from me. There was no mistaking the look on his face. Guilt - the look of a small boy who's been caught out doing something he knows is wrong. He caught my eye and shrugged apologetically. Liam, married? Liam, has kids? The woman, his wife, was still shouting at me.

'Did you think I didn't know about you? I knew he would bring you here tonight. He always brings them here.' She was fumbling with the lid on the coffee cup, digging her fingernails into the rim to ease it off. 'Well, perhaps now you'll think twice about fucking a married man!' She raised her arm, ready to throw the contents in my face. Liam grabbed her arm again and she stumbled slightly, overbalanced by her own pregnant belly. I turned my head and closed my eyes, my hair whipped against my face and I felt the cold liquid hit my skin.

At first all I could feel was the freezing coldness of it. I thought, oh, that's OK, she's only thrown cold coffee at me. I hoped it would wash out of my favourite top. Then I began

14

to feel the heat. I tasted it on my lips as it began to burn its way into my mouth. Metallic, toxic. My throat began to close up immediately. The heat intensified and I was on fire. My entire face was awash with flame. I could feel my skin shrinking and bubbling as the acid began to eat its way into my flesh. I screamed, loud and long. I clawed at my face, desperately trying to wipe the pain away. I didn't dare open my eyes which were burning as well. Falling to the ground I tried to cool my face on the cold concrete. It was only slightly damp but felt like heaven against the hell of my scorching skin. I was dimly aware of someone kneeling down next to me and talking to me calmly, trying to soothe me. Another splash of cold liquid and I recoiled, screaming again. I thought it was the crazy woman, Liam's wife, back to attack me a second time.

'Shhhhh, shhhh love. It's only water. It'll help stop the burning,' a kindly voice soothed. I lay on my side, whimpering in pain and fear, letting a complete stranger dribble water onto my face. The kindness of strangers. That's what was going through my mind at that point. I never did find out who he was, just that he was calm and steady with a gentle voice that I clung onto as the last light of consciousness left me as the shrill sound of emergency sirens filled the foggy night air.

CHAPTER THREE

I wandered in and out of consciousness, catching snippets of conversation around me.

'- Sulphuric acid attack.'
'- two clicks of Morphine,'
'- woman's been arrested.'
'Jesus, she's a right mess!'
'Leah, can you hear me? Can you open your eyes?'
'Leah?'

No way. No way was I going to open my eyes. They were still burning. They were still on fire.

'Leah? Open your eyes for me, dear. Just a little bit. Come on, try for me Leah.'

I sensed rather than saw the light of the small torch being shone through my eyelids. I felt a gentle tugging, two fingers, one above my right eye and one below. A sliver of white light slammed into my brain and I screwed my face up tight again. I couldn't feel most of it, the left side felt almost totally numb. Blessedly so. My throat was closed and painful and I was so desperately thirsty. I opened my lips to ask for water but instantly closed them again as I felt the different-ness of them, the total WRONGNESS of them. They weren't my lips; this wasn't my mouth - what have you done with my mouth?

'Shhhh, Leah, don't try and talk. There's been some damage to the area around your mouth, nose and lips. We've had to fit a tube into your throat while we assess the scale of your burns and to make sure your airways haven't suffered any long-term damage. Now that some of the swelling has gone down, I expect we'll be able to remove the tube very soon and you'll be able to have a nice, long drink.'

A squeeze of my hand. Whoever was speaking had warm, gentle hands that held mine firmly. I clutched at them, panicking, and beginning to gasp uncontrollably. I was fighting the tube in my throat, feeling for the first time the IV line in my hand and pulling against that too.

'Shhhh, calm down now, Leah. You're OK. You're going to be OK.' The warm hands soothed my fringe away from my brow. 'I know it feels weird right now, but you're in good hands. You just have to trust us. As soon as the tube is removed and you feel comfortable enough to open your eyes then we can start to talk about your injuries and, more importantly, your recovery plan OK?'

Injuries? Recovery plan? I had a banging headache and a dreadful thirst but the rest of my body felt OK. Apart from the pinching of the IV line, the rest of me felt normal. It was just my face that was wrong. It felt like I was wearing a cheap, plastic Halloween mask - one that had caught fire and had melted into my skin, sealing itself tightly and permanently onto my head. For the first time it began to occur to me that I wouldn't look the same as I did when I set out for that ill-fated date with Liam, with a bounce in my step and overflowing with confidence. I may never look the same. The words that the gentle voice had used came back to me over and over again.

I had INJURIES.
I had DAMAGE.
I had BURNS.

I had no idea what I looked like now.

It wasn't like I was stunningly beautiful before anyway but I thought I was decent enough looking. A good figure, made firm by walking to work every day and running up and down the stairs instead of taking the lift, and dark hair which I made more interesting with the help of the

17

occasional red rinse and some wacky coloured highlights. I had large, expressive blue/grey eyes which people often commented upon and good skin, courtesy of my mother, who only ever used Ponds cold cream and had the softest, smoothest skin I'd ever seen on a sixty-year-old. Sure, I fretted over the odd spot on my chin and wondered if those laughter lines around my eyes could, in fact, be technically termed 'wrinkles', but overall, I was doing pretty damn good. An attractive, moderately successful twenty-something who had her whole life ahead of her. I had a great job in marketing - well, OK, I had a great job working on the reception desk at a marketing company, but that didn't mean I wouldn't be able to move sideways into a sales role in the future.

The future. What future did I have now?

I thought about my friends during those long hours of hospital twilight. I had great friends, great groups of friends. There were my work friends with whom I went for lunch or Friday drinks. My old school friends, who admittedly were dwindling down a bit now as we all settled into our adult lives and some had invariably moved away, had families and dropped off my social radar. I had my family, and extended family, as my two older brothers had both found themselves life partners and began to have conversations about mortgages, school capture zones and "doing up the third bedroom as a nursery". With their girlfriends came a whole lot of new family members - in-laws, step-in-laws, cousins, aunts and uncles - people who swelled the numbers during our frequent family parties and then became family to me themselves. Would my friends stand by me? My family would, I knew. They had to; they had no choice.

I shivered as I pictured a future family gathering. Everybody talking to me slightly too loudly, determinedly not looking at my ruined face and treating me like an invalid with a terminal disease. I would be an object of pity, a subject to be talked about over dinner or afternoon tea. People would pretend not to notice, pretend not to see the burn scars but the truth would be in their sad, shocked eyes and in their over-bright voices. This would be my future from now on.

I couldn't even cry with that damn tube down my throat and my eyes steadfastly refused to well with the tears I wanted so desperately to release.

CHAPTER FOUR

After my throat tube had been removed and I was able to finally wet my parched mouth with water, sipped through a straw, I started to feel just a tiny bit better. I woke up one morning after a long dreamless sleep, helped by the sleeping pills prescribed to me by the ward doctor, and opened my eyes for the first time since the attack. Just a bit. Just enough to see the bright blue sky outside the hospital window. But it was enough to lift my low spirits. My eyes were OK. The acid hadn't touched them. My eyesight was fine. That was one worry I hadn't dared to voice aloud, that I had been blinded in one or both eyes by the attack.

Now that I could see, I took stock of my surroundings. I was in a small room on my own and for that I was profoundly grateful. I couldn't begin to fathom what my recovery would be like if I had been on a busy ward full of other curious patients and their goggling visitors watching my every move. There were a smattering of cards lining the windowsill. Bright images of flowers and cartoon animals bearing the words "Get Well Soon". There was a small locker next to my bed holding a jug of water and the glass with the straw. The room was bright, almost pleasant even. I noticed the grey plastic call button had been placed close to my hand and I pressed it down, hoping it would summon the nurse with the gentle hands and friendly voice.

'Hey there!' You're awake!' She bustled into the room cheerfully. 'How'ya feeling?' She checked the fluid bag on the drip stand and made some notes on the chart attached to it. Her blue name badge said Jayne.

'What do I look like?' I asked. My voice was rough, rusty from disuse. My mouth struggled to form the words and I could hear myself slurring. Even worse was the dribble of saliva that I could feel running down the side of my chin.

She glanced at me sharply, then her glance slid away.

'No need to think about that just yet. You've got a lot of healing to do.'

She fussed with the water jug and topped up the glass, handing it to me with the straw facing me. 'You just concentrate on feeling better.'

'Don't!' I said as loudly as I dared. 'Don't do that! Don't patronise me. Please, just tell me. What. Do. I. Look. Like?' I enunciated each word carefully and slowly, my mouth and lips not quite obeying my brain so they came out blurry and distorted. I could feel a sharp puckering and pulling with every slight muscle movement.

She hesitated, then came to sit on the side of my bed companionably.

'I probably shouldn't be talking to you about this. In fact, we've been told not to talk to you about this. But I can see how upset it's making you, so I'll tell you the facts - as much as I'm able to anyway.'

She took my hand in hers. Again, I felt its warmth and its strength and I was grateful to her for giving me something strong to cling on to.

'As you probably know, you were the subject of an acid attack in which undiluted sulfuric acid was thrown at your face.'

'By my boyfriend's crazy wife, I know. I had no idea he was married by the way,' I interrupted her, needing her to know that it wasn't my fault. 'Where did she get the acid from anyway? I mean, I know she must have been planning it, the way she tracked us to the restaurant and had the acid in that coffee cup, but isn't it hard to get hold of? Would she have had to buy it off the dark web or something?'

The nurse had been watching my mouth as I spoke, her brow furrowed in concentration as she struggled to understand me. Then she laughed. She had a pretty laugh which suited her. She was quite a big lady with blonde hair and pink cheeks and she oozed capability and compassion in equal amounts.

'Nah,' she said. 'You can buy it at any chemists for a fiver. It was probably a spur of the moment thing. She wouldn't have had to plan very far ahead. She just bought it, decanted it into an empty coffee cup so as not to raise any suspicions, and trotted along to the restaurant to confront you.' She plucked at the bedcovers with her fingers.

'Anyway, after she threw it at you - you were lucky, the husband had a hold of her arm so she didn't quite get to fling it at you properly - you collapsed on the ground. Someone at the scene administered first aid treatment to your burns by pouring water on them, and by doing so he probably limited the damage considerably. You were thrashing about, swiping at your face, which would have only succeeded in spreading the acid around even further and doing even more damage.'

That word again - lucky. How lucky I am, I thought bitterly.

'So, what's the damage? Truthfully, I mean.' I looked her in the eye and, to her credit, she looked back at me unflinchingly and with complete honesty.

'Your hair took the brunt of it, which saved your eyes, but you have damaged areas to your left cheek, your left ear and your lips and mouth.' She looked hard at me as she continued. 'You have a long, long road ahead. There will be months of treatment, possibly skin grafts and almost certainly a number of operations to help you regain full use of your mouth. All of this will take time. This is why we don't want you seeing yourself just yet - this is the worst you will look, right now, but you will look very different in a few months' time when the scars have healed.' She smiled. 'OK? Do you trust me?'

'OK.' It would do for now. 'Thank you. For your honesty, I mean.'

'No problem.' She jumped up off the bed with an easy grace that seemed at odds with her size. 'We're going to be seeing a lot of each other from now on. I hope we'll be friends,' she grinned.

'I'd like that.' I tried to grin back but my mouth just wouldn't work.

The first time they changed the gauze bandaging covering my burns, I vomited with the pain. The vomiting put pressure on the fragile skin surrounding my lips and mouth and I could feel the damaged tissues splitting and tearing, breaking down even further. The next time was no easier and I began to beg the doctors to knock me out. If it wasn't for Jayne's kindness and patience I wouldn't have been able to bear the pain, but at her insistence we took things ever so slowly, literally working on a millimetre at a time and resting in-between until gradually, moving with glacial slowness, the old gauze was removed and the new one strapped into place. I began to get bored lying in bed all day. My mother had tried to visit several times but interaction with other people was limited until I was considered past the risk of infection. Instead she sent me care parcels; sweets I couldn't chew, grapes which went mouldy in their plastic bag and bottles of fizzy Lucozade, which tickled my nose and made me sneeze, splitting my tender skin and making me drip blood on the pristine white sheets. Jayne kept up her constant stream of bubbly chatter and began bringing me magazines from the small hospital shop. They were the kind of ones where people write in with stories about how horrendous their lives are, like it's a competition over who's had the worst upbringing or the most horrific medical problem. Printed on cheap paper, they had lurid covers and boasted headlines like "My REAL father is a garden gnome!" and "I had a baby but then they had to chop off my head!" We would sit next to each other on my bed and laugh hysterically at all the gory, ridiculous details.
'Maybe I should send my story in?' I half-joked. 'It's exactly the type of thing they love - a jealous wife, a cheating husband, the poor, innocent girl caught up in the middle -

and look, it says they pay up to two thousand pounds for true stories!'

'Maybe you should,' Jayne nudged me. 'Not just yet, but when you're all healed up. You could even get them to do one of those "Then and Now" makeover whatsits. You know, how you looked before and how great you look after.' Jayne was always encouraging me to think positively. She brought me in magazine features on Katie Piper, the former model who was partially blinded and severely disfigured in an acid attack by her ex-boyfriend. Katie has undergone numerous surgeries to help repair the damage to her face and now appears on TV regularly as a presenter or advertising beauty products. Her face, while still bearing the scars, is completely beautiful and her smile is as wide and bright as ever. She went on to marry and have children, and still works tirelessly for her foundation, aimed at helping other people with body disfigurements. She is an inspiration, but I have a very long way to go before I will feel brave enough to show my new face to the world. I hadn't even seen it for myself yet.

CHAPTER FIVE

Jayne and I grew ever closer. She began to sit with me during her break times and we would talk and talk, putting the world to rights as good friends are wont to do. She told me all about her husband Matthew, and her two children, Alice - who is four, nearly five, and will be going to school soon, and Noah - her cheeky, chubby one-year old son. When Jayne first showed me some photos of them on her phone (strictly NOT allowed during her working hours but by then we were firm friends and I wouldn't have grassed her up anyway), I gasped. Alice was a little beauty, light blonde hair, beaming smile full of baby teeth but Noah, Noah was something else entirely.

'It's a haemangioma, a strawberry nevus,' Jayne explained. 'It's a type of birthmark, although it doesn't always appear at birth. It usually starts developing a few weeks afterwards, like it did with Noah.'
I stared at little Noah in the pictures. A dark red, raised blob covered a quarter of his face, from his hairline, down over one eye to halfway down his cheek.

'Poor little thing!' I said softly. Jayne snatched her phone away.

'No! Don't you say that! He's not a poor little thing at all. He's healthy and happy and has no idea that he looks a bit different,' she snapped. 'Anyway, it'll most likely fade away by the time he's ten.'

'Can you not do anything about it?' I asked tentatively. 'Can't it be removed by lasers or something?'

'No, it's a cluster of blood vessels all tangled up together so it would be impossible to get rid of it surgically, especially with it being over his eye. It's not painful, or contagious, and causes him no bother. It's a part of him, a part of our lovely boy, and I wouldn't change him for anything.'

'But...' I had to venture carefully. It was obviously a very touchy subject for Jayne. 'But, what about when he goes to school? Aren't you worried about the other kids teasing him, that he'll be bullied?'

Jayne sighed.

'Of course I am. Kids can be right little shits sometimes. But it's the parents who are the worst. I've already lost my place at the nursery for Noah before he's even started! Some of the parents objected to him being in the same nursery as their own kids - like it's catching or something!' she spat. 'Actually, I've found that younger children are the most accepting. Take Alice for example. A little while ago she asked what was wrong with Noah's face. Just like that, all matter of fact. "What's that on Noah's face, Mummy?" We sat her down and said it was just a birthmark and no, it didn't hurt him and no, she wouldn't get one too. And she accepted it completely. Never mentions it unless we're out with Noah in his stroller and she sees people staring at him, then she marches right up to them with her hands on her hips and shouts "It's just a birthmark, you know!". Right at them! I'm so proud of her.'

'She sounds like she gets it from you.'

'She does, I think,' Jayne agreed. 'Matt's so easy-going, he just lets everything flow over him. I'm a lot more sensitive. And gobby! I'll quite happily tell people when they're being ignorant twats!'

After some time, the doctors decided that it was time for me to leave the hospital. My face was healing nicely, they said, and I was no longer at risk of picking up an infection. I would still have to attend a lot of outpatient clinics, and I would have plastic surgery on my mouth in the future to try and stop my lips from twisting inwards even further as the skin healed. I still hadn't seen myself in a mirror. I think I thought that the longer I could put it off, then I wouldn't have to deal with it. My release from the quiet

26

safety of my room on the ward presented me with a whole set of new challenges.

I would have to let other people see my face. I would have to learn how to deal with the stares, the stifled sniggers, the whistles and the catcalls and the questions. And before I could learn to do that, I would have to learn to accept how I looked now myself.

On my last morning in the hospital, Jayne brought in a carrier bag of goodies from her home. With infinite gentleness, she washed my hair and blow-dried it smooth and straight, making sure it fell in soft flicks over my bad cheek. She expertly plucked my eyebrows. She made up my eyes with a touch of mascara and liner, not too much, and no eyeshadow. She wasn't about to turn me into a freakshow, she muttered. I laughed out loud. Only Jayne could say that I wasn't already a freakshow. When she pronounced herself finished, she said 'Ta da!' and whipped the final item from her carrier bag - a hand mirror.

'Are you ready?' she asked me gently.

I nodded and took a deep breath. It was now or never. In a few seconds I would see what the rest of the world would see when I walked out into the street this afternoon. I took the mirror's handle from Jayne and slowly turned it to face me.

I screamed.

'Oh my God! Oh my God! Oh no! Oh my God, no!' I started to gasp for breath. I couldn't draw in any air.

'Why didn't you tell me?' I screamed at Jayne, who was standing there with tears streaming down her face. 'Why didn't you say something? Why didn't you tell me how bad it was?' I collapsed on my bed, still gasping. The mirror fell from my hand to the floor and smashed into pieces. 'Oh no, no, no no, no nooooo...' I whimpered. 'Oh my God. This can't be happening. This can't be how I look.'

I looked up through my hair at Jayne who was trying to pick up the broken glass.

'Is this really true? Is this it? Is this the best they could do?'

'Leah, you have to understand.' I felt her sit on the bed next to me. 'The acid got into your mouth.' She went on gently, sniffling, still crying. 'It did a lot of damage in an area where the skin is especially thin and vulnerable, and where there are hundreds of tiny muscles that control the movement of your lips and mouth.'

'You should have told me,' I wept. 'You should have prepared me for this.'

'It's really not so bad....' She started helplessly but I cut her off with a snarl.

'Not so bad? I look like a RABBIT! A fucking RABBIT!"

It was true. The acid had eaten into my top lip and twisted it upwards towards my nose. I had a split from the centre of the lip to my nostrils and the lip had been drawn up and under, revealing my two top teeth underneath. I couldn't close my mouth over them and I looked like I was screwing up my nose to make a funny rodenty face as a joke. But it wasn't a joke. My face looked like a caricature of a rabbit, a cartoon, a child's drawing of a rabbit. But perhaps the cruellest cut of all was the shiny pink scar that covered my cheek. It was round at the bottom with two long thin upward strokes - one which just touched the bottom of my eye and one which leaned towards the bridge of my nose.

It looked exactly like the Playboy bunny logo.

Oh yes, I was just so damn lucky, wasn't I?

CHAPTER SIX

I sat on the orange candlewick bedspread that covered my single bed. My mum had had these same bedspreads ever since I could remember, along with the pastel colour-striped sheets. This used to be my bedroom, back when I was growing up. Now, it still holds my old bed, but it shares the room with mum's sewing machine, a dusty cross-trainer and a growing family of suitcases. The same full-length mirror sits on the opposite wall though, still with a couple of cheap costume jewellery necklaces that I must have decided weren't sophisticated enough for my new grown-up life in London when I eventually left home. I stared into that mirror for hours, locked into a trance almost. I sat on the bed, my hand unconsciously picking at the orange threads, and looked at my face, all day. I had been doing this ever since I moved back into mum's house in Tunbridge Wells three weeks ago.

When I first left the hospital, via a side entrance with a cardigan over my face like a celebrity or a criminal, I was determined to go back to my flat. Well, it wasn't mine, I rented it, but it was my space. Mine, just me. That's how I wanted it to be from now on - just me. Someone had been in during my time away, cleared out the fridge and thrown away the mouldy pastries that I had bought for mine and Liam's first post-coital breakfast. Someone, Mum probably, had made sure there was fresh milk, fresh fruit and a freezer full of homemade ready meals. Soups, cottage pies, stews with tiny, easy-to-chew pieces of meat - all thoughtfully made with my poor deformed mouth in mind. I still had trouble with solid foods; things like apples and crusty bread were definitely out. I still dribbled when I spoke, and food fell out of my mouth unexpectedly, so I tended to live on vitamin milkshakes and tea, drunk through a straw. Best diet ever.

I was encouraged by the number of cards and messages of support that lay in a tidy pile on my kitchen counter. Cards from friends, letters from charity support groups, and even a letter from the Katie Piper Foundation offering me advice and counselling if I felt I needed it. Details of my attack had briefly made the national papers and a lady from Edinburgh, a complete stranger, had set up a crowd-funding page for me to help with my everyday costs while I was getting back on my feet. There was a decent amount of money in the fund and I made a mental note to contact the lovely lady as soon as I could, in order to thank her. The kindness of strangers, again.

Missing from the pile of cards though, noticeably so, was anything from my work. The company I worked for was based in Hammersmith, a short tube ride, or twenty minutes' walk away from my flat, and I had been there for almost three years. I had thought I was well-liked, popular even, so I was surprised that no one had even bothered to organise a card signed by everyone in the office. It was what we did for people on maternity leave or when somebody left the company so it hurt a bit that no one had bothered to think to do it for me.

I drifted around my flat for a few days, blinds closed against the sunlight outside. Jayne phoned me every day. Mum phoned me every day. They both kept telling me to keep positive, that there was no reason why my life couldn't carry on exactly as before. They were proved wrong at the very first hurdle, when I ran out of milk.

My local shop was less than a minutes' walk away, on the corner of my street, and I had been popping in there on most days ever since I moved to London. I didn't know the staff there by name, nor did they know mine - London's just not like that - but we knew each other by sight and always gave a friendly nod or 'hello' whenever I went in. I dithered at home in my flat. I toyed with the idea of asking Mum or Jayne to get me a few bits and drop them off later but I wanted tea now, not later. I went online to see what supermarkets delivered but found out I had missed the same day delivery deadline, and they wouldn't be able to deliver until tomorrow. There was nothing else I could think of. If I wanted tea, I would have to go out and get the milk myself.

Even though the day was bright and sunny the weather forecast still predicted a cold wind so I had the perfect excuse to wear a big scarf, which I wrapped around my neck several times, and covered my face up to my nose. With my hair down and hiding the stub of my earlobe and the pink scar on my cheek I felt I was sufficiently concealed enough to not bring any attention to myself. It still took me the best part of an hour to pluck up the courage to open the door to my flat and peek down the road. There were very few people about, I noticed with relief. Eyes down, bag slung over my shoulder and breathing deeply into my scarf, I half-walked, half-ran to the end of my road and into the shop's front door. It was empty apart from one elderly lady perusing the pet food section, and the man behind the till. He looked up from the paper he was reading when the door's bell tinkled my arrival. I raised my hand in a wave and quickly turned away towards the fridges at the side of the shop. Milk, just a pint of milk, that's all. I can do this, I thought. I don't even need to speak to him, I can just hand over the money and leave, pretend I'm in a rush. I picked up a carton of skimmed milk and fumbled in my bag for my purse. Damn, I didn't have the right money. I would have to hand over a five-pound note and wait for my change. He rang up the sale slowly.

'One pound, twelve please,' he said. 'And how are you today? Not seen you for a while?'
I didn't want to speak. I could feel my scarf slipping away from where it was hiding my twisted lips. With one hand I held it in place and replied.

'No, ah, got a touch of flu,' I said through the material. 'Don't want anyone to catch it.' I gestured lamely to the scarf.

31

'Fair enough,' he said, and counted my change into my open palm. 'Eighty-eight pence and three pounds makes five.'

'Thanks,' I muttered and stuffed the coins into my pocket. Turning around with the milk in my hand I felt the scarf snag on something, the corner of the Perspex lottery scratch card stand. To my horror, the man behind the counter lifted his hand to help free it and before I knew what was happening the scarf had fallen away from my mouth, leaving my deformed face exposed to his view.

'Fuck me!' he muttered, mouth open in shock. I don't think he meant it. 'Sorry love, I mean, I didn't know like...... fucking hell, what happened?' He was still staring at my scars.

'Um, an attack,' I whispered. 'Acid.'

'Oh, fuck a duck, you poor thing. Did they catch the bastard?'

'Yeah. She's been arrested anyway.' I tried to twist my lips into a brave smile but he winced and hissed between his teeth. The old lady, clearly sensing something interesting was happening at the till, came bustling over

'Oh my Gawd! Look at you, you poor, poor girl!' She came right up into my face and squinted hard at my mouth. 'Is it permanent?'

I was feeling sick. I could feel the panic rising up in me, breathing shallow, heart racing.

'No.....um.... they, the doctors, think they can make it look a lot better. With time.' I added.

'Well, I should think so!' the old lady barked. 'Never catch a husband looking like that! You look like a rabbit!'

'Um....excuse me.... I have to....' I fled the shop, feeling the tears running down my face and the saliva pool uncontrollably in my mouth and slide down my chin. I ran home and slammed the door. With shaking hands I called my mum.

'Mum? Mum, can you come and get me please? I want to go home.'

Jennet's Story

Jersey 1603

Are you faring well, Sister?

Yes, I will continue.

I must have been nearing my seventh year when my mother did something I had never seen her do before. She stopped working.

My mother usually worked from sun-up to sun-down, lighting the fires, baking the day's bread, cooking the main meal, cleaning our hovel as best she could with a rag and water drawn from the well. She was busy all through the day and never had time to rest. As I was small for my age, I could not as yet take on some of the heavier chores she had to do. I couldn't manage to lift the heavy washing as it came out of the soapy tub, nor could I lift more than a half pail of water, let alone carry it down the hill to our house. I tried to be a help to her but was usually met with a push or a slap and told to go outside and let her alone. My uselessness was often commented upon by the man they called my father and my mother did little to defend me.

'She can help me with the cooking now,' she would say in a voice that betrayed her impatience and revulsion of me. 'There's no strength needed to shell peas or stir the pot.'

I could do these little things for her but I could not skin a rabbit or knead bread with any competence so I was put to sweeping the hard-packed dirt on the floor, and tasked with keeping the firewood stacked by the hearth, which I gathered from the floor of the woods nearby.

On this day I was sitting at the rough-hewn table, picking over some early blackberries I had found near the

33

churchyard. The berries were not yet ripened and the ones I shoved greedily into my hungry mouth were bitter and dry on my tongue. My mother had never eaten a blackberry again after the day of my birth but, for some reason, they were my favourite. She stood by the hearth adding lumps of greening turnip, foraged from the sides of the farmer's field after dark, to the stew pot. I looked up from my berries as she gave a sigh. Then she stretched her back, turned from the fire and came to where I sat silently, looking up at her curiously. She reached out once as if to stroke my hair. I pulled away. She had never touched me with kindness before. Her hands were always slapping and pinching, pulling my hair or poking hard into my skin. She stopped just before she touched the tangled mess of black hair on my head.

'What could have been, if not for that cursed hare,' she murmured, not to me but to no one in particular. She spoke above my head, still unable or unwilling to look at my ruined face. 'Jennet, I am going now. Your life won't be easy without me here to shield you but, with God's grace, it will be mercifully short. Try to follow the righteous path, Jennet, for the Devil himself waits to claim you as his own daughter.'

I remained silent. I knew not how to reply. What did she mean she was going now? She was Mother, and Mother was always here, in the cottage. She looked at me a moment longer before turning away and moving over to the settle bed where she slept with my father. She sat down. I watched as she lay down on her back and crossed her hands over her stomach. She breathed in deeply once, twice. Then......... nothing. Her chest remained still. Her eyes lay half open.

A long minute later I opened my mouth in astonishment as I saw her soul sit up, leaving her earthly body lying motionless on the bed. It was see-through and hazy but it was definitely my mother. I could make out her greying hair and her worn, patched gown. The shadow floated upwards and moved towards the small square window set into the thick wall.

'Mother? Mother? Mama!'

I clambered down from the bench and ran to catch up with the wispy form, which was almost level with the window. There was no glass in the square. We could not afford such luxury, but there was a worn piece of linen nailed to the wooden frame which served to keep out the worst of the draughts and driving rain. The form seemed to dissipate, like smoke, through the small aperture and then it was gone, leaving me alone with the body that had once been my mother cooling rapidly on the bed beside me.

Do you believe me Sister? Do you believe I saw my mother's soul ascend to Heaven? You believe in the immortal soul, do you not, or else you would not be here trying in vain to save mine? If you believe in the immortal soul, is it not so hard to believe that there may be people who can see it?

I sat next to her for hours, waiting to see if she would come back and my mother would sit up again, declare herself starving and bustle over to the stew pot to check on the daily meal. I sat there until the stew pot boiled dry and a rancid smoke filled the tiny cottage. I watched as the long evening shadows passed over our faces. My mother's face was already sunken and grey, her lips beginning to pull apart, exposing blackened teeth in a rictus grin. How could she have left me? How could she have just lain down and died? The ill-fitting wooden door to the cottage banged open behind me and my father lumbered into the room. He stank after a long day working in the fields and with the pigs on the farm.

'Girl, what'cha doing there?' he shouted at me. He always called me Girl. I don't think he even knew my name. There was no love lost between us.

'Mother's dead,' I stated baldly.

35

'*Dead? She can't be dead. She was all right this morning. What've you done to her, you Devil's whore?*' *He rolled over to take a closer look. He had spent many a year as a seaman and the rolling gait had never quite left him. An accident with some cargo had left him with a crushed leg and put an end to his seafaring days. He limped badly now but his brute strength enabled him to work as a farm labourer for Monsieur Chevalier at the big house. His first love was the sea, and he never recovered from the bitter blow of having to become a land worker. Monsieur Chevalier owned the cottage we were in also, and it was fit for neither people nor pigs.*

He peered at the body on the bed. Disbelief settled over his blunt features, making him look even stupider than as was normal for him. He poked at my mother's shoulder, then grunted in annoyance.

'*Damned woman can't up and die. Who's to look after my needs now?*' *he asked. I didn't answer him. There was no grief in his face, just irritation.* '*Up and fetch the Connétablé,*' *he said to me.* '*Don't want them saying it's an unnatural death. I'll not be taking the blame for this, it's you they will be looking at. You and your witching ways!*' *He raised a fist and clouted me on the side of the head.* '*Go!*' *he shouted.* '*Fetch them here but I won't be paying for a leech man, mind. Just need 'em to say she's dead proper and ready for the communal pit. You'd better fetch old Ma Le Brun as well. She can be doing the laying out an' all.*' *He stomped over to the water pail and poured a ladle of fresh water over his head and neck. Noticing the burnt remains in the charred stew pot he aimed a kick at my retreating backside as I skittered past him and out the door into the lane.*

'*An' get me some dinner on the way back! I can't be working my fingers to the bone and then come home to no meal, ya lazy bastard!*'

Forgive me, Sister. My language offends you.

I ran all the way to the parish church, where the Connétablé had his office to the side. There was no answer to my timid knock so I ran around to the main church doors, which were propped open with shafts of wood. The priest was there with a boy I didn't know. They both stared at me – a small, ragged child with birds-nest hair and a dirty hare-cursed face - and I gulped back my fear of other people to stammer out the news that my mother had died.

'Name?' barked the priest.

'Jennet,' I muttered, staring at the ground.

'Speak up, girl! And address me properly!' The priest slapped me across the face with the back of his hand. I stared at him, silent and mutinous.

'I know who she is, Father!' the boy piped up, in a clear high voice. 'She's the daughter of the man who sees to the pigs on my father's farm. His name is Pyke, sir.'

'Pyke?' The priest looked at me as if I were verminous which, in all fairness, I was. 'Yes. I know of the man. You say your mother is dead?' He asked me loudly and slowly, as if I were an imbecile. I managed a small nod. 'How did she die?' he asked me, again as if talking to an idiot.

'She just lay down and didn't get up again,' I whispered. 'Sir.' I said, just in time to stop another blow to my cheek.

'Hmm. Well. I suppose I had better come and see for myself.' He moved to the doorway, his robes flowing behind his corpulent body. The boy had been staring at me, hopping from foot to foot in his excitement at there being a dead body to go and see. As he rushed to follow the priest, he brushed past me and grabbed a hank of my hair, tugging hard.

'Hare-witch!' he hissed in my ear. 'You're a witch and an abomination and I'm telling my father. He'll throw you out, or get you burned at the stake!'

That was my first meeting with Matthieu Chevalier.

CHAPTER SEVEN

Leah

The doorbell went, downstairs, and broke into my trance. I looked at my watch. I had been sitting on the bed for over four hours. The sounds of Jayne's bright voice carried up the stairs and I heard Mum's equally bright reply as she let her in. For the past weeks, Jayne had made a point of visiting me whenever her shifts at the hospital allowed it. At first, she brought me books and articles on other women who have been facially disfigured and gave me pep talks on "getting back out there" and "living your best life". A phrase I came to detest. Then, when this didn't pull me out of my self-imposed isolation, she ordered me to stop feeling sorry for myself and to pull myself together. Other people had injuries far worse than mine so who was I to wallow in self-pity? I did nothing but shrug at all her attempts to shake me out of my pity-party for one, and she finally gave up, spending her days off sitting next to me on the couch as we stared dumbly at the monotonous reliability of daytime TV. Jayne's husband, Matt, worked for himself and liked to be at home in the early afternoons to spend time with their children before heading back off to work for a few hours in the evenings after Jayne got home. It meant they didn't see much of each other but it also meant that the number of hours Alice spent at nursery was affordable. A nurse's salary and a self-employed builder's wage didn't go a long way with two kids. Today, however, I heard the unmistakable sound of a little girl talking loudly followed by the shout of an excited baby. It seemed Jayne had brought the kids with her today. She'd never done that before; I wondered, why now? As I clumped slowly downstairs, I could hear Mum exclaiming happily over the two children. Alice was telling her about a doggie she had seen from the car on the way here, and Mum was replying with absolute fascination, her conversation peppered with 'Really?!'s and

38

'Well I never!'s. I peeped around the door frame and Jayne caught sight of me straight away.

'Leah! So sorry to dump this on you but Matt's been called away on family business so I'm taking a few day's leave from work to stay at home with the kids. I didn't think you'd mind if we popped in for an impromptu visit.....?'

'What's 'promptu, Mumma?' Alice came up behind Jayne and looked at me. I'd not met her kids before, nor Matt, but I'd heard so much about them I felt as if I'd known them since they were born. However, Alice had not seen my face just yet and this would be the first time since coming to live at Mum's that someone outside of my family and Jayne had seen it. I braced myself for the shock, maybe tears of fright, but Alice came dancing up to me and grabbed my hand like I was a favourite friend.

'Hello. My name's Alice. What's yours?' She grinned up at me and swung on my hand. 'Mummy said I'm not to be cheeky about your face but now that I've seen it, it's not nearly as bad as I thought it was going to be.'
She studied me closely.

'Bend down so I can see properly,' she demanded. I did so, holding my breath as she lightly traced the outline of the burn mark on my cheek with her index finger before lifting my hair so she could see the wrinkled nub of my ear. She nodded to herself as if it was what she had expected all along before finally moving her finger along to my mouth and touching my deformed upper lip with determined gentleness. She stepped back, grabbing my other hand in hers and swinging both of our arms playfully.

'You know what?' she asked. 'I think you look so cool. I'd love to look like that. Mum, can I look like that too?' she asked Jayne, who shook her head no. Undeterred, Alice wittered on. 'Rabbits are my favourite animals, well, rabbits AND hares, and you look like a hare and I think that it's just soooooooooo cool!'

I couldn't help it. I laughed with delight. And relief. Jayne and Mum started laughing with me and Mum went forward to take Noah out of Jayne's arms.

'Who's this handsome chappie, eh?' She cuddled Noah to her, her eyes taking in the large red birthmark but she never once showed one ounce of pity or shock. It was at that moment that Jayne fell in love with my mother. And I fell in love with Alice.

Later, sitting in the lounge with cups of tea and a packet of digestives, Jayne and I watched out of the windows as Mum played happily in the garden with Alice and Noah. Poor Mum. None of us kids had made her one wish come true and given her grandchildren yet. She had lived a lonely life since we lost my dad a few years ago to a heart attack at fifty-four. He was tinkering with the lawnmower in his shed when it happened, and the coroner had told Mum that the attack had been so massive, my father had been dead before he'd hit the floor. Mum tried to keep busy, with her tennis club and her volunteering for various charities, but she was still waiting to be a granny, waiting for the good news so she could knit and sew and make the spare (my) room into a grand bedroom for the grandkids. Well, sorry Mum, but you're going to have to look to your sons for that - I can't see myself in a baby-producing relationship, not now, not ever.

I turned to Jayne.

'So where's Matt gone?'

'Jersey,' she said.

'Jersey?' I repeated. 'As in, the Channel Islands?'

Jayne nodded, taking another mouthful of tea.

'I didn't realise he had family connections to Jersey'

'He was born there,' she explained. 'But his parents moved to London when he was about Noah's age. He's still got some elderly relatives there - which is why he's been called back. A great-uncle about to peg it apparently, and he's asked Matt to go and see him before he dies.'

'Bit weird,' I said. 'Or are they close, Matt and the uncle?'

'Great-uncle,' she corrected me. 'And no, they've never met. So you're right, it is a bit weird, but Matt's like that. Can't say no to anyone. We were going to go as a family, you know, take a few days break and make it a bit of a holiday but his great-uncle said no, it was just Matt he wanted to see.'

'Weirder still,' I frowned. 'Maybe he wants to see Matt because he's his only living relative and wants to bequeath him his massive mansion and his even massiver fortune before he goes,' I grinned, making light of the subject. Jayne laughed.

'I wish!' she said. 'Property on Jersey goes for mega-bucks. That would solve all of our money problems for life. But, no, I'm sure it's just the sentimentality of an old man wanting to see his great-nephew for the first and last time. Anyhow, changing the subject, have you given any more thought about what you're going to do with your life, you know, now that you're unemployed and all?'

I rolled my eyes. It was a sore point with both Jayne and my mother. Soon after I arrived at Mum's I went through the anger phase of my recovery. Well, I could hardly do denial and I was a long way off acceptance - anger was a good one for me to really get my teeth into. I fired off a vicious email to my employers asking why no one had bothered to get in touch out of courtesy and, no - don't bother your arses about me now, I was handing in my notice, effective immediately. The almost instantaneous reply I got from the Human Resources department was one of intense gratitude. Seriously, I could almost see them all in the boardroom exhaling with relief that I had given them a way out of keeping my job for me. Yes, they bleated on about intending to find me a new job role "in the back office", meaning out of sight, but they respected my decision and would pay me a month's salary in lieu of notice as a goodwill gesture. I stuck two fingers up to their goodwill gesture. Of course they didn't want me back, not on reception anyway, not anywhere. Who would want their clients scared off by the staff member with the disfigured face? That left me jobless.

I also made myself homeless too. I just didn't see the point of paying rent on my London flat, not when I wouldn't be earning a wage any longer. I gave notice to the landlord and guilt-tripped my brothers into going up there and packing up my stuff. The furniture all came with the flat so everything I owned fit into a few boxes and some suitcases. It was now all crammed into the spare (my) room with me until I figured out what to do.

'I mean, it's great you have the money that people donated to you through that crowdfunding page....' I just knew there was a 'but' coming. '..... but, that money was given to you in good faith, to help you get on with your life. It wasn't meant to provide you with a way to stay hiding in your mum's spare room for the rest of your life.

'MY room,' I corrected. 'And it's not for the rest of my life. I just need to figure out what kind of life I have now. In all seriousness, what chance have I got of getting a good job now, eh? In what kind of industry? There's no career out there for someone like me.'

'Defeatist,' Jayne scoffed at me. 'There's plenty you could do. You could work in a call centre...' I huffed my disdain for call centres. '.... you could start your own business and work from home, you could become a housekeeper or a nanny for someone and live-in.' She ticked off my many opportunities on her fingers. 'Or you could just get over yourself and get out there. Once people have seen your face they'll get used to it and they'll be like "oh, it's no big deal. Leah's a lovely person and she's good at her job!"' Jayne folded her arms across her ample chest and glared at me. 'OK. Let me tell you something. As a friend.'

When someone said they were saying something "as a friend", you can guarantee it's something you're not going to want to hear.

'Leah, you are fast becoming my best friend and I'm thankful that your accident brought you into my life...'

'Wasn't an accident, I was attacked,' I said mutinously, and under my breath.

'WHATEVER!' Jayne soldiered on. 'But you are using your scars as an excuse. They're really not as bad as you think they are. The longer you take to realise that and take the steps to build a new life, the harder it will be. OK, so it's not what you had planned for yourself. Get over it! Two kids and a crippling mortgage is not what I wanted for me either, but I'm getting on with it. Life is hard. It's not fair and it has a habit of kicking you when you're down, but it's the only one you're going to get, Leah, so get off your lazy arse and DO SOMETHING WITH IT!' These last few words were delivered with hard taps to my head with the magazine she was holding. We glared at each other for a minute before bursting into giggles, which became big belly laughs and then we were both keeling over, crying with laughter until we could no longer breathe. When the hilarity had subsided we lay next to each other on the floor.

'But you know I'm right.' Jayne always had to get the last word. And she was.

Now that Alice had so sweetly broken the ice between us, I started spending more and more time with Jayne and her family. I was invited round for dinner at least once a week and mum encouraged me to go at every invite.

'I'm fed up of you moping around here all day, getting under my feet,' she would tell me gruffly, but she meant it kindly enough. I met Matt for the first time, briefly, when he was rushing out to price up a job. Jayne must have warned him because he didn't stare, he shook my hand

43

warmly and looked me in the eye with a broad smile on his face.

'At last! I was beginning to think she was having an affair and that she'd made you up as a cover story!' he laughed. Jayne poked him in the ribs.

'Oi! You should know I'm too old, too tired and too fat to have an affair!'

She quite often made remarks about her weight like this. Disguised as poking fun at herself, she would describe herself as fat, obese or 'a whale in a blonde wig!' It was only when you looked closely at her face when she was saying such things that you could see the sadness and shame in her eyes.

We sat down to a takeaway in front of the TV when she had put the kids to bed. I was slowly increasing my solid food intake. Living with Mum, she made it her job to provide me with easy-to-eat but nutritious meals. I ate a lot of soft pasta and soup, and I was managing fairly well with the special fried rice we were sharing now.

'So, how did Matt's trip to Jersey go?' I asked.

'OK. A bit odd, she said.' Jayne chewed on a chicken wing. 'His great-uncle is in a care home until, you know, the end, and he wasn't making a lot of sense. Kept on telling Matt that he had to come home to Jersey, carry on the family line.'

'And is that an option?'

'No! No, no, no. There's no way we could afford to live there. I could get a job in the hospital easily enough but Matt would struggle getting work I think. Still, it is supposed to be a beautiful place. Lovely beaches, year-round sunshine. I'd love for the kids to grow up somewhere like that.' She put down her plate and turned to me.

'Matt's uncle did say something else a bit weird though,' she said. 'He kept calling Matt by the French version of his name - Matthieu - and saying "she" wanted him to come home.'

'Who's "she"?'

'No idea. Matt said it didn't make sense. Anyway he's Matthew, the English spelling, not the French way.' She shrugged it off. 'The delusional ramblings of a sick old man, I suppose.'

It turned out to be anything but the delusional ramblings of a sick old man. Jayne called me in a flap one day a few weeks after that conversation.

'Leah!' She sounded breathless. ' Can I ask you for a huge, huge favour?'

'Of course!' I said brightly. 'What do you need? A model for the cover of Healthcare Weekly magazine? Advice on what colour your next ghoonghat should be?' I had taken to wearing the brightly coloured Indian headscarves at all times. They were made from the softest brushed cotton, came in a myriad of jewel-like colours and best of all, they draped over my head and covered most of my face. With them on, I had managed to summon up the courage to accompany Mum to the supermarket twice a week. She had talked me out of buying a full burqa, which I thought was a brilliant idea at the time.

'You are not a Muslim woman!' Mum had hissed. 'It would be an insult to their culture.'

Jayne laughed at my joke now.

'No, no, although when I need that advice I'll know where to come. Can you look after Alice and Noah for me? For like, a few days, and overnight?'

'Ummm, I guess so.....'
Jayne had never asked me to babysit the kids before. She and Matt never went out. They couldn't afford it.

'Oh, you lifesaver!' she gushed. 'Matt's Great-Uncle Pierre died yesterday. We're all going to Jersey for the funeral, me and Matt and Matt's mum and dad, but we don't think it's right to take the kids.'

45

'Fair enough. How come you're going too? I thought you'd never met the man?' I wondered.

'I haven't. But the old man was quite specific in his last lucid moments. He wanted us there because he's left Matt something in his will! Isn't that great? We might get a nice little windfall, maybe enough for us to have a nice holiday, take the kids to Disneyworld or something.'

'Yeah, great!' I echoed. 'So what time do you want me there and for how long?'

'We thought we could leave on Thursday night - there's an eight o'clock flight from Gatwick. The funeral's on Friday and the reading of the will is to be straight afterwards, at the wake. So we should be back on Saturday or Sunday, depending on which day works out cheapest to fly back.'

'OK. What if I come over late Thursday afternoon? Will they be all right with me looking after them, the kids?'

'Oh yeah, they'll be fine. I'll leave you a few notes to help you, otherwise Alice will have you convinced that chocolate ice cream is perfectly acceptable for dinner and that her bedtime is midnight!'

'Fine, OK then. I'll see you Thursday!' I hung up, feeling strange. I was needed, I thought, I was useful. It had been a long time since I had felt useful and it felt good.

It was some time later that evening that it occurred to me that Jayne had never once mentioned her own parents. All those conversations, both in the hospital and since, when we'd talked about everything under the sun and I'd never heard her say 'My mum.....' or 'Dad says.....'. If both her and Matt, and Matt's folks, were all heading to Jersey, and she'd turned to me to ask for help, then maybe they weren't in the picture. I raised the subject with her when I borrowed Mum's little Fiat and drove to their tiny, two-bed terraced house on Thursday afternoon. We were having a quick cup of tea while the kids played with big Lego on the floor. Alice was doing a great job of building a wall whereas Noah was having a great time bashing one brick against another and shouting 'Bah!' at the top of his voice. He was just about walking, standing and wobbling on bowed legs as he grinned at us, delighted at his own cleverness.

'He can walk a few steps. He just takes after Matt in that he's too laidback to bother.' Jayne held her arms out to the chubby toddler. 'Noah, come on. Walk to Mummy, Noah!' Noah just went on bashing the bricks together, giving up on the effort of standing up and thumping down gently onto his bottom.

'You never talk about your own family,' I said to Jayne. She immediately stiffened.

'Nothing to talk about. I grew up in care,' she said shortly.

'Oh, sorry. I didn't mean to pry. I was just wondering.'

'Yeah, well, I didn't do too badly, did I? Good career, my own home and a family to raise.' She half-smiled. 'Sorry, I can be a bit touchy about it. You never really get over the rejection of your parents not wanting you.'

'Is that what happened?' I asked gently.

'I was signed over to Social Services when I was only a little bit older than Noah is now. They couldn't cope, apparently. I don't remember anything but being at the children's home. It's true, you don't miss what you never had, I suppose.'

'Well, you're more than making up for it with these two. I've never seen someone so devoted to their kids!' I rubbed her shoulder gently. 'Are you sure you trust me with them for three whole days?'

'Yeah. You'll be fine. Alice loves you, she calls you her "rabbit Aunty" and keeps asking when you'll be here next.' I smiled. It didn't sound like an insult when it came from a not quite five-year-old.

'Well, if I get stuck with anything I can always call my mum. She's itching to get her hands on your offspring! They're her surrogate grandchildren.'

47

'You're so lucky. Your mum's so great.' Jayne said seriously.

We waved them off in the taxi and I carried Noah back into the house while Alice skipped up the steps in front of us. Jayne had left me a long list of instructions. Tea at 5.00pm - vegetable pasta bake, in the fridge all ready to re-heat - then bath and bed for Noah at 6.30pm, followed by Alice at 7.00pm. 7.30pm at the very latest. Alice had pre-school in the morning, so I just had Noah to look after until we picked her up at 2.30pm. It all went swimmingly well until I went to turn out the light in Alice's room.

'Aunty Leah?' she whispered. 'Does your face still hurt you?'

I sat back down on her bed, her teddies and stuffed animals making a big pile around her.

'Well, it doesn't hurt on the outside anymore,' I said, wanting to be honest with her. 'But it still hurts in here sometimes.' I pointed to my heart, 'and in here,' pointing to my head. She smiled sadly at me.

'Noah's face doesn't hurt him on the outside, but I think it will hurt him on the inside when he gets older too.'

'Maybe,' I said truthfully. 'But you'll always be his big sister, and as long as you and your Mummy and Daddy all love him, then I'm sure he'll be fine.'

'Yes, and if anyone stares or laughs at him I'm going to beat them up!' she said seriously, in an angry voice. 'So if anyone stares or laughs at you, you just tell me and I'll beat them up too!'

I smiled and gave her a big hug.

'Thanks, little bunny.' My pet name for her. 'I'll hold you to that one day.'

I had a blast that weekend. It had been such a long time since my life had any structure or purpose and looking after Alice and Noah, following Jayne's many pages of written instructions to the letter, kept me so busy that I barely gave my own desolate life a thought. As well as making sure they were adequately fed and clothed, I bustled around the little house throwing washing into the machine, tidying the kitchen work surfaces and running the Hoover over the carpets, marvelling at how much mess two small people can make.

I made sure we had fun too. We walked to the park to play in the playground and look at the ducks on the lake. I would still only go out with one of my Indian scarves draped across my hair and face, but in multi-cultural London, no one ever gave me a second glance. Back at home, we made forts in the lounge using the cushions from the couch and the covers from Alice's bed. Noah chuckled in delight, shuffling on his bottom into the covered den and playing peek-a-boo with both Alice and I from inside his hidey-hole. On Saturday night I made popcorn and we all snuggled up, cosy in our pyjamas, to watch Frozen again for the umpteenth time, singing along at the tops of our voices. Both of them were fast asleep on the couch when my phone rang with a call from Jayne.

'Hi, everything's fine. They're both still alive,' I joked.

'Oh my God, Leah, you're not going to believe what's happened!' Jayne squealed down the phone.

'Oh my God, what?' I asked, thinking that maybe she'd messed up their flight bookings and weren't flying home tomorrow as intended.

'Matt's Great-Uncle Pierre - he's only gone and left us everything!' she screeched.

'WHAT?'

'I know! All of it, his farmhouse, some land and everything else he owned.' She was babbling in her excitement. 'It caused a right stir at the reading of the will. Matt didn't realise he had so many relatives on Jersey still; they all turned up hoping for a piece of the pie but it all got left to Matt. I can't believe it! A whole house, worth millions!'

'So what are you going to do with it?' I said, getting caught up in her elation. 'Will you sell it, do you think?'

'I have no idea. We've barely had a chance to take it in so we haven't discussed it. Matt's going to stay on here for a few days but I'll be back tomorrow as planned. The lawyer for the estate is going to show him around the house on Monday, and there's tons of paperwork and red tape to go through before we even get the keys.'

'Oh Jayne, that's so exciting! I'm so pleased for you both. Just think, you might be able to give up work and become a lady of leisure, swanning around your big house in your designer wardrobe!' I teased.

'Oh my God, I just can't believe it,' Jayne's voice had a wobble to it. 'It's like winning the lottery or something. I haven't stopped shaking since we were told. I can't believe we've been so lucky.'

'You deserve a bit of luck,' I said firmly. 'I can't think of two nicer people who could use a lucky break.'

'Aw, thanks Leah. It all seems a bit surreal at the moment though. Kiss the kids for me and I'll see you tomorrow.'

Jennet's Story

Jersey 1603

Hey-la, the sun still rises each day and now we have a new king. Old Queen Bess has gone to the Devil still claiming her virginity and leaving no English heir to inherit the throne. The new King has been King of the Scots for a long while but now claims the English crown for himself, and we are bound to him and his laws as we were bound to the old English court. We are late hearing the news as it takes time for it to reach us on our lonely island but I hear the guards above our heads talk of it as they fling open the grate to throw down our daily portion of hard, black bread and water. The water is stale and has more than a touch of brine to it as the well is dug so close to the sea, but it is drinkable. The bread I do not touch. The guards here make sure I am given the hardest baked end of the loaf and I could as much gnaw on a piece of granite stone than I could tear off the smallest piece and swallow. I have no vessels here, no cup or bowl, so I cannot even soak the bread in the salty water to try and ease my hunger. It matters little. Soon they will come for me and my death will be a most welcome release.

Sometimes I move, as far as I am able to in my chains, to the far wall of the oubliette. The old stones of the castle have many gaps that let in the wind and damp but that also let me press my nose to the cold wall and smell the fresh air straight off the sea. Sometimes I am lucky and I can see a glint of sunlight through one of these cracks, see the blue water sparkling like jewels over the channel to France. The calls of the seabirds echo all around us and remind me of how it feels to be free and I do smile. For I have a secret, Sister Marie-Therése, one which I have kept to myself even whilst I was enduring the trials by cross, fire

51

and water. My own secret to hold, deep down inside my belly, it lies quietly in the dark. For now.

Yes, Sister, my hands still pain me but I do not like to talk of it just now. Thank you Sister, a salve would be very welcome. It is the irons, you see. They chafe against the skin where the boiling water and fire burned my hands and wrists.

After my mother's death my life became a lot harder. My father expected me to see to all the household work she had once done and my days became a drudgery of lighting the fire in the morning, baking bread and cooking the daily meal, as well as fetching the water from the well. I was still a child, thin and underfed, and it soon became apparent that I was not able to keep house like my mother had. My father found a woman from the nearby village of Gorey to come in every day and she soon took my mother's place in my father's bed also. Madame Gouyet was a lazy slattern, and she had little interest in cooking or cleaning and even less in caring for a hare-cursed brat like me. I became even more ragged, my hair was a knotted mass of black, thick with dirt and bits of twig and leaves. I only had the one dress and no apron, and I never took it off, not even to wash, so I began to stink as badly as my father did after a day looking after his pigs. As I was not of much help to Mme Gouyet she declared to my father than I was to shift for myself - she wasn't going to slave to feed me as well. My father agreed and the same day they turned me out of the cottage to sleep in the lean-to barn, attached to the grain store a few paces away. If I continued to fetch them firewood every day, then they would provide me with a piece of bread in return, but no more. I was not to live with them again.

The rickety wooden lean-to became my home. It wasn't warm for I had no fire, and it wasn't dry as the rain came through in all places. I made a bed as best I could from some mouldy straw and a patched blanket I had stolen from the trunk that had been my mother's before she wed that fat pig. I foraged for food, and stole what I could from the bordering fields but with no fire I survived on raw vegetables and sour apples, taken from the old apple trees in Monsieur Chevalier's orchard. Sometimes I begged from the cook at the big house. She would answer the door to my timid knock and, more often as not, fetch me a bowl of fresh milk to drink and some soft bread to eat. She always crossed herself and made the sign of the evil eye before I left. As I had been doing all of my life beforehand, I survived. But I did not thrive.

CHAPTER EIGHT

Leah

Once the taxi had deposited Jayne on her doorstep and she had spent a good fifteen minutes hugging and kissing her children to death, we settled down at the kitchen table with cups of tea to discuss their good fortune.

'I still can't believe it,' Jayne said over and over again. 'I had a quick look in the Jersey paper at property prices and, my goodness, houses can go for millions over there. I know places in certain areas of London can cost an absolute fortune but this is on a different scale altogether. Matt said he'd email photos of the place as soon as he could. I can't even begin to picture what it might be like.'

'Did you get a chance to speak to Matt about what you might do with it?'

'Only briefly. The lawyer said something about there being a lot of covenants and clauses in the will, so we might be restricted in what we can do.' Jayne took a sip of tea. 'Bloody hell Leah, you should have seen the faces on Matt's relatives when the will was read out. We had an entire room of strangers glaring daggers at us. Apparently, they seem to see Matt as some kind of outsider, even though he was born there, and they looked at me as if I was a gold-digging floozy! There's one cousin in particular, he seemed to think it was all going to go to him.'

'What about Matt's mum?' I asked. 'Did she mind? I mean, the great-uncle was from her side of the family so maybe she was expecting it to go to her.'

'Nah, Linda's not like that at all,' she said. 'She was thrilled for us. Matt's family history goes back hundreds of years. They can trace it back to practically the middle ages. She's just pleased that her grandkids can be a part of that family history too.'

'I can't wait to see it!' I said excitedly. 'I've never known anyone who's inherited a whole house before. You said something about getting everything else as well?'

'Well, yes, there's some land, a few fields I think, that adjoin the house. And we get everything inside the property. The will said "All chattels, interiors, everything in-situ and all its entails", or something like that anyway. I don't remember the actual wording and the will was written in French. We did ask for a copy of the English translation so the lawyer's working on that too.'

'Wow, so you don't just get a house, you get everything in it too? What if it's stuffed full of priceless antiques? You might be multi-millionaires!'
Jayne sighed happily.

'Just the money from selling the place would be enough for us. We could sell this place, pay off the mortgage and get something bigger. I suppose it would be our responsibility to sort through what's in the house first. There might be some family pieces that we could give to Matt's cousin, sort of soften the blow a bit.'

Saying goodbye to Alice and Noah, I left Jayne to it. Although the kids were happy to have their mother back they were still upset when I told them I had to get back to my own house.

'I don't want you to go home, Aunty Rabbit,' Alice cried as I cuddled her on my knee. 'Why can't you come and live with us? Mummy won't mind.' I caught Jayne's eye as we both tried not to giggle. I rocked Alice gently.

'That's a lovely thought, sweetheart, but I have my own home to live in. My mummy will be lonely if I'm not there - she's all on her own. I'll be back to see you in a few days' time, OK?'
Noah looked at me with big, sad eyes and held out a piece of rusk to me as a parting gift.

'Thank you, sweet boy.' I kissed his face, accepted the soggy biscuit offering and surreptitiously passed it behind my back to Jayne, who took it from me and deposited it in the bin. 'Don't forget to phone me as soon as Matt sends you the photos,' I reminded Jayne. 'I want to see this mansion of yours.'

'Oh, I will,' she said. 'You just wait - it'll turn out to be a wooden shack in a field or a rusty caravan.'

'Yeah, right,' I scoffed, hugging her briefly. 'Or it might turn out to be a chateau or a flipping castle with solid gold floors.'

'No one's that lucky,' she told me.

A few days later I was back at Jayne's kitchen table, pouring over the photographs of their ancestral home on her laptop.

'Bloody hell!' I muttered as Jayne clicked through picture after picture. The house was enormous. It was a solid, no-nonsense structure, square and blocky. Consisting of two rectangular wings set at a right angle to each other, it was built of the local granite with neat rows of sash windows in perfect symmetrical order. Two stories high, or two stories plus additional attic space as the large dormer window high up in the tiled roof suggested, it looked nothing like the simple farm house we had both been imagining. There was something quite unlikable about it though, I thought. It was as if it had been designed by a child; a door in the middle, windows on either side, pitched roof with a chimney stack on top. It squatted in the middle of a large scruffy garden, surrounded by huge trees. The driveway had once been neatly covered with gravel but now it was choked with weeds and there was a large circular feature in front of the house, again made using the Jersey granite. It had a big stone wheel in the middle of it and looked like it may have had a functional purpose, some kind of mill or press perhaps.

'This is all yours! Has Matt been able to find out any more about it?'

Jayne had lost some of her sparkling giddiness. She looked tired, and her face was pinched with dark shadows under her eyes.

'Yes, unfortunately.'

'That doesn't sound good,' I said.

'It's not that it's not good,' she replied. 'It's just that it's not what we expected.'

'I can see that,' I said, gesturing to the screen. 'It's far bigger than I thought.'

Matt had tried his best to get the whole house in one photo but even at an obvious distance away, he still hadn't managed to capture it all.

'For a start, we're not allowed to sell it. Out of the question, according to the man handing over the estate. The house has been in Matt's family ever since it was built in the mid 1500's and we're only the custodians, he says, until we pass it on to our heirs and they pass it on to theirs and so on and so on, forever.' Jayne's voice was heavy with disappointment.

'OK, so that's a non-starter. What about renting it out?' I offered. 'Surely you're allowed to do that?'

'Not in the state it's in at the moment,' Jayne said. 'Even though Matt's great-uncle lived there his whole life he only occupied a small part of it. He never married or had children. Sometime in the 1970's it was divided up into flats and bed-slash-sitting rooms, known as bedsits; nine units in total, and rented out but they've all been empty for the past fifteen years or so as well.'

'So,... if you spruced it up a bit you could rent the flats out again?' I asked. That didn't sound too bad. I don't know what the rental market was like in Jersey but having money coming in from nine flats would surely add up to a decent income.

'The place is in a mess, Matt said.' Jayne tapped her fingers absently on the table top. 'Whoever converted the place did a proper cowboy job of it. Flimsy stud walls, dodgy electrics, cheap fixtures and fittings - Matt says that

57

the flats as they are wouldn't meet any of the required building regulations these days. And, ... oh Leah, I could hear it in his voice when he called me today, Matt's fallen in love with the place. He's already visualising how it could be if we renovated the property back to one big manor house, as it was when it was built. He wants to do the work himself.' Jayne covered her face with her hands and let out a sob. 'He wants us all to move there. To Jersey. To live in the house while he does it up.'

I put my hand on her shoulder and rubbed it, trying to comfort her.

'But what's the point of that? If you can't sell it?'

'That's what I said but he won't listen. He's talking about how grand it will be when it's all finished. I have no idea where he thinks we'll get the money to restore it from. I told him there's no point living in a big, fancy house if we can't afford to put food in the kids mouth's. But Matt's stubborn. When he makes his mind up - and I think he already has on this - there's no changing it.'

I sat silent for a moment, letting Jayne cry. They were tears of tiredness. Too much had happened to her in such a short time and she was overwhelmed by it all. After a minute or two, Jayne sniffed and sat up, wiping her eyes with the back of her hand.

'Anyway, this won't get the baby bathed, as my old matron used to say. Matt's coming home tomorrow so we can talk it all through then.'

She called me late the following day.

'It's all decided,' she said dully. 'We're going. We're moving to Jersey.'

'Oh my God Jayne, Matt only got back today. Why has it all been decided so quickly? He's not bullied you into it or anything, has he?' Even as I spoke the words I knew it was not in Matt's nature to be a bully. He was the most laid-back guy I'd ever met and he adored Jayne and the kids to bits. He wouldn't force her to do anything she wasn't happy about.

'No, of course not. It's just that ..... it's ..... he put it all so reasonably, I couldn't argue. I couldn't find fault with his plans. And it does all make sense, both financially and for the kids' sakes. We move to Jersey this summer, Alice can start school there in September and I can work part-time hours at the hospital while Matt works on the house. With me working reduced hours and Matt at home all day we'll have loads of time to spend together as a family. No more tag-team parenting. And Jersey's so safe, there's very little crime there and almost zero violent crime, it's a great place to bring up a family.' Jayne sounded desperately like she was trying to convince herself, and not me, of Jersey's charms. 'The beaches are beautiful,' she went on, 'and it's only an hour's ferry ride to France. Matt's right; we can have a great life there with no mortgage hanging over our heads.'

'What about paying for the work to the house? You said you were worried about that,' I butted in.

'My salary will cover some of it. Matt thinks there may be a local grant available to help with restoration projects to historic buildings. The Grange is quite an important house in Jersey's history so I'm sure we'll be able to get some help from somewhere. And besides, we've still got the gargantuan task of clearing the house out first. There might be some things we can sell to help with the bills.'

'The Grange? Is that the name of the house? Seems a bit tame for such an important place. And not very French.'

'Yes, I thought that too. According to Matt, the locals call it Harewich House for some reason. I think I like that a bit better. Maybe we can change the name back when we get there.'

59

So it was all arranged and they threw themselves into their plans for their new life in the Channel Islands. They rented out their little house in Shoreditch to cover the mortgage payments on it and they packed up all their furniture and belongings, shipping them over to Jersey, before driving down to Portsmouth to catch the slow car ferry over the channel. They had aimed for June but, due to some last minute hold-ups and a mistake over Jayne's notice period at the hospital, they didn't actually make it over until the beginning of July. I spent their last few days in London drifting around their house like a lost spirit, offering to help with the packing but clearly getting under Jayne's feet. I already felt lost without Jayne and I would miss the kids dreadfully.

Mum and I were getting on each other's nerves all the time, living in the same house. She just couldn't understand why I hadn't moved on from the acid attack and forged myself a new life. Preferably somewhere else, away from her house.

When the day came to say goodbye, both Jayne and I were in floods of tears.

'Promise you'll come and visit when we're settled?' she asked, hugging me long and hard.

'Of course I will.' I told her. 'Just try and keep me away.'

I hugged Matt briefly and then both Alice and Noah much more tightly. Alice had taken the move in her stride, no doubt won over by the promises of beaches and all the ice creams that she could eat, and was excited to be finally going. They piled into their car, every inch of it crammed with boxes and piles of bedding. Smiling bravely, I waved and waved as they pulled away until they turned the corner at the end of the road and were gone.

CHAPTER NINE

For the next few weeks or so, I went backwards. Without Jayne and the children to break up my week, I had nothing to look forward to and I retreated back into the shell I had created when I first left the hospital. Mum and I tiptoed around each other, coolly polite when we did meet in the kitchen or on the way to the bathroom, but it was clear that Mum had reached the end of her tether with me. She kept leaving the local paper lying about for me to find, with red rings circling around the job vacancies and flats available which she thought might be suitable for me.

I had a phone call from the police sergeant who was investigating my attack out of the blue one day. Liam's wife - Marianne, that was her name - had pleaded guilty to all charges which was good news, he said, it meant I wouldn't have to give evidence in court. I was thankful for that small mercy but he went on to ask me if I could write some kind of victim statement, an open letter to Marianne telling her how the attack had impacted on my life.

'We're also going to show photos of you before and after the attack,' the sergeant said. 'We've got some from the hospital of how you looked when you were first admitted but it would really help our case if you could send me a photo of how you look now.'

The last thing I wanted to do was to take a selfie. I tried talking my way out of it but he was very persuasive.

'We want to get the best result possible for you,' he said 'and that means getting her the maximum sentence. We're asking the court for a minimum of twelve years. Now that she's had the baby she will be able to serve out her sentence in custody.'

The baby. I'd completely forgotten that Liam's wife had been heavily pregnant when she threw that cup of acid at me. Who would look after the baby if she was in prison, I wondered. What was Liam doing in all this? I never did hear from him again after that night. Not a card, not even a text saying sorry. His wife had ruined my life, no, HE had ruined my life by pretending to be single and making me fall for him. Suddenly I wanted him to see what his lies and irresponsibility had done. I snapped a few photos on my phone making sure to include a few close-ups of my mouth so he could see the way my lips twisted up and inwards. I took pictures of my ear, puckered and deformed, and of my cheek, with its comedic Playboy logo scar marring my skin. I took photo after photo, my face serious and sad in all of them. I just hoped he would be there in the courtroom to see them and realise just how badly he had let me down. I emailed them to the police sergeant and told him he'd have my victim impact statement within a few days. I wanted to really take my time and put down the exact words about how Liam's selfishness had ruined my life. I had had so much potential, the world was indeed my oyster, and I had gone from being on the cusp of having everything to my world crashing down to nothing. My life was now limited to the rooms within my mum's house, the highlight of my week being a trip to Waitrose.

I texted Jayne regularly. They were having a battle getting Wi-fi installed in their new house but as soon as it was up and running Jayne promised to email me photos, and to Skype me once a week so I could see Alice and Noah. There was just so much to do, Jayne said, what with getting Alice ready for school in September, applying for nursing jobs at the Jersey General Hospital and generally finding their way around the small but baffling island. They hadn't realised just how expensive things were there; food especially was way more than what they had paid at home and just little things like figuring out the complicated parking system and learning that they had to register with the local government in order to apply for jobs meant that what they thought were small things became much more complicated.

Jayne sounded harassed in her texts. She complained about the state of the house constantly. They were living in the biggest flat, the one Matt's great-uncle had lived in before being moved to the old people's home. It was run-down and shabby with very little in the way of mod-cons, Jayne said, and every room was packed full of Uncle Pierre's junk. Boxes and boxes of broken china, dead clocks, calendars years out of date fought for space alongside towers of yellowing newspapers and furniture full of woodworm. She and Matt had spent the first two days moving everything into one of the empty bedsits next door just so they would have somewhere to sleep. She sounded exhausted already and they had only been there a few weeks. I tried to text her positive thoughts; that it could only get easier. Surely when Alice was at school all day it would free Jayne up a bit more. I asked if they had been to one of the beautiful beaches yet. Jayne responded with a single 'No.' I asked if she wanted me to come over and help. My phone rang instantly. Jayne was sobbing and laughing at the same time.

'Oh God, yes please, yes, yes, all the yes in the world! When can you come? And how long can you stay?'

'I'll get a flight tomorrow if I can,' I said. 'It's not like I have anywhere else to be. And I really miss you guys. It makes sense to be there and helping instead of just hearing about how hard it is and how much there is to do. Besides,' I went on. 'I'm dying to see this house you've been lumped with!'

Jayne sniffed and let out a wet snort.

'Ha! Don't get too excited. Matt's determined to do all the restoration on his own, well, as much as he can anyway. The place is in such a state it'll take him fifty years just to clear the rooms! But seriously, Leah, if you could stay and help for a while that would be a Godsend. I'm on the list for bank staff at the hospital and they are offering me shifts but the problem is I don't have much advance notice of when I'll be working so we can't make plans for childcare.

63

It will be better when Alice goes to school and there's just Noah to think about although we've been looking at the cost of nursery places over here and it's extortionate! I'd be working just to pay for Noah's fees. And I know he'd never say it but Matt's already beginning to resent having to look after the kids when I'm working - it's like he can't bear to be dragged away from his precious house!'

'It's probably just the excitement of having such a massive project, and it being all his,' I soothed. 'He just wants to throw himself into it and crack on, I get it. But listen. I'll look at flights now and text you the details. Will one of you be able to pick me up from the airport?'

'Yes, of course. That's one thing about this place I suppose. Everywhere's close to everywhere else. The airport's only about fifteen minutes away.'

We hung up and I felt a glow of anticipation. Matt and Jayne needed me. The children needed me. I pictured myself arriving at their place to rapturous hugs and kisses, rolling up my sleeves and taking charge. I'd help Jayne, take the kids off her hands to free her up and maybe I could help Matt as well. I quite fancied sorting through boxes of old stuff, looking for treasure, and I could lend a hand with the demolition work too. Just give me a sledgehammer, let me picture Liam's guilty face and stand back!

The flight over was easy. It was a clear sunny day and we hugged the south coast all the way before nipping over to hug the French coast for a while. I stared down at the miles and miles of sandy beaches from the plane's tiny window. It was less than an hour's flight; I hadn't realised the Channel Islands were so close. I'd never really given them much thought before. I picked up the in-flight magazine and read a little of the information on the islands. Jersey was a crown dependency I learned, although it was self-governed and had its own treasury, meaning it printed its own money although it was still in pounds sterling. It was small, only nine miles long by five miles wide and had a long and turbulent history, having been bitterly fought over by the French and English for centuries. Its principal exports were Jersey Royals, the small sweet new potatoes that fetched exorbitant prices in the supermarkets each spring; Jersey cows, which were famous the world over and various other agricultural products. It was famous for being an offshore finance centre, for the eighties TV series of Bergerac and for being the birth place of the famous actress (although she was probably more famous for being the then Prince of Wales's main shag) Lilly Langtry, 1853 - 1929.

I was wearing one of my colourful headscarves; this one with a paisley pattern in reds and oranges. There was only one low point in my journey so far and that was when I was asked to remove the scarf for the security camera at the passenger checkpoint at Gatwick airport. I knew I had to do it, it was the law, but even so, the look of pity and disgust on the security guard's face when he saw my scars made my stomach sink. I imagined him describing me to his colleagues later in the staff room.

'Yeah, you should have seen her. Poor bitch looked exactly like a rabbit.'

I had to undo the scarf again just before I went through to the gate but the mumsy-looking woman barely gave me a glance. She just mumbled the gate number at me and avoided looking at my face again.

Now, as the plane began its descent I felt excitement rise up in me again. The pilot swung around in a big arc and I saw my first glimpse of Jersey as we flew over the island from the east. Patchwork fields, sparkling seas and, as we got lower, big pastel houses with swimming pools in their gardens. It looked like a peaceful paradise and I just knew my life was finally beginning to look up.

Matt greeted me in the small arrivals hall. He gave me a quick one-armed hug but I noticed his smile didn't quite reach his eyes.

'Leah, thanks so much for doing this,' he said as he took my case from me and we walked out of the hall into the bright sunshine. The air was clean and clear after polluted old London, and a slight breeze ruffled my scarf and lifted it away from my head, as if the wind wanted to see what I was hiding underneath. I could smell salt from the sea straight away and I breathed in deeply, cleansing my lungs of the stuffy, plasticky smell of the airplane. Matt threw my case in the back of his car.

'I know Jayne's been finding it harder than she thought it would be,' he said, leaning over to push the car park ticket into the machine at the barrier. 'But, to be honest, I feel like she's not really given it a chance yet.' He turned left and we passed green fields and wooded hills.

'She can't see what I can see,' he went on. 'We're in a beautiful place with a great big house we own outright, the kids can grow up safe and happy, get a good education and imagine this as their playground!' He gestured to our right, where we were driving alongside the prettiest beach I'd ever seen. White railings topped grey concrete walls as they framed a huge half-moon shaped bay, golden sand leading to clear blue sea. The beach stretched into the distance where I could make out the slightly more built up vista of the main town, St Helier.

'No problem, Matt. You know I'm happy to help. Jayne has been sounding kind of stressed though. I hope me being here will cheer her up.'

'Yeah, well, don't think you're getting a free ride,' Matt joked. 'There's enough work to keep us all busy until we get to retirement age. Feel up to sorting out some junk? I've got the biggest skip I could hire just waiting to be filled.'

'That's the bit I'm looking forward to the most!' I said. 'And spending some time with the kids too, of course. Hey, Matt?' I was looking at the immense grey sea walls, noticing for the first time that here and there they had bits that stuck out awkwardly, with small slit-like windows cut into the walls. 'What's with the giant concrete walls?'

'Defence bunkers,' Matt told me. 'A souvenir from the Occupation, when Jersey was taken over by the Nazi forces.'

My mouth dropped open in amazement.

'Jersey was occupied?'

'Yep. For most of World War Two. You'll see bunkers everywhere, all over the island. And there's a cool tunnel museum - Jersey War Tunnels. The Nazis' used slave labour to dig massive tunnels that all linked up. There's even a whole hospital there, underground. We'll go and see it one day, although I doubt it's suitable for the kids. Maybe just us then.' Matt tapered off then shrugged. 'Jayne doesn't seem interested in exploring our new home just yet. That's why it's so great that you're here. We could do with some help with Noah when Alice goes to school and Alice has been playing up recently. She's a bit unsettled from the move, I think.'

We hit a line of traffic and crawled along the seafront at a snail's pace.

'One thing I didn't expect,' Matt sighed. 'The traffic's terrible here. You get traffic jams everywhere. Too many cars on such a small island.'

I didn't mind going so slowly though. I was enjoying taking in the new and unfamiliar sights. The narrow roads, the grand houses and hotels, and the road signs - all in French. It was both comfortably British yet exotically French at the same time. The sight of a huge castle sitting regally in the calm waters of the bay made me gasp and point.

'Look at that! That castle's in the sea! How did it get there?' I wondered. Matt laughed at me.

'That's Elizabeth Castle. When the tide goes out you'll be able to see the causeway from the beach this side to the gate on their side. So it's not always in the sea.' He punched my arm gently. 'It just looks like it is when the tide's up.'

'Sounds like you're already quite the expert on this place,' I said. He shrugged again.

'I love it. It feels like home to me. Maybe it's my Jersey blood coming out in me but .... it's hard to explain .... it's like I've known this place all my life, not just arrived a few weeks' ago. I already feel a part of it. I don't think I'll ever leave.'

'Not even if Jayne's unhappy being here?' I asked quietly.

Matt was silent for a second.

'Well, we'll just have to convince her how great it is, won't we?'

We drove through the St Helier tunnel and passed a few suburbs before, in no time at all, we left the town behind as he drove a short way into the country parish of Grouville before indicating to turn right. All I could see were two matching gateposts. Once a brilliant white, they were now grey with age and green with moss. Overgrown trees flanked a driveway, through which a sloping roof and several tall chimneys could be seen. We pulled up outside their new home, beside a lopsided wooden sign with "The Grange" picked out in tatty adhesive letters. I looked out of the car window and gazed up at the stone house in front of me. It was seriously huge. I mean really, really big. Intimidating.

Matt unbuckled his seatbelt and opened his door, going to the boot to get my case. The afternoon sun had already disappeared behind the thick wall of oak trees, which surrounded the lawned garden, and cast long shadows over the patchy gravelled driveway. Tucked under the tall oaks beside the house were some outbuildings, reduced to not much more than rubble now but one old structure was still fairly intact, its three stone walls drowning in ivy and brambles.

'Are they very old?' I asked him.

'I think so,' he replied. 'I'm not sure what's what yet. I know that there has been a house belonging to my family here since 1544 and that the house you see now is a result of centuries of additions and improvements. Those outbuildings are definitely older than the main house is though. I'm hoping there will be something about the history of the house in the piles of junk Uncle Pierre left. I'd love to be able to find out what this place looked like when it was first built.'

Jayne was at the sink when I opened the side door to the kitchen and dragged my case in. Noah was in his high chair gnawing messily on a rusk while Alice was busy with her colouring-in book at the table. It would have been a welcome picture of domesticity if it weren't for the fact that Jayne was slamming dishes into the sink with such force I thought they might break in half. Her whole body radiated tension and unhappiness. Her shoulders were so hunched they almost touched the frown lines on her forehead. It wasn't quite the warm welcome I'd expected.

'AUNTY RABBIT!' screeched Alice, scattering crayons and paper in the rush to get down from the table to greet me. She ran over and hugged my legs, beaming her gappy smile up at me. 'Mummy said you were coming to stay at our house with us! And that you were going to look after Noah and me! Will you show me how to do a plait in my hair? Aunty Rabbit, look at where my teeth falled out!' She pulled her lower lip down so I could see where she had lost one of her baby teeth. She was undeniably cute. She had on flowery leggings and a white t-shirt with a unicorn on the front, her long blonde hair loose and falling in tangled waves down her back. I leaned down to give her a hug.

'Aunty Rabbit, it's my birthday soon. Will you be here for my birthday?'

'I hope so, little bunny,' I replied.

69

Alice danced around me, chattering excitedly about all the things we could do together and even Noah joined in with a loud 'Bahhh!'

'Shhhh, Alice! Stop bothering Aunty Leah. She doesn't need you jumping all over her,' Jayne said sharply. She turned to me, some of the tension leaving her face. 'Oh Leah, it's so good to see you!'

'Are you OK, Jayne?' I asked, concerned at how pale she looked. She had big dark circles under her eyes and they had certainly lost most of the sparkle I was used to. Jayne's chin began to wobble and her eyes filled with tears. She whirled around, grabbing the kitchen sponge and began to wipe at the counters furiously.

'I'm all right,' she said thickly. 'THAT one is just getting on my last nerve, that's all.' She jerked her chin at Alice who seemed oblivious to the tension and the fact she was the cause of her mother's mood. 'Put your case in your room and we'll have a cuppa. Come on, I'll show you where it is.'

'Me do it, Mummy! Me, me me!' shouted Alice as she grabbed me by the hand and pulled me towards the narrow passageway.

'Alice! Stop it, please! You're giving me a headache.' Jayne put both hands to her face and pressed hard on her temples. 'Sit at the table nicely please, like I asked you to.' Alice pouted and was about to protest but Jayne gripped her upper arm and sent her back to the kitchen with a light tap on her behind. The little girl screwed up her face and let out a loud wail but Jayne pointedly ignored her, picking up my bag and leading the way down the dim hall.

'Sorry about that,' Jayne said over her shoulder. 'She got a bit overexcited about you coming to stay.'

'It's fine. Don't worry about it,' I replied, not liking to add that I didn't actually think Alice deserved a smack on the bum just for wanting to show me my bedroom. I had never seen Jayne hit either of her children - not ever.

70

'She's just been …. oh, I don't know ….. so difficult since we got here.' Jayne turned left into another short hall and stopped outside a door. 'She's been doing a few hours in a holiday club each week before school starts. I needed to get her out of my hair! And since she's been going there she's been so naughty! Answering back, lying to us, that sort of thing. God only knows who she's picking it up from.' She stepped aside to show me the bedroom she had already made up for me. A single bed hard up against the far wall, covered in a plain cream duvet. A small bedside cabinet with a reading lamp and a clock/radio. A wooden chair. A rickety white single wardrobe leaning precariously back against the other wall. It was functional, practical, but there was not a shred of warmth nor welcome within the four walls.

'Thanks Jayne. It's, er, great!' I tried to put as much enthusiasm into my voice as possible.

'It's not much, I know. But it's the same for Matt and me. We're stuck in this awful flat until he can get a big chunk of the work done and we can move into the main house.' Matt had disappeared back to work as soon as he had left the car and I could hear a distant hammering and the faint burble of his radio as he knocked down another partition wall.

'How long before you can move into the finished rooms?'
Jayne rolled her eyes.

'Ages. There are all sorts of problems with the plumbing and electrics apparently. Whoever split the property into flats did a proper cowboy job of it. And then there's all the paperwork and planning permissions from the Planning Department. Not to mention that some of the local history people are already sticking their noses in, wanting to know what we intend to do.'
I tried hard to be sympathetic, to put myself in Jayne's shoes and understand the trials of living on a permanent building site with two small children.

'Anyway, how about that tea?' She turned and went back towards the kitchen, where Alice was still howling at the injustice of it all.

Jayne seemed more like her normal self after we'd had several cups of tea. She moaned about the house, about how weird and antiquated some of the rules in Jersey were, and about how many hours Matt was spending in the bigger wing next door.

'He spends every minute he can there,' she complained. 'I see him at breakfast, then he grabs a sandwich for lunch and then I don't see him until five o'clock when I shout him that dinner's ready. As soon as he's finished eating he's off again! Working until ten o'clock at night! Since we've been here he's not once offered to help with the kids so I can get a bit of peace, and when I suggest he take a few hours off so we can do something as a family - go for a walk or to the beach and explore a bit - he snaps my head off!'

'That's no good,' I frowned. 'I know he was working long hours in London and doing night work because that's the only way you could make it work when you had to make the mortgage payments each month, but you don't have that hanging over your head now. What you need to do is sit him down and work out what hours he can work on the house, and what hours he needs to be here helping you. And seeing his kids! Maybe that's why Alice is acting out? She doesn't see enough of her dad. She's probably picking up on the tension between you two as well and being a bit cheeky pulls the attention back to her.'

'Do you think?' asked Jayne. 'Yeah, that would make sense. Maybe you're right. Matt should set working hours for the house and stick to it. I'd be happy if he worked eight to five each day and set at least one day a week aside for us to do family things.'

'I'll take the kids out for a walk tomorrow, give you time to talk.' I grabbed her hand over the table. 'Don't worry. I read somewhere that moving house is one of the most stressful things people can do. I'm here to help - whatever I can do.'

She squeezed my hand back.

'I feel so much better already,' she grinned.

Dinner was a subdued affair. Jayne spent most of it silently spooning mashed up sweet potato into Noah's mouth. Matt sat at the head of the table, patiently cutting up Alice's sausages into small pieces while she wriggled and whined that she didn't like sausages anymore. The strain between the couple was obvious.

'Shall we open a bottle of wine?' suggested Jayne, over-brightly. 'Celebrate Leah's first night with us?'

'Not for me.' Matt barely gave her a glance. 'I'm going back to it as soon as I've eaten.'

'Oh Matt, couldn't you give it a break? Just for one night?' Jayne whined.

'No, I couldn't,' Matt said shortly. 'Anyway, I'm sure you two have lots to catch up on. I'll just be in the way.'

Jayne caught my eye and made a "see what I mean?" gesture. I kept quiet. Something was most definitely not right with this little family, whom I loved as much as my own. Matt jumped up as soon as he had forked the last bit of food from his plate and left without another word.

'See?' Jayne hissed. 'He won't even stay long enough to help me with the washing up. I've been asking him about Alice's birthday for weeks now. It's next week and I want to do something really nice for her. She doesn't have lots of family and she's made no new friends here yet so it seems a bit pointless having a party - not that I'd invite people to this dump anyway. The local zoo seems really nice and they do birthday things for kids there so I thought we could all go there, have a nice day out.'

She started wiping Noah's messy face roughly.

'Mumma, I want to go to the zoo!' Alice shouted. 'Will they have hares there?'

'She's still obsessed with hares, as you can tell,' said Jayne.

'They're my favourite!' confirmed Alice.

We cleared the table and I went to the kitchen sink to make a start on the dishes.

'Mummy, is it time for my cake yet?' Alice asked.

'Oh, sweetie, I'm sorry! I nearly forgot!' Jayne pulled a huge frosted concoction from the fridge. 'Ta-da!' she sang.

'Yay!' said Alice. 'Is Daddy going to have some with us too?'

Jayne took her phone and quickly sent a text.

'There! I've told him to hurry up or there won't be any left.'

'Is that how you communicate with each other?' I asked, flabbergasted. 'By text?

'It's the only way. I could spend days looking for him otherwise. This house is just too damned big!'

I made a big deal out of Alice's rainbow cake, declaring it the best cake I had ever had. She beamed at me with pride.

'I did all the colours! I mixed them in.'

'I can tell,' I said to her. 'Look how good the colours are!'

After dessert had been eaten and the mess cleared away, I went with Jayne to give the children their bath. Noah had a special seat, which sat him safely upright, and he splashed happily, kicking his fat little legs in the water. He was such an easy baby, I remarked to Jayne.

'Yes, he's a dote,' she said fondly. 'Such a difference compared to....'

She jerked her head at Alice, who was in her own little world of Barbie mermaids and plastic fish. 'She ran me ragged for the first year, never stopped screaming. There were times when I thought I'd made a huge mistake, having kids.' Jayne swirled her hands in the soapy water. 'You know, looking back on it, I can completely understand why my birth parents gave me up. If I was anything like...' She nodded her head at Alice again. 'then I don't blame them.'

'Jayne, you don't mean that!' I said, shocked to the core. Jayne had never been anything other than the perfect mother to both children. If anything, she could be a little bit TOO perfect.

'Oh, I know. I'm only being maudlin,' Jayne said wearily. 'I'm just tired. And homesick, I guess.'

'This is your home now,' I said firmly. 'Like it or not, this is what you have. Once you start working proper hours and both kids are settled it will be a lot better, OK?' She looked at me sceptically, as if I didn't quite understand just how bad things were.

CHAPTER TEN

I lay in the darkness, finding sleep impossible. I turned onto my good side and watched the red digital numbers flick over to 3.04 am. Eventually, my full bladder won the battle and I knew I wouldn't be getting any more sleep that night. I might as well get up, have a wee, get some toast. I went to the bathroom at the end of the hall. It was ridiculously old-fashioned, with the cistern high up on the wall behind the toilet. It made far too much noise so I neglected to flush and then padded down the hall to the kitchen. It was far enough away from the bedrooms not to disturb anyone if I turned on the light and pottered around for a while. The strip light, a throw-back to the seventies when the flats were built, fizzled and stuttered but eventually settled into its job of shining a harsh, unforgiving light over the kitchen surfaces. I put the kettle on to boil. It sounded far too loud in the early morning quietness.

While I waited for the water to heat, I cupped my hands around my face and looked through the bare window at the darkness outside. There was a faint orange glow from the distant lights of the town but it was not enough to make out the shapes of the trees or the outbuildings in the garden. I could barely see the corner of the east wing where it sat at a right angle to the wing this flat was in. The light from the kitchen window threw an arc onto the gravel in front of me but beyond that there was just the rusty night sky. A flicker of movement caught my eye and I held my breath as a hedgehog trundled into the square of yellow light. Its tiny eyes were lit glowing green as it silently observed me at my post, before it lurched clumsily away. It was enough to make me smile briefly. For a few seconds I didn't feel quite so alone.

With my cup of tea in my hands, I sat at the kitchen table and took stock of my situation. The sniping and cold silences between Matt and Jayne had continued when he had briefly come back into the kitchen, grabbed a slice of cake, ruffled Alice's hair and then promptly disappeared back through the door into the bigger part of the house where he was working. If I could help, take care of the kids for Alice, in return for bed and board - I could almost be like a kind of au pair for them. I didn't want them to treat me as a guest. I genuinely wanted to work for them. They wouldn't have to pay me, I still had money from the crowdfunding that would see me through for a while. It saved me the bother of going through the pointless rigmarole of trying to find a proper job. I knew I didn't have a hope of getting anything like what I was qualified for and working for Jayne would be a win-win situation for us both. I resolved to make some notes the next day and approach her with my idea. This house was big enough for me to have my own space, I wouldn't be in their faces all the time. Maybe we could work out some hours for me, just like she was going to do with Matt. Maybe I could stay forever.

A noise made me jerk my head up painfully, pulling on my scars in a way that made my stomach churn with nausea. I listened into the oppressive silence. Nothing. Must have been something outside, an animal or a tree branch against a window. The silence grew even louder as I cocked my head to the side. Breathing. Not mine, I didn't think so anyway. Small, gulpy breaths that then rose up into a crescendo of wailing. Noah had woken up and I was hearing him through the baby monitor. I heard someone, Jayne or Matt, get up, shuffle down the hall towards Noah's room and open the bedroom door a fraction. For a second the noise rose, and then it fell away as the door was shut again and the sleepy baby was picked up and cradled safely against his parents' chest.

'What are you doing?'
I gasped in fright and then let out a murmured 'Fuck's sake!' before turning to see Alice in the doorway.

'Alice, bunny, you made me jump,' I whispered. 'What are you doing out of bed?'
She rubbed her eyes with the back of her hand sleepily and then toddled over to crawl onto my knee. She smelled of milk and biscuits, of bedtimes and bubble bath.

'I heard Noah and then I saw the light on in the kitchen so I came to see if there was any cake left,' she finished hopefully.

'It's not time for cake,' I grinned against the top of her head where she had tucked herself under my chin. 'It's very early. Too early for breakfast, so too early for cake.'

'Oh,' was all she said as she stuck her thumb in her mouth and closed her eyes drowsily.

'Come on. Back to bed for a little while, ok?'
She clung to me in monkey-fashion as I stood up and held onto her tightly. I walked with her down the hallway and met Jayne, who was closing Noah's door softly. Alice was all but asleep again on my shoulder.
'Just putting her back to bed,' I whispered. 'Sorry. I got up to make a cup of tea. Hope I didn't disturb you.'
Jayne smiled wanly and shook her head.

'No. It's a rare night when both of them sleep through and don't need me in the night. Alice wakes up more since we moved in here. I don't know if it's the house that unsettles her, or if she wakes up because Noah has.' Jayne looked fondly at her sleeping daughter. 'She can't bear to miss out on anything so she quite often comes in when I'm giving Noah his night feed and demands a story or a drink.' She moved to take Alice from me, lifting her into her own arms. Alice stirred and let out a sleepy 'fuck's sake' before settling down again. I caught Jayne's eye and she gave me a stony glare.

'Sorry. My fault.'
What else could I say?

After breakfast at a more reasonable hour, I asked Matt to show me the rest of the house. He agreed readily, itching to show off his latest trophy, and led me through the temporary plastic-sheeted door just off the kitchen. He handed me a hard hat.

'It's a proper building site. You'll need this,' he said We were standing in a cavernous hallway in a dusty grey light. There were stained glass panels around the impressive metal-studded oak front door, which threw pools of red and green in a random pattern around the floor.

'This is the main entrance hall,' he said, quite unnecessarily as even I had worked that one out. 'The original grand staircase is still here, look.' He ran his hand over the smooth, chestnut coloured wood of the newel post at the bottom of the staircase. It was beautiful, I agreed. It curved up to the right, while its twin on the other side of the hall curved up to meet it on a level landing, before both sets of stairs twisted even further up out of sight. The floor was covered in painted terracotta tiles which were chipped and cracked.

'I'm still at the stage where it's more about demolition than renovation,' Matt told me. 'It's the fun part! Ripping down walls and pulling away the nasty modern fabrics to get to the real building underneath. Look! This is one of the first things I found.' He showed me a carved wooden panel. It sat gracefully next to the wide doorway and echoed some of the patterns in the door frame. I touched it reverently.

'Is it what they call linenfold panelling?' I asked. Matt nodded, pleased at my interest.

'Yes, I think so. I don't know much about the history of houses on Jersey. I really need to get to the local library and find some books on the subject. You never know, it could be one of the first examples of linenfold on the island and of major historical importance.'

79

'Do you know much about the house?' I looked up at the double-height ceiling. 'Who built it, who lived here?'

'All I know is that it has been called The Grange since Victorian times, before that it was called Harewich House and it appears on the early survey maps of Jersey as being owned by a Monsieur Gabriel Chevalier.' Chevalier was Matt's mother's maiden name. I remember him telling me that it was from the old French word for soldier, a horse-mounted soldier.

'There's a box of old papers that came with the house when I signed the legal documents but I haven't got round to sorting through them yet. There might be some more information about the house in them.'

A cloud must have passed over the sun as the hall suddenly grew dark and I shivered.

'Show me the rest,' I said, leading Matt away from the hall and its shadows. We crawled through holes in walls and climbed creaking stairs. In most of the house there was not much to see, just a mish-mash of old flats with stained carpets and cupboards with doors hanging off. Here and there I could see flashes of the older house, where Matt had knocked down the flimsy dividing walls and uncovered panelled walls or dressed granite blocks underneath.

'I'm working on the main entrance at the moment,' Matt said. 'It's on the opposite side of our flat. The wing we're staying in was the smaller of the two and would have housed the kitchens and the more functional of the rooms. This side was the grander side where guests would have been brought in. I think there was a kind of great hall here, on this side.' He indicated to where another empty flat lay. 'It seems to have had a new floor here, in between the two flats when they were built, which tells me that the early room must have been of double height originally.'

'It's absolutely fascinating!' I said, genuinely meaning it. It didn't take a lot to see what the house could be like when it was brought back to its original lay-out.

'You haven't seen the best bit yet!' Matt teased, leading me up to the top floor via a narrow wooden staircase set deep into the house walls. There was a cream-painted wooden door at the top. Matt flung it open with a grand gesture. 'The attics!' he laughed.

I stared around the vast room in front of me with awe. Dimly lit, with only one window on the right side to let in light, the room went back as far as I could see. I couldn't even see the far wall, probably partly due to the entire room being stuffed full of dusty, cobwebby treasure. Well, I say treasure, which it was to me, but it was actually mostly pieces of furniture, old travelling trunks, packing chests and old, rolled up carpets. It was like that bit in the Indiana Jones films, where he finally stumbles across that inner chamber holding mountains of gold and jewels and precious icons.

'Wow!' I breathed, wanting to grab the nearest box to me and start rifling through it.

'Yeah. It is a bit wow,' said Matt. 'Fancy helping me go through it?'

When we had finished our house tour, I went back to the kitchen while Matt went back to his sledgehammer. As promised, I took charge of both the kids so Jayne and Matt could have the space to talk. Alice promised to show me the grounds of the house and we could have a walk over the adjoining fields before heading back for lunch, when I would tell Jayne of my plans to stay on. The ground was rough going, the once pristine lawns had been ravaged by generations of moles and I soon abandoned Noah's stroller and hoisted him on my hip, carrying him carefully around the piles of fallen bricks and rusting machinery that littered the ground.

We explored the gardens and poked around the ruined outbuildings. They were not in any fit state to use as storage so they had just been left to fall down of their own accord. In the curious three-sided structure, I could see the remains of a chimney stack and fireplace. There was a small square window set into the wall but the rest of the space was filled with broken glass and rusted metal farm tools.

'Careful!' I said to Alice as she picked up a stick and began to prod at the debris. 'There's sharp things in here so don't pick anything up, OK?'

'OK,' she said. 'I come in here a lot though. It's my favourite place. I think a witch lived here in the olden days.'

'What makes you say that?' I smiled, loving her creative imagination. She shrugged.

'Don't know. I think someone told me. Or maybe I saw her once.'

'You saw her? What did she look like? Did she have green skin and a big warty nose? Did she have a black cat and fly on a broomstick?' I poked Alice under her ribs to make her laugh and she squirmed away in delight.

'No, silly!' she told me. 'She looked like a normal girl. She had dark hair but it was all messy. She had a funny dress on too.'

'What do you mean – funny?' I was curious now. Her description was so vivid. Maybe it was something she saw on TV once and she'd convinced herself it was real. Alice screwed up her face as if trying hard to find the right words.

'It was very dirty. And like it was made up of lots of bits of other dresses.'

'Like patchwork, you mean? Like Poppydog?' Poppydog was Alice's favourite baby toy which she still clung to when she was feeling sad or upset. It was a soft toy made from pieces of different fabrics, which were stitched together in patchwork form.

Yes!' Alice said triumphantly. 'Like Poppydog! Except not as nice.'

'When did you see her?' I asked her.

'When I was in here one day. She was just standing there.' She pointed to the old fireplace. 'And then she was just gone.' Alice opened her arms wide. 'Gone!'

82

'That must have been scary?' I said, carefully choosing my words. Alice nodded a bit, but then shrugged indifferently.

'No, not really. I felt sorry for her.'

'Sorry for her? Why's that?'

'Well, it wasn't very nice for her, having those nasty heavy chains on her arms and legs. She lifted up her dress and showed me.'

We strolled around the grounds until my phone blipped with a text from Jayne.

Lunch time

'Righto guys. Back we go. Mummy's got our lunch ready.'

I pushed Noah's stroller back over the uneven ground and we were at the kitchen door within minutes. The walk had done the children good. They both had rosy cheeks and sparkling eyes, and Alice declared herself to be starving. After a flurry of pulling off wellington boots and washing hands we settled around the table, falling ravenously on the sandwiches Jayne had made.

'I've just got a call from the hospital. I've got a shift tonight - six through to six tomorrow morning. Will you be OK if I take it?' Jayne asked.

'Of course I will,' I said. 'In fact, there's something I want to run by you. Both you and Matt really. Did you get a chance to, you know, thrash things out?'

Jayne was on her phone, presumably signing up for the shift. She didn't look at me.

'Not really. Tell you about it later.' She jerked her head at Alice who was following our every word.

With Noah down for his nap and Alice inspecting bugs on the gravel, Jayne and I sat on the dilapidated plastic chairs just outside the kitchen door, basking in the afternoon sun.

'He did say he'd try,' Jayne opened the conversation. 'You were right about him being like a kid with a new toy. He said it's like he can't pull himself away from the house, like he's addicted to it.'

'That doesn't excuse him from neglecting his wife and kids though,' I said.

'Yeah, he knows that now,' Jayne sighed. 'Anyway, at least I got him to agree to work daytime only, and not to go disappearing next door again after dinner. What would we have done tonight if I'm at work and he can't go for ten minutes without hammering something or smashing a wall down, if you weren't here to help?'

'That's kind of what I wanted to talk to you about.' I turned to face her. 'How would you feel if I stayed on, long-term I mean? As a kind of au pair.'

'What do you mean as an au pair?' Jayne asked, mystified. 'You're our guest and a very welcome one. I don't want you to start thinking you're our staff! We couldn't afford to pay you anything, anyway!'

'I wouldn't want paying,' I said. 'Think about it. I'd live here with you guys and, in return for bed and board, I could look after both the kids and do a bit of housework, that kind of thing. That way, you could look for more regular hours at the hospital, Matt could still work on the house during the day and I'd have a proper job to do. What do you think?'
Jayne turned it over in her mind. I could see she was thinking of the pitfalls, as if there were any.

'I wouldn't get in your way,' I gabbled on. 'I could move into one of the empty bedsits so I'd have my own space and I wouldn't be treading on yours and Matt's toes all the time. I'm sure there's a bit of furniture up in the attic I could use, I only need a bed and a couch really, and I could buy my own television. Oh go on Jayne, say yes, it's the perfect solution.'
A slow smile crept across Jayne's face.

'Do you know, I really think that could work,' she said. 'As long as you don't mind, of course.'

'No, of course not,' I squealed. 'I'd love it!'

'We'd have to work out some ground rules though,' Jayne went on. 'Proper working hours and things. I don't want you to become our Cinderella! But if we stick to things like taking Alice to school, looking after Noah during the day and maybe a bit of light cleaning, that would be absolutely fantastic!'

We grinned at each other and then hugged, laughing.

'One thing I will have to insist on though,' Jayne went on, mock-seriously. 'Please do not teach my babies bad words! Can you imagine if Alice rocked up at school in a few weeks and started telling people to fuck off?!'

We both chuckled.

'I know. I'm so sorry about that. It just slipped out. She gave me a fright!'

Later that day, after the children were in bed and the chores done, I realised I never asked Alice why she used the word 'witch' when she was talking about the girl in the stone building.

'Matt?' I turned to him. He was slumped on the couch in front of an old Grand Designs repeat on the television. 'What were the buildings out in the garden?

'Hm? What?' he said distractedly. 'Why do you want to know?'

'Just curious,' I said. 'Alice was showing me them today. I just wondered what they were built for.'

'Probably for animals,' he said, not turning from the screen. 'I think one was used as a grain store, not sure.' He yawned loudly. 'They're not very interesting. I'll probably demolish them at some point.'

'Did you say you thought that they were older than some parts of the house?' I asked.

'I would think so,' said Matt. 'They're built of the same granite as the original part of the main hall, so they were probably built at the same time.'

'They might have been cottages. For the farm labourers?' I ventured. He nodded absently, his attention was clearly elsewhere. I gave up, and tried to concentrate on the programme, but the image of a ragged waif in chains would not leave my head.

I went to bed quite early. We had talked about fixing up the bed-sit next door for me, and Matt was going to knock through one of the walls and create a new door into their flat so I wouldn't have to enter it via the vast entrance hall. We would move the bed I was in now into the bedsit and Matt had seen a reasonable couch I could have, left behind by the owners when they moved out of one of the other flats. I would need to go shopping for a telly, and things like bed linen and towels. The bedsit had a decent shower room and I was relishing having my own bathroom again. I phoned Mum with the news that I would be staying on for a while and she nearly cried with relief and happiness at having her house back. She agreed to pack up some of my clothes and bits and pieces, and send them on to me here in Jersey. We hung up on much better terms than when I had left.

I tried to read for a bit but when the words began to jumble themselves up and start dancing over the page I gave up, and switched off the bedside lamp. Sleep came swiftly. It was a bit like falling through deep, warm, dark water. Drifting down and down, nothing but silence and peaceful darkness.

I was forced into wakefulness again by someone prodding me on the injured side of my mouth. Whoever they were, they were trying to hook their fingers under the twisted portion of my lips and pull upwards. The pain of it, combined with the anaesthetic effects of a deep sleep, made the world rock for a moment and a wave of nausea washed through my stomach. Opening my sticky eyes slowly, all I could see was black. I could feel someone there though. A presence in my room, next to my bed. I reached for the switch of the lamp and a mellow light filled the room. Alice was standing over me, eyes wide and fingers primed, ready for another poke at my face.

'Alice! What are you doing? That hurts!' I said angrily. 'You know I've got a poorly face and you shouldn't be trying to touch it.' She said nothing. She didn't even blink, just swayed gently on her little feet, her eyes fixed on my mouth.

'Alice? Alice?' I clicked my fingers under her nose and she didn't react at all. Taking a closer look at her, I could see that her pupils were dilated and fixed. She was not seeing anything – she was fast asleep. The clock clicked over to 3.04. I rubbed at the good side of my face wearily. I felt jetlagged. Slowly and quietly, I got out of bed, talking gently to Alice all the time. 'Come on, little bunny, time for bed.'

I went to lift her onto my hip, intent on putting her back safely in her own bed. She turned at my touch and hissed like a scalded cat, ducking out of my reach. She ran to the door and pulled at the handle. She's moving in an odd way, I thought. A kind of scuttle, not like her usual graceful young stride at all. 'Alice? Have you hurt yourself? What's wrong?' I caught up with her and took her gently by the hand, thinking she might have stubbed her bare toes against the bed frame as she walked in her sleep. She stared at me unblinkingly for a second, and then raised my hand to her mouth and bit down hard. She didn't let go, but kept biting down onto my index finger as hard as she could. I yelped, and pulled my hand away, but not before I could see the beads of blood welling up in the small crescent-like indents on my finger.

'Alice! No! That's naughty!' I was trying not to shout. I didn't want to bring Jayne running to my door. Alice slid past me and continued her strange crab-like run down the hallway towards her own bedroom. I debated going after her but after that little debacle I decided to leave her be. My hand was throbbing and my head began to throb in perfect time. Groaning, I flopped heavily back into my bed, but not until I propped the back of the wooden chair underneath the door handle. I did not want a repeat performance of the night's baffling events. Cradling my injured finger in my good hand, I closed my eyes and prepared to drift off again.

The last thing I heard before sliding back into sleep was a muffled giggle, coming from outside my door. It didn't sound like Alice's hearty chuckle. It was more low-pitched, and there was something slightly desperate about it. Then my brain flooded with sleep again and I was gone before I could think about the eerie laughter anymore.

At breakfast I slumped, heavy-lidded and yawning over the table. Jayne looked at me quizzically.

'Not slept well?' she asked.

'I'm fine. I was getting a great night's sleep until Alice woke me up by coming into my room in the middle of the night, sleepwalking.'

'Sleepwalking?' Jayne paused, the spoon full of baby food hovering in mid-air as Noah obediently opened his mouth to receive it. 'Alice doesn't sleepwalk. Are you sure?'

'Yeah. She woke me up by poking at my face but when I turned the light on it was like she couldn't see me. Her eyes were totally blank.' I held back on mentioning the nasty bite Alice had inflicted on my hand. I was curious to see if she remembered anything about last night. 'I tried to steer her back to her room but she just ran off and went back to bed on her own.'

Jayne did her frowny face again – the one I was seeing more and more often.

'How very strange. She's never done that before. She must just be a bit unsettled with all the changes at the moment....'

She broke off as we heard Alice charging down the hallway, Matt following at a more leisurely pace. She looked fine that morning, normal. She sat up at the table in her little blue and white Tottenham shirt and started on a bowl of cereal, slopping milk over the sides of the bowl in her haste.

'Alice, do you remember coming into my room last night?' I asked her gently. She frowned and shook her head.

'No I didn't.'

'You did. I woke up and you were there by my bed.' She thought hard but shook her head again.

'I never! And it's not nice to tell fibs!' She scowled at me, mistrusting. I thought I saw something in her eye though, a spark that told me she knew exactly what I was talking about.

'I think you were still asleep. That's probably why you don't remember.' I laid my hand on her shoulder but she pulled away from me sharply. 'It's OK. I'm not angry at you,' I said gently. 'I was worried you'd hurt yourself because you looked like you were limping. Can I see your feet? Did you bang your foot on something?'

She considered this, and consented to lift her feet up for me to see. They were already encased in white socks and I couldn't see if there was any evidence of stubbed toes or bruised soles. When I thought of how she bounded into the room just then though, it's clear she didn't have any pain in her feet now.

'Well, they look fine to me.' I gave them a little tickle and she couldn't help but giggle. 'I guess I was just imagining things.'

She nodded. I didn't mention the bite marks on my hand just yet. That was something I wanted to tackle later, when I was alone with her.

Alice was going to the holiday club for a couple of hours that morning and I told Jayne I would be fine to take her, it wasn't far to walk. With Noah buckled into his stroller we left the house, with Alice's little school rucksack bouncing on her back. Jayne had bought it for her for when she started school but Alice loved it so much she took it out at every opportunity. As we walked in the direction of the hall where the club was held, Alice kept sneaking little glances at me, or rather, at my hand on the stroller handle.

'Aunty Leah?' she asked, sugary sweet. 'What happened to your hand?'

'I don't know,' I replied. 'I think I must have knocked it in the night.'

She clapped her hand over her mouth and stifled a giggle.

'But it looks like a bite,' she said delightedly. 'It looks like you were bitten really, really HARD!' She was shaking with laughter now.

'You know,' I said slowly. 'I think you might be right. I think I was bitten really, really hard by a very, very naughty little GIRL!'

Alice rocked on her heels and doubled over, she was laughing so hard.

'It wasn't ME!'

'Oh? So was there another very naughty little girl in my room last night who bit me so hard I have tooth marks and bruising?' Alice nodded her head vigorously.

'There was! There was another girl. My friend Jenny. She was very naughty, wasn't she?' Alice turned her innocent blue eyes to me. 'I told her not to do it, but you touched her and she didn't like it, so she bit you.'

'Who's Jenny?' I asked. 'Is she someone from holiday club?

Alice rolled her eyes

'Nooooo, I just told you. Jenny's my friend. She lives in our house too.'

'Why haven't I seen her then?' I said

'Cos she's imbisable!' Alice groaned at my stupidity. 'She can see you but you can't see her until she lets you. Do you know something, Aunty Leah?'

'No. What?' I asked cautiously. I was trying to work out if she was playing pretend with me or if she really thought there was another girl called Jenny in the house - like an imaginary friend.

'Jenny's face is like yours.' Alice's simple words stopped me in my tracks.

'What do you mean, her face is like mine?' I gasped. Was Alice being cruel, or did she have a vivid dream about my scars and somehow invent another little girl with the same flaws.

'She has a face like a rabbit too. She's sad about it, like you are, because people are not very nice to her because of it.'

I wish I knew more about the way kid's mind's work, but to me this felt like some kind of disassociation – knowing what she did was wrong so she was inventing another girl, a naughty version of Alice, in order to absolve herself from any blame. I had no idea what to make of Alice transposing my scarred features onto this imaginary girl's face and hoped it wasn't because Alice still harboured some fears about my looks.

'Well, I'm not sure I like this naughty girl. This, this Jenny!' I huffed. 'I don't like little girls who bite.'

Alice didn't react guiltily, as I thought she might, even though she had just all but admitted she knew she had bitten me last night. Instead, she gave me a thoughtful look.

'That's OK, Aunty Leah. She doesn't like you either.'

Jennet's Story

Jersey, 1603

I am well, Sister. I just need to shift my legs. I have been sitting here so long they grow numb and I cannot feel the rats nibbling on my feet.

No, Sister, that was not a jest. Truly, the rats will eat living flesh as soon as eat dead.

Where was I in my story?

My little lean-to shelter became harder to bear as the winter snows drifted in and draped heavily over my makeshift roof. I could not have a fire and I was still wearing the same one dress I had, so my feet were bare and blue with cold. I spent as much time as I could in the woods gathering firewood. Some I gave to my father and step-mother in return for a little food, and some I hawked door to door at the cottages in the little hamlet further down the coast. Most times I got the door shut in my face and a hissed threat to keep my ugly hare-cursed face away, but sometimes I had a lucky day and earned a piece of bread or a small amount of pottage. As the cold season set in and the days grew ever shorter, firewood became scarce as other families were sending their children out into the woods to find small pieces of kindling for their own hearths. I ventured as far as I dared, even combing the pebbly shores of the beach for driftwood and other burnable pieces which might have washed up after heavy seas. I lived this way for many months.

One day, I was walking through the frosted trees when I heard the tell-tale crack of a branch being stepped on somewhere behind me. Creeping as quietly as I could

92

on my bare feet, which were hardened to leather, I crawled under the drooping fronds of a low-growing bush. Moments later, I heard another crack and the well-dressed form of Matthieu Chevalier came into my view. He was wearing a thick padded coat and sturdy boots and walked slowly, placing one foot carefully in front of the other as he searched the trees on either side of him for something. What was he doing out here? Was he hunting? He didn't have a bow and arrow that I could see, nor a knife or dagger. He moved past my hiding place stealthily, pausing only to peer around thicker tree trunks, his face unable to hide his disappointment at not seeing whatever it was he was looking for.

It was not in my nature to call attention to myself. If I saw other people in these woods it was my natural instinct to hide. I had been on the receiving end of too many kicks and curses should someone unexpectedly see my face. But on this day something bubbled up inside me, something rebellious. I had not forgotten how Matthieu Chevalier had pulled at my hair and hissed threats at me when I saw him at the church with the priest. Perhaps it was time he should know what it is like to be the one in receipt of pain and fear, for a change. Reaching out my hand I found a lump of soil, hardened by the frost so it was like a rock, and took careful aim and threw it at his head. He was wearing a cap which covered his head but it left his ears unprotected and it was on his left ear that my weapon found its mark. Matthieu jumped and hollered, spinning around to glare at the empty woods, for he could not see me where I crouched under the thick branches of the bush. For a time it looked as if he was going to cry as he rubbed his ear and I saw bright red blood mixed with the dirt on his hands. Matthieu took another look around him but, still not seeing me, he turned away and began his slow stalking pace through the trees once again. I slipped away from my hiding place and followed him, keeping out of sight and completely silent for I was always

93

light on my feet. Using the thick foliage for cover, I got a few paces ahead of him and this time my fingers found a pine-cone, which I swiftly hurled at his face. It found his cheek and he squawked in shock as the sharp points dug in and drew more blood. Disbelievingly, he stared at the blood on his gloved hand.

'Who's there?' he demanded, but the tremor in his voice gave away his fear. 'Who dares mark the son of the man who owns this land?' he said, a bit more imperiously. I threw another pine-cone, smaller this time and not so hard, but it still caused Matthew to jump and brush at where the dirt had landed on his sheep's wool coat. The look of incredulity on his spoiled face was so funny I could not hold back a giggle.

'Who's there? Come out, I demand you!' His shout was thin and reedy and there was a look of petulant disbelief on his face, his lower lip trembling. 'Who's there, I say!'

The laughter inside of me burst out and I stepped forward, revealing myself from behind the thick tree trunk. His eyes opened wide in alarm and fear and he made the sign of the cross at me.

'Witch! Hare witch! Go away!' he yelled at me. The sight of him, face covered in blood and dirt, bellowing like a baby with a full clout, made me laugh even harder and I bent over double with the joyous pain of it in my stomach. He stood, not knowing whether to stand his ground or run away as he dearly wanted to do.

'Why are you laughing?' he demanded. 'What is so funny?'

I couldn't breathe for laughing and I gasped out my answer in short painful bursts of breath.

'Your.... you.... your...... fuh... fuh... fuh... FACE!' I collapsed once more, unable to stand for mirth. He scuffed his boots on the ground.

'It is not so funny,' he said sulkily. 'Not as funny as you sound, for when you laugh you sound exactly like a GOOSE! So there!'

And then I thought the laughter would tear open my stomach as that set another bout of cackling loose, for he was absolutely right. I did sound like a goose! I had never noticed it before because I could not remember ever having cause to laugh so much in my life before. I started to hiccup and snort and I raised my arms up and flapped them down as does a goose and pretended to strut about as if on webbed feet. Matthieu watched me in amazement before he too started to laugh.

'Goosey, goosey gander!' he cried, slapping his legs with glee as I flapped and strutted and honked around him. 'Here, goosey, goosey!' He held out his hand and I went up to him and pecked it as if it held seeds and we both laughed and laughed and laughed.

When we had finally run out of breath we sat companionably together upon the trunk of a fallen tree.
'What are you doing here?' I asked him. 'Were you looking for something?'
He picked up a thin stick of wood and began to make shapes in the dirt on the ground.
'I was looking .... I heard..... my father's servants, they say the woods are haunted by the ghost of a French soldier. They say he was captured by the guards at the garrison as a spy, so they brought him here, to these woods and then they cut off his head!' He demonstrated with the stick as if it was a great sword, and swiped it down hard towards my neck.
'Why would they bring him here?' I asked. 'Why did they not just kill him where they captured him, or throw him into the dungeons at Mont Orgueil castle like they do with all other French spies they catch?'
He shrugged. He did not know. He had thought it was a good story and he had wanted to see if he could see the soldier's ghost.
'Fool,' I scorned. 'Ghosts only come out after dark, everyone knows that.'

He looked uncomfortable. I had made him look a simpleton and I was sorry, for I had never had a companion of my own age to talk to and I wanted him to stay and talk with me some more. 'I am in these woods for many hours each day and I have never seen the ghost, even when I am here after nightfall.'

'Why are you here all the time?' he asked. I showed him my pitiful bundle of firewood, wrapped in my tatty skirts.

'If I do not get wood for the fire, I do not eat,' I said simply.

'What do you mean?' he frowned. 'Does your father's woman not provide for you?'

I made a noise halfway between a bark and a hoot.

'Madame Gouyet will not have me in the cottage. I have a bed of sorts in the lean-to and she gives me a little food in exchange for wood, but mostly I have to fend for myself.'

Matthieu looked incredulous.

'But how do you live? What do you eat?'

'I forage. I beg. Sometimes I steal,' I admitted. 'But not much, only apples and such.' I said hastily, lest he thought about handing me over to the connétablé for theft or, even worse, to his father. He sat, looking at me curiously.

'Are you very hungry all of the time?'

'Yes,' I said truthfully. 'All of the time.'

When the sun began to dip below the horizon and the woods began to darken, Matthieu said he had to go. He would be expected at home shortly, he said, as if making me an apology.

'But if you were to be here again tomorrow, here in this clearing, it might be that I will be here as well,' he said, indifferently.

'I will be here,' I told him, joy creeping into my heart. I so hoped he would meet me again and I thought that he would, for in truth, he seemed as lonely as I.

CHAPTER ELEVEN

Leah

I settled into my new responsibilities easily enough. We still had the long, hot summer holidays to get through before school started again, and I tried to find fun things to do with Alice and Noah. Alice went to holiday club two days a week, and our outings were limited to when Jayne was sleeping after a night shift, when I had use of the car. It was better for all of us, if I took the kids out somewhere where they could shout and play as loudly as they wanted to, without having to shush them all the time and remind them that Mummy needed to sleep.

Negotiating the narrow Jersey roads took some getting used to, and I tended to stick to places where parking was easy and free. I had driven past a lovely old castle, situated above a picturesque harbour, a couple of times and resolved to take the children there next.

'We're going to a big, big castle today!' I promised Alice, as she picked out a summery dress to wear that day.

'Will it have princesses?' she asked excitedly.

'Maybe,' I told her. 'It's very big and very old, and there'll be a lot of steps to go up, so we'll put Noah in his backpack, OK?'

The castle loomed above us as the harbour came into view.

'Look, it's so pretty!' I enthused, pointing out the pastel houses lining the harbour, and the boats bobbing merrily in the sparkling blue sea. Alice didn't reply. She was looking up at the castle walls with abject fear on her face. 'Come on, it's not THAT scary!' I teased her. 'Let's get parked and walk across the lovely grounds to the gate.'

We followed the neat path to the ticket desk, Noah already a dead weight on my back. As the children were both under six, there was no entry charge for them, which made my rather hefty admission fee a bit easier to swallow.

'Look, Alice! They have a dressing-up room! You can wear a princess dress as we look around if you want.'
I expected Alice to jump about in excitement, but she clutched my free hand tightly and whispered 'Don't want to.'
'OK, sweetie. You don't have to. It was just an idea.'
We entered the castle proper, under a huge stone arch. It was so beautifully kept, with tidy lawns and gardens, and I could hear mediaeval flute music being played somewhere above us. The castle stood on a cliff looking over towards the coast of France, and the coastline was so clear it was as though we could paddle across the channel and be in France in time for lunch.
'Where shall we go first?' I asked Alice, who was still clinging fearfully to me. 'Up the big stairs? Come on, let's see if you can find the top of the castle!'
Alice made a moaning sound deep in her throat. I looked at her closely. This wasn't just Alice in a grump, something was scaring her out of her mind.
'What is it, little bunny? What are you afraid of?' I asked her gently. She took a series of quick, panicky breaths and her bottom lip started to wobble. She pointed upwards, towards something in the middle ward.
'Don't want to go up there,' she cried.
'What's up there? What is it that's making you so scared, darling?'
Alice whined with fear.
'The room,' she whispered, so quietly I had to strain to hear her. 'The dark room. I don't want to go in there again.'
'What do you mean, again?' I asked her, confused. 'We've never been here before. Let's just go up these stairs and take a look. There's nothing to be afraid of, you'll see.'
I tried to lead her towards the wide granite steps, but Alice refused to move. She pulled back against me and whimpered.
'Not the pit again, don't want to go in the pit.'
'Alice! What on earth….?'

I looked on in shock as a stream of warm urine ran down Alice's leg. She crouched down, moaning and shaking, so thoroughly scared that she had wet herself. Something that hadn't happened in a very long time.

'OK baby, don't worry. We don't have to go up there if you don't want to.' I fussed around her, wishing I had thought to pack some spare, dry clothes for her.

'Want to go home,' Alice whined tearfully. 'Want to go home, Aunty Leah!'

'OK darling, let's go,' I soothed her. Carrying Noah on my back meant I couldn't bend down to pick her up and give her the cuddle she so desperately needed. 'We'll go home.'

We left the castle grounds straight away. As soon as we were in the car, Alice picked up almost immediately and she chattered away as I drove back towards The Grange.

'What was it in the castle that made you so scared?' I asked her later that night, as I was tucking her in. She stared at me in confusion.

'What castle?' she asked.

'The castle we went to today,' I reminded her.

'We didn't go to a castle! Silly Aunty Leah, we went to the long sea place!' she laughed at me. She meant St Catherine's, a long breakwater that we had visited a couple of times. But not today, we hadn't gone anywhere near there today.

'But...' I started, then broke off as I saw the fear flash in Alice's eyes. 'Never mind. Sleep well.'

With the school term starting in just over a weeks' time and Alice's fifth birthday this weekend, there was plenty for me to do. Jayne wrote lists and lists and lists of things we needed to get and we made the quick journey into the town of St Helier to try and get Alice's school uniform. We had settled on the idea of a family day out at Jersey Zoo on Sunday for the birthday girl, and Jayne had arranged for a cake and some party food to be set out at the cafe inside the zoo grounds - even though there were only going to be five of us in the party. Matt's mum and dad were supposed to make the trip over to see their eldest grandchild turn five and to wave her off on her first day of school, but they had both come down with rotten colds that quickly turned into chest infections. Reluctantly making their excuses, they put the visit off until the Christmas break, when they promised to stay longer.

Strolling around the picturesque St Helier streets, we were so busy exclaiming over the quaint little shops and enjoying the cleanliness of the main precinct of King Street, that we were hardly aware of the attention we seemed to be attracting. Gradually though, we became aware of the stares of the other shoppers and one elderly man even raised his walking stick to point at us.

'Just look at that!' we heard him exclaim to the dowdy woman by his side, whom I assumed to be his wife. 'What's wrong with them?' he asked no one in particular. Groups of people turned their heads to gawp as we pushed Noah along the granite path; women caught my eye and openly stared as they tried to make sense of what I was hiding under my headscarf. Alice skipped alongside Jayne, one hand on Noah's stroller, oblivious to the looks and sniggers coming from other members of the public. Feeling increasingly uncomfortable, we were grateful to finally be at the little shop which would sell us everything we needed for Alice's first day at school. The young woman serving behind the counter took us all in with a single glance - Jayne carrying far too much weight, me with my scarf hiding my face, Noah's birthmark and Alice, perfectly formed Alice. The young woman broke into a genuine smile.

'Good morning! I bet I can tell which one of you is going to school next week!' she trilled. Alice stepped forward shyly, sucking on the sleeve of her jumper.

'You are?' the woman carried on. 'Well, what a big girl you are, going to school! And which one of you ladies is

Mum?' She beamed, looking at Jayne and me where we hung back, taking refuge among the rail displays of school blazers. Jayne raised her hand slightly.

'Righto, Mum, do you have your list? Of the bits and bobs you need to get?'

She fussed around Alice, measuring her and pulling out packages of white shirts and the blue and white gingham pinafores that made up the uniform of Plat Douet school. She had an endless stream of cheerful chatter that soon had Jayne and I at ease, and we relaxed as we watched Alice try everything on. After talking her out of the straw boater that wasn't compulsory as part of the uniform and handing over a small fortune, we said a grateful goodbye to the nice shop lady and went thankfully back to where our car was parked, before our allotted time was up. It was one of the weird things about Jersey. Parking was at a premium and you could only park in town for up to three hours - no more. It meant rushing around trying to get everything done but after the unwelcome stares and rude sniggers we'd overheard, we were both glad to be leaving town and get back to The Grange.

Alice's birthday dawned bright and sunny and we were all looking forward to seeing the famous Jersey Zoo, even Matt, who had pointedly locked the door from their flat to the main house with a flourish.

'No work today. It's my baby's birthday!' he whooped, lifting Alice up high in his arms. She giggled and brushed the ceiling tiles with her hands.

'I'm not a baby, Daddy! I'm five today!'

'Oh my goodness, I'm so old to have a five year old daughter!' Matt cried in mock alarm. 'What do you say we swap you for one of the monkeys at the zoo, eh? Leave you there in the monkey cage and bring home a nice little baby monkey instead?' Alice shrieked and laughed until Matt slid her down his body and set her gently on the floor.

'No, Daddy! You don't want a baby monkey!' she protested. 'They smell even worse than Noah!'

We all laughed and packed up everything in the car. She was going to unwrap her presents when she had her cake at the cafe, all of them except the pink Barbie bicycle I knew Matt and Jayne had got her. That was going to be a last surprise when we all got home much later that day.

The zoo was set in large, mature grounds and was getting pretty busy by the time we rolled up. Armed with a map of the layout, Alice directed us to the meercats first, followed by the gorillas, the flamingos and then on to the stunning indoor butterfly house. We were due at the Dodo Cafe for our party at one o'clock and by that time we were all hungry and thirsty, and beginning to feel the burn of the sun on our skins. The cafe was busy and noisy. Our table was reserved in the far right corner and the staff had decorated it with a bright tablecloth, and 'Happy Birthday' balloons festooned the chairs. Alice gasped when she saw it, especially when she discovered the gold plastic tiara that had been placed reverently on the chair at the head of the table.

'Is that for me?' she asked, disbelievingly.

'It certainly is!' her father said. 'A crown for a princess to wear on her throne.' He bent low in a mock bow. Alice hugged herself and jumped up and down in excitement. The staff had forgotten to provide a high-chair for Noah so Jayne set about trying to locate one amid the hustle and bustle of the other families eating lunch. When we were all seated we ordered pizzas to share and lots of cold drinks, which came in blessedly tall glasses and were clinking with ice.

'Cheers!' We all said and touched glasses, even Alice with her cardboard carton of juice and Noah's sippy cup. Other children started drifting in closer to our table to watch as Alice opened her birthday presents, and they joined in the singing when the waitress brought out a huge chocolate cake topped with five blazing candles.

'....Happy birthday to youuuuuuuu!' we all chorused as Alice blew out her candles, extinguishing them with two deep breaths. Families at the other tables clapped and cheered and Alice sat, beaming with pleasure at all the attention.

Full of sugar and excitement, Alice begged to be able to go and play on the playground a short distance away from the cafe patio. A few of the children from the cafe were already there, swinging upside down on the monkey bars and climbing the wooden fort, and Alice sprinted over to join them where she immediately started organising a complicated game of soldiers, bossing the other children around in a loud voice.

'Oh my God, listen to her!' Jayne laughed. 'Where does she get the bossy gene from?' We watched the kids tear around, pretending to shoot each other and take others prisoner, where they were kept in the 'jail' under the treehouse fort. Sat at the table surrounded by the party debris of wrapping paper, leftover cake and presents torn open, only to be discarded a moment later when the next gaily wrapped parcel was pounced on, we looked at each other happily. It had been the perfect birthday for Alice.

'I can't wait to see her face when she sees her bike later!' Matt grinned. 'I bet she wants to take it out straight away.'

'Yes, well, we need to make sure she knows she can't ride it without, one: her knee pads, elbow pads and helmet, and two: not unless there's one of us with her at all times,' Jayne said firmly. 'I know she's got all the space on the driveway to learn how to ride but it's not exactly the smoothest surface to ride on.'

We were startled out of our conversation by a loud scream. A small dark-haired girl came running into the cafe doors and threw herself at one of the women sitting at the table behind us.

'Mummy, mummy, she's hurting Matthieu!' the child wailed. 'She's sitting on him and won't get up and she's making him eat leaves and dirt from the ground!'

The woman got up, lifting the girl up onto her hip as she craned her head to see where the children were playing.

'Oh my God!' she screeched, and ran towards the doors, hampered by the weight of the little girl. Matt got up too and followed her.

'I'll check on Alice,' he said. Jayne was already lifting Noah from his high-chair.

'We're coming with you.'

The four of us puffed our way down the slight slope to where the playground lay, increasingly concerned at the growing number of parents who were gathering at the end by the swinging tyres. The woman with the dark-haired girl was there, now lifting up a small boy and gathering him close against her breast. We heard her shouting long before we got close to them.

'.... What the hell were you doing?' the woman screamed. 'You could have killed him! He might have suffocated!'

The little boy looked no older than three or four and he was howling steadily, his little face marked with dirt and scratches, some of which were beginning to seep with blood. As we got nearer, the crowd of children and adults parted and we were able to see who the woman was ferociously berating.

Alice.

She stood with her head down, one hand pulling on a strand of her hair as she twirled it around her fingers. She wasn't crying, as one might expect. She was shuffling her shoes on the ground and looking like she wished this awful woman would just go away, so she could get on with the serious business of playing.

'What's going on here?' Matt pushed through the last few parents and went to stand behind Alice, putting his hands on her shoulders as if to warn the shouting woman that she was under his protection.

'Is this your daughter?' the woman shrieked. Matt nodded silently. 'She just tried to kill my son!' A collective gasp went up from the growing crowd. 'She was stuffing clumps of dirt into his mouth and telling him to swallow them!'

Matt crouched down and turned Alice to face him.

'Alice, is this true? What happened? Tell me, tell Daddy.' he asked her softly and gently.

'No, Daddy,' Alice replied, her eyes wide and innocent in her face. 'We were just playing and he fell down. I was trying to help him up.'

'That's a lie!' shouted one of the other children from the side lines, an older boy of about nine. 'I saw her! He was running and she tripped him up on purpose. Then she sat on his stomach and pushed things into his mouth. He couldn't breathe and started coughing and she just kept on trying to push more and more dirt in.'

'He was just playing,' put in another girl. 'We were all playing soldiers, and he was going to put her in the dungeon. She freaked out for no reason, and kept screaming about not being a witch and asking him why he lied! She's a weirdo!'

'I think we had better leave,' Matt said to the impatiently waiting woman, with a rueful smile on his face. 'I'm sure Alice is sorry she scared your son. I think it's just a case of rough play. She's a bit overexcited. It's her fifth birthday today. Alice, say sorry.' He nudged Alice forward towards the woman, who was clutching her sobbing son as her daughter clung to her leg. Alice looked up at her. She didn't look in the least bit sorry, I thought.

'I'm sorry,' Alice said clearly. 'I'm sorry your little boy's a puling weakling and I'm sorry your little girl's a mealy-mouthed brat!'

And with that she stomped off back towards the cafe, leaving us adults looking helplessly at each other. Jayne took charge.

'I'm so, so sorry. I can't apologise enough. I really don't know what's got into her.....' The woman cut her off in mid-sentence.

'Your child needs locking up! What's wrong with her? Has she got one of those syndromes where she can't understand social interactions and behaves inappropriately towards other children? Does she go to a special school? I certainly hope so - she's a danger to others! She shouldn't be allowed to play with normal children.' The woman's face was growing redder and redder as she increased her rant. Matt turned away and walked off, unable to stomach the woman's vitriol.

'I'm going to find Alice,' he threw over his shoulder. Jayne put her hand up in a 'stop' gesture at the woman.

'Look. We've apologised. We are truly sorry. But when I feel that my daughter - my intelligent, sweet, kind and loving daughter - needs a professional diagnosis, we'll go to someone who isn't an ignorant bigot, OK?'

She stalked back to where Matt was sitting on one of the outside picnic benches with a very small and sorry-looking Alice beside him. The woman goggled with disbelief, then opened her mouth and drew in a deep breath while turning towards me - I was clearly the next intended target for her outrage. I scarpered in the same direction as Matt and Jayne, leaving the weeping woman behind to be comforted and consoled by the other parents.

'What in the hell.....?' I said, as I joined the despondent little group.

'I have no idea. She's not speaking,' said Jayne, as Alice hunched over with her arms crossed defiantly over her chest and a mutinous expression on her face.

'Alice wouldn't do something like that. She's never played rough before. Her nursery in London always commented on how kind and helpful she was to the other children,' Matt said gloomily.

'Where did she learn words like that? Puling weakling? Mealy-mouthed brat?' I said, completely baffled. Jayne raised an eyebrow as she looked at me. 'No way. Not from me. I've never said stuff like that in front of her. I've never even heard words like that before.'

'She must have picked it up from something on the television. It's the only thing I can think of.' Jayne said.

'What was she watching? Baby Shakespeare?' I asked, incredulous.

'Well, something happened to that little boy, and all the fingers were pointing to Alice,' Jayne commented grimly. 'Anyway, I've explained to Alice that zoo time is over for today. We're going home. Oh, and there'll be no more birthday presents for her either. Not until she tells us what she did to that poor boy.'

Alice's face dropped the rebellious look and she screwed her mouth up in a sob. Fat tears began to run down her cheeks. She still wouldn't look at any of us and she never said a word while we traipsed solemnly to the car and drove away. The second we got home she ran to her room and slammed the door hard. Jayne sighed.

'I thought things didn't get this hard until they reached their teens,' she half-joked, but I could see she was trying not to give in to tears herself.

'Maybe it was just too much excitement and too much sugar. Anyhow, let's put the kettle on. It'll all seem better after a nice cup of tea,' I promised.

CHAPTER TWELVE

Matt made use of the unexpected free afternoon to go back to his hammering. Neither Jayne or I felt like eating much, but Jayne put on some fish fingers and heated some mixed vegetables for the children's' dinner. Alice's bedroom door remained firmly closed throughout the afternoon and Jayne moved the little pink bike back to its hiding place in her wardrobe, firmly resolute in following through on her promise of no more birthday presents today.

'If she can be like this today, what on earth is she going to be like at school on Tuesday?' Jayne wondered. 'I have no idea why she's behaving this way all of a sudden. She never had any problems making friends and playing nicely in pre-school.'

'It has to be the move,' I said. 'Think about it, a new house - a very big and somewhat spooky house at that, a whole new place to get used to. You're stressed, you and Matt are bickering....'

'We're not bickering!' Jayne grumbled . 'You have to be speaking to bicker.'

'Then there's the whole starting a new school thing. It's bound to be frightening for her.'

Just then we heard Alice's door open and a second later she bounded into the room, full of smiles and still wearing her plastic tiara from lunch.

'Hello Mummy, hello Aunty Leah! What's for dinner? I'm starving!' She leaned into Jayne affectionately. Jayne and I exchanged a look. Jayne cleared her throat.

'Fish fingers. But first I think we need to talk about what happened today.'

'What do you mean, Mummy?' Alice sprawled over her lap. 'I love fish fingers! Do you like fish fingers, Aunty Rabbit?' she giggled, using her pet name for me

'I mean,' went on Jayne, 'what happened at the zoo today. With the little boy at the playground?'

Alice frowned.

'What little boy? I never went to the playground.'

'You did, Alice! Remember? We had lunch in the cafe with your birthday cake, then you wanted to go and play with some of the other kids. And the little boy got hurt because you did something to him.' Jayne turned Alice so she was facing her. Alice was looking scared and confused.

'But Mummy, I didn't go to the playground. I stayed with you and Daddy and Noah and Aunty Leah all day.'

Jayne looked at me with utter helplessness.

'OK little bunny,' I took over. 'Let's go through exactly what we did today, starting from when we got to the zoo, OK? I'll start; we went into the zoo and got our tickets and a map of all the animals, and then.....' I prompted Alice.

'Um, then we saw the meercats?' Alice said in a tiny voice. I nodded encouragingly. 'And the plamingos.'

'Flamingos, and yes, we did that too. What next?' Painstakingly, we revisited every animal we saw that morning before we finally got to the point where we were having the birthday lunch at the cafe.

'And then everybody sang Happy Birthday to me and we looked at the map again and went to see the bats and the bears and the stripy monkey things!' Alice finished triumphantly. 'And then we came home.'

'No, no Alice. That's not what happened. We never got to see the bats or the bears or the.......stripy monkey things...'

'Lemurs,' I put in helpfully.

'...yes, those things,' Jayne said. 'We came home just after lunch because you did something naughty in the playground. Don't you remember?' she asked Alice warily. Alice shook her head, beginning to get truly distressed.

'No, I never did, Mummy!' she cried. 'I never went to the playground and I never saw a little boy. Why are you saying that I did?'

109

She burst into noisy sobs and clambered onto my lap, turning her back on her mother. I stroked her back gently.

'I really don't think she does remember,' I said to Jayne softly. 'Either that or she's the best little actress I ever saw.'

'Do you think she's blocked it out?'

'Possibly,' I said. 'Maybe she's had some kind of E-number induced black-out?'

OK, so it was a long shot, but we were both truly disturbed at how Alice didn't seem to remember being in the playground at all; at how she invented a whole new alternative afternoon of seeing the animals instead. I shivered involuntarily. I wouldn't ever admit it to Jayne but I was looking forward to moving into the bedsit on my own, my own space safely away from Alice.

The morning of Alice's first day at school we rushed around, finding shoes and bits of school uniform and chivvying Alice into getting dressed. The promised plaits I put in her hair sealed the deal, and after Matt had taken a million photos of Alice we set off, the four of us, with Noah in his stroller and Alice clinging tightly to my hand. It wasn't far to her school, probably only a ten-minute walk, but it seemed much further as Alice stopped so many times along the way to look at things in the hedgerows.

'Look! A worm!' she announced, poking at the dried-up thing with her finger.

Alice! Leave that please! It's dirty!' Jayne frowned and stopped pushing Noah long enough to grab Alice by the arm and drag her away from her prize. Alice bounced from new discovery to new discovery, exclaiming over everything she found.

'Look! A bottle. And look, flowers!' she pointed to some bedraggled dandelions. She skipped ahead of us as Jayne called to her.

'Alice, stop there please! There's a road up ahead.'

Alice obediently stopped and waited for us to catch her up. The road that lead to the school was teeming with other mothers and children all heading in the same direction. A lollipop lady saw us all safely across the busy crossing and we joined the others at the school gates, waiting for the caretaker to unlock them and signal the start of a new school day. I glanced nervously at the groups of yummy mummies waiting with their children a short way away from where we stood. They all looked so well put-together, with their swishy sundresses and their big sunglasses. One particular group of women were eyeing our little group up silently, before obviously judging us to be no one useful to know, and they turned back to each other and whispered snidely.

'Morning!'

A cheery voice called out behind us. We all turned to see a tall, dark-haired man holding the hand of a very sweet looking little girl with her equally dark hair in high pigtails.

'First day?' he asked.

'Yes,' Jayne replied gratefully. 'New school for us. We've only just moved to Jersey so Alice here hasn't met any friends her age yet.'

The man pulled his daughter forward so she was standing in front of Alice.

'Hi Alice. Welcome!' he said. 'This is my daughter Gracie. She's starting big school today too and she's a little bit scared. Do you think you and Gracie can be friends so maybe it's not so scary for either of you?'

He cocked his head at Alice. Jayne and I both held our breath, dreading Alice lunging at Gracie and taking a chunk out of her hair. Alice smiled a big smile and gently put her hand out towards the smaller girl.

'Hi Gracie. We can be friends today, best friends!'

Gracie shyly put her hand in Alice's and both girls skipped towards the door to the reception class, where a cuddly looking teacher was ringing a handbell and calling them.

'Phew!' said the dark-haired man. 'Glad that went so well. I was expecting all sorts of tears and tantrums today. Thanks for letting your little girl pal up with mine.'

'No, no, not at all,' simpered Jayne, because he really was very good looking when you looked closely. 'Thank you for breaking the ice. I don't know who was more terrified about starting school - me or Alice!'

He held out his hand.

'Hi! I'm Ben. Ben Markham. Single father, master craftsman, terrible cook.'

We laughed and introduced ourselves.

'Jayne Cooper, mum of two, nurse, not so bad at cooking.'

'Leah Harrop, nanny to Jayne's two, not so good at anything!'

'Now I'm sure that's not true,' Ben said, shaking my hand.

And this is Noah!' Jayne said brightly, gently wiggling the stroller handles to make Noah laugh. Ben bent down and took his hand.

'Pleased to meet you, Noah. He's a happy boy, isn't he?' Ben straightened up. I felt Jayne tense beside me as she waited for the inevitable 'considering his hideous birthmark...' comment but Ben said nothing about it. The other parents were beginning to drift away now, and one of the over-dressed and over-styled mothers walked over to us.

'Ben! How lovely to see you! Awww, wasn't little Grace looking gorgeous this morning?' she drawled, clinging onto his arm like a limpet and completely blanking Jayne and me. Ben looked uncomfortable and tried to pull his arm away but she deftly turned him around and began to walk back towards the cars, giving him no option but to fall into step alongside her.

'Well! That was rude!' exclaimed Jayne. 'Nice of him to speak to us though. Notice none of the other parents bothered? Come on, let's get back. I've got a meeting with the recruitment people at the hospital.'

'At least we met one friendly face,' I said. 'Now we only have to get through the day without a phone call from the school saying Alice has beaten Gracie up!'

Jayne glared at me.

'Joking!'

Matt had kindly put off working on the main hall while he knocked through the wall of my bedsit and put in an adjoining door that would lead me straight into the corridor of their flat. I was still sleeping with my chair wedged up against the door handle in my bedroom, in case of any more nocturnal wanderings by Alice. I hadn't heard her trying the handle at night but I had heard someone walking the hallway restlessly, and I thought she might still be having bouts of sleepwalking. With Noah safely down for his nap, Matt got me to stand in the corridor while he tapped on the walls of the bedsit, trying to find the best place to put a great big hole in the wall.

'Here?' I thought I heard him say but his voice was too muffled. Tap, tap, tap. I tapped back where I thought his taps were coming from. More tapping from his side.

'I'm going to put a nail through the wall,' he shouted 'then I'll come over to that side to see where it comes out.'

'OK!' I shouted back, waiting to see the tip of the nail as he hammered it into his side of the wall.

'See it?' he asked.

'No!' I yelled.

'I'll do another one then.'

Again I waited. I could hear the dull thuds of the hammer but there was no sign of the nail, no cracking of paint or puff of plaster dust.

'Anything?' Matt hollered.

'Nothing!'

I heard him drop the hammer on the floor and a minute later he appeared in the hallway beside me.

'That's weird.' he said. 'It should just come straight through. It's only an interior wall made of plasterboard. I don't think they would have bothered knocking two walls up and insulating between them. The building work in this place is just too shoddy. You can tell it was done on the cheap.' He tapped on this side of the wall. 'Come to think of it, it does sound a bit hollow. I'll go back next door and put a hole in the wall that side, see what I can see.'

I waited obediently. I heard a couple of thuds followed by a dry cracking noise which I assumed was Matt pulling away the plasterboard with the claw end of the hammer. There was a moment's silence.

'Leah? I think you should come and see this.' Matt shouted, sounding closer now but still there was no sign of any hole on my side of the wall. I put some shoes on and went through the door into the main hallway, Matt's workspace. The hall was dusty and littered with the debris of Matt's renovations. It was a chilly area and I was grateful to step into the lighter rooms that had been earmarked for my bedsit. Matt was there peering through a hole, several inches wide, in the wall.

'Can you find me my torch please?' he asked me without taking his eyes away from the hole. 'I think there's something through here.' His torch was sitting next to his tool bag on the floor by the bedsit door. Handing it to him I watched as he attempted to aim the beam through the hole while still trying to look through it himself. 'It's no good. I'll have to make it bigger. Is my lump hammer there?'

'What's a lump hammer?'

He tsked at me good naturedly and picked up a wooden handle that was attached to a solid metal bar. It was indeed a hammer, a large one.

'Lump hammer.' he told me, brandishing it at the wall. 'Stand back!'

Matt aimed the lump hammer at the small hole and swung heavily, the plasterboard giving way without protest. He kept on swinging a few times until there was a hole roughly a metre square in the wall. Sweating, he put the hammer down and picked up his torch again. There was room now for both of us to look through the hole. The first thing the torch beam illuminated was the timber frame and boarding of another wall opposite us, perhaps two feet away.

'That's the wall to our flat.' Matt muttered. He moved the torch left and right. To our left the walls both ended abruptly with another set at a right angle to them, which made up one of the walls in my bedsit. To our right, the torch showed a dark tunnel, festooned with cobwebs and seemingly unending. We leaned into the gap as far as we could, straining our eyes.

'I think there's something down there.' Matt breathed.

'Like what?' I couldn't see anything. The darkness was absolute. I could feel a cold breeze coming from the tunnel.

'Feel that?' asked Matt. 'Fresh air. That means this leads somewhere. It doesn't just end like it does on that side.' He moved the torch back to the left side. As soon as the light left the tunnel I felt as if the darkness was engulfing me, crawling malevolently over me and drawing me in. The breeze grew colder. I could see my breath in front of my face.

'Feel like exploring?' Matt was already pulling at the broken plasterboard, ripping it off the stud walls and making the hole big enough for us to crawl through.

'You aren't serious?' I said. 'You don't know what's down there. It could be dangerous! And look at the size of those spiderwebs - do you really want to meet the spiders who made them?'

Matt made a brrrkkkk noise like a chicken.

'Won't know what's down there until we take a look. Come on! Where's your sense of adventure?' He wriggled into the tunnel through the timber frame and, with some difficulty, turned himself sideways until he was standing in the gap between the two walls. 'Have to go this way. It's too narrow to walk down otherwise.' He started shuffling along the gap, soon disappearing behind the remainder of the wall completely.

'Oh, wait for me then!' I said crossly. At least he was going first and clearing a path through those cobwebs for me. I shimmied into the gap. The first thing I noticed was that there was a step down from the floor of the bedsit to the floor of the tunnel, and that it was freezing cold. Matt bent himself over awkwardly and touched the ground.

'Flagstones!' he said, sounding thrilled. 'They're the original flagstones I think. This side of the house was where the kitchens were and all the side rooms that went with it.'

'What sort of rooms?' I asked, curious and feeling a bit braver now that Matt's warm body was between me and whatever was at the end of the tunnel.

'They would have had different rooms for different purposes.' he said. 'Besides the kitchen there would have been the dry store pantry, the wet pantry for milk and cheese and things, various scullery rooms, storerooms.' He shuffled along a few more feet. 'There was probably another way out of the house too, a back door.'
We continued our slow progress down the tunnel.

'Hang on.' Matt held up his hand to me. 'Stop here for a bit. I want to shine the torch down there.' He clicked on the torch and the beam caught on something glinting in the distance. 'I think there's a room here!' he said excitedly. 'I can see a window.' He clicked the torch off again. 'See? There's a little bit of light at the end there.' I couldn't see past him to look. He continued his sideways steps, getting faster and leaving me struggling to catch up. I could feel the webs brushing my hair and my feet stumbled on the uneven slabs on the floor. Finally I could sense a widening in the passageway and I took one more step and bumped into Matt where he had stopped abruptly.

'Oh my God!' I exclaimed. We were in a small, square room. It had whitewashed stone walls, now a dirty grey and covered in grime. One small rectangular window was high up on the exterior wall and it was almost completely obscured by dead leaves and ivy growing right across it. This was where Matt had seen the chink of light reflecting in the torch beam. The flagstone floor was smooth with years of wear and there was a curious dip in it, like a drain or a channel running around the sides of the room. Even curiouser were the loops of iron fixed to the floor in various places which mirrored the loops fixed to the ceiling, some still draped with rusty chains. 'What is it?' I asked Matt, who had gone very quiet.

'Not sure. From the hanging loops though I think it might be a game store, where they hung meat to mature before eating it. They would have had all sorts in here - beef, pigs, rabbits. It's naturally cold, from the stone. And the channel around the sides would have been to flush the blood away.' He brushed his hand against the wall as I shivered and felt sick. Indeed the room smelled as if it had witnessed death on a daily basis, but I thought I must have been imagining the coppery stench of blood which still seemed to permeate the air.

'What about the loops on the floor? What would they have been used for?' I asked Matt as he strode around the room, measuring and tapping the walls.

'Probably just something to hoist the meat, I suppose. Loops for the chains.' He stopped pacing and put his hand on the left-hand side wall, opposite the outer wall with the window. 'Do you know, I think I've worked out what's on the other side of this room.'

'What?'

'Alice's bedroom.'

CHAPTER THIRTEEN

Filthy dirty and freezing cold, we shuffled back up the tiny passageway and back into the sunlit warmth of the bedsitting room.

'It's not a problem,' Matt said. 'I'll just create a small hallway here,' he indicated the gap between the two walls, 'and fix a doorway into our hall. I'll board up the tunnel for now. I can always knock it down again when I've finished the main part of the house and we've moved in there.'

I felt uncomfortable, being just on the other side of a flimsy wall to that dank, dark space. There was a very odd feeling to that stone-lined room. It didn't feel like an innocent store room to me. Maybe I was tapping in to the ghosts of the animals who had met their grisly end in that room but, whatever it was, just knowing what was in there and so close to me at night was enough to give me nightmares.

'Is there... er... another bedsit I could use?' I asked Matt. 'Just... feels a bit weird.... this one.'

Matt thought for a moment.

'Well, it's the only one that joins onto our flat, which is why I thought it would be the best choice, but you could choose one on the next floor if you wanted too. It just means me devising some way of you getting up and down safely. The main stairs are off limits while I strengthen the supports, but maybe we could cut a hole in the floor, put a fireman's pole in for you?' He grinned to show me he was joking. I grinned back.

'Nah. It's OK. I'll stick with this one, thanks.' But in the back of my mind I was still picturing the grim little room next door and it troubled me.

'Want to see if we can find the window on the outside?' Matt said, still buzzing after our discovery.

'I'll just check on Noah,' I said. 'If he's awake he could do with some fresh air and sunshine so we could take him with us.'

We traipsed around the back of the house, Matt swiping away tree branches as he went.

'Follow my footsteps,' he commanded, as I carefully carried a curious Noah with me. 'There could be all sorts of rubbish hidden in the grass. I don't want you to slip or tread on something nasty.' We skirted around the side of the flat, counting the windows out loud as we did so.

'Your room, bathroom, Alice's room.' Matt said. 'If that's Alice's bedroom then the window should be right around the corner.'

We found it after Matt climbed a small tree and pulled away some clinging tendrils of ivy where it smothered the walls. The little window was hard to see, it blended in with the walls so that it was almost invisible, but as we searched our eyes made sense of what was granite wall and what was glass and the window became more noticeable.

'I wonder what else we'll find,' Matt mused out loud. 'Any more hidden rooms, do you think?'

'With this place, anything's possible.'

I hugged Noah tightly to me. Looking at the blank glass of the window, I couldn't help but feel uneasy. Like there was someone, or something, looking back out at us.

Alice's first day at school was a raving success and she regaled us with stories all through dinner.

'Me and Gracie,' every sentence seemed to start this way, 'we played in the painting corner after break and she painted a dog and I painted a hare. Except the stupid teacher called it a rabbit and when I said it wasn't a rabbit, it was a hare, she told me they were the same thing!' She threw her arms up in a big shrug. 'How can they be the same thing when they're totally different things?' she asked me.

'Don't call your teacher stupid,' Jayne said automatically. Alice carried on as if she hadn't heard her.

'Me and Gracie, we're best friends and some other girls wanted to be our friends too but we said no 'cos we only want one best friend and we don't want to share.'

'Did you do any learning today or was it all playing?' asked Matt, teasingly.

'Um, we did singing and we had a story and we all had to run in a circle when we had games outside,' Alice said, as if this cleared everything up.

'So, did you like school?' I asked her.

'Yes,' she said, after thinking about it for a moment. 'I shall go again tomorrow.'

The next day I took Alice to school on my own. Jayne had texted me when her nightshift ran over and said she wouldn't be home until after nine. It was my job anyway, what I was employed to do, so I strapped Noah into his stroller, packed Alice's schoolbag with her lunch and snacks, and we headed down the long drive towards the main road. Alice seemed overjoyed to see her 'best friend' Gracie again and the two of them hugged each other cutely as soon as we reached the crossing. Ben walked with us towards the school gate, looking tanned and relaxed in a faded surf T-shirt and board shorts. I should have felt self-conscious in my green and blue headscarf but his easy chat put me at ease and we talked of nothing much until we reached the road by the school gates.

There was that one particular cluster of mothers' there again, gossiping and swapping salacious tales behind one another's backs. When they saw me they huddled in closer together, forcing me to manoeuvre Noah's stroller into the busy road, rather than moving aside to let me pass. I heard the whispered words as I went by.

'Look out, here comes the Addams family!'

There were some quiet sniggers amongst the group

'What does she think she looks like in that ridiculous scarf?' Louder this time.

'It's got to be better than what's underneath. I heard she has a big open wound instead of a mouth!'

'...and look at that baby! It's just gross. It turns my stomach looking at them both.' This last comment was said at a normal volume, designed for me to hear, and came from the same woman who had monopolised Ben and dragged him away yesterday.

I ignored them and fixed my gaze on a point in the distance, not daring to look at Ben beside me. Surely he would not want to be seen with us; he was probably thinking of how he could melt away without a fuss.

'Morning Kate!' His cheery voice rang out. The woman flushed prettily and flashed him a big smile.

'I see you've not been hitting the gym lately,' Ben went on. 'Your arse is getting HUGE! And your stomach's flapping over the top of your jeans; you can't hide it with that top. And you, Felicity, have you not persuaded your hubby to get you that chin tuck yet? More rolls than a bakery, you have!' He hadn't changed the tone of his voice, it was still friendly and jovial, but the words he was speaking to these women were delivered with a steely note. They gaped, the crowd of nasty bitches, and the woman called Kate visibly sucked in her stomach while the one called Felicity automatically lifted her head higher. 'See. Not so much fun when someone else is commenting on your flaws, is it?' Ben put his hand casually on my shoulder and steered us past the now silent group.

'I can't believe you just did that!' I gasped at him.

'They deserved it,' he said. 'They're a nasty bunch. Ignore them. They won't dare to insult you again if I'm with you.' He smiled down at me. 'I think your scarf is lovely, but you shouldn't have to hide your face. What was it? Road

121

accident?' His voice was gentle and serious now. 'You don't have to tell me. I know it's none of my business.'

'Acid attack,' I blurted out. 'Four months ago.'

He winced and gently pulled my scarf from my mouth and I let him. I let him look at my scars and he brushed my hair away from my cheek to see the scar there.

'It's so cute!' he grinned. 'It looks just like the...'

Playboy bunny, yeah I know,' I finished for him.

Thank you for showing me,' he said seriously. 'Thank you for trusting me.'

He kissed my cheek, right on the scar, and walked away from us, whistling.

'See you after school!' he called. I held my hand to my cheek, still feeling his gentle kiss.

I decided to walk Noah the long way home, down the lanes that run behind the fields at the back of The Grange. It was a beautiful late summer morning. Fresh but sunny, with the promise of warmer temperatures later in the day. Noah was crowing happily as we swooped around puddles and went off-roading in the fields. He stared with absolute fascination at a group of cows, who had strolled over to gaze at us curiously, and now stood nonchalantly chewing their cuds.

From this lane I could see the back of the house where it peeped through the trees. It looked far less grand from this side. It was only built to look imposing from the front, so the back was a hodgepodge of uneven lines and odd angles. I could see more dilapidated granite structures from here too. More outbuildings, I supposed, maybe pig sties or storage sheds. They were mostly in ruins, like the ones at the side of the house, but I still wanted to explore them. Maybe a day when I didn't have Alice or Noah in tow, though. There could be all sorts of dangers lurking in those overgrown walls, not to mention they don't look particularly stable either, and I could clearly picture a sliding mass of granite blocks collapsing onto tiny limbs and fragile skulls.

We carried on walking, expecting there to be a lane to the left which would meet up with the main road and from there, lead us back to The Grange. We didn't find one for ages, but what we did find was an old communal water well. Set into the side of a small hill and surrounded by carved blocks of the island granite that seemed to make up most of the buildings on Jersey, it looked almost like a church alter. It hadn't been touched in decades by the look of the climbing vines that nearly camouflaged it completely. I could just make out the old carvings, etched into the surrounding granite alcove. Leaving Noah parked safely to the side of the lane, I picked my way through a tangle of blackberry bushes and nettles to take a closer look. There was a date carved into one of the stones, but all I could make out were the numbers '1' and '5', the rest was illegible – worn away by centuries of wind and rain. The actual well itself had been made safe with a metal mesh cover, which must have been added in fairly recent times. Leaning precariously over a clump of nasty-looking, rusty barbed wire, I tried to peer through the squares of the mesh down to the long drop below. I could just make out a faint sliver of blue, where the reflection of the sky sat on top of the water. It wasn't that far down, maybe fifteen feet, and I could see the outline of my head, rippling in the water's gentle movement. I watched for a moment, enjoying the peace of the fields, peppered only with bursts of jubilant birdsong.

A shadow passed across the water.

There was another shape down there; another reflection on the water next to mine. Another figure echoed in the silver light. There was someone standing right behind me.

Whirling around too fast, I lost my footing and wobbled dangerously. About to fall, I threw my arms out in an automatic reflex and reached for something, anything, to hold onto to keep me upright. My hand found a solid shape and I clutched it instinctively, crying out in pain and alarm when the rusted knots of wire pierced my palm. In my panic I had grabbed onto the piece of barbed wire fencing and, despite its age, the spikes were still capable of perforating skin.

I was alone. There was no one there.

I regained my balance quickly, adjusting my footing for a more secure stance. Slowly, I unclasped my fist where it gripped the wire, wincing at the stinging in both my hand, and my foot, where I had brushed against a patch of nettles. I didn't see it at first. I was too busy looking at the holes in my palm. But when I looked at the strands of wire where they disappeared into the bushes, I saw feathers. Not just a few feathers, when I took a closer look, but a whole bird. It was a blackbird, or maybe a crow. It was too decomposed for me to tell the difference and it was stretched out grotesquely along the top line of wire, as if in full flight. Poor thing, I thought, what a way to meet your end. Something was bothering me though about the way it was hanging on the wires. It can't have just flown into them by accident. Leaning closer I saw that there were finer, thin strands of wire circling its outstretched wings, fixing them to the rest of the fencing. More wire was looped around it's drooping neck. The bird hadn't met an untimely death by flying into the disguised barbs, it had been strung up there. Deliberately. Flies buzzed lazily around its exposed ribcage and I backed away hurriedly, feeling sick at this mutilation of an innocent creature. It was only Noah's outraged wailing that brought me back to the present, and I hurried back to where he sat, red-faced and indignant in his stroller.

'Oh Noah, I'm so sorry darling!' I leant over and unbuckled his straps, then hauled him up into my arms. 'Did you think I'd gone and left you? Did you think I wasn't coming back?' I crooned, kissing the soft downy hair just above his ear as I jiggled him to try and stop him crying. 'I wouldn't do that, darling. I wouldn't leave you alone.'

His wails turned to occasional hiccups and his breathing turned slow and sleepy. Gently, I placed him back in his buggy, secured him in and turned him around to push him home.

'Bah!' Noah shouted, twisting in his seat and pointing back towards the well. 'Bah!'

'What are you pointing at, funny boy?' I said, catching hold of his hand. 'There's nothing there.'

'Bah!' he insisted.

I felt a cold breeze hit the back of my neck, and the feeling of being watched was unnerving.

'No one there,' I sang, determinedly. 'No one here but us chickens.'

Back at The Grange, Jayne was at the kitchen table eating toast and looking bleary-eyed after a long night at the hospital. She fussed over my wounded hand.

'Look at the state of it. You've ripped half your hand away!'

She filled a bowl with warm water and swirled some disinfectant in it, then found a half-pack of cotton wool and gestured for me to sit down at the table so she could give it a good clean. She swabbed at my hand roughly. 'You'll definitely need a tetanus shot, rusty barbed wire is one of the worse things you could have picked.'

'I didn't exactly 'pick' it – I lost my balance and it happened to be the first thing I grabbed. But it was so weird, that well.' I told her about the bird strung up on the wire and she grimaced in disgust.

'That's bizarre. Who would want to do that? Why?'

'No idea. Maybe it's a local thing?' I guessed. 'You know, keep other birds away by showcasing a dead one.'

'Whatever,' said Jayne. 'It doesn't sound like a safe place to explore, what with rusty wire and rotten corpses, so maybe just stick to the grounds around here, eh?' She finished her ministrations and wrapped a gauze dressing around my hand. Yawning, she stretched her arms above her head. 'I'm knackered. I'm off to bed. Although how I'm supposed to sleep with that racket going on, I don't know.'

Matt had made a start on the passageway to my bedsit and was hammering, drilling and sawing with great and noisy enthusiasm. I put Noah down in his playpen and gave him some cloth books to look at. He liked to suck on the corners but it kept him happy and occupied while I tidied up the kitchen. I fussed around, spraying surfaces with citrus cleaner and tidying Alice's discarded toys in the lounge. The hours until I picked her up from school seemed endless and I decided to take up Matt's offer of picking through some of the boxes containing his great-uncle's belongings. After all, all I had to do was look after Noah until we had to collect Alice and he was happy with his toys and had a nap in the afternoon anyway. When Matt came in looking for coffee, I got him to fetch me a couple of crates from where they had stored them in another flat. He willingly obliged and soon I was sitting cross-legged on the floor of the lounge, about to dive into the contents of the first box. Old newspapers spilled out of the sides and there were a number of paper-wrapped shapes nestled in there, just waiting for me to discover them. I couldn't think of a better way to spend the day.

Jennet's Story

Jersey, 1603

He was there the next day, Sister, and the next and the next.

Each time he waited for me in the clearing where we had first met and talked, and each day he had a little gift for me. The first time, he brought bread and soft cheese, enough for two, and we drank small beer from his pewter flask. Then there were hard boiled eggs and pieces of smoked chicken pilfered from his father's breakfast table and wrapped in the softest linen cloth. Best of all, he once gave me a honey cake made by their cook fresh that morning, and my mouth rejoiced over the delicate sweetness of it. I cannot recall ever having tasted such richness before and the memory of the finely grated grains of sugar melting on my tongue will stay with me for the rest of my miserable life.

We spent many hours exploring the woods and then venturing further than I usually dared. We combed the coastline, paddling in the gentle seas and looking for shellfish at low tide. When I told Matthieu that I did not have a fire to cook upon, he immediately took it upon himself to find me a small kettle and a tripod over which to set it above a blaze, and laboured with his own hands to dig a hole next to my rough shelter and lined the small pit with stones we lugged from the beach. With my own meagre supply of dry sticks I was able to make a small fire - enough to heat the kettle and cook a simple soup of whelks and foraged greens, sometimes thickened with a carrot or turnip stolen from the farmer's field. He found me other treasures too. Once a worn feather comforter stolen from under the housekeeper's nose.

'It is too faded and old for use now. She had the maids put a bundle of old bedlinen up in the attics. No one

will ever even know it is missing!' he claimed triumphantly. It was heavenly to me, to roll myself into its plump depths each night, the duck feathers warding off the cold and damp. Matthieu had taken one look at my inadequate dwelling and promptly returned with hammer and nails, pieces of good wood and some old thatch which he had scavenged from the pile waiting to be burned. Within a day he had patched up the holes which let the rain in and mended the gaps in the rotten planks where the wind whistled through at night and left me shivering in my bed. He worked methodically, whistling a merry tune. He liked working with his hands he told me, he often helped the estate carpenters whenever he could steal away from his tutor and his tyrannical father. My father came out of the cottage once when he heard the hammering and almost fell over himself trying to get back inside once he saw Matthieu, the son of the Lord, but not before he had tugged at the sparse hair on his head in a gesture of respect. Matthieu glared darkly at him.

'I can order him to take you back in, you know. He has a duty to provide for you until you are of age.'

'Please, do not bother with him. I am used to being by myself now. If I were to move back into that cottage with him and his woman I would feel as though I am in chains,' I begged.

With a dry space to sleep and the means to cook myself a meal, I was living better than I had in a long while. The stolen treats from the big house kitchens provided me with fat and starch, things which had been sorely missing from my daily diet, and with this good food I began to fill out and gradually lost the thin, pinched look from my face. My ragged dress became far too small for me as my body blossomed. I never grew much taller than I had been as a child but I began to look healthy, making the grotesque scar on my face all the more prominent as the hare-like features drew attention to my good teeth underneath.

One summer's day Matthieu gave me the best present of all. It was a thin sliver of soap. I had never even seen real soap in all my life and this was of good quality, the kind only rich men and ladies can buy. It was not much, only a nub, but it was scented with roses and glided over my skin leaving a waxy trail in the ingrained dirt there.

'We can go to the beach by La Roquebourg,' Matthieu coaxed me. 'It is such a fine day, we can swim and you can bathe in the rockpools.'

It was such a new feeling for me to be clean. Clutching the tiny piece of soap I ducked my head under the warm waters and rubbed it over my hair and face, exalting in the feel of the dirt and filth washing out of my body. I was fully clothed, so my dress got a dunking too as to bathe in my ragged shift in front of a boy would have been unseemly. The soap dissolved into nothing as I scrubbed and scrubbed and then we lay in the warming sun to dry.

'I will have to find you some other clothes to wear.' Matthieu ran his eyes over my newly cleansed body where my rags clung wetly to my burgeoning curves. 'That garment is not fit for scrubbing the floors.'

He was true to his word and a few days later he presented me with an armful of cloth.

'But, Matthieu, where did you get this?' I asked him, both drawn to the pretty fabric and fearful at the same time. 'I cannot take this. I will be accused of theft and sent to the scaffold!'

'Pah!' Matthieu scoffed. 'It is a cast off from my sister, Agnes. It was stuffed into one of her old chests in the attic. She has been married these past five years and has never had need of it so I doubt she even remembers it is there.'

The dress was of wool and full skirted, with the bodice and sleeves laced together with fine leather. It was a little worn and showed some evidence of moth so I did not doubt his tale of it being stored away for some years. It was a beautiful moss green which went well with my black hair and would be useful for hiding amongst the trees and bushes in the woods. I had no apron to cover it and no boots for my feet but I felt as rich and grand as a lady gently born as the folds of soft wool caressed my bare legs.

I had never had someone who looked after me as Matthieu did. He stole food to keep me fed, and cloth to keep me clothed. No one had ever shown me as much care in my life before and, although I knew it was charity, I took these things gladly for I would have starved or frozen to death without them. I thought Matthieu was providing for me out of responsibility - he was the son of the lord of the manor house after all and had a duty of care towards all who lived and toiled on his land. I like to think he felt guilt too, at having so much when I had so little. And I hoped it was because he perhaps cared for me a little.

But the truth of the matter was much darker. Matthieu liked to steal. He enjoyed the thrill of pilfering from the cook, and the housekeeper and, most of all, his father whom he hated. He loved seeing their confusion, their bafflement, when items went missing. When the blame was laid on the scullery maid or the dairy maid or the laundry maid, he would bite down on his fist to stop himself laughing at their stupidity, even if it meant those poor innocent unfortunates were turned out from their jobs and their home. He was careful not to take too much and too often but the temptation was always there - if he encountered an opportunity to steal something, he would have it away and secrete it about his person until such a time as he encountered me in the woods to pass it on. Poor, starving, shunned little Jennet who was ever grateful for Matthieu's "gifts" and would receive them with a gasp of delight and a shy smile. Poor, stupid, trusting little me.

CHAPTER FOURTEEN

Leah

Several hours later, I was surrounded by rubbish. And I mean, it was total rubbish. The old yellowing newspapers were just old copies of the local daily paper, the Jersey Evening Post. They went back a few years but a quick flick through them highlighted nothing of interest. I scanned them quickly for any mention of the Chevalier family, thinking maybe Great-Uncle Pierre had kept them for this reason, but there was no mention of the old family name. The promising paper-wrapped parcels only held old glass tumblers, none matching, and an assortment of what can only be described as "tat". Plastic ashtrays with garish pictures of Spanish dancers - souvenirs from a long-ago package holiday to Benidorm; a carved wooden horse with its tail broken off and missing; old mugs, chipped plates and one of those executive desk toys from the eighties - silver balls on wires that snapped against each other for no apparent use or reason. I had a binbag full of things to throw on the skip, and a box of slightly better things to give to a charity shop, if and when we came across one.

'Any luck?' said Matt, as he put down his tools and took a break. 'Found any lost treasure or family heirlooms we can sell?'

'Not unless there's a niche market for tacky Spanish souvenir goods, no.' I replied.

We declared a lunchbreak and made our sandwiches companionly, side-by-side in the kitchen. Matt even offered to feed Noah his banana and yoghurt as I made a proper pot of tea for us both. I had thoroughly enjoyed my morning, poking through the left-behind detritus of an elderly man I didn't know, and I was keen to get stuck into another couple of boxes.

'Woah, at this rate you'll have the attic cleared in no time!' Matt teased but he obligingly fetched me more crates to sort out. We put Noah down for his nap and in the peaceful sunlit lounge I sifted through more boxes of cheap china ornaments and old Christmas cards until the reminder on my phone prompted me to get Noah up and walk down to the school for Alice.

Ben waved when he saw us at the school gates and came to stand next to me. The cluster of designer-clad, overly made-up yummy mummies' pointedly ignored us both. Alice and Gracie came running out to meet us joyfully, their brightly coloured school bags ricocheting off each other.

'Can Gracie come to our place for tea?' Alice asked breathlessly, as Gracie shyly nodded behind her.

'Not today, sweetie,' Ben told her. 'I'm sorry but we have to see our Aunty Debbie today, don't we Gracie?' Gracie nodded again but this time her little face was etched with disappointment. Alice looked disappointed too.

'Awwwwww,' she whined. 'I wanted to show her my bedroom and the place outside where Jenny lives.'

Ben looked at me quizzically at the mention of Jenny. I was perplexed too, as Alice had gone a week now without mentioning the name and I thought that, with all the excitement of starting school and making some real friends, her imaginary one had been forgotten.

'Who's Jenny?' Ben asked me, a puzzled smile on his face.

'Imaginary friend!' I mouthed back at him, hoping Alice wouldn't see.

But she did.

'Jenny's not 'maginary!' She stamped her foot and pouted at me angrily. 'She lives in a house in the garden and she comes to see me in my bedroom.'

'OK, whatever you say,' I said to her, rolling my eyes at Ben. 'She lives in the garden but she also lives in the house.'

'Yes, she does!' Alice insisted firmly. 'Just because you can't see her! She only likes me so I'm the only one who can, but I know she'll like Gracie too.' She folded her arms across her chest and turned away from us, in a right sulk now.

'Come on then. Let's get home and then you can play with Jenny if you want to.'
I said goodbye to Ben and swung the pushchair around and Alice reluctantly took my free hand as we neared the zebra crossing.

'I know you don't believe me,' Alice said darkly. 'But you will soon.'

'What do you mean?' I asked, concentrating on getting us across the road safely and not really paying attention.

'Nothing,' she said, and clammed up, refusing to speak to me for the rest of the journey home.

I didn't think any more on Alice's strange outburst as my phone had started ringing. The call was from a London number.

'Hello?' I answered, still pushing Noah's stroller with one hand and putting Alice's hand firmly on the handle so she couldn't run off ahead of me.

'Leah? Hi, it's DS Shead here,' said a male voice. 'Just wanted to update you on your case. It went to court this morning and we've got a result.'

'So soon?'

'Yes. It was all just a formality really, seeing as Marianne Walsh pleaded guilty.'
There was a pause.

'Did it not go well then?' I asked quietly.

'Not as well as we'd hoped,' the police sergeant admitted. 'She got eighteen months, suspended sentence.'

'What?!' I yelled. 'You told me she'd get twelve years!'

'I told you we were HOPING for twelve years. The judge felt there were sufficient circumstances to show some leniency in this case. No previous convictions, no evidence that the attack was premeditated, husband's a faithless twat...,' He broke off and cleared his throat. 'Anyway, I just wanted to let you know the outcome.'

'Did she mention me at all?' I asked. 'Did she apologise at least? Did he?'

'No, I'm sorry. In my opinion neither of them gave you a moment's thought, even after the photos were shown.' The photos. They had looked at my torn and twisted face in those photos and shown no remorse. They had heard the words of my victim impact statement and had not been moved, had not felt guilty, had not shown the least concern that they had both ruined my life. And now she had got off, scot-free, more or less. She was free to carry on living her normal life, with her normal-looking face, raising her normal-looking children.

For a moment I was so angry, so distraught, that I was blinded by my rage. I stopped walking, breathing hard as I punched the end call button on my phone and shoved it deep inside my bag. I bent over the handles of the stroller as the anger formed a hard, cold knot in my stomach and I cried out with pain. It's true that when you feel badly let down it's like a kick in the guts. Noah looked around with big, worried eyes.

It's OK, sweetheart. Leah's just got a tummy ache.' I said, forcing myself to stand up and keep pushing. We were only a few minutes from home. Alice was nowhere to be seen. 'Alice?' I shouted, cupping my hands to my mouth. 'Alllliiiicce?'

She wasn't on the path ahead of us and when I looked around, she wasn't behind us either. The road was on our left and to the right was a low granite wall, with high hedges hiding the empty field behind them. Surely I would have noticed if she had run into the road, even if I was distracted by my phone call.

'Alice? ALICE?'

'Ahhhhhh-eeeeeeeeeeeeeeee!' Noah joined in the yelling.

We walked a few steps forward, calling all the time. I was beginning to panic. Even if she had run straight home she wouldn't be able to get in the house without my key. She would probably wander around the building to where Matt was working and he would see that she was on her own and be so angry with me.

'ALICE?'

I saw a gap in the hedgerow and stuck my head through. We were just outside the field which bordered the house and I could see the solid walls of the east wing through the trees. The ramshackle granite forms of the old animal pens stood out starkly from this side, far more than when I had glimpsed them from the other edge of the field, by the well. From here I could see their former symmetry and how dangerously they leaned to the side now. A movement near them made me hold my breath. A glimpse of blonde and blue in between the pinky-brown blocks.

'Alice?' I hollered. She peeked out from behind one particularly nasty-looking wall. I thought I heard her giggle. 'Alice, you get back here RIGHT NOW!'

Frustrated, I pulled my head painfully from the thorny hedge and stalked down the road a few more yards. There had to be an opening to this field somewhere, a gate or a track. We were so close to the house that we could have cut across the overgrown lawns and found a way into the field that way. At last, the low wall and hedge came to an end by an old pathway which, judging by the length of the long grass, hadn't been used for some time. It was too rough, impassable for a toddler in a stroller, so I unclipped Noah and hoisted him on my hip while I stalked through the dense weeds towards where I had seen Alice near the ruins. I struggled to keep hold of him tightly as I stumbled and slid on pitted ground littered with old rabbit holes. More barbed wire curled around my legs as it tried to trip me up and now and then I stubbed my toes on a camouflaged loose block of granite.

Alice was sitting serenely on a small pyramid of bricks and old wooden beams.

'Alice? What the hell....?' I shouted at her. 'Why did you run off like that? Get down from there! It's dangerous!'

'I like it here,' Alice said calmly. 'I can see for miles when I climb up on the wall.'

'That "wall" is going to fall down any minute and I don't want you to be under it when it does, so GET DOWN!' She scrambled down off her perch but didn't come over to where Noah and I were waiting; instead she disappeared behind another loose section of granite. I climbed gingerly around the fallen pile of stones after her. She was on her hands and knees, using a broken roof slate to dig at the ground in the corner of one of the pens.

'Alice, what in the world are you doing? You're getting filthy, look at the state of you.' I put Noah down gently on the ground and went to grab Alice's arm to pull her away from whatever she was doing. She jerked away from me and continued digging in a frenzy.

'It is here, I know it is,' she muttered under her breath.

'Alice, what are you looking for? Come on. Enough now. Let's go.' I reached for her again and she turned her face towards me in a snarl.

'Get AWAY from me!' she hissed, before whirling around and digging, digging madly at the dirt in the corner. I recoiled sharply. That had not sounded like Alice. The voice was deeper, rougher, and with a slight accent. She continued to jab ferociously until the slate she was using snapped and she leant back on her heels, panting hard. 'It has to be here. They will believe me then. They will have to tell the truth.' Alice moaned. I was wrong; it wasn't an accent she was speaking with - it was a speech impediment. Not quite a lisp, more like she couldn't make certain sounds without sounding like she'd had a shitload of Novocaine at the dentist.

'Alice?' I said quietly. 'Alice, what are you looking for?'

She stilled at the sound of my voice, frozen on the ground with her hands and school pinafore black with dirt. She didn't move for a long moment until she hiccupped and I noticed her shoulders were shaking and she had tears running down her face.

'Aunty Leah?'

She whispered so softly I had to crouch down to hear her.

'What am I doing here?'

A short time later we were back at The Grange, having successfully avoided running into Matt, and Alice's school uniform was tumbling merrily in the washing machine. She was still quiet and pale, sitting listlessly at the kitchen table while I fussed around making hot chocolate for comfort.

'Aunty Leah, why don't I remember?' she'd asked me, confusion and fear on her tiny face. 'I remember walking home from school with you and Noah, but then.... it was like I fell asleep.... and then I woke up..... and I was all dirty and I didn't know where I was.'

I sat beside her and put my arm around my shoulders. She snuggled into me and I was glad that, at least, she had stopped being mad at me over Gracie not being able to come home with us.

'I don't know, little bunny. Maybe you were daydreaming? Maybe you dreamed there was buried treasure in those buildings - you were certainly looking for something in there. Look, it doesn't matter now. You're safe

137

and here with me, and Daddy, and Mummy will be awake soon, but please promise me you won't go in that field again.' I squeezed her tight. 'Those ruins are really dangerous!'

'I promise,' she said solemnly.

It was a weird thing altogether, I thought to myself. Had I imagined the low, growling voice coming from Alice's mouth? Did she genuinely not remember digging in the ground, as if desperately searching for something she was adamant was there? When I thought about this episode, and the one that had happened at the zoo, I was beginning to wonder if Alice was suffering from blackouts. Could they be an underlying symptom of something more serious, I thought, should I suggest taking her to a doctor?

Alice giggled.

'What?' I said to her, smiling and hugging her tight.

'Jenny's laughing at you!'

I didn't want to worry Jayne by telling her about Alice's latest weird behaviour. She got home from her shift at the hospital the next day with big dark circles under her eyes, looking absolutely exhausted, and slumped down at the kitchen table. I passed her a cup of tea and got a wan smile in return.

'Cheers.' She cupped her hands around the mug. 'God, I'm so knackered. There's an outbreak of Norovirus on the wards. Most of the Health Care Assistants are off sick with it so we're run ragged.' She took a sip of tea. 'At least it means more shifts for me.'

'Don't go running yourself into the ground though,' I warned. 'The last thing we need is for you to get sick too.'

We were interrupted by the sound of a car pulling up on the gravel outside. Glancing at each other in surprise - we never got visitors at The Grange, we didn't know anyone here in Jersey - we looked through the window at the sleek, silver Audi. A tall, familiar-looking man unfolded from the driver's seat and raised a hand in greeting.

'He looks familiar,' Jayne said.

'Yeah, you're right. He does,' I agreed.

'Jayne, hello!' the strange man called. 'Sorry to just drop in like this but I don't have your number.' He loped casually through the kitchen door like he'd done it a thousand times before.

'Hi there!' He held out his hand for me to shake. 'I'm Gabriel, Matt's...um...second cousin I believe.'

'Of course! Gabriel! Sorry, couldn't place you for a minute,' flustered Jayne. 'We met at the funeral.'

'Hi, pleased to meet you. Would you like some tea? We're just having one.' I grabbed a clean mug and clicked the kettle on again.

'I'll go and grab Matt.' Jayne said, already on her way down the hall to where Matt was working. Gabriel accepted tea gratefully and sat down next to me at the table.

'So, ... how are you getting on here?' he asked me. He was open and friendly, with a nice smile and hair which flopped lazily into his eyes. He was dressed in what I like to call "rich man in down time" clothing - designer jeans teamed with a tasteful check shirt and a fitted blazer over the top.

'Oh, fine, you know,' I fumbled. 'I like helping out, looking after Alice and Noah.'

As if on cue Alice burst into the kitchen, the lure of a visiting stranger was too enticing to ignore.

'Hello!' she blurted out, grinning. 'I'm Alice. Who are you?'

'I'm your Uncle Gabriel.' He held out his hand and Alice took it with a giggle. 'Well, not strictly an uncle but close enough,' he said.

Jayne returned with Matt in tow and I realised why Gabriel had looked so familiar - when he and Matt stood side by side the familial resemblance was uncanny. Both had the same olive skin tone and hair colour, the same high cheekbones.

'Gabriel! Good to see you again!' Matt clapped him on the shoulder.

'Well, I must admit I'm a little curious to see what you've done to the old place!' Gabriel said genially.

'Come on, come on! I'll give you the grand tour!' Matt led him back towards the hallway and they both disappeared into the gloomy depths of the grand hall, their voices fading as they went.

'I'd forgotten,' said Jayne 'just how much of a babe he is! Don't you think?'

'He looks too much like Matt. That's why you think he's a babe!' I laughed.

'Maybe, maybe,' mused Jayne. 'He was supposed to inherit, you know, not me and Matt. You should have seen his face at the reading of the will when he discovered the old man had turfed him out and put Matt in his place instead!'

'Really? Well, he doesn't seem to be holding a grudge. He was perfectly friendly just now.'

'Hmmm, I don't know,' Jayne narrowed her eyes thoughtfully. 'There's just something about him.... something I don't trust.'

'Jayne, you hardly know the man. You've met him, what, once before?'

'I think Mummy's right.' We'd both forgotten Alice was still there, hanging on our every word. She looked up at both of us in earnest. 'I don't think Uncle Gabriel is a very nice man.'

'What makes you say that, sweetie?' Jayne smoothed Alice's hair.

Jenny ran away when he came in. She's scared of him. He looks like the man who chained her up in the room and was very angry with her,' Alice finished. Jayne and I looked at each other in complete puzzlement.

'Oh, that's too bad. Poor Jenny,' Jayne said to Alice and I echoed her.

'Yes, poor Jenny.'

140

An hour later, Matt and Gabriel surfaced from the building site of the wing next door with identical grins on their faces.

'Gabe's been telling me a bit about the history of this place,' enthused Matt. 'Fascinating, absolutely fascinating! Did you know, Jayne, that the Nazis took this house over during the war and used it as a brothel? Poor Uncle Pierre's father was allowed to stay but only if he moved up into the attics, but he didn't want to be seen as a collaborator so he moved into Gabe's great-grandfather's house instead!'
Gabriel, now Gabe apparently, laughed at the expression on Jayne's face.

'No need to look so shocked, dear, it happened all over the Channel Islands. And it was your Great-Great-Uncle's house too, Matt. Pierre's uncle.' He paused. 'Matt tells me you haven't been to any of our stunning beaches yet?' he said to Jayne. Jayne went slightly pink.

'No, well, we just haven't had a chance yet. What with me working and Alice's first day at school and .....' she tailed off uncomfortably.

'Well, it's a beautiful day and it'll stay warm for another couple of hours yet, so why don't I take you now? Show you some of the best ones?' Gabriel offered, addressing us all. Alice jumped up and down.

'Yay! Yes please! Mummy can we go please?'
Jayne looked at Matt helplessly.

'Do you know what? That sounds like just the thing. It's time I took a break anyway. What do you say, love?' Matt turned to Jayne. 'We can let the kids have a run about on the beach and get fish and chips on the way home for dinner.' Jayne visibly brightened at knowing Matt was willingly taking precious time away from his work to join them.

'Yes! OK then, that sounds great!'

'Great!' Gabriel repeated. 'Why don't you grab what you need and follow me down in your car? I don't have any child seats in mine, but Leah can come with me if she wants.'

I didn't want. I would rather squash into the same car as Jayne and Matt and the kids than spend an awkward ten minute drive with a complete stranger.

'Good plan!' Jayne decided. 'Right then, what do we need? Alice, see if you can find your swimsuit. I'll grab Noah. Matt, find some sunscreen and some towels. Oh, and Noah's nappy bag too.' She gave the orders to everyone and we scattered in all directions to dig out appropriate beachwear, and find all the other paraphernalia that comes with taking two small children out for a few hours. Fifteen minutes later, armed with buckets and spades, bottles of water, sun hats, bags of crisps and flip flops, we loaded Matt's car and I climbed gingerly into the passenger seat of Gabriel's pristine Audi. It smelled of leather and polish, and was absolutely spotless inside and out.

'My pride and joy!' Gabriel explained as he glided the car down the rough driveway and onto the sealed road. 'I love this car. It's like my child.' he laughed.

'It's very nice,' I agreed.

'A bit unnecessary for such a small island, and the speed limit's only forty miles an hour here, so I have to take her to France to really enjoy her.'

I hated men who called their cars 'her' and spoke about them like they were an illicit lover.

'I hope you don't mind,' he went on. 'Matt told me a bit about your.... um…,' he gestured at his mouth. 'It must have been a difficult time for you,' he said sympathetically. 'He wasn't gossiping, just so you know, I asked him why you were wearing a headscarf, and I saw a bit of your scar on your cheek.'

'Doesn't matter,' I said stiffly. 'I was attacked, had acid thrown at me, and now I'm deformed for the rest of my life. There, now you know everything.'

142

'I'm sorry if I spoke out of turn,' he apologised. 'My father is a surgeon. He has good contacts with other surgeons who specialise in...... injuries like yours. I was wondering if perhaps he could suggest someone who could help, take a look and see if they can make things a bit better for you?' He sounded so sincere, and was obviously mortified at upsetting me, that I softened.

'Thank you. I don't know if there's much room for improvement. The hospital I was in in London was supposed to arrange for plastic surgery for me, but no one's ever called. But I'll be glad to go and see your father's contacts. I'd like to hear what they think. Can you give me the number of his office, so I can make an appointment?'

'No need. I'll get him to give you a call if you give me your number.' He leaned over and flipped open the glove box, taking out a black and gold Faber-Castell pen and a notepad. I scribbled down my mobile number and handed it to him.

'Thank you.'

'No problem. You're family after all. Sort of.' He gave me a crooked smile and I could see that the features which made Matt seem so cuddly and brotherly, sat better on Gabriel's thinner face, and made him quite extraordinarily handsome. He was just that little bit too suave though, too confident, for me to find him really attractive.

We cruised along a long stretch of coast road. The tide was out so far I could barely see the water on the horizon.

'It's so far away!' I exclaimed.

'Tides,' Gabriel replied. 'Jersey has one of the biggest tidal ranges in the world. The island practically doubles in size when the tide's out. Don't worry, it's on the way back in. You'll be swimming in no time, it comes in so fast.'

We indicated right and turned into a tiny car park filled with boats and empty boat trailers. Matt and Jayne joined us a second later. There was a gently sloping granite slipway which led down to the golden sand of the sheltered bay, and a large round tower standing sentry over the sea.

'Le Hocq!' Gabriel announced, putting on his sunglasses and helping Matt unpack his car. 'Safe for the kids to swim, when the tide comes in. It'll be better then anyway as the water warms up when it comes in over the sand.'

We hauled all of our beach stuff down to the warm sand. Jayne set up HQ by putting down several towels on the sand and promptly started to slather Noah in sunscreen. Alice had already changed into her pink Little Mermaid swimming costume and was excitedly running toward the distant shoreline. Matt dumped the supplies he was carrying and followed her.

'Alice! Not too far, OK?' he shouted after her, but she was already just a pink speck in the distance. Jayne sat Noah safely in a sandy hollow where he was promptly mesmerised by the feel of the grains between his fingers and toes, and he grinned happily.

'Come for a walk?' Gabriel said to me and indicated to a rocky outcrop at the end of the sweeping bay. 'There's something I want to show you.'

Curious, I slipped off my sandals and followed him as he set off towards it. Although it was nearing three o'clock, there was still plenty of warmth in the sun and I lifted my head to feel the heat on my skin. My scarf fluttered loose in the breeze and I unwound it, voluntarily showing my face in public for the first time since the attack. Gabriel looked at my scars briefly but he showed no signs of disgust or shock. We walked in tandem, getting closer to the shoreline.

'The tide will probably cut us off on the way back, but we can walk along the footpath.'

Gabriel led me through a patch of sharp granite boulders and we walked around the headland and into another sweep of perfect beach. He pointed to the end of the bay, where a turreted Gothic monstrosity of a house perched upon the clifftop. 'That's Roqueberg.' Gabriel said. 'The house I mean, and at the end of their garden there's a pointy bit of rock, can you see?'

I shielded my eyes against the sun and looked in the direction he was pointing to.

'Yes, I see it. It looks like all the other rocks around here.'

'Ha! It does to the uneducated eye, I suppose, but that rock is known as Rochers de La Sorciere; the Witches' Rock. It's just one of the old Jersey legends.'

'Tell me then,' I asked, interested in why this unassuming piece of granite was the stuff of local legend. Gabriel settled himself on the sand and patted the space next to him. He had taken off his blazer and rolled his jeans up, but he still looked incongruous against the other beachgoers in their shorts and swimsuits.

'Well, it's always been associated with witches and devil worshippers. They say that there's one part of the rock where you can clearly see the outline of the devil's hoofprint. But the main legend is that a coven of witches lived on this cliff, and they would only allow fishermen to pass safely, and not be dashed to pieces on the treacherous rocks underneath, if they were thrown every thirteenth fish of the fishermen's' catch. One day, a particularly brave fisherman picked up a five-legged starfish from the catch, cut of one of the legs so it had four legs and formed the shape of the cross, and threw it at the witches shouting "This cross is my pass!" It landed among the witches who screamed and disappeared in a puff of smoke and were never seen again.' Gabriel leaned back on his elbows and smiled. 'There's loads of witch stories in Jersey. There's one about The Grange, actually.'

'What about The Grange?' I demanded. 'Are you serious? A witch story?'

'Yeah.' Gabriel turned on his side to face me, his golden eyes on mine. 'It's true. I mean, I don't want to scare you, but ....'

'I'm not scared,' I said instantly. 'Just... interested.'

'OK, well, the house hasn't always been called The Grange, that's a fairly recent change.'

'Oh, I know about that!' I interrupted, scornfully. 'It was called something else. Hare-something house.'

'Harewich House,' he corrected. 'Hare. Witch. House. So, the family lore has it that way back in the day, one of the first Chevaliers to live in the house did something to upset a local witch and she put a curse on the family forever.'

'What's a hare-witch? And what kind of curse? Did it come true?' I bombarded him with questions.

'Supposedly, a hare-witch is a witch who was born with the facial features of a hare. And the curse was something to do with the male line of our family doomed to die out - but, as you know, that hasn't happened, so I think the curse has run its course.'

A sudden sick feeling entered my stomach coldly. The facial features of a hare. Was he making fun of the way my face looked like now, like a rabbit? I jumped up, scattering him with fine grains of sand.

'Are you taking the piss?' I yelled, my eyes blurry with tears. 'The face of a hare? Are you seriously sitting there and telling me some bullshit story about a witch with a face like a hare?' I grabbed at my scarf where I had tucked it into the pocket of my shorts and wound it around my face quickly. 'How fucking dare you? Just fuck off, Gabriel, fuck off and don't speak to me again!' I took off back towards the headland, my feet making angry tracks in the damp sand.

'No, Leah, wait!' I heard him cry. 'I didn't mean.... I wasn't... oh, FUCK IT!'

He ran to catch up with me and tried to grab my arm. I shook him off roughly and walked quicker, wanting nothing more than to put as much distance between us as possible.

Jayne must have noticed my reddened eyes as I huffed back to where she was sitting on a towel, and flopped down beside her, but she knew my moods well enough not to pry. She grabbed my hand and squeezed it.

'All right?' she asked. I shrugged and said nothing. I didn't know what Gabriel was playing at. Was he just playing a mean trick on me? But, why? He only met me a few hours ago, why would he single me out and be so horrible? He must have known how touchy I am about my looks. I sat there, thinking about the way he said "hare-witch", wondering if I had missed a subtle inflection in his voice, looking retrospectively for any clue that he was having a sly dig at me. When I looked up, the tide had started to come in and was close enough for us to see where Matt was playing with Alice and Noah in the shallow breakers. Alice was laughing, jumping over the tiny waves and splashing down on her tummy. Matt was lifting Noah high in the air then dipping him down to dangle his pudgy feet in the calm water. A cool breeze was licking over us and I shivered, suddenly feeling a chill despite sitting in full sun. Jayne noticed and began to pack up.

'Time to go. They'll be freezing in that water.'
She hauled herself to her feet and wrapped a towel around her middle self-consciously, before plodding down to the water's edge to chivvy Matt and Alice into getting out of the sea. It was a tired and happy little bunch who wandered back towards me, although Alice's lips were turning blue and she was shaking with cold.

'Aunty Rabbit, the sea is so much fun!' she said to me, eyes sparkling. 'Daddy said he's going to get me a special board so I can ride on top of the waves. We can come down here all of the time!'
We rubbed both of the kids down with the sun-warmed towels and picked our way back to the car. There was still no sign of Gabriel. He had given up on following me back.

'Can I come back with you guys?' I asked. 'I don't want to wait for Gabriel.'

'Sure,' said Matt. 'We're going to find a chippy on the way home anyway. Nothing like fish and chips for tea after a big swim in the sea!'

'Daddy, that rhymes!' Alice said delightedly. 'Like this - I am a fish and my tail goes swish!'

'Erm, I am a crab and I like to GRAB!' countered Matt, as he grabbed Alice around her waist. She collapsed into giggles and they were so infectious, we were soon all giggling along with her. We packed up the boot of the car and settled inside, all of us feeling the after effects of the salt and sun on our skin, but all of us feeling we had had a little holiday, a break from the strain of our everyday lives.

CHAPTER FIFTEEN

We didn't see Gabriel again for a while but, the day following our beach visit, a florist's van pulled up outside The Grange and delivered a posy of sweet summer flowers. The card was addressed to me.

I'm sorry if I offended you, that wasn't my intention. Please forgive my insensitivity. Gabriel.

I crumpled it up in my palm, still unsure what to make of Gabriel and his sudden interest in us and The Grange. I went over the witch story again and again in my mind. Hare-witch - a witch with the features of a hare. What did that mean? Surely it was just folklore, a long-forgotten tale that had been exaggerated and added to through the centuries with each re-telling.

Ben had taken to waiting for us on the corner of the road to school each morning. Alice and Gracie would join hands and run joyfully towards the school gates together, leaving Ben, Noah and I to follow along behind. Alice had still not given up asking if Gracie could come and play at our house after school one day and Ben and I both agreed that we would have to organise something soon.

'It's difficult for me sometimes, balancing work and Gracie,' Ben confessed one day. 'My aunt helps me out a lot. Gracie goes there most days after school so I can get a few more hours work in, but Debbie doesn't like to drive much these days. Her eyesight is quite bad. I tend to drop Gracie off and pick her up at about seven; we usually have something to eat with Debbie - she's a great cook, used to be a chef and had a restaurant with one of her ex-husbands. She's the reason I don't bother to cook for us at home. Gracie much prefers Aunty Debbie's food!' he laughed.

'She sounds amazing,' I said. 'I think that's what Jayne and Matt are missing the most, not having that extended family here in Jersey to fall back on.'

'That's why I'm sure they're so glad to have you,' Ben said warmly. 'You must be a Godsend to them at the moment.'

I flushed pink.

'I suppose. But I love being there with them and looking after the kids, even though Alice has her moments.'

'You need your own life too though. It's not healthy spending all your time with them. You should get out a bit more, do some evening classes or something,' Ben suggested. 'I'll happily show you some basic woodworking if you want. I'd love for you to see my workshop anyway.' I laughed.

'I can't imagine me making things with wood,' I said. 'but I'd love to see your workshop.'

We walked on for a bit, an easy silence between us until Ben stopped suddenly and put a hand on Noah's stroller to stop me too.

'I was wondering if you'd like to go for a coffee with me sometime? Just us, without the kids. You could drop Noah off after the school run and we could meet at the park down the road. It's got a nice cafe, not too busy.'

I stared at him, dumbfounded. Like a date? I wondered. No, he can't mean it like that. He's just being kind. After what he just said about me needing my own life he's just offering me the opportunity to get out and spend time with other people. As friends. Just friends. Oh God, I hope this isn't a pity invite.

'Well?' he grinned. 'Say something!'

'Oh...ahm... sure. That would be...um...great.'

'We don't get to talk properly during the walk to school, too many people around.' I looked around and, sure enough, Kate and Felicity and their little group of hangers-on were looking our way curiously and whispering to each other. 'Why don't we say tomorrow?' Ben suggested.

Tomorrow was Friday. Jayne didn't have to be at work until the middle of the afternoon so she could take Noah for an hour or so in the morning.

'OK, tomorrow,' I agreed.

'I'll wait on the corner for you as usual, we can walk to the park together....unless you'd prefer to meet me there?'

'No, no, we can walk together,' I said, much preferring to be with a friend when I walked into the cafe. I could just imagine the hush which would settle over the other customers as I walked in with my headscarf over my face.

'Great! Maybe we can sort out that play-date for Gracie and Alice over our coffees.' Ben leaned forward and pressed his cheek against mine, the bad one, for a second, then squeezed my shoulder and jogged away in the direction of town.

Jayne was thrilled for me.

'He likes you,' she said simply when I over-analysed his invitation and was openly wondering why he had asked me. 'He wants to get to know you better, not just as another parent or childminder at the school gates either.'

'It's more likely because he feels sorry for me,' I stated baldly. 'He's one of those nice guys who collects lame ducks and "projects".' I made the commas in the air with my fingers.

'Bollocks!' argued Jayne. 'So, you meet for a coffee, you talk, you find out more about each other, you find things in common and BAM! You discover you like each other and coffee becomes dinner, dinner becomes romantic nights in, romantic nights in becomes a serious relationship. You meet his family, start staying overnight at his place and before you know it, you're engaged and planning the wedding with your gorgeous new step-daughter begging for

151

a purple flouncy bridesmaid dress. That's how dating works!'

'No way!' I disagreed. 'I wouldn't get your Matron of Honour outfit planned just yet. It's just a coffee. Because he's making a point of being friendly when all those other bitches at the school are making a point of being unfriendly.'

'You'll see,' Jayne proclaimed. 'I'm right about these things. I'm always right.'

I was on the verge on cancelling when I saw Ben at school the next day, but he was so enthusiastic and clearly looking forward to it that I didn't have the heart.

'Meet you at the top of the road in half an hour!' he called loudly across the playground after we had seen the children into their classrooms safely. Heads turned, and I could feel their eyes on me as I nervously steered Noah back towards home. I could almost hear them muttering amongst themselves, wondering why someone as handsome and lovely as Ben was meeting someone like me outside of the normal school duties. I wouldn't put it past some of them to wait and follow us to the cafe; it would have made good playground gossip on Monday.

My heart was beating fast as I waited nervously on the corner for him twenty minutes later. I was early, I knew that, but it still didn't stop me from imagining Ben not coming, picturing him standing me up. I was ridiculously grateful when I spotted him walking up the road towards me.

'Hey!' he smiled.

'Hey.'

'It's this way,' he said, turning back to the way he had just come from. 'Have you been to the park yet? It's small, but a really nice space, very well kept and you wouldn't know you were in the middle of town.'

'No. I've hardly seen any of Jersey yet - just St Helier and we went to a beach the other day, Le something?'

'Everywhere's called Le something!   Give me something else to go on,' he laughed.

'Um, we walked around some rocks and there was a kind of cliff thing with a Gothic-looking house on it. It had a famous story about some witches?'

'Oh, that'll be Rocqueberg. You must have been near Le Hocq then.'

'Yes! That was it. Le Hocq,' I repeated, feeling the unfamiliar words swirl around in my mouth.

'Cool,' he said. 'But the best beaches are out west, St Brelade and St Ouen'

He pronounced St Ouen as 'Sint Won'.

'I'll take you out there one day. We'll take a walk along the Five Mile Road.'

We had reached a church surrounded by tall trees and beautifully manicured grounds.

'It's in here,' Ben said, indicating the gravel path to the side.

'A church?' I asked, surprised, and disappointedly thinking that maybe he was going to turn out to be one of those evangelistic, religion-obsessed God-botherers who preyed on vulnerable and lonely people. People like me.

'On the other side of the church. Don't look so worried! I'm not about to ask you if you have accepted our saviour Jesus Christ Our Lord into your heart,' he grinned, reading my mind. We strolled down a tree-lined path that gave occasional glimpses onto a large oval expanse of green. Lush planting on both sides dulled the noise of the passing traffic enough for us to hear the twittering birdsong and the gentle splash of the decorative fountain in the middle of another lawn to our left. We turned right up a small slope and then we were suddenly inside a walled garden full of roses. The late, blowsy blooms bobbed in the breeze as their perfume filled the air. Wooden walkways covered in purple wisteria led a path through this wonderful space, out the other side, and brought us to a Victorian building complete with a conservatory. A swinging blackboard sign welcomed us to the Rose Garden Café and promised us all sorts of delicious treats.

'Do you want to sit inside or out?' Ben asked. There was no one sitting at the white cast-iron tables and chairs which were spaced around the lawn. I could see a couple of people at the tables indoors.

'Out, if you don't mind,' I decided. If I didn't have to sit next to other people, I wouldn't. We settled at one of the tables in the sun. Bees buzzed lazily around the garden and I relaxed, at peace in these beautiful surroundings.

'I'll get the drinks. What would you like?' Ben asked.

'A latte please. Oh, and Ben?'

'Yeah?'

'Could you ask them for a straw please? It's easier for me to drink hot drinks. If I have a straw….' I trailed off, embarrassed.

'Sure,' he said and disappeared through the cafe doors to place our order. I could, in fact, drink perfectly well from a mug but I was reluctant to remove my scarf, so a straw would allow me to drink my coffee underneath it and take away the awkwardness of strangers seeing my face. Ben returned with a wooden spoon, the number four written in marker pen on the base, and propped it up in the jar of daisies in the centre of the table. 'I took the liberty of ordering some scones as well. Strawberry jam, Jersey clotted cream - you can't beat a cream tea!'

While we waited for our order, I took the opportunity to study Ben. His t-shirt showed off his broad shoulders and toned arms, tanned from the summer sun. His hair, while mostly dark, had little glints of a lighter brown where the sun had lightened them. His face was friendly and open with laughter lines in creases around his eyes. He was easy-going, bordering on scruffy when I compared him with the smooth and polished Gabriel, but somehow a million times more attractive. He caught me looking and smiled.

'So, shall we swap life stories?'

'Well, mine's easy,' I said, leaning back as the waitress brought over our drinks on a tray. I waited until she had set out the plate of scones, with the tiny pats of Jersey butter and pots of cream and jam, and left the bill on the table before I spoke again. 'Normal childhood, grew up just outside of London. Two brothers, Dad died a couple of years ago, Mum still lives in the family home. Moved into the city proper when I got a job in marketing. Met someone on Tinder, thought he was the real deal, however his wife decided she'd had enough of his philandering and turned up uninvited on one of our dates to specifically throw sulfuric acid at me. The end.'

'That's not the end. Your life hasn't ended because of that. You forgot to add - "moved to Jersey, loving your job here and, oh yeah, just met a great guy who has no secret wife around to throw acid at you",' Ben finished.

'OK, sort of that as well,' I said shyly. 'So what's your story?'

'Rough childhood. Poor, not abusive or anything. Dad took off before I could walk. Mum moved us to Jersey from Plymouth when I was five and we moved in with Aunty Debbie. Mum died of cancer when I was fourteen and I left school as soon as I could to help Debbie out with the bills. Got an apprenticeship with a local firm of joiners and learned my trade from the best. Met my ex-wife, Adele, when she asked for a quote to have some wardrobes built in her bedroom. We got married five months later when we found out Gracie was on the way. Adele took off with the carpet fitter soon after Gracie was born. She didn't "do" motherhood apparently. So it's just been me, Gracie and Debbie since then. We get by. As I said before, Debbie helps out a lot. I don't know what I'd do without her.' Ben stopped talking and shoved half a scone into his mouth. I buttered mine carefully and broke it up into more manageable pieces.

'That's appalling!' I frowned. 'Is she, Adele, still in Gracie's life?'

155

'Nah. She sent a birthday card for the first couple of years but then they stopped coming. Last I heard she was living in Portugal with the carpet fitter.'

'Doesn't Gracie ask about her mother?'

'Sometimes,' he nodded. 'I try and tell her the truth as much as possible. I tell her that her mum is living a long way away and can't come and see her. I tell her that, when she's eighteen, she can try and track her mother down if she wants. I don't tell Gracie that her mother loves her. That wouldn't be the truth. Adele's conveniently forgotten she ever had a child and I don't want Gracie to grow up with unrealistic dreams of an emotional reunion with the mother she doesn't even remember.'

'That's a bit harsh,' I said.

'It's how things are,' Ben shrugged. 'Like I said, thank God for Debbie. You should meet her, she's brilliant! She volunteers at the Jersey Archive four days a week, grows every fruit and vegetable known to man in her garden, goes on archaeological digs whenever she can and practises, what she calls, hedgerow medicine.'

'What's that?'

'She makes her own medicines with plants and herbs and things she finds growing in hedgerows,' Ben explained. 'She mixes them up and makes ointments and potions and stuff for healing. Some of it's pretty good! Her ointment for cuts and bruises is miraculous.'

'Sounds like witchcraft to me!' I joked. 'Hey, that reminds me, I found out that The Grange has a story about witches attached to it. There's a curse on the Chevalier family that goes back centuries.'

'Interesting!' Ben raised his eyebrows. 'Something else you can talk to Debbie about. She'll probably be able to give you the complete history of the house, the family and the curse.'

'It is quite a weird place,' I told him. 'We found a secret room hidden behind the modern walls.' I described the way we had inched sideways down the narrow space

156

and found ourselves in the room full of hooks and loops of iron. 'It was such an odd room. A really weird feeling, like someone had just been there moments before us and was waiting for us to leave before they returned.'

'Creepy!' Ben gave a theatrical shiver. 'There are a lot of weird old places in Jersey. Once I had to do a job at the museum and I was up on the fourth floor on my own; I heard someone whistling and then heard them run up the stairs towards the room I was working in but when I looked around the corner there was no one there. The girls in the office there told me there's a ghost called Sid who haunts the older side of the museum - the bit which was a merchant's house in the 1840's - and that there's a brass bell high up on the wall in the main hallway, really high, about fifteen feet up, and it rings by itself all the time.'

'I don't know if I believe in ghosts. I mean, I can't say I've ever seen one but my mum reckons she has. She used to see a little girl in Victorian clothing standing on the stairs in the house she grew up in,' I replied.

'I don't know either,' Ben said. 'Debbie certainly does though. She's got loads of stories about ghosts and witches and big, black devil dogs who haunt the island bays!'

'OK, you've sold me. I have to meet your Aunty Debbie now. You've mentioned her in nearly every sentence today!' I laughed and Ben blushed.

'I know, I'm sorry. She's just done so much for me, you know? So much for both of us, me and Gracie. I'm just so grateful for her, and she really is a fascinating lady.'

'So let's make a plan then. Do you think she'd mind meeting me?'

'No of course not, she'd love it! She already nags me about working too many hours and not spending any time with friends so she'll be delighted that I've met you. I've got an idea. Why don't we kill two birds with one stone and arrange Alice and Gracie's playdate at the same time? You can take Gracie home with you and Alice after school with you one day next week and then, when I come to pick Gracie up after work, I can take you to meet Debbie and we can have a bit of dinner at her place?'

'Won't she mind? I don't want to impose,' I said.

'Hey, she used to be a chef, remember? There's nothing she likes more than showing off her cooking skills!' Ben held my gaze. 'Go on, I really want her to meet you. And she'd love to tell you more about your house if she can.' I couldn't tear my eyes away from his. He was looking at me with such warmth but there was something else there too, a vulnerability, a rawness that lay just below the surface. He had been badly hurt by his ex-wife, I saw, and he was in no rush to throw himself into another passionate relationship. An easy friendship with someone like me, someone who wouldn't expect more, who wouldn't demand any more from him, was all he could offer for now.

'That sounds.... like a plan! Alice is going to be so excited.'

'So is Gracie. We'd better do it soon or neither of us will hear the end of it.' He rolled his eyes and I laughed along with him, feeling better than I had in a long time. Feeling normal.

Jennet's Story

Jersey 1603

I am sorry, Sister. Some parts of the next telling may be offensive to you.

> *'Why do you not come to church?'*
We were on a hillside, looking out over the dark blue sea and warming ourselves in a sunny hollow away out of the chill wind. I looked over at Matthieu where he was chewing on a blade of grass.

'You know full well why,' I remarked as he grinned impudently at me. 'I am not welcome at the services. The priest told me so himself. You were there when he did.'

'He is a fat fool,' Matthieu said dismissively 'He preaches godliness and holiness and orders us to follow the commandments yet he spends his days in sloth and gluttony. And he is sinful in his pride, I have seen how much he delights in the church's treasures like they are his very own. Do you know, he has a special silver chalice he likes to drink his midday wine from?'

I did not abstain from church deliberately. Indeed, not attending holy worship was punishable by a fine but the priest overlooked this and did not insist my father bring me to church or pay the charge. Once, not long after my mother's death when I was feeling very alone and needing the company of others, I tried to creep in to one of the services. I tiptoed in through the open oak door and tried to hide behind one of the pillars at the back. Everyone was looking towards the front to the priest in his pulpit, and I thought they would not notice me amongst the shadows and the dust at the very back of the stone wall, but all it took was for one man to move slightly and see me out of the corner of his eye. He turned and gaped at me, and his wife turned also to see what was distracting him from the word of God. She let out an almighty screech when she saw my face half-

hidden in the gloom and then more and more people turned to look behind them at the commotion. Children wailed in fright, women screamed and men hissed at me, crossing their fingers in protection against the evil eye. The wave of sound from the frightened parishioners rippled upwards towards the priest and he stopped in the middle of his droning prayer, looking up in annoyance at the interruption.

'It's the hare-witch!' someone shouted.

'She comes to this holy place to mock us!' screamed another.

'Pretre! Father! The witch has looked at me and I fear I am cursed!'

I stood, frozen by fear and unable to move as the townspeople surged towards the alter in their desperation to get away from me. One rough-looking man in a dirty shirt spat at my feet and it glistened wetly on the stone-flagged floor.

'Witch! Hare-witch! Devil's spawn!'

The shouts went on and on and I finally found the strength to step towards the door and into the forgiving daylight beyond when I heard the priest's voice.

'Witch! Thou shalt not suffer a witch to live!' he roared, pointing at me. His loud voice, trained to carry across large empty spaces, was like the voice of God himself. 'Get thee gone, you devil! Bother these good people no more! We will NOT succumb to your evil ways nor follow you into the pits of Hell as you so desire! You are cast out! You are not welcome in here, in this holy house of God. You will leave this place and never show your hare-cursed face here again!' His face was puce as if he had been boiled and spittle ran down his chin as he ranted against me. I took one step, and then another, then another until I was on the steps on the other side of the church door and free to flee into the sanctuary of the cool, inviting woods. The cries and screams of the people inside faded to blessed silence as I tripped and stumbled over roots and stones in my haste to get as far away from the hateful, fearful faces

as possible. One face had stood out amongst the rest. The memory of seeing Matthieu, his mouth open in shock, his father's hand clamped tightly upon his shoulder, would never leave me.

'I think you are lucky, not having to go to church like the rest of us.' Matthieu flipped over onto his stomach.

'I may not be welcome inside God's house but that does not mean I do not pray to Him,' I said piously.

'Do you?' Matthieu probed. 'Or do you have your own God you pray to?' He made a grinning, leering devil's face and wiggled his eyebrows. 'You pray by the light of the full moon and dance naked in worship! You sign the Devil's book and suckle your familiars and rain curses down on the heads of us mere mortal men!' He laughed heartily at his own humour.

'Fool,' I muttered, uncomfortable at his voicing out loud the very crimes other people do suspect me of. 'You know I am no witch. If I was a witch, would I not be living a fine life? How many spells have you seen me cast, eh? In truth, I would not know how.'

'Do not fret, I am only jesting with you.' Matthieu slapped me gently on my rump. 'Do you not think that if you were truly a witch then I would be asking you to hex my father and have him die a sudden death?

'Hush, Matthieu, do not say such things.'

Matthieu's hatred of his father had only grown stronger in the years we had known each other. He was a third son. His eldest brother, Guillaume, would inherit the land and the estates, the houses and the title from Matthieu's father. Guillaume was away in England learning how to run such an estate for when the time came. His next brother, Jeanne, had been given to the church as is usual in these families and had been sent away to France to join a monastery there. Then there was his sister, Agnes, whose cast-off dress I wore. She was married off at fourteen and now lived

161

with her husband and his family over in St Peter. As the third and much later son, Matthieu was useless to his father, and he suffered the additional fate of being the reason for his mother's death, for she died when Matthieu was born and his father never ceased to remind him of this every day. There was no estate for Matthieu to inherit, no trade he could learn to free him from his father's iron fist. The only chance he would have to make his own way in life was to join the King's army and he relished the thought, making me play at sword fights with sticks for hours on end.

'What will you do? When I am gone away, fighting the French for the King, whom will you see?' It was not meant cruelly but I felt the barb none the less. Matthieu had been my constant companion and indeed we had grown up together. He had taught me basic letters and numbers, drawing them in the damp sand over and over until my eyes made sense of them. I had taught him about nature, and how to find the creatures who live in the woods out of sight from most. Together we had roamed the island as far as we dared, for to be seen together would be our undoing, especially now we were grown older and not children anymore.

I had begun my bleeding times a few months earlier. When I crouched in the woods to pass water, my belly ached with a new pain which was not caused either by hunger or a swift kick to my middle. I bent over and breathed through each cramp, thinking I had eaten something gone bad, or had mistaken a bad mushroom for a good one. It was only when I saw the blood on my thighs, thick and dark, that I feared this new pain was a sickness inside me, and that I would surely die from it. Although I was scared, there was something in my heart, a female voice, which told me this was not something I should share with Matthieu. I do not know how I knew, but this voice told me to seek out another female, that this was women's business. I ran through the woods and skirted the low cottages of the village at twilight.

It is the best time to move about unnoticed; when the candles are lit inside and folk are sitting down to eat they are not likely to look far from their tables. I ran across the common to the hovel where Ma Le Brun lived. She was sat outside her door, smoking her clay pipe and reeking of sour, unwashed bodies. When she saw me creeping through the bushes towards her, she opened her mouth and the clay pipe dropped to the ground. I saw surprise and fear in her eyes and saw how she wanted nothing more than to run inside and bolt her door, but she stayed. She was crouched, and fearful of me, but she stayed.

'Ye have no business here with me, hare-child,' she called and made the sign of the cross. 'I'll not be dancing with the likes of you!'

'P...p..pl...please, Mother Le Brun,' I stammered. 'I am in need of your wisdom. I mean no harm.'
She looked me over and I imagined I saw a softening in her face.

'What do ye need? Ye have no pennies so I cannot sell ye a cure, if that is what you are after.'

'I have a great pain. And blood comes. Oh, Madame Le Brun, I am so afraid.'

'Blood? From where?' I saw her nose twitch in curiosity. I blushed as I pointed to under my ragged skirts.

'From here. And pains, in my belly and privy parts,' I whispered. I had never spoken of such things to another living creature and to do so now made my face flame red. Ma Le Brun paused and studied me carefully, eyeing my newly rounded form under my shapeless clothing. She took in my growing breasts, my soft hips and lean waist. She slapped her thighs hard with her hands and barked out a laugh.

'Ha! Ye need not fear, ye simple maid. Ye are having Eve's curse, that is all! Did your mother not speak of this to you?'
I shook my head mutely and she grew sober.

163

'Aye, aye,' she muttered. 'You were just a pippin when she went, God rest her soul.' She made the sign of the cross again, this time in memory of my mother's early passing rather than in protection against my evil ways. 'How old are ye now, girl? Thirteen, fourteen?'

I shook my head again and shrugged. I did not know my true age for I counted the years as seasons in the woods, and not in birthdays.

'Going on for fourteen, I would say. It's late, later than most, for certain, but it happens that way when the body lacks proper nourishment in its youth.' She picked up her pipe, tapped it against a stone and stuck it firmly in her mouth again. 'It is something all women must bear. A reminder of Eve's great sin. T'will happen every moon time and ye must take care not to be around men then, or surely they will sniff you out, as a dog sniffs out a bitch."

'But, what do I do? When it comes?' My mind was racing at the thought of this pain and shaming blood happening over and over every month. 'Why does it come?' I asked, confused.

'It is God's way of telling a woman that they are ripe. They are ready to fulfil their duty and take a husband and labour hard to bring forth the babes. Not that ye will ever know the pleasure of that!' she snorted, hawking a yellow plug of phlegm up and spitting it on the ground. 'Not for you, the secrets of the marriage bed nor the making of a child. But a woman ye are now, it seems. Hmmm, I would have thought a hare-witch would know all about moon magick, the blood rituals.' She turned to go indoors, for we had been conversing long enough, dangerously so. 'Rags,' she muttered. 'You use rags for the blood and rinse them clean for the next moon. Now, off with ye! Afore I set the connétable on ye.'

And with that she slammed the rotten wooden door shut and I was left to wander back to my hut, my mind churning over her words again and again. Marriage, husband, babies. Was it so - would these things never be mine? In truth, I did not know that I wanted them until I was told I could not have them , and then, well - it was all my heart could think of.

Did you not dream, Sister? As a young girl, did you not dream of a husband and babies? Oh, I know you are married to God and I am sure you find this a great honour, but does your body not cry out for a child to suckle?

I am sorry, Sister, I can see I have offended you again.

CHAPTER SIXTEEN

Leah

Matt had finished working on my bedsit and it was finally ready for me to move into. In the sunlight, it was a cheerful space, with white painted walls and high ceilings. Matt had thoughtfully created a wall of wardrobes and storage space which stretched along the length of the same wall which hid the secret passageway and strange stone room. Maybe he had picked up on my uneasiness about that weird place, or maybe he was just thinking practically, but either way the cupboards created a barrier between me and that room and I felt much better about living in the tiny flat. With my bed moved in and my new television delivered, the room felt instantly warm and cosy. It joined the corridor in the main flat but the door was fitted with a sturdy lock and only I had a key.

'It's your space,' Matt had assured me. 'Jayne and I won't go in there without your permission. And the kids won't go in there at all - promise.'

With my own private room it was easier to feel like I was an employee, with my job as an au pair to the two children, rather than treading the fine line between guest and unpaid nanny that I had been walking. It was easier too, to take myself away from the ever-growing chilly atmosphere between Matt and Jayne. Easier to walk away and close my door rather than curl up awkwardly in my chair in their living room as they sniped and bitched at each other. Jayne refused to talk about it, her lips clamped in a tight line if I so much as mentioned Matt's name. A couple of times I had caught her on her mobile, whispering and giggling into the phone with some unknown person, but she would turn away and snap the phone shut as soon as she saw me. She managed to look both defiant and guilty as fuck at the same time, and her message was clear: It's not your business, stay out of it.

 Ben texted me most days, mostly with an update on the best day for Gracie to come over, and for me to join him, Gracie and his Aunty Debbie for dinner. We decided on the following Wednesday and told both girls when we dropped them off to school on the Tuesday morning.

 'Yes! Yes! Yes!' chanted Alice as she bounced up and down on her toes. 'Gracie, you're coming to my house to play tomorrow!'

Gracie grinned up at us through her thick, dark fringe. Naturally quieter than Alice, she didn't jump about or shout but her beaming smile said it all. She swung on Ben's hand and did a little dance, and when Alice grabbed her hand and tugged her towards their classroom she waved shyly at me before following Alice in - always Alice's little shadow.

 'Debbie's really looking forward to it,' Ben told me. 'She's had all her old cook books out, planning something special for you.' He nudged me gently. 'Don't be surprised if she tries to matchmake - it's been a very long time since I've brought a girl back to meet her!'

 'I'm sure she'll realise that's a waste of time when she sees me,' I said archly. 'You have told her, haven't you? About my face? I don't want to shock her.'

Ben touched my cheek gently.

 'Yes, I've told her. About your face, about the attack, all of it. She's been digging around her garden, determined to make you a salve to help with the scarring.'

I was relieved in a way. At least I wouldn't have to go through the whole story again while she stared at me with pity over the dinner plates.

 When Noah and I got back to The Grange I found a missed call on my phone. I had left it charging while I walked the kids to school and the call was from a local number I didn't recognise. I called it back.

'Mr Harlow's office, how may I help you?' the cool tones of a receptionist greeted me.

'Um... hi.... I just had a missed call from this number? It's Leah Harrop.' I waited as she checked.

'Oh yes, Miss Harrop. Mr Harlow asked me to call you to arrange an appointment. Mr Chevalier asked him to take a look at your case.'

'Mr Chevalier?'

'Yes, Gabriel Chevalier? I believe he's related to your, er, employers.'

'Oh! Right, yes, Gabriel, of course,' I stuttered, having completely forgotten how he had suggested he ask his eminent surgeon father for a recommendation of a doctor who could help me.

'Mr Harlow can see you on Monday the 24th, at 9.30 am. Would that be convenient? His consulting rooms are on the second floor of the Lumiere Building, near the Liberty Wharf shopping centre.'

It was almost two weeks away but I accepted readily. I wanted, no - I needed - to hear if there was any hope, anything at all that could be done to magically reverse the damage to my face.

In my free time - the time that wasn't spent looking after Noah or doing housework - I continued to sort through the boxes that had been left behind by Pierre. It was interesting work, even when there was nothing of particular interest to find, and I occasionally did find something that warranted putting to one side to show Matt later. There was the bundle of letters in a sloping hand, dating from the war years; a pile of old carbonised rent books showing the payments from the tenants who previously rented out the flats. In one dusty box which was in danger of falling apart, I found reams and reams of old paperwork as if someone had opened a drawer or filing cabinet and dumped the whole lot into this box without even glancing through it. Bills from over thirty years ago, church pamphlets, an Order of Service for the funeral of one Richard (Dick) Bertie in 1978, a bus timetable from 1984 - all of it piled randomly on top of each other with no discernible system or date order. I leafed through each piece carefully, scanning the pages for mention of the Chevalier name and for anything which could be connected to the history of the house. It seemed that Pierre had been the type of man who kept anything and everything, and he often made little notes in the margins of old newspapers or on scraps of lined paper.

"... milk, tea bags, tin of soup" – a shopping list scrawled on the side of a TV guide dated August 1995, and "Remind T about rates" penned neatly on the back of a flyer for the church fête. Right at the bottom of this box, I found an A4 writing pad with about half of its pages filled with the now familiar cursive script that Pierre wrote with. I flicked through them with half-hearted interest until my eye caught on one particular word - *Harewich.* Starting again from the beginning, I found that I was looking at an attempt by Pierre to chart the history of the house, and the Chevalier family. Names and dates filled the pages on both sides, and Pierre had tried to sketch out a family tree but had only succeeded in going back to the late 1800's. I skimmed over the branches, noting how the same names kept cropping up with almost every generation - Pierre, Matthieu, Jeanne, even Gabriel - they all appeared with monotonous regularity. Was it family tradition to name your sons after their fathers and uncles, or were the Chevaliers' just spectacularly lacking in imagination?

 The paragraphs where Pierre had written down what he knew about the house were much more interesting. The name was changed to The Grange in 1869, after being called Harewich House since the seventeenth century. Apparently, according to Pierre, the house was originally called Le Manoir des aux Cadeau des Reines when it was first built - The Manor is a Gift From the Queen - which was a bit of a mouthful and no wonder they changed it, but it was clearly the first Chevalier's way of showing off. He had been gifted the land and built his fine house through the favour he had been gifted by the queen, Elizabeth I, and by saddling his house with such a grand name he made sure the rest of the known world knew exactly how he had risen so high in the queen's service. The name of Harewich House first appeared in the early 1600's and next to this fact Pierre had written "local name for house? Hare-witch legend?" which echoed what Gabriel had told me on the beach that day. The pages became less coherent and the writing slanted so hard to the right that it was becoming difficult to read. I could pick out the odd word, mostly because Pierre had written in capitals or underlined them several times.

"MATTHIEU!"
"Family line!"
"HARE WITCH"
"CURSE"
"CURSE"
"CURSE"

The last pages were full of disjointed ramblings, as if Pierre had lost the ability to think rationally, and consisted of random sentences which stopped in the middle of nowhere.

"She follows me about the house. I see her...... Her face haunts me....I know I am not long for this world..... I must get Matthieu back.......she calls for him....... she is still here...... he is my only hope for rest .... a great wrong has been done .... she will never stop as long as there is a Chevalier living! WE ARE CURSED."

The fine hairs on the back of my neck stood up and I shivered, even though the room was warm and the sun was shining through the windows. Poor Great Uncle Pierre was haunted in his last, confused days, wittering on about witches and curses.

A distant shout drew me out of my thoughts. Matt was hollering my name.

'Leah! LEAH! Come over here, quick.'

He was in the other wing of the house and I picked my way through carefully between the piles of rubble and scrap wood. Matt was standing at the far end of the wing. He had busted through the walls of the two flats on the ground floor and opened up the space into one large room. The ghosts of former walls were speckled with old plaster, and redundant electric cables. A pile of light fittings lay in a corner waiting to be hauled out to the skip. There was a big hole in the wall at the end of the building, showing large granite blocks on the other side.

'Look!' Matt gasped, pulling down his face mask. 'I'm just about to take down this last wall and look what's on the other side!'

He swung his torch beam through the gap and illuminated a deep cavernous hole in the blocks.

'What is it?' I asked, curiously and not a little bit fearfully, as that strange little stone room at the other end of the house was still very much on my mind.

'It's a fireplace! The original one, I think! Look at it, it's big enough to roast a horse!' Matt was buzzing, delighted with his latest find. 'Look out, I'll take the rest of the wall down and show you.' He swung his hammer into the flimsy modern wall then picked up a crowbar to wrench the rest of it away. Through the newish wooden framing, the shape of the fireplace began to emerge. Matt was right. It was enormous. He put his tools down and bent to pick up an electric saw. Slapping my hands over my ears against the shrill, harsh noise, I watched as he deftly sawed through the wooden joists one by one until they lay in a heap on the floor. We both stared at the sight of the impressive hearth. The granite blocks on either side had been dressed to create a smooth frame. The fireplace itself went back about

171

five feet but it was the lintel which was the most startling sight. It was a huge granite block, supported on either side with smaller blocks, and had been carved into a decorative motif of flowers and leaves. Matt moved to inspect the stones close up.

'Is it safe?' I asked, fearing that the whole lot was about to come tumbling down on top of him.

'I should say so. It's been here for over four hundred years. Christ, it's big! Must have taken whole trees to light a decent fire.' He pulled out a tape measure from his pocket. 'Look, it's six feet wide and almost the same in height.' He crouched under the lintel stone and stood directly in the middle of the hearth. 'I can almost stand up straight in here. Come on, come and have a look. There's plenty of room for both of us.'

Tentatively, I stepped over the pile of debris and stepped onto the cold stone. Even though there was ample head room, I still crouched and ducked my head, listening for any rumblings of disturbed bricks and expecting to feel pieces of crumbling masonry hit me at any moment. Matt was moving around the space, tapping stones and feeling for spaces in between them.

'I can't see daylight up there. The chimney must be blocked. Probably decades worth of old birds' nests. I'll have to get someone out to have a look and make sure it's structurally sound at the same time.' He continued feeling his way around the walls of the fireplace, checking for cracks in the pointing. There was another large stone at the back, squared off so it sat like a low table.

'What's that for?' I asked, thinking it out of place.

'Dunno, could be where they heated water or baked bread, not sure.' Matt had stepped onto the block and was using it as leverage to get his head higher into the black space above us.

'Matt, what the hell are you doing? For God's sake! Be careful, please?'

He had almost completely disappeared into the darkness now, using the uneven surfaces of the stones as footholds to climb up.

'There's something up here,' he cried, his voice muffled by the thick granite. 'A space, in the back of the lintel.'

I watched as he swung dangerously against the wall.

'I can't quite grab it.' His face, streaked with grime, appeared above me. 'Hand me the torch, and that long piece of wood.' He said, indicating to where one of the old joists lay. I passed them both to him, one by one. I could see he was bracing his arms against the chimney, and he grunted with the effort of balancing while trying to poke the wood into the small space above the fireplace. 'Got it!' he called triumphantly. 'Here, take this.' He handed back the wood first, then the torch, then finally he jumped down off the wall, cradling an object to his chest.

'What is it? Is it treasure? Like gold or jewels or something?' I squealed with excitement.

'Whatever it is, it's wrapped up tight.' Matt moved to a clear space and we both crouched on our haunches to see what he had found. It was a small parcel, about the size of a shoebox, but lumpy and wrapped up in a waxy material. As Matt turned it this way and that, looking for the best way to unwrap it, I was struck by a sudden thought.

'Should we be doing this? I mean, what if it's of historic importance? Shouldn't we give it to an archaeologist or someone? We might be damaging it if we try and unwrap it without really knowing what we're doing.'

'Nope. My house, my treasure!' grinned Matt, and then he said 'Aha!' as he found his way into the creased material and started picking away at the resinous coating. 'Looks like it's been coated in wax. It's old too, bloody old!' The fabric gave way, literally fell apart in Matt's hands as he turned the object carefully over. A glint of shiny green showed through. 'It's a bottle!' Matt said, sounding a little disappointed, as if he had been expecting a tumble of golden coins.

And it was.

A misshapen bottle with a globe shaped bottom and a tapered top. It was a pale green, and had a blob of wax sealed across its mouth to keep in the contents, which we could see still moved around inside. Matt held it up to the light. Spiky shapes clinked inside the bottle's stomach, a puddle of dark viscous liquid slopped up the sides and a matted ball of what looked like hair or wool rolled lazily around as Matt turned the bottle over and over.

It made me feel sick. Instantly nauseous, like I was about to throw up my breakfast right there on the floor.

'Matt, I don't like it. Wrap it up again, please?'

'What IS it?' Matt said curiously as if I hadn't spoken. 'Should we open it, do you think? Find out what those bits are inside.'

'NO!' I shouted, my hand clamping over my mouth. 'It's making me feel ill. Put it away, for God's sake.'

'I think I'll take a look on the internet, see if I can find out what it's for.'

'Whatever. Just... just put it away. I can't look at it anymore.'

'What is it?' Jayne asked, wrinkling her nose in distaste. Matt had put the strange bottle on the kitchen table while he searched the internet for clues as to what it could be. I still couldn't look at it without my stomach rolling dangerously and bile filling my throat.

'Ummm... I think... I'm not sure but I think it could be a witch bottle.' Matt scowled at the screen in front of him. 'It looks similar to what I've found here, but I can't say for certain.' He swung the laptop around so the screen faced me. He was on Wikipedia and the page was full of photos of similar looking green glass vessels.

'Witch bottles began as countermagical devices used as protection against other witchcraft and conjure,' I read. 'Historically, the witch's bottle contained the victim's (the person who believed they had a spell put on them, for example) urine, hair or nail clippings, or red thread from sprite traps.'

'What's a sprite trap?' I wondered aloud, before picking up the description again. 'Later witch bottles were filled with rosemary, needles and pins, and red wine. Historically and currently, the bottle is then hidden at the farthest corner of the property, beneath the house hearth, or placed in an inconspicuous spot in the house. It is believed that after being buried, the bottle captures evil which is impaled on the pins and needles, drowned by the wine, and sent away by the rosemary.'

'Ewww, gross!' Jayne made a disgusted face. 'Urine, nail clippings and red wine?'

'The witch bottle was believed to be active as long as the bottle remained hidden and unbroken,' I read on. 'Maybe we should put it back. We've taken it from its hiding place.'

Matt had picked up the bottle again and was tilting it slowly, making the contents slide from one end to the other.

'It does look like nails, and the liquid is quite dark so it could be red wine.' He made the bottle tilt again. 'That looks like hair though, human hair I'd say.'

'Well, whatever it is, it's not staying in my kitchen!' Jayne huffed. 'Put it back or find somewhere else for it to go, Matt.'

'Hey, wouldn't it be cool if I made a glass case for it? I could take out some of the fireplace lintel and we could put it back in there but we could have a glass brick in front of it so it's still on show. What do you think? That way, it will still be back in its rightful place but we could still see it.'

'It wouldn't be hidden though,' I muttered darkly. 'Wiki says it only works as long as it's hidden.'

Matt and Jayne stared at me for a second before they both burst into laughter.

'You can't mean to say you actually believe in this stuff,' Jayne giggled. 'It's only a superstition from hundreds of years ago. What, do you think we'll be inundated with witches if we don't stick to the witch bottle rules?'

'Yeah, it's not real, Leah,' Matt broke in. 'Don't worry, I won't let the bad witches get you. Wooooooooooo!' He waved the bottle in front of my face and my stomach churned again.

'It's just creepy. That thing creeps me out. I can't stand to look at it,' I said, bad-temperedly. 'Jayne's right, put it somewhere else.'

'I'll keep it in the lounge for now.' Matt got up and mercifully, took the bottle with him. 'But I really like the idea of having it on show again when the great hall is finished.'

CHAPTER SEVENTEEN

I didn't like to confess to Jayne and Matt just how much that horrible little bottle disturbed me. Not only did I feel sick every time I looked at it, but an overwhelming feeling of dread came out of nowhere and hung over me like a poisonous cloud. Matt had put it high up on top of a shelf in their lounge where Alice's curious little fingers couldn't reach it but I caught her looking at it, really staring at it, with a sly smile on her face.

'What's that, Daddy? Can I see it?' she would ask each day.

No, Alice, I've told you - it's not for little hands,' Matt would reply. 'It's very, very old and only for the grown-ups to touch, OK?'

'Ok Daddy,' Alice would say, the very picture of innocence. 'I won't touch it, I promise.'
Only I could see her fingers were crossed behind her back.

The treat of having Gracie come over after school the following day temporarily drew Alice's attention away from the witch bottle. Both girls were giddy, high on life, when I picked them up at three o'clock and they insisted on holding hands the whole way home.

'Aunty Rabbit, can we play outside when we get home?' Alice asked me. She turned to Gracie. 'Aunty Rabbit is my funny name for my Aunty Leah. She looks like a rabbit, or maybe a hare, but I like the way she looks. Can Gracie call you Aunty Rabbit too?'

'Gracie can just call me Leah, if she wants. She doesn't have to call me Aunty Rabbit. I'm not her Aunty am I?' I smiled down at both girls.

'Yeah, but you're not my Aunty either,' Alice pointed out. 'And I still call you Aunty Rabbit because I love you like my Aunty.'

'True, I'm not your real Aunty. But I love you like I am, too. That's why I call you Little Bunny, it's my special name for you, just you.'

'We need to have a special name for Gracie,' Alice declared. 'If I'm Little Bunny, she can be Little Hare!'

'No, I want to be Little Birdie!' Gracie piped up in her quiet voice. 'That's what my Aunty Debbie calls me.'

'Perfect! Little Birdie it is,' I declared. I loved it when Alice was like this, at her best, being her sweet, kind little self and not running off to dig holes or batter other children. If only things could have stayed that way.

When we got back to The Grange I made the children a snack of sliced-up apples with raisins, followed by an iced cupcake each as a special treat. I put Noah down for a late nap and settled the baby monitor on his chest of drawers. I took the other half with me into the lounge where I was busy packing up Pierre's old glassware and ceramic knick-knacks ready for the charity shop. Alice and Gracie had disappeared outside to run around the garden and I had made Alice pinky-promise not to take Gracie any further than the trees at the end of the lawn, and most definitely NOT to go in any of the old outbuildings or the fields at the back. I listened to Noah's happy burbles through the monitor. He was such a good baby, content to lie quietly and watch the sunlight ripple on the ceiling as the gentle breeze made his airplane mobile swing above his head. I rolled glass in newspaper mindlessly, already thinking of all the crates and boxes in the attic that needed sorting out. There was some furniture up there too; I'd spied an old sloped writing desk half hidden behind rolled-up rugs that I was itching to get hold of. I was sure there were more house secrets stored away somewhere and I was determined to find them.

My daydreaming was interrupted by Alice's voice.

'... and this is Noah's room. I got a bigger room but Daddy says we'll have even bigger rooms when we move upstairs after he finishes all the work.'

I heard Gracie say 'Hi Noah', and then I heard the sound of his musical stuffed bear singing his silly tune as the girls moved around Noah's room playing with his toys. All went quiet and I assumed the girls had moved on, perhaps going into Alice's own room and out of range of the baby monitor.

'La-La!' I heard Noah yell. 'La-la, la-la, la-la!' This was his word for Alice. He couldn't manage to say Alice fully yet so he settled on La-La. He sounded tearful, distressed. I got up off the lounge floor, stretching my cramped limbs, ready to go down and check on him when I heard Alice on the monitor again. She had obviously heard Noah shouting and had gone to soothe him, I thought, and I turned around and crouched on the floor again.

'Wahhhhhhhhhhh!'

A shrill scream made me bolt upright and I was at the door just in time to see Gracie sprint past me and into the kitchen. Jayne was just coming home from work and literally had one foot in the door before Gracie cannoned into her, sobbing and wailing. Jayne's motherly instincts took over and she promptly dropped her handbag and shopping and picked Gracie up, shushing her gently and rocking her on one hip. Gracie buried her face in Jayne's neck and sobbed piteously.

'What's happened? Jayne looked at me, bewildered.

'I have no idea,' I said. 'The girls were in Alice's room and I was in the lounge and I heard Gracie scream and run into the kitchen.'

'Alice?' Jayne called down the corridor but Alice didn't answer.

'Let me take Gracie and you go find Alice.' I held out my arms to take the terrified little girl but she looked at me, and my uncovered face, and screamed in fear again.

'NO, no, no, no, no, no, no!' she wailed, hiding against Jayne's shoulder again.

'Shhhhh, Gracie, it's just me,' I cried. 'It's just Leah. Come on, come to Leah.'

'NOOOOOOOOO!' Gracie howled, and kicked out when I tried to prise her from Jayne's arms. 'NOOOOOOO, you look like her! You look like her!'

'Er, I'd better look after Gracie,' said Jayne apologetically. 'You go see where Alice is.'

Feeling unbearably hurt by Gracie's rejection, I walked down the hall towards Alice's room.

'Oh dear,' I heard Alice's voice on the baby monitor as I passed the lounge. 'I don't think Gracie wants to play with us,' she said sadly. I waited, listening. Alice was in Noah's room after all. I heard her go to Noah's cot and try to lift him out. He was a chunky baby so she wasn't able to lift him fully and she grunted with the effort. 'I can't pick Noah up. Do you think Noah would like to play with us instead? Can you lift him out of his cot and we can take him outside to play?'

Who was she talking to? I wondered. Matt was still working on the other side of the house, Jayne was in the kitchen with Gracie - that just left me, Alice and Noah. Before I could move I heard a deep guttural voice coming from the baby monitor in the lounge.

'Yes,' it said. 'He can play too.'

I freaked out. My breath froze in my lungs and my skin crawled. Who the hell was in Noah's room with him and Alice? I broke into a run as I covered the last few steps to Noah's door.

'Alice?' She was standing by Noah's cot. There was no one else in the room besides her and Noah.

'Yes, Aunty Rabbit?' she asked innocently.

'Who was here, just now? Who were you talking to?

'Nobody,' she replied. 'Gracie ran away. She was crying.'

'Yes, I know. Do you know why?'

An icy chill ran down my spine. I did not believe what I was seeing. Noah lay face down on the soft rug on the floor. He was moving, trying to lever himself upright and he managed to get into a crawling position. He heard my voice and let out a loud cry before falling over onto his back and holding out his arms for me to pick him up, his little face red and scrunched-up. I pulled him safely into my grasp.

'Alice, how did Noah get out of his cot?' I kept my voice soft and light, hiding the fact that I was terrified. 'You can't pick him up yet, and you're not tall enough to reach into his cot properly anyway, so how did he get on the floor?' Alice looked at me and guilt flashed across her face. She bit her lip and I saw that she was trembling.

'It's OK, I won't be mad. I just need to know how this happened. It's very dangerous for you to try and pick up Noah, OK? He's heavy and you could drop him by accident.'

Alice stayed silent but I could see she was near to tears.

'Alice, I'll ask you one more time. How did Noah get out of his cot and onto the floor?'

Alice looked at the floor.

'Jenny lifted him,' she whispered.

'Leah!' Jayne's voice filled the hallway. She sounded worried. 'Did you find Alice? Is she OK?'

'Yes!' I called back. 'We're coming now.' I heaved Noah onto my hip and jerked my head at Alice. 'Come on,' I said to her. 'You can tell your mum what happened to make Gracie so scared like that.'

Alice dragged her feet, crying quietly, but she obediently followed us to the kitchen. Jayne was now seated at the table with Gracie on her knee. Gracie's sobs had faded to the occasional hiccup but her eyes grew wide with fear again when she saw me. I hurriedly put Noah in his playpen and wrapped my scarf over my face.

'Leah, look,' Jayne said quietly to me. She moved Gracie around slightly so I could see her face. Gracie had three livid scratches down her right cheek. They were just beginning to ooze blood.

'How did she do that?' I gasped. Oh God, Ben was going to go mental when he saw.

'She keeps saying the witch lady did it. Those were her exact words - the witch lady did it.'

'Gracie,' I said very gently to the frightened child. 'Can you tell me and Alice's mummy what happened please? Can you do that? I know you were in Noah's room, and that's OK, you're not in any trouble, we just need to know how you did that to your face.'

Gracie looked at me, torn between trusting the lady she knows from the walk to school yet still clearly terrified by me for some reason.

'Was it Alice?' I prompted. 'Did Alice hurt your face?'

Gracie shook her head. Alice let out a small noise of protest.

'It wasn't me. I would never hurt Gracie.'

'Alice, shush. Let Gracie talk please,' Jayne said firmly.

'Gracie,' I tried again. 'Did you fall? Did you bump your face?'

Again, Gracie shook her head. She leaned against Jayne, trying to make herself as small as possible.

'The witch lady did it,' Gracie said in a tiny voice, her eyes filling with tears again. 'Alice was talking to the witch lady but I was scared of her. I tried to run away but she scratched me. She didn't want me to leave so she scratched me with her hands.'

Jayne and I looked at each other, both lost for words.

'Who is this lady?' Jayne asked, rocking Gracie soothingly.

'I don't know. Alice calls her Jenny. I didn't like her. She looked so scary.' Gracie looked up at me in confusion. 'She looked like you.'

I sat down with a bump, a hard lump in my throat, and struggled not to cry.

'What do you mean, honey?' I asked Gracie, my voice cracking. 'What do you mean she looked like me?'

Gracie hesitated. Then she brought her index finger up to her mouth and pushed her upper lip up towards her nose, exposing her baby teeth. I let out an involuntary sob and turned away, unable to look. Jayne saw how upset I was and lifted Gracie up, carrying her over to the kitchen counter.

'Come on, sweet pea. Let's get your poor face cleaned up. I'll put some nice cream on it so it doesn't hurt, OK?' Jayne reached for the first aid kit high up on a shelf. 'Don't worry - she's just had a fright,' she said to me over her shoulder. 'She's not scared of you, not really.'

I wiped the tears from my cheeks.

'I didn't realise,' I said. 'I didn't realise she saw me that way. I have to call Ben, let him know Gracie's been hurt.' I grabbed my phone and hurriedly left the kitchen, going outside to make the call.

'Hello?' His voice was cheery but tinged with concern. 'Everything OK?'

'Ben... hi,' I said lamely. 'Listen, I'm so sorry about this but Gracie's had a fright and... well, I think it might be better if you came and picked her up.'

'A what? A fright, did you say?' Ben sounded confused. 'What sort of fright?'

'She and Alice were playing and Gracie got hurt...' I heard his intake of breath. 'Not badly, a scratch on her cheek,' I hastened to add. 'But she's upset and wants to go home.'

'I'll be there in five,' Ben said and hung up.

Gracie's face looked much better after Jayne's ministrations. The scratches weren't deep, they looked like a cat had lashed out at her, and they would heal quickly and without scars. The little girl sat forlornly in the kitchen waiting for her Dad, her face only cheering up when she heard his car in the driveway.

'Daddy!' she cried, running to the door and throwing herself into his arms as soon as he got out of the car.

'Hey, baby,' he crooned. 'Hey baby girl, what's happened eh? Let me see.' He smoothed her hair away from her face and inspected her cheek. 'Oh, it's not so bad. How did that happen, sweetheart?'

'The witch lady.' Gracie said solemnly. 'The witch lady did it, Daddy.'

Ben looked at me for the first time, confusion on his face.

'Come on in,' I said. 'You'd better hear the whole story.'

We sat round the table with mugs of tea, Ben, Jayne and me. Gracie was glued to Ben's lap, thumb in her mouth and Alice was sitting on the floor against the wall playing with her stuffed toy, Poppydog. She had a ferocious scowl on her face and was carefully listening to every word we said. I told both Ben and Jayne what I had heard through the baby monitor, about the mysterious voice, and how I had gone into Noah's room to find him on the floor, and not in his cot.

'Alice keeps talking about this Jenny person,' I said urgently. 'I know we thought it was an imaginary friend but I'm not so sure now. How could Alice have lifted Noah out of his cot? She can't!'

'So what do you think's going on?' Ben asked. 'I mean, are we talking about a ghost here or...'

'Don't be ridiculous!' Jayne cut in. 'Alice is just making up stories.'

'So it was Alice who made the marks on Gracie's face?' Ben looked at his daughter's cheek. 'You think Alice was playing a game, pretending to be a witch, and she scratched Gracie?'

Gracie shook her head.

'Not Alice, witch lady,' Gracie was adamant.

'There's something else Gracie said,' I swallowed down my shame. 'She said the witch lady looked like me. She had a face like mine.'

'What does that even mean?' Jayne said in exasperation. 'It's clearly a case of overactive imaginations, getting carried away while playing a game about witches. To say it's anything else is utterly absurd, it's laughable!'

'But there's been other things, Jayne,' I pleaded. 'You know there has. Alice's weird behaviour - that day at the zoo, and the thing she did the other day, digging in the field.'

'What digging in the field?' Jayne demanded. I remembered too late that I hadn't told her about it, because I didn't want to worry her after a long shift at the hospital.

'Alice ran off, when we were walking home from school,' I admitted. 'I found her in the field behind the house, digging in the old ruins there. She was digging like a mad thing, and talking in a really strange voice, the same voice I just heard on the monitor.'

'So, she was making it up!' Jayne protested. 'That just proves that it was Alice you heard, not some witch or ghost. She was just playing a game, for God's sake! Will you stop talking like you think my daughter's possessed!'

'But that doesn't explain how Noah came to be out of his cot!' I said.

'You probably didn't put him in,' Jayne blamed me. 'You probably changed him on the floor, then left him there!'

'No way!' I defended myself. 'I checked on him a few times. He was in his cot, Jayne, and then he wasn't.'

'Look, this isn't getting us anywhere,' Ben butted in calmly. 'I don't know what went on today but I can see Gracie isn't badly hurt. I'm inclined to think it was just an accident, just Alice acting in high spirits. I'll take her home and I'm sure she'll have forgotten all about it by tomorrow.'

'Where's Alice?' Jayne asked suddenly. We turned to where she had been sitting a moment earlier. The space was empty. 'I hope you haven't upset her by saying she hurt Gracie. 'Alice? Allllliiicce?' Jayne called.

I got up and looked down the hallway. I heard a clink and a small thump from the lounge and then Alice appeared carrying the witch bottle. She must have climbed up the shelving to get it.

'Alice, put that back! You know you're not supposed to touch that. You promised your dad, remember?'

Alice ignored me and stalked straight past me to the kitchen where she stood in the middle of the floor. She glared at each of us in turn, even Gracie, who shrank back against her father. Alice raised the bottle above her head and, without giving us time to react, she let out a piercing scream and threw the bottle onto the tiles with all her strength. The old bottle shattered immediately on impact and shards of glass scattered across the floor, along with the bottle's contents. A foul smell, iron and blood, filled the air as the blackened liquid trickled over the tiles. We jumped back, not wanting to get the disgusting fluid on our feet. Alice smiled with grim satisfaction.

'Now you'll be sorry.'

CHAPTER EIGHTEEN

'Well, that was intense.' Ben was strapping Gracie into her child seat in the back of his car.

'Ben, I'm so sorry,' I apologised. 'I completely understand if you don't want anything to do with us, after this.'

'What? No, don't be sorry. None of this is your fault.' Ben put a hand on my arm. 'You're still coming to Debbie's for dinner tonight, aren't you?'

'I really don't think that's a good idea,' I said. 'Gracie's too frightened of me. It wouldn't be fair on her, if I came tonight.'

'Gracie's not frightened of you, Leah! Come on, after today I think you need to talk to Debbie more than ever. She's got a lot of knowledge about ghosts and witches and what have you. She can probably make some sense of what happened in there today.'

'Ben, I don't want Gracie to be scared...'

'Gracie, are you scared of Leah?' Ben turned to his daughter. She shook her head. 'See?'

I crouched down to meet Gracie's solemn gaze.

'Gracie, it's OK if you are. I know I don't look ... quite like other people. If you don't want me to come with you to your Aunty Debbie's house, then that's OK too. I won't come.' Gracie looked into my eyes seriously.

'You're not her. You're not mean, like her,' she whispered. 'I want you to come to Aunty Debbie's house. She'll know what to do. She can tell you how to make the witch lady go away.'

'Are you sure?'

Gracie nodded her head again.

'Great! That's that sorted. Pick you up at seven.' Ben jumped into his car and reversed up the drive. Gracie waved at me from the back seat and I waved back, heart still heavy and knowing that the dinner was a bad idea, but wanting more than anything to be out of this house for a few hours.

When I went back into the kitchen Jayne was on her knees, scrubbing at the worn tiles where the bottle had smashed. She looked up as I came in.

'You're right. There is something weird going on in this house.' She slapped the wet cloth onto another patch of floor. 'Honest to God, I'm beginning to wish we'd never come here.' She sniffled and her face crumpled. 'Alice, the Alice we saw today... that's not my Alice. I don't know who she is but it's not my Alice!'

I persuaded her to leave the floor for now, the worst of the black liquid was gone, leaving just a faint grey smear. I would give the floor a good clean later but for now, Jayne needed to let the floodgates open.

'I'm sorry,' Jayne sobbed. 'I'm sorry I yelled at you. I know things aren't right with this house, what with me and Matt barely speaking. Do you know that since we've been living here, we've not had sex once?'

I made a sympathetic face.

'He barely touches me,' she went on. 'And the things you said, about all the weird things going on, it's true. I haven't told you, because I was sure there was a simple explanation, but things have been happening to me too. Silly things. Like, when I'm in the bathroom brushing my teeth, I swear I see someone else reflected in the bathroom mirror. Not a real person as such, more a...'

'... feeling of a person,' I finished with her.

'And it's the same when I get home after a nightshift. I'll go to walk down the hallway and I get the impression that someone's just turned the corner at the end, into Alice's room, but when I check, there's no one there. But I feel like I'm being watched all the same.'

I reminded her about the time I was at the old well, when I'd seen the reflection of someone in the water with me, and the overwhelming feeling of being watched, even though I was alone.

'That well is a part of the land that goes with the house, it's on the boundary papers we got from the lawyers,' Jayne said thoughtfully. 'Do you really think we've got a ghost?'

'We've definitely got a something,' I said firmly. 'Ben thinks his aunt may be able to shed some more light on it. She knows all about these things apparently. I'm going to meet her tonight.'

'Well, I hope she can help us. If it wasn't for Matt's obsession with this place I'd happily lock the doors, take the kids and go back to his parent's place in Surrey. For good.'

'I know it sounds weird, and a bit daft, but do you think we should be doing something to protect us - burn sage or chant prayers, or get a priest in to bless the house?' I asked doubtfully, not even believing I was suggesting it. Jayne sighed and shrugged.

'No idea. Let's see what Ben's aunt says tonight and go from there. I can't even believe we're having this conversation, to be honest,' she said, echoing my own thoughts exactly.

When Ben picked me up later I checked his face carefully for any signs of coolness with me, but he was the same as always; upbeat, cheerful. He smiled warmly at me.

'Well, today was a bit weird, wasn't it?' he stated. 'Although, I'm finding it all quite interesting. Do you really think there's something supernatural going on?'

'I can't think of another explanation,' I replied, filling him in on some of the other things that had happened in the house, and the grounds since we moved in.

We drove through St Helier and onto what the locals called the Avenue, a straight piece of four-lane road which headed east to west. The speed limit on the island was a leisurely forty miles an hour, which was slow enough to appreciate the tranquil waters of the sweeping bays. We climbed a hill, turned right at an intersection graced by a cannon and a memorial plaque, then into a small, green lane. Ben indicated left at the top of the hill and I found us in the forecourt of a large, two-storey house, with panoramic views of the sea.

'It's lovely!' I enthused.

'It's falling down,' remarked Ben.

Gracie came running out to meet us and to my intense relief, she showed no signs of being scared or shy with me. In fact, she took my hand and pulled me towards the door.

'Come and see my Aunty Debs,' she ordered.

Her cheek looked so much better, the scratches looked like they were scabbing over already and the redness had completely gone.

'So, you're the one I've been hearing so much about,' boomed a voice. I looked up from Gracie to see a small, wiry woman standing in the hall. She had strawberry blonde hair, cut short, almost in a pixie cut. Her accent was cultured and she spoke with the precise pronunciation of someone who has had many years of elocution lessons. But she was smiling and her eyes were warm with welcome.

'Hello! Lovely to meet you! I'm the decrepit Great-Aunt, but you can call me Debbie.'

'Hi, I'm Leah,' I said, taking her outstretched hand.

'Well, Leah, Ben and Birdie here have been telling me some tall tales about your house. Terribly interesting! I have some ideas but we'll talk later.' She mimed zipping up her mouth. 'Little pitchers have big ears!' She stage-whispered, nodding her head at Gracie. 'Come in, come in! I hope you like Boeuf Bourguignon?'

'Yes, lovely!' I replied, and allowed the hallway to swallow me up.

The house was vast and shabby. The carpets were so worn in places that the floorboards underneath were visible. Wallpaper sagged, curtains drooped and it was rammed full of furniture. Books were piled on every available surface and were stacked in towers on the floors, hiding the worst of the carpet damage I assumed. Overstuffed sofas jostled for space amongst spindly-legged tables and straight-backed chairs, but it was warm and cosy and welcoming - a far cry from the frosty grandeur of The Grange. A large ginger cat was curled up into a perfect circle on one of the chairs. Gracie patted his head as she ran by and he didn't even open an eyelid. The table in the dining room was set with sparkling glassware on a snow-white tablecloth, low bowls full of summer flowers gracing the centre.

'I hope you're prepared for this, Leah,' Ben raised an eyebrow. 'Debbie's been cooking all afternoon. Looks like we're in for one of her ten-course tasting menus.'
Debbie gave him a friendly slap on the arm.

'Silly! It's only a bit of stew,' she said. 'Goat's cheese soufflé to start and poached pears for dessert. And a few nibbley bits in between.'
Ben shot me a conspiratorial look.

'See! Ten courses, like I said.'

'Now, Leah, will you have some wine with me? Ben's always so boring about drinking and driving, and I've got a wonderful bottle of St Emilion going begging.'

'Oh, yes please. I could use a glass of wine after the day I've had.'
Debbie seated us all at the table. I took in the polished silverware and the freshly ironed linen napkins.

'You didn't have to go through so much trouble for me,' I said, feeling slightly awkward.

'Nonsense!' Debbie bellowed. 'We always dine like this.' Ben shook his head at me and mouthed 'No, we don't'. The light in the dining room was muted, with only a few uplighters casting a soft glow. I was glad; I was still wearing one of my headscarves and I knew I would have to take it off to eat properly, so I was pleased that I wouldn't be sitting under a harsh overhead light. Debbie brought out baskets of homemade walnut bread, complete with decorative swirls of creamy Jersey butter. A vast tureen of fragrant beef dominated the middle of the table, with dishes of Dauphinoise potatoes and freshly steamed vegetables either side of it, like bridesmaids flanking the bride. As we all helped ourselves, I self-consciously unwound my scarf, glancing across at Gracie to gauge her reaction. The last thing I wanted was to frighten her again but she hardly flinched and gave me a brave smile. I could feel Debbie's shrewd gaze from across the table as she studied my face.

'That's something else we can talk about later,' she murmured.

The ginger cat was weaving between my feet, drawn in by the delicious savoury smells. He gently clawed my leg and looked up at me with hopeful green eyes.

'Sorry, puss,' I said as I removed his claw from my jeans. 'This is all far too good to share.'

'Harry!' Debbie looked under the table and flapped her napkin at the cat to shoo him away. 'Sorry about that, he's too used to getting his own way. Young Madam there is a particularly soft touch.' She nodded to Gracie who giggled as she was caught in the act of passing a delectable morsel of meat to the appreciative Harry. 'He's really called Henry the Eighth, on account of being fat, grumpy and ginger, but Harry is what he answers to.'

We all laughed and I relaxed. The food was truly outstanding. Each dish was perfect and complimented all the other dishes, each flavour highlighting another. Debbie had us in fits of laughter as she regaled us with tales of her time 'treading the boards' with the Jersey Amateur Drama Club saying 'I only joined up to find husband number three, darlings, but all the men were either gay or spoken for!' She spoke fondly of her volunteering with the Jersey Archives - 'I'm so nosy, Leah! And all that information, all that history, is just waiting to be discovered and gossiped about!'

I could totally see why Ben had been so convinced Debbie and I would get on well. As the dinner went on, I felt more and more at home. Debbie was fascinating, so knowledgeable and so funny, and yet I could feel she was subtly appraising me, silently assessing me, even as she was telling us another funny story. I found myself looking forward to after dinner, when Gracie was put to bed and we could speak openly of the things that were happening at The Grange.

'Ben tells me you're into herbal medicine?' I asked Debbie as she topped my wine glass up again.

'Hedgerow medicine - yes, I've used it for years,' she replied. 'I put some of my remedies on Gracie's cheek before. Gracie, show Leah your scratches.' Gracie obediently turned her face so I could see.

'Yes, I noticed that when I first saw Gracie tonight. It looks so much better! What did you put on it?' Debbie gave a small self-depreciating shrug.

'Just a bit of chamomile to wash them out, a bit of flowering yarrow afterwards to promote quick healing. I use whatever's growing in the garden or the field. I find that Mother Nature has the answer to most minor injuries.'

'Well, it certainly looks like it works. Poor Gracie had such a fright today, didn't you sweetheart?' I looked over at the little girl. She nodded firmly and went back to concentrating on her dinner plate. 'I'm so sorry this happened,' I said to Debbie. Debbie looked at me, as if she was about to say something, but then shook her head and mouthed 'later' at me.

After a sublime pudding of pears poached in wine, with ice cream instead for Gracie, we leaned back in our chairs completely stuffed to the gills.

'I don't think I can move,' I groaned. Ben, next to me, patted his flat stomach.

'Look what she's done to me! She's a feeder, wants me to get so fat I'll never be able to leave!' he teased, as Debbie stood and began to clear our plates. 'No, I'll do that. You and Leah stay a while. Come on Gracie, you can help me with the dishes and then I'll put a DVD on for you. What one is it going to be this time?'

'Frozen!' cheered Gracie.

'Frozen!' echoed Ben. 'For the thousandth time!'

Debbie waved the nearly empty wine bottle in my direction and I accepted. She split the remainder between our two glasses and we settled down for a long chat.

'Right. Where shall we start?' Debbie said. 'I've been waiting to talk to you about this all evening. Why don't you fill me in from the beginning?'

And so I did. I told her the whole story. How I had come to know Jayne and Matt, how we had come to be in Jersey after they inherited The Grange. I told her about all the little things that had been happening in, and around, the house. When I got to the part about the strange feeling I had encountered at the old well, and finding the dead bird strung up on the wire fence, Debbie nodded.

'I've heard of that before. It's a very old farming custom. Some say it stops other birds from hanging around, if there's a dead one of their number hanging up, but others will tell you that it has a much more sinister purpose, that it keeps unrested spirits at bay.'

'There's a mesh covering the well so I don't see why anyone felt the need to string that poor bird up as a warning; it's not like other birds could have gotten inside. And I just had that feeling, you know... that feeling I wasn't alone,' I tried to explain.

We talked about Alice's strange behaviour, and I explained how Jayne thought it must have been Alice who inflicted those scratches on Gracie today. Debbie interrupted when I got to that part.

'No, no, I don't believe that, Leah. Alice was not the one who scratched Gracie.' Debbie took another gulp of wine. 'I had a good look when I cleaned Gracie up. Those marks were not done by a five year old child. They were too far apart.'

'So, you think this Jenny person, whoever or whatever she is, might be real?' I asked cautiously.

'Yes I think she must be,' Debbie sighed. 'I know it sounds highly improbable, if not impossible and slightly insane, but I do believe you have an entity of some sort in that house. I know the place, of course, everybody who knows Jersey history will have heard of The Grange at some point, even if they don't realise it. They're more familiar with its historical name - Harewich House.'

'I know there's supposed to be a curse attached to the house, or the Chevalier family in particular,' I said. 'Gabriel told me a little bit about it.'
Was it my imagination or did her face close up a little when I mentioned Gabriel's name?

'Yes, there supposedly is. Do you know why it was called Harewich House?' Debbie asked. I shook my head. 'A hare-witch is a very old term for someone who has been hare-cursed. In less enlightened times, people believed that someone who was born with a cleft palate, or a hare-lip as it used to be called, was hare-cursed. That they were marked out in the womb by the devil and would grow up to be a witch. Stuff and nonsense to us nowadays, of course, but you can see how folk might have made the connection - a hare-lip does make the face look a bit like a hare.'
The penny dropped.

'So THAT'S why Alice and Gracie said this Jenny person looked like me! She has a hare-lip, and with my face being the wreck it is now, I can see why they thought that.'

'Your face is not the wreck you think it is,' Debbie told me patiently. 'But that is another conversation, to be had later. Back to the house, the old story goes that one of the early Chevaliers did a young girl a great wrong and the girl was supposed to be a witch who cursed the Chevalier name for all time. Of course, Jersey is no stranger to witches, even today. Do you know, back in the 1930's, some chap decided to map all the ley lines that ran through the island. He had a dowsing rod which told him where the ley lines were, and he discovered that if he marked all the lines on a map, they formed the shape of a pentagram! Jersey's always been a mystical place, right from Neolithic times. Anyway, back to the real subject, the fact that Alice calls her "friend" shall we say, Jenny, and has described her as having a hare-lip along with her telling you that this Jenny had chains on her arms and legs...'

'Yes, that's right. Why? Do you think Jenny is somehow connected with the house and the curse?' I jumped in.

'I think that, well, someone who was in chains - they must have been convicted of a crime and imprisoned at some point. And when you add the first name of Jenny, who was hare-cursed or had a hare-lip, she's got to be on record somewhere. Her crime, whatever it was that got her chained up, should have been recorded. I might be able to find something in the archives. We've got loads of old papers dating back centuries from the assizes detailing all sorts of crimes and their allotted punishments.

'Do you really think you can find her?' I asked excitedly.

'Hopefully,' Debbie said. 'The problem is, we don't really know what year we should be looking at. All we know is that the legend refers to an early Chevalier, so if I look up when the house was built, that should give me a date to work from.'

'That would be amazing, Debbie, thank you so much!'

Debbie held up her hand.

'Steady on, I haven't found anything yet. You'd better give me your number so I can call you if I do.'

Ben came back in to the dining room from the kitchen, a tea towel slung over his shoulder.

'I've put some coffee on. Should be ready in a minute.' He leaned against the back of my chair companionly. 'Hey, I meant to ask you before but in all the kerfuffle I didn't get a chance! What was that bottle that Alice smashed so dramatically today?'

'Matt found it a couple of days ago,' I explained. 'He was knocking through the end wall of the ground floor flat and found the original fireplace to the house. It's a bloody great big massive thing, it is! Anyway, we were poking around and he found a glass bottle, wrapped up in waxed cloth, hidden in a secret cavity inside it.'

'A witch bottle!' Debbie exclaimed.

'Yes! Well, that's what we think it was. Matt was doing some research online but what we found out about witch bottles all adds up. It was really old, super old, and had things like nails and hair and some black liquid stuff inside it.' The red wine I had drunk sloshed uneasily inside my stomach and my mouth suddenly tasted sour. 'Matt put it in a safe place high up on some shelving, but Alice must have climbed up to get it, the little monkey. She dropped it on the tiles today to smash it - deliberately.'

'What was it she said? Something about now we'll be sorry?' Ben asked.

'That's just Alice being a little drama queen.'

'I'm not so sure,' Debbie said thoughtfully. 'People used to hide witch bottles in their houses to protect them from a particular witch or curse. They're supposed to be a powerful spell, that is until they get broken, and then the protection is lost.'

'Alice wouldn't have known that though. I doubt she even knew what the bottle was,' I said.

'Not necessarily,' Debbie argued. 'She might well have heard you calling it a witch bottle and, if she is being haunted by the ghost of a hare-witch...'

'You really think this is a haunting?' I asked sceptically.

'Well, yes I do. That's the only thing that would explain it all. Whoever Jenny is, she died a long, long time ago. As I was saying, if Alice is the only one who can see or hear this Jenny, then it may be possible that she's being

197

manipulated into doing what Jenny wants her to do - like smashing the bottle. If the witch bottle was put there to protect the family from Jenny herself, then by breaking the bottle she's breaking the spell.'

'You mean she could hurt the family, since we don't have that bottle protecting us anymore?' I gasped. Debbie held up her hands.

'I'm just saying, be careful. That's all. It sounds like Alice is being used by Jenny for some reason.'

'But what does she want? This Jenny?' I asked fearfully.

'I don't know. If I can find out some more about her I might be able to help. Until then, I think you should keep your wits about you.'

'Do you think I should tell Matt and Jayne?' I asked them both.

'Depends. Do you think they'll believe it?' Ben queried.

'Jayne might. Matt? Definitely not.'

'Maybe you should just let things lie for the moment. Until I have the chance to find out some more at the archives,' Debbie suggested. 'I don't suppose you've come across any papers relating to the history of the house, have you?'

'Only a notebook belonging to old Pierre Chevalier, Matt's great uncle. Full of ramblings, and not making much sense.'

'Keep an eye out. See if you can find a family tree or better still, any information on the early Chevalier's.'

We called it a night then. Gracie had long since fallen asleep in front of the TV in the next room and my mind was overcrowded with all we had discussed tonight. Before I left, Debbie pressed a small jar of yellowish cream into my hands.

'It's a special recipe I invented - just for you,' she said. 'It should help with reducing the redness of the scarring on your face.'

'Thank you,' I said, touched by her thoughtfulness. 'What's in it?'

'Oh, the usual. Lavender, rosemary, calendula, a bit of dandelion, some chickweed, a touch of eyebright,' she rattled off the ingredients.

'Eye of toad, toe of newt,' Ben stage-whispered behind me and Debbie laughed.

'Mock me if you will, my boy, but you've seen the benefits of my witchery many times! Just a small amount twice a day, Leah, and you should start seeing an improvement within a day or two.'

'Well, thank you, I really appreciate it,' I leaned in to give her a hug. 'Actually, I have an appointment with a surgeon in a week or so. I'm hoping he'll be able to do something about my twisted lip.'

'Hey, that's great news!' Ben beamed at me. 'But I have to say, I was kinda getting used to Leah the Playboy bunny...'

Debbie and I both slapped him that time.

Ben carefully laid the sleeping Gracie on the back seat of his car as we prepared to go home.

'I had a great time tonight,' I said shyly. 'Debbie's everything you said she would be. I love her. I want her to be my aunty too!' I broke off, embarrassed by my blunder. 'Sorry, I didn't mean.... I mean, that would be weird.'

'Yeah, we'd have to get married for that to happen,' Ben teased me dryly.

'Or, she could adopt me,' I suggested. 'Then we'd be, what, cousins or something?'

'Neh. I kinda like the getting married idea better,' Ben said casually.

I stood awkwardly, dumbfounded into silence.

'All good to go,' Ben announced as he finished strapping Gracie in with the seatbelts and turned to open the passenger door for me. I made to move past him towards the car but he stopped me with a gentle hand on my arm.

'Hey,' he said softly. I looked up at him and he brought his lips down gently to meet mine. 'Is this OK?' he asked, his voice barely a whisper. I nodded, unable to speak, and he kissed me again. He caressed my cheek with the lightest touch.

'Put that poor girl down!' Debbie shouted from the doorway, and we broke apart, laughing and embarrassed.

CHAPTER NINETEEN

I could hear the raised voices before I even left the car. Jayne and Matt were arguing furiously in the kitchen when Ben dropped me home.

'Will you be alright?' Ben asked me anxiously. 'You're welcome to come and stay with us tonight, if you want. I'll take the couch.'

'No, no it's fine,' I replied. 'I've never heard them argue like this before though, but I suppose all couples argue sometimes. Maybe me walking in might make them stop.'

I opened the kitchen door as quietly as I could.

'Oh good, Leah's home,' Jayne sounded relieved. 'Maybe she can make you see some sense.'

'Don't go dragging Leah into this, Jayne. This is for us to discuss between ourselves. Leah's not even...' Matt broke off, looking awkward.

'Family,' I finished for him. 'Yeah, you're right Matt. I'm not family and it's not for me to get involved, but I could hear you two shouting from outside in the car. And if I can hear you then so can Alice and Noah.'

'I'll go check on them,' Jayne began.

'No. I will,' I told her forcefully. 'That's why I'm here. It's my job. But can I suggest you two either take this next door where we can't hear you or, better still, stop acting like children yourselves and discuss whatever it is you're fighting about calmly and rationally, like adults?'

They both looked at me, shocked into silence.

'Sorry, I've, er, had some wine. I probably shouldn't have said that,' I mumbled.

'No, it's fine,' Matt said. 'Actually it's probably exactly what we needed to hear. Look,' he said to Jayne. 'This isn't getting us anywhere. We should talk about it tomorrow, after we've had some sleep.'

'When tomorrow?' demanded Jayne. 'You're always in the bloody wing next door. I barely see you and when I do, you don't bother to talk to me.'

Feeling like a third wheel, I tried to inch my way past Matt to the corridor so I could check on the children. Jayne hadn't finished, her voice becoming louder still as she berated Matt.

'I'm telling you now, Matthew, I'm taking the kids and going! I've had enough of this house and enough of this island, with its narrow-minded, ignorant bloody people. You can choose, either you give up this ridiculous idea of restoring this .... this fucking monstrosity, and come back to London with us or you can stay here on your own!'

You're not taking my kids anywhere!' Matt roared back at her. 'This house is their family legacy, it's their inheritance.'

'It's a bloody curse, that's what it is!' Jayne shouted at him. 'You must feel it, Matt, something's not right here. Look, keep it if you must but why can't you rent it out? Put back the flats you've ripped out and we can rent it out as a house of multiple occupancy, make a good income from it, but be back in London where we were happy!'

'There's nothing wrong with the house. It's in your imagination! All this stupid talk of ghosts - it's just you and Leah getting each other worked up over nothing. Bloody hysterical women!'

I balked at my name being used as a weapon in their war.

'Alice is just acting up because she's moved house and moved schools and things are unsettled for her, that's all. There's no ghost called Jenny telling her to misbehave. It's all her imagination. She gets it from you!'

'Matthew, I am going home, to London, either with or without you but at this moment I would be happy if it was without. You've been insufferable since we moved here.'

'You can't go back to London anyway,' Matt said, sounding triumphant. 'I've sold the house there.'

There was silence, complete and utter cold silence.

'You've done what?' Jayne said, in a voice so low I could barely hear her.

'Sold the London house!' Matt crowed. 'We needed the money for the renovations. Your job isn't bringing enough in and the rent from it was only just covering the mortgage, so I sold it.'

'But that is OUR house, Matt! It belongs to both of us! How? How could you have sold it without me signing something? It was in both our names,' Jayne raged.
Matt smirked.

'Didn't need to. The mortgage was in both our names but the deeds to the house were in my name only. I didn't need your signature for anything. I sold it and paid off the mortgage. Made a decent profit on it too, enough to finish the downstairs entrance and great hall and make a start on the bedrooms upstairs.'
I couldn't believe it. Matt was discussing the sale of their family home in London as casually as if he was talking about buying a newspaper or a pint of milk. Jayne stared at him with pure hatred on her face.

'I can't believe you've done this. I can't believe you made such a momentous decision without even mentioning it to me first.'

'I knew you would say no, so I didn't bother to ask,' Matt shrugged flippantly.
Without another word Jayne whirled on her feet and crashed heavily down the hallway. She slammed the door to their bedroom so hard we could feel the flimsy walls shake. I looked at Matt in horror.

'Matt, what have you done?' I whispered.

'Don't start on me, Leah. Or you can pack your bags and fuck off too,' he warned.

'Don't tempt me,' I said. 'The way you're going, you'll have nobody left!'
He opened his mouth to retaliate but before he could get another word out we both heard the bedroom door open

again. Jayne came walking out calmly, a small holdall in her hand and her phone to her ear.

'Yes, OK,' she said into it. 'I'll wait outside in the lane. Can you pick me up as soon as you can? OK, thanks. Yeah, I know. See you in a minute.'

Without a single word or a glance in Matt's direction Jayne sailed through the kitchen and walked out of the door. We watched as she continued to walk down the dark driveway towards the main road.

'Well?' I said to Matt. 'Aren't you going to go after her?'

Matt's face was twisted with pain and something else - anger, jealousy and a righteous indignation.

'No,' he said flatly. 'If that fat cow wants to go off running after him, she can go. More fool him for taking her on.'

'Who? Who's she gone running off to?' I said, totally bewildered.

'Didn't she tell you?' Matt's voice was mocking. 'I thought she would have, with you two being best friends and all.'

'Matt, I have no idea what you're talking about. Where has she gone? And with who?'

'She's gone to Gabriel. My cousin, Gabriel.' Matt's eyes glowed with rage. 'They've been having an affair for weeks.

I retreated to my room, unable to process what had just happened. Jayne and Gabriel? I mean, I knew Jayne could be secretive, in fact, she'd been downright cagey when I caught her talking on her phone sometimes. But Gabriel? He hadn't been to the house ever since that trip to the beach. And Jayne was working so many hours, when would she even get the time to...

Oh. I got it then. She hadn't been working so many shifts, she wasn't needed to work on after her shift finished as overtime. Those were just excuses. Lies. When she told me she had to work late, she'd been hooking up with Gabriel.

Feeling betrayed, I sat down on my bed and wondered if I should go home, return to Mum's house and leave Jayne and Matt to sort themselves out. But who would look after the kids? If Jayne had left, which I didn't believe for one second - she'd never leave her children - who's going to look after them?

I heard Matt walk down his hallway and open the door to Noah's room. A couple of seconds ticked by and then I heard him cross the hall to Alice's room. Faint voices - one high and scared, the other deep and reassuring - told me that Alice was awake, and she had probably heard a great deal of her parents' argument. I undressed and got into bed. The rich food I'd so enjoyed earlier tonight lay heavily in my stomach and I curled up uncomfortably, thinking it would be ages until I could sleep, but I dropped off almost straight away.

The baby was still crying when I woke up. I was wrenched out of sleep and out of a nightmare in which a small child, about Noah's age but I instinctively knew it wasn't Noah, crawled around naked and crying in a dusty attic room. In my dream I was standing behind it and when I went to pick the baby up, it turned to face me only for me to see that it had no eyes, just bloody holes where the eyes should have been. I sat up gasping, my heart racing, relieved it was only a dream.

But I could still hear the baby's cries.

It must be Noah, I thought, looking over at my alarm clock. The luminous numbers glowed 3.04 am. The thin wailing was relentless and I groggily turned back the bedcovers and reached for my robe. Just as I unlocked the connecting door to the main hallway, the crying stopped. Matt must have got up and settled Noah, I thought gratefully. Tiredness pulled at me and I wanted nothing else but to crawl back into my bed and sleep for a few more hours. Just as I turned to go back to bed, a soft knock at my door startled me.

'Leah?' I heard Matt whisper. I unlocked the door. He was standing there in his own dressing gown, his face blurry with sleep. He stank of whiskey. He must have hit the bottle hard after Jayne left. 'What's wrong with Noah? I heard him crying but he stopped so I thought you must have taken him into bed with you.'

'No, I heard him crying too but I thought you must have gone into him.'

'Oh.' Matt seemed confused. 'No. I guess we should check on him now.'

I followed him down the darkened corridor to Noah's room. Matt quietly pushed open the door and we both saw Noah, on his back, arms splayed above his head, snoring away in a deep sleep.

'It's funny, but it didn't sound like Noah.'

'No, I thought that too. It sounded too young to be Noah,' I replied. 'It sounded more like a new-born than a one-year-old.'

'Must have been something outside, a bird perhaps,' Matt said. We tiptoed back along the hall. 'Leah, about before. I'm so sorry. We shouldn't have made you get involved.' He sounded hoarse and heart-broken.

'It's OK,' I said. 'Although I had no idea about Jayne and Gabriel, Matt. You have to believe that.'

'I know, I know,' he sighed. 'I only found out myself by accident. Jayne left her phone by the bed one night after she got home from the hospital. She was in the shower and I heard it ping with a text. I don't know why I looked, I've never done that before, but I did. It was him. Gabriel.'

What did it say?' I asked, horrified. Matt closed his eyes in pain.

'It said, "Thank you for another wonderful night", and there were kisses, three of them.'

'Oh Matt, I'm so sorry.'

He nodded, unable to speak for grief. We were back at my door and were about to say goodnight when the crying started again. It was a thin, reedy wail; the kind made by a very young baby.

'That's not Noah,' Matt said and I shook my head in agreement.

'I think it's coming from Alice's room,' I said. We both padded down the hall towards Alice's bedroom. The crying continued even as we opened her door. She was sound asleep in her bed, curled up under the covers.

'It sounds like it's coming from behind this wall,' Matt whispered as he tapped it lightly.

'You know what's on the other side of that wall, don't you?' I said. He nodded.

'The stone room. But there's nothing in there,' he said.

'Could an animal have got in?' I offered. 'It sounds a bit like a seagull.'

'It sounds like Noah did when he was just born and had colic. It sounds like a tiny baby in pain,' Matt replied. He opened the door to my room and started pushing at the wall covering the secret passageway.

'You're not seriously thinking what I think you're thinking, are you?' I stuttered in disbelief. 'Matt, you are not breaking down that wall in the middle of the night!'

'I don't have to break down the wall, I left a loose panel when I built your doorway. Just in case we needed to get to the stone room.' Matt hit the wall hard with the flat of his hand and the panel moved inwards.

'What possible reason could we have had for needing to get back into that creepy little room?' I hissed.

'Oh, I don't know. How about an animal getting trapped in there during the night and us needing to rescue it? I don't want a dead animal stinking up the house so, whatever it is, we need to go in and set it free.' He pushed at the loose panel some more and it gave way. He hauled it out sideways and then we were looking into the impenetrable blackness of the flag-stoned corridor.

'Do we have to go now?' I whimpered. 'Can't we wait a couple of hours until daylight and go then?'

'You don't have to come with me. I'll be fine on my own. I'll just grab my torch.' Matt backed up and walked quickly down the flat's hallway, then shoved aside the temporary door which led into the other wing of the house. I shivered in the darkness. The crying had stopped again. An unnatural cold seeped up from the tunnel and enveloped me.

'Hurry up, Matt!' I whispered, crossing my arms and hugging myself, and almost sagging with relief when I heard him blundering back down the hall. He climbed over the gap clumsily with the torch anchored in his armpit.

'Coming?' he asked me.

'What? No way!'

'I'll let you hold the torch,' he waved it invitingly. 'I'll go first. Come on. We might need both of us to catch it, whatever it is.'

I glared at him but I knew he was right.

'Oh bloody hell, all right then,' I said crossly. 'Give me a hand to get over this wall.'

The dark gap between the walls seemed smaller than before. At least that time, when we first found the passage, it had been daylight and the tiny window in the stone room had given us a bit of grey light to see by. Now, there was nothing. The darkness was absolute. The bright beam of Matt's torch seemed to get sucked up by the pitch-black space, as if the darkness was made of something solid, and the floor was icy cold on my bare feet. Slowly, we slid along the wall towards the creepy little room. I tried not to think of what I was rubbing against, feeling spun-silk webs brush my face. The passage seemed endless, although we both knew the room was just down there, to the right.

'Shhhhh!' Matt shushed me and stopped abruptly. 'Hear that?'

The piteous wailing started up again. It sounded louder as if, indeed, there was a new-born baby just around the corner.

'This is impossible,' I grumbled. 'There's no way there could be a baby in that room.'

At last, we found the doorway and Matt's body warmth left my side as he ventured into the room first. I followed hesitantly, not wanting to go in there but not wanting to be left on my own in that black passageway either. The crying stopped immediately. The torch beam swung around the empty room. We searched all four corners, tested the firmly closed window, and scanned every inch of the ground. There was nothing in the room. It had the same iron hooks in the ceiling and the same iron loops on the floor, but otherwise it was exactly the same as we had left it.

There was no sign of any animal having got in, nor was there any crying baby.

'Weird,' Matt said.

'Very weird,' I agreed. 'Come on, let's go. There's nothing here.'

Matt was busy running his hand over the granite blocks, tapping one now and then with his fingernail.

'What are you looking for now?' I said in exasperation. I was cold, annoyed and desperately wanting to leave this place and go back to my warm, safe bed.

'Just seeing if there are any loose bricks,' Matt said seriously. 'Maybe there's a secret hiding place in here as well.'

'What? With a live baby inside it? I don't think so, Matt.'

'It might explain the noise we heard. It could have been the wind blowing through a gap in the wall, making a sound like a baby crying,' he reasoned.

'Matt, look outside.' I gestured to the small window where the leaves of the tree growing just outside it were perfectly still. 'There is no wind tonight.'

'Just a thought,' Matt shrugged. 'Otherwise, I don't have a clue what made that noise.'

'Well, it's stopped now. Can we just forget about it and go back to our beds please?'

Matt took one long look around the room.

'Yeah, sure,' he said, and I was relieved when we reached the end of the passage and had climbed back over the hole in the wall to my room again. Matt hefted the panel back into place and the passageway was sealed once again.

I crawled wearily into bed. There was no more crying that night.

Jennet's Story

Jersey 1603

Bonjour again, Sister, and how do you fare today?

I must thank you for the soup. No, it matters not that it was cold, it was most welcome.

Do you remember, Sister, of me telling you of a great secret I have? I have been thinking, Sister. I have little else to do in here but think. I feel I have TWO secrets, Sister. One I may share with you today, but one I must keep to myself for now, for it is such a delicious feeling to have a secret and to know that no one else knows it but you.

Where was I in my story? Ah yes, I had just become a woman.

This was a time of great change in my life. Not only did Matthieu and I begin to act differently with one another, but there were other happenings which heralded the beginning of all that occurred later and brought me low to this place.

As you know, Matthieu was older than me by some months and there were changes to his appearance also that did not go unnoticed by me. His shoulders became broader and his legs longer and leaner. He started to grow the beginnings of a beard and his voice was deeper whereas before it had been higher and more girlish than my own. He was fascinated by all things military and took a great interest in the newly built Elizabeth Castle, that marvellous fort in the bay named for the late queen. Indeed, he twice went with his father to dine with Sir Walter Raleigh, the Governor of Jersey, who resides in the Governor's House there. Matthieu had never wanted anything more than to be a

211

soldier and, as he was so far down the line of inheritance, it was certain that this would be his predestination. But this was all to change.

In our newly adult bodies, we were shy with each other now. We no longer swam in the warm tidal pools together nor lay drying in the sun afterwards. The green dress Matthieu had given me long ago was starting to rot and I was reluctant and shy in asking him for another. For one, I did not want to draw attention to the places on my body which now peeked through the gaping rents in the dress and for two, I did not want him to steal for me again.

Matthieu's penchant for taking things that did not belong to him had grown ever stronger and he now did not restrict himself to stealing from his own home, but had broadened into swiping whatever took his fancy from the mean houses in the village. He once took a jug of rough cider that was sitting on a windowsill and we shared it at our secret place in the woods until we were clumsy and laughing. He went for larger things now, no longer satisfied with cakes from the cook's pantry, and often came by with things that I knew would be sorely missed by its hardworking owner. When he appeared one day with a bundle of cloth, I knew he had stolen a poor woman's wash from her drying line outside. The garments were patched and faded but would still be easily recognised by their owner and I begged Matthieu for a needle and some thread so I could patch the worst areas of my green dress, and in doing so, would render the clothes into nothing more than indistinguishable squares of dirty linen. At once, he pilfered a poke of needles and pins from the laundry maids in his father's employ, and a selection of fine cotton threads. I tried not to think of their confusion when these things were discovered gone, and their fear when the finger of suspicion pointed at them, but my need was greater than theirs at that moment.

Matthieu and I would still play the games of our childhood when we were together but the games of soldiers and prisoners, or kings and court, changed into something more worldly as we grew older. Now, instead of besting me at swordplay and pretending to take me prisoner, Matthieu would wrestle me to the ground and cover my body with his. He would hold my wrists tightly above my head and lie fully on me so that I felt his hard body hot against mine. When I wriggled beneath him, he would groan and close his eyes in bliss. Once, he tied me with rope to a tree and bid me beg him to let me go. I squirmed and whimpered as if I was helpless as he ran his hands over my curves, lingering on my breasts and daring to snake between my legs.

Such feelings, Sister! Oh, I know this is sinful talk, Sister, but is this not what you came here for? My confession? This is part of my confession, Sister, for I confess to the sin of lust. I have already confessed to the sin of stealing, or enticing another to steal for me. I have so much more to confess, Sister.

Matthieu leaned his body into mine and looked deep into my eyes.
'Can you kiss, I wonder, with that mouth of yours?' He pressed his lips to mine and moved them slowly against my mouth until we were tongues entwined and tasting each other. It did not matter, in that moment, that I was cursed with the face of a hare. Indeed, that was the one time in my life when I felt like any other maid would do when being kissed by the man she loves. I wanted him to kiss me some more, and hold me, and tell me I was his own true love but that was not what happened next.

Can you imagine, Sister, what Matthieu did next? I am sure you do, Sister, I am sure you do.

Matthieu grabbed the skirts of my green dress in his fist and lifted them high. *Remember, Sister, that the green dress was the only item of clothing I had, and that when he lifted it up I was completely naked beneath his gaze.* I felt him fumble with the opening of his own breeches and then I felt a pushing. He moved to lift my legs so they were wrapped around his waist and the pushing grew stronger. I wriggled, as it was not so comfortable for me, Sister, being tied to the rough trunk of a tree whilst being hoisted into the air by my legs. Matthieu lunged at me hard and I felt myself break, then he was inside me and groaning and crying out in pleasure. He pushed again once or twice then sagged against me, breathing heavily. He stayed still for a long while. I felt him slide out of me and a wetness, different from the wetness of my bleeding times, trailed down my thigh. Matthieu eventually roused himself and released the rope which bound my hands.

'Don't tell!' he warned as he turned and crashed through the undergrowth, hasty to be away from me. I stood against that tree trunk for the longest time, savouring the feel of him, the soreness between my legs as proof of him being there.

I did not tell. For whom would I tell?

No, Sister, this is not the secret I spoke of earlier. I am coming to that.

Matthieu stayed away from me for a couple of days after that time. I continued my routine of foraging for food and firewood in the woods but my heart was light and I found myself humming as I worked. I rarely saw other people in my wood but there were times when I skirted close to the edge of the village and the conversations of the common folk drifted over to me through the trees. I heard two women talking in the lane outside their houses and they were speaking of a strange occurrence at the manor house.

'...heard tell that one of their hens laid an egg with two yolks, which is a sign of devilment as we all know, and that the master gave the order to have all the hens killed as it would have been impossible to tell which of them was the bewitched hen, so they were all under the axe.'

'Aye, I heard that too,' replied the other woman. 'Only I also hear that all those hens were burned on a bonfire so as not to end up on the dining table. A waste of good meat if ever I heard of!'

'Ah, but you yourself would not have wanted to eat the flesh of a hen who was witched. I cannot say as I blame them. And that is not the only sign of witching I hear of,' the first woman said. 'The Pallot farm had a cow who gave birth to a calf with five legs last week!'

'Five is the number of witches!' her companion hissed. ''Tis surely dark times we are living in, Madame, dark times indeed!'

They both clucked their tongues and carried on their ways. They would have been shocked to know I was just there, just out of sight in the dark green of the trees, and listening to their prattle of devilments and witches. In truth, I was uneasy to hear their village gossip for any talk of witchery brought my hare-cursed face to mind. I resolved to be more careful from then on, and stay well-hidden and near to my home.

I was crouched down behind a fallen tree slicing at some mushrooms which had sprouted in the damp ground underneath it when I heard the crack of a twig being stepped on. Thinking it was Matthieu, for only he knew where I foraged, I lifted my head above the tree's trunk. A tall man in a blue riding coat was walking along the half-hidden path, looking around him in confusion. I ducked down and stayed quiet, hoping he would pass me by without seeing me. A long moment went by and I heard no more movement so I slowly peeked over the fallen log again. The man in blue was standing on the other side of the tree staring back at *me. I yelped and ducked away again but I knew he had seen me so I cautiously raised my gaze to meet his. He was still looking dazed and it was then I noticed he had a large wound to the side of his head. It must have pained him greatly but he appeared not to notice it.*

'Can you tell me where I am?' he asked me, as if baffled to find himself in the middle of a wood.

'In the woods, Sir, of Grouville. Near the parish church, Sir,' I told him.

'And have you seen my horse?' he says and I shook my head.

'Nay, Sir, there has been no horse here. I would have heard it.'

He muttered something unintelligible and paced a step or two. The injury to his head was very bad, I did wonder how he was still standing, but it was then that I saw how he was not a living, breathing man.

This is my secret, Sister. Do you recall, the telling of my mother's death, when I described how I saw her soul ascend to Heaven? Yes, you huffed at me and disbelieved me. But it was the same for this man, Sister. I was not seeing a solid human form, I was seeing his shade, Sister.

The man was pale of flesh but I thought this was in part due to the loss of blood from his head wound. As he muttered and paced I saw that he was not a solid shape but a hazy form I could almost see through. Like a piece of cloth that has been washed so many times, the pattern fades and the cloth becomes washed out and thin. Like that, Sister. I can see you do not want to believe me, Sister, but hey-la! - listen to this next piece and then doubt me.

The man lumbered away, still muttering and cursing. He became lesser as he moved away from me and it was not so much he disappeared behind the trees, but more that he disappeared INTO them. One moment he was there and the next he was not and I was alone once more apart from the slight breeze rustling in the leaves. He was a dead man, Sister. I should have known it from the start when I saw the wound in his head as no man could suffer that and live. It was the following day when Matthieu found me in my shack, grinding acorns to make a rough flour. He looked the very picture of misery, and when he spoke he was Matthieu the boy again, and not Matthieu the man who had taken my maidenhead roughly against a tree trunk.

'Guillaume, my brother, he has been killed,' he told me, his voice wobbling. 'He went out riding yesterday and did not come home when it was dark so my father sent the grooms out to look for him.' He picked at the skin around his fingernails. 'They think his horse stood in a rabbit hole and stumbled, throwing him off. His head was caved in by the rock he landed on. His horse had to be killed, its leg was badly broken.'

I knew then who the man in the blue riding coat had been but I did not speak of it to Matthieu.

'This changes everything,' Matthieu went on uneasily. 'Guillaume was my father's heir. They are writing to Jeanne now, to see if he will give up his vows to God and come home to take his place as the next heir. But if he doesn't, Jennet, and he does not have to if he believes his calling is to serve God, it will be me,' he said miserably. 'I will be Father's heir and he will make me stay here and learn the ways of the estate, and I shall be bound here for my whole life.' He broke off with a sob.

'But, Matthieu, would that be so bad?' I wondered. 'You would be a very great man. You would be the Lord after your father dies and you will be one of the highest men on the island and sit on the parish councils.'

'I do not want that, Jennet! All I ever wanted was to be free from my father.' He ground his fist into the hard-packed floor of my house. 'I wanted to be a soldier, and to come back in many years' time with a fortune of my own making. I wanted to show my father that I do not need him.

I can make my own way in life. I am not the useless wastrel he thinks me.' He gave in to his tears then and I held him close as he sobbed into my neck. The wheel of fortune had turned for Matthieu, and I did not know it then, but it turned for me also.

So you see, Sister, that is one of my secrets. I can see the dead when they leave this earthly plane. You remember Frances, the boy who was here before? He died of his fever a day ago, Sister, and I saw him too. But it was the strangest thing - I did not see him as he breathed his last here in this fetid pit. I did not see him when they hauled his wasted body out and took him away to throw him off the cliff behind us. I only saw him much later that night. I had my eye to the gap between the stones in that far wall, which is as far as my chains will allow me to move, when I saw Frances outside. He smiled and waved to me, and did a little dance, and I saw that his own chains had been removed in death. So I wonder, Sister, I am wondering if the chains make a difference? I am in irons as they fear me as a witch, and these chains are supposed to stop me from flying free and away from here. Do you think it is possible, Sister, that the iron stops our souls from leaving our bodies when we die? I know I am fanciful, Sister. But I still think this is so.

Will you promise me something, Sister?

The dawn of my death draws close. Will you promise me to make them remove these chains from my body before they kill me, Sister? I am so afeared my soul will be trapped within my blackened mortal remains forever, Sister, if they are not cut off me. Do you? Do you promise me, Sister?

CHAPTER TWENTY

Leah

It was almost impossible to get Alice out of bed for school in the morning. She looked as tired as I felt, with big purple shadows underneath her eyes.

'It's not fair,' she said crossly as I made her breakfast. 'The baby kept me awake all night with its crying. And Jenny kept walking through the wall into my room and walking around, waking me up.'

'Did you hear the crying too last night?' I asked her, curiously. Whenever Matt and I had looked in on her she appeared to be sound asleep.

'Yeah, stupid baby,' she muttered.

'Did you see the baby?' I wondered.

'No. That's why Jenny was walking around so much. She was trying to find the baby.'

Before I could question her any further, Matt walked into the kitchen. He was dishevelled and unshaven, and had obviously slept in his clothes. He poured himself a coffee without a word.

'Where's Mummy?' Alice asked him.

'At work,' he grunted.

Alice looked as if she was going to argue but took in his grim face and wisely kept her counsel. Noah was the only one of us who wasn't suffering the after-effects from the night before. He pulled himself up on his fat little legs and stood unsteadily, grinning at us from his playpen.

'La-la!' he shouted happily. 'Da-da.'

Alice giggled through a mouthful of toast.

'Daddy, Noah said your name!'

Matt's face lit up and lost its sullen look and he smiled widely as he swept Noah up in his arms.

'Who's a clever boy, then? Where's your dad, eh?' He chuckled as he jigged Noah up and down. Noah burst into delighted laughter and pointed to Alice.

'La-La!' he announced.

'Yes, Alice!' agreed Matt. 'Who's this?' he asked, pointing at me.

'Zhee... Zhee... aaaaa!' declared Noah, looking at Matt for confirmation.

'Yes, Leah! That's right, clever lad. Who am I?'

'Da-Da!' shouted Noah gleefully and poking his pudgy finger into Matt's face.

'Oof! Yes, Daddy! Mind my eye, Noah. And who is this?' Matt asked finally as he gently poked his own finger at Noah's tummy. Noah looked down thoughtfully, then looked up and suddenly pointed at the far corner of the kitchen.

'Jenny!' he said, as clear as day.

'We've got to talk to Alice about this Jenny,' Matt said firmly as I got back from the school run with Noah. 'It's one thing talking about her like she's an imaginary friend but I'm not having Noah start with it as well.'

Matt was leaning back against the kitchen counter, arms folded across his chest. He was usually knee-deep in rubble and wood by now. It was rare for him to still be in the flat when I got back from taking Alice to school.

'I really don't think Jenny is imaginary,' I said. 'What about last night? That pitiful crying.'

'It must have been the wind, like I said,' Matt replied. 'Or else air in the old water pipes. That can sometimes sound like a human cry.'

'Oh, bullshit, Matt!' I rounded on him angrily. 'Why can't you just admit that there's something in this house? Something we don't understand. Your children... BOTH your children can see it. We have heard it. How do you explain the voice on the baby monitor, huh?   Or the scratches on poor Gracie's face?'

'Only you heard the voice on the monitor, Leah, and I'm pretty sure it was Alice who scratched Gracie,' Matt said calmly. 'I'm sorry, but I just don't believe in any of that shit. Ghosts, witches, the supernatural - it's all too far-fetched to believe in. We need to sit down with Alice and tell her that she is not to mention Jenny again.'

'Matt, that's not my job. It should be you and Jayne sitting down with your daughter - together!' I reminded him. 'What are you going to do, Matt?'

'About what?' He argued stubbornly, and looked me in the eye. 'She's made her choice. But she won't get the kids. They are MY kids and they will stay with ME in MY house!' he said, spitting the words at me. 'So when you go running to her telling tales, tell her THAT!'

'Matt, I'm not going to choose sides. I told you last night that I had no idea about her and Gabriel, and that's the truth! It seems to me that you both need me more than ever at the moment. I don't see you taking time off from your precious renovation work to look after your son or take your daughter to school!' I threw at him venomously. He pushed himself away from the counter and strode towards the door to the other wing.

'I don't need this shit! Just get out of my face, Leah,' he shouted as he grabbed his hard hat and pulled on his work boots.

'You can't just keep disappearing when things get tough!' I screamed back, following him through the temporary door into the main hall. 'So you're going through a rough patch, so what? It happens to us all. Trust me, I know that better than anyone! For fuck's sake, Matt, grow a pair and deal with it!'

I had just stepped through into the old part of the house when we heard an enormous crash coming from the kitchen. We stopped bickering and looked at each other in horror.

'Noah!' we both said at the same time, and turned on our heels, almost falling over each other in our hurry to get back to the kitchen. Matt got there first, just in front of me. He paused in the doorway, but when I went to push past him, desperate to get to Noah and wondering why Matt wasn't moving quicker, he put his arm back to stop me going in.

'Wait! Stop. Don't go in,' he said. He took one cautious step. I leaned around him and craned my neck to see what it was that was stopping Matt from running in to rescue his son.

Every single kitchen cabinet door was hanging open.

We both took another small step inside the room and looked around in disbelief. The small pile of breakfast dishes that were waiting to be washed by the sink now lay strewn across the floor in pieces. The small pots of seedlings, previously in a sunny spot on the windowsill, were upended, their pots cracked in half and useless. The wooden kitchen chairs were stacked in an untidy tower against the kitchen door when, moments ago, they had been in their proper place around the dining table.

'What in the hell...?' Matt murmured. He stepped over the debris on the floor and went to check on Noah, who was sitting wide-eyed and completely unmoving in his playpen. His little face crumpled when he saw his father and he held his arms out to be picked up. I bent down to start picking up the sharp shards of broken crockery from the floor.

'Leah, look,' Matt said quietly to me. I looked at where he was pointing to and gasped in terror. The big carving knife, the one from a set given to Jayne and Matt as a wedding present and usually kept safely in a locked kitchen drawer, was sticking upright out of the toaster. It looked like it had been jammed in there with some force, and the toaster was still plugged in and switched on. A pair of scissors from the same set - big, chunky, sharp scissors, designed to crunch through chicken bones and tough cartilage, were embedded point-first into the top of the table. Deep scratches had been gouged into the table's surface, three of them, eerily mirroring the three scratches on Gracie's face.

'We keep that knife set locked away!' I said to Matt as he surveyed the room gravely.

'I'll turn the power off. Don't touch the toaster until then.' He carried Noah out of the room in search of the fuse box. As they passed me, Noah laid a sleepy head on Matt's shoulder.

'Jenny,' the little boy whispered.

'Believe me now?' I said to Matt's stiff, retreating back.

'... and then the whole kitchen was completely trashed!'

Ben was sitting opposite me at the little table in the café garden. We had Noah with us as I couldn't very well leave him in Matt's care for the morning. He was happy in his stroller, looking around with interest at the bright flowers as he contentedly sucked at his sippy cup of water. I had just finished telling Ben everything that had gone on last night, and this morning. He gave a low whistle.

'And here's me thinking that the most exciting thing to happen last night was when I kissed you!' He raised one eyebrow rakishly. 'I'm afraid I can't compete with poltergeist activity, so...'

'Are you dumping me?' I teased, throwing my paper napkin at him.

'Never!' he grinned. 'But it does sound like things are starting to get out of hand. I really don't like the idea of you being there if things are going to get dangerous. And with things the way they are between Jayne and Matt...'

223

'Yeah, I know. Part of me thinks I would be better leaving them to it, to sort things out between them without having me there. It's too convenient for them to ignore what's happening if I'm there to see to the kids every day.'

'And the other part of you?' Ben asked. I let out a big sigh.

'The other part of me thinks that I'm the only one who can protect those kids. It's all tied in with the house, Ben, I know it is. If only I could just find something, something which could tell us who Jenny is and what she wants.'

'I still don't like it, Leah. You don't know what you're dealing with. Are you sure you won't stay with me and Gracie for a few nights? Leave Jayne to calm down and go home?' Ben took my hand across the table.

'I can't, Ben. Not now, not until I can find a way to get rid of Jenny, for good.'

'Well, then would you accept some help?' He searched my face. 'I can spare a couple of hours today. Maybe we could go and have a poke around the attics?'

'Would you do that?' I beamed with pleasure. 'I can't think of anything nicer.'

'Will Matt mind?' he asked.

'Matt will probably steal you away, have you holding the measuring tape or put you on rubble-dumping duty. He'd love to have another man about to help him, although he'd never admit it.'

Matt looked surprised to see Ben but was welcoming enough.

'Let me know if you get bored playing at ghost-hunting,' he said good-naturedly. 'I've got plenty to keep you busy. I could use a master craftsman's advice.'
I nudged Ben.
'See!' I told him. 'You boys chat for a minute,' I said to both. 'I'll put Noah down for a nap.'

Pocketing the baby monitor, I led Ben up the old staircases to the main attic door and flung it open with a creaking flourish.

'Ta-dah!'

'Woah! Oh my God, I thought you were exaggerating.' Ben gaped at the vast room crammed with old furniture, closed trunks and boxes upon boxes of mystery items. 'Where does it end? I can't even see a far wall.'

'I know. It's the same size as the entire ground floor of the house. I've only taken a few boxes from up here so far, maybe ten or so, but it'll take years to clear the whole attic.'

'What should we look for first?' Ben said, scanning the length of the attic.

'Well, everything I've looked at has been pretty recent, but it looks like there's no system, you know? All the paperwork I've found has been jumbled up into boxes with other random stuff.'

'It would make sense to start at the back,' Ben suggested. 'I would guess that's where the oldest stuff will be. Generations of Chevaliers have probably been dumping stuff in here for centuries, just shoving it in front of whatever was already here.'

'Now, why didn't I think of that?' I mused. 'Although it's not the best idea to start clambering over everything else to get to the back. I'm not sure how safe the floor is in here.'

'That's why you need me,' Ben said flippantly. 'Stand back! Master carpenter and wood expert at your service.'

He stood on the seat of a straight-backed chair and wobbled dangerously.

'Shouldn't we tie a rope around you?' I joked. 'So you don't get lost and I can pull you to safety if you get trapped.'

Ben stepped awkwardly onto the top of a wooden packing crate, grabbing the back of the chair for balance.

'I can do this,' he assured me. 'I'll find a path, you follow, but stand EXACTLY where I stand, OK?'

I saluted.

'OK boss. Let's do this!'

Together, we slowly picked our way through the years of accumulated and unwanted belongings, stopping often to pull open the lids of dusty steamer trunks and rummage through their contents.

'Look at this!' I exclaimed, holding up a length of yellowing fabric. 'It's a nightgown, Victorian by the look of it. Look at the lace on the sleeves!'

'You could get five of you in that,' remarked Ben. 'It's hardly sexy bedwear.'

'I think that was the point,' I laughed. 'Victorian ladies were supposed to wrap themselves in so much material, from head to toe, so it was impossible for a man to find their way in.'

We hopped from chair to box to sturdy table, occasionally finding a bare patch of floor which Ben tested for safety by slowly leaning his entire weight on it. He held my hand as we clambered clumsily towards the back of the attic. Ben whistled whenever he found a particularly impressive piece of furniture.

'Just look at that carving around the inlay,' he said, running his fingers over a small round table, intricately decorated with mother of pearl and different coloured woods. 'I'd love to be able to take a proper look at that. I love carving but it's so time consuming.'

'What sort of things do you carve?'

'Mostly just stuff for myself. It takes too long to do to be lucrative. I'm experimenting at the moment with some carved panels for a bookcase. I'll carve you something one day,' Ben promised. 'Something special, made for you.'

'Would you?' I asked, touched by the sweet gesture. He squeezed my hand fondly.

'Of course. I'd love to.'

We continued our crazy zig-zagging pathway across the attic.

'Do you think some of this furniture could be worth something?' I said. 'There's so much stuff here. Some of these must be valuable?' I pointed to where a stack of elaborate gilt picture frames leaned against each other. They were facing away from us so I couldn't see if any of them still held their original paintings.

'Most of it has woodworm, I'm afraid,' Ben grimaced. 'Only fit for a bonfire.'

'Oh well, it's Bonfire Night soon. Maybe we can have the island's biggest bonfire,' I said, slightly disappointed.

'Got to get through Halloween first,' Ben grinned. 'Gracie's already pestering me for a costume. She wants to go as a black cat.'

'Alice hasn't mentioned Halloween yet,' I said thoughtfully.

'Probably enough spooky things going on in this house already. You don't want to encourage any more.'

The problem was that we didn't really know what we were looking for. I very much doubted we would simply stumble across a seventeenth-century chest with 'Chevalier Family Treasure' printed upon it. Ben was right about the layout of the attic though. The further back we went, the older things seemed to get. We found a couple of tapestries, rolled up and laid flat. We tried to unroll one but the backing material was so cracked and fragile that we stopped, afraid we would be doing irreversible damage.

'I have no idea how you'd get any of this stuff out,' Ben muttered as we stepped gingerly over a pile of mothed material, which looked like bed coverings.

'Do what I was trying to do, I guess. Start at the front and take things out one by one,'

'Most of this stuff must be museum material, though. We need the experts to come in to do what we're doing, and conserve any of the really historically important things. It would be criminal to just let everything crumble into dust, especially the textiles. If they were moved out now, they might be saved,' Ben fretted.

'Ben, I agree with you, but it's not up to us. It's Matt's house, and everything you see here is Matt's, for him to decide what to do with,' I reminded him. 'I think he thinks there'll be enough antiques and original family pieces to furnish the place when he's finished the restoration.'

Ben sighed.

'I know. It's just a crying shame, you know.'

We were stunned into silence by the sound of something sliding across a wall and falling heavily onto the floor.

'What was that?' I asked, looking over in the direction of the far left corner. No light penetrated this corner and it was inky black. I could almost make out the form of a large dresser, the type you find in kitchens, full of china, but beyond that there was only a solid darkness.

'We must have dislodged something with our poking around and it's fallen over,' Ben said. 'I wish we'd thought to bring a torch up with us.' He changed direction and started picking out a path towards the area of the noise. He had moved a few feet towards the corner when the sliding noise happened again, and this time I was sure I saw movement in the shadows.

'Ben, I don't like this! It sounds like there's something moving over there.'

'It's most probably mice or, at worst, squirrels,' Ben reassured me. 'A house this old and decrepit has got to be full of rodents.' He moved a few more feet in the direction of the noise, and was almost on the edge of the darkness when there was a resounding crash and something flew towards him. I screamed in fright. Ben ducked and the thing, a long cylindrical object, bounced off the back of a tattered chaise lounge behind him and landed with a clatter at his feet.

'What the hell was that?'

He looked at me in complete bafflement.

'That thing!' I gibbered. 'It came flying out of that corner and almost hit you!'

Ben leaned down to look at the mysterious item.

'Don't touch it!' I cried.

'It looks like a container of some sort,' he said, ignoring my pleas to leave it alone. 'Look, it ties at the top and there's a lid that comes off. Looks like it's made of leather.'

'What is it, some kind of early golf club bag or an umbrella stand?' I joked feebly, my eyes still open and alert for any more movement from the corner. Ben had lifted the case onto the flat surface of a wooden bench that wouldn't have looked out of place as a pew in the local church. I followed the route he had taken and perched next to him, looking at the object in his hands. It was about three feet in length, roughly octagonal in shape with a tightly fitting lid at the top. Made of tooled leather, it was beautiful in a way, but the leather was beginning to crack and showed signs of coming apart at the seams in some places. There were long tassels woven in and around the edge of the lid and they were knotted firmly together. It was clear we were going to have to unpick them in order to see what was inside. Ben shook the case gently. There was a dull rustle from inside but it didn't give any clues for us to hazard a guess at what the container held.

'Do you want to open it here, or shall we take it downstairs?' Ben asked me, turning the case around towards me.

'Let's try and open it here,' I replied. 'That way, if it's nothing important we haven't dragged it all the way downstairs only to have to drag it back up again.'

We picked and picked at the leather ties with our fingernails but they were swollen and dried out with age, and they would not yield in the slightest.

'Looks like we'll have to take it downstairs anyway,' Ben admitted. 'We need a large needle and some tweezer's so we can work the knots loose enough for us to unravel them. Do you want to go down and have a look now or keep looking around up here for a while...?'

As he spoke, a china bowl that had been resting on top of its wash basin stand suddenly flew sideways and smashed against the wall, coming to rest in a hundred pieces scattered over the dust-sheet draped shapes behind us.

'Looks like something wants us to open this case as soon as possible,' he said calmly.

'How can you be so cool about this?' I demanded. 'A bowl just moved by itself and smashed into the wall!'

'Could have been worse,' he shrugged. 'It could have smashed into one of us. Believe me Leah, I might look cool, calm and collected on the outside but inside I'm shaking like a leaf. Let's get out of here!'

Between us, we carefully carried the cylindrical case back over the obstacle course of the attic's contents, and managed to get it safely to the door. I took one last cautious look around but we had not seen anything else move of its own accord since the flying bowl. From the safety of the doorway, the far left corner couldn't even be seen, but that did not distil the distinct feeling that we were being carefully watched from within the shadowy depths.

Back downstairs in the bright sunlight of the lounge, I felt safe enough to brave the kitchen - now cleared of the chaos of this morning - to make us both a restorative cup of tea. Taking both mugs into the lounge, I found Ben examining the leather case carefully.

'Look, there's some initials stamped here, on the base,' Ben said. I peered closely and could just make out a cursive G followed by C.

'The C could be for Chevalier, couldn't it?' I ventured.

'Highly likely,' agreed Ben. 'Do you have some tweezers and a large needle, like a darning needle?'

I fetched the tweezers from the first aid kit and searched through various drawers for a suitable needle. All I could find was a small sewing kit, pilfered from a hotel at some point, and it only contained tiny needles barely bigger than a pin. Something tugged at the back of my mind, and I remembered one of the boxes of Pierre's I had gone through. Loose inside it was an old, rusting tin which had once held tinned tomatoes, but now boasted an odd assortment of pens, nails, dried up highlighters and a couple of large, curved needles. Locating the tin in one of the "To be Binned" piles, I dug out the needles and showed Ben.

'Ah, perfect!' he smiled. 'These look like old saddlery needles, made for working with leather so they should be just the thing.'

I watched as he worked the tip of a needle into the middle of a knot and manipulated it around. He held the tweezers lightly and used them to pull gently at the loosening leather ties. It was a slow and laborious endeavour, and the fragile leather threatened to break apart time and time again, but after an hour of patient enterprise Ben had succeeded in unravelling the cords enough for us to pull them away from the fitted lid. Ben tried pulling the lid away from the top of the container but it was stuck fast.

'I think it must have been up in the attic for decades,' Ben said. 'It probably swelled up with damp during the winters and shrunk again during the hotter weather. I doubt we're going to be able to get the top off at all.'

I poked around the old tin of random items and came up with a metal nail file.

'Here, try this,' I told him. 'If you can manage to slide it up between the lid and the case you might be able to pull the two apart.'

Ben wiggled the end of the nail file into the lid at a place where the leather was sewn into a seam. He used the file as a lever and carefully worked his way around the octagonal shape, moving the file a few millimetres at a time. With the lid loosened like this it began to give and, with a bit of effort, the seal of time was broken, the top popped off and we were looking into the depths of the canister. Curled up inside was a tightly rolled length of paper, tied with a ribbon that had once been red but was now dulled to a rusty brown. Ben tipped the leather case up and the coiled parchment slid into his hand.

'Quick, find some things to weigh it down as we unroll it,' suggested Ben. 'We have to be careful. This hasn't been touched for God knows how long.'

We scurried around, gathering heavy glass candle holders and hardbacked books from the shelves around the lounge. When we had enough, we cleared a space on the floor and Ben solemnly pulled at the ribbon to untie it. Gently, and ever so slowly, we laid the paper on the floor and weighed it down at the top and sides, unrolling and laying more weights on it as we went.

'It's a plan of the house!' I gasped, as the bold black outlines began to make sense. 'Look, La Manoir des aux Cadeau des Reines, 1610, ' I read the heading at the top of the paper. 'That fits with what I read in Pierre's notes. It's the original name for the house.'

We had reached the end of the parchment and it lay fully unrolled in front of us.

'Matt's going to love this,' Ben whistled. 'He's got the full plans for the whole place right here.'

We pored over the drawings. Although simple in their design, every room was named according to its function, right down to the store rooms and the attics.

'Let's try to figure out what this flat was then,' I suggested. We found the kitchens easily enough and, as Matt had already suspected, the area the modern day flat covered was once home to not only the kitchens, but the wet larders, dry larders, still rooms, dairy and butchery. A back entrance way to the house showed the layout of the kitchen gardens. We worked out that the room we were in now, the lounge, would have housed the still rooms, where simple medicines and tonics were brewed to see to the health of the entire household.

'Alice's room was the dairy,' I commented, pointing to the plan. 'And next to it was the, what's that?' I looked to where the room's title had been roughly scored out. 'I think it says the hanging room. That must be the stone room that's been blocked off! Matt said he thought the hooks in the ceiling were to hang meat and game from.' I shivered from a sudden chill. 'A bit of a grim name to call it though, the hanging room. Why has it been crossed out?' I wondered.

'Look what someone's written next to it though,' Ben pointed out. Sure enough, when I looked closer at the little square which was once called a hanging room, the words "Le Chambré de la Sorciére" had been etched inside the black lines instead. 'Le Chambré de la Sorciére - you know what that means, don't you?'

I shook my head.

'It's French. It translates as The Witch's Room.'

Jennet's Story

Jersey 1603

No, Sister, I have not changed my mind.

The more I think on it, the more certain I am that it is these irons which imprison my soul within my mortal body. Just promise me, Sister, that you will do all you can to see these chains struck from my wrists and ankles before I go to the stake? They can tie me up again with rope, if they so wish, I do not mind. A hemp rope will not tie my soul to this earth as iron does, and I can go to your God as a free spirit.

Thank you Sister, that is indeed a heavy weight taken from my mind.

Where to go to next... ah yes, Matthieu's change of fortune.

Matthieu did indeed become his fathers' next heir. His only hope, his older brother Jeanne, had declined the call in favour of his position in the church, for he was high in favour and standing, and he wished to undertake a pilgrimage to the Holy Father's palace and study under the university there. Notaries were called for, and the right of succession was duly transcribed and witnessed and Matthieu was tied to his father's house and lands as surely as if he were bound in golden chains.

Matthieu did not accept this turn of his fate well. His thieving became ever more desperate and more than once he came by with a clinking bag of coin and plate. He cajoled me into hiding these for him and we buried many fine things in the hard dirt beneath my shack, and in the softer ground in my father's pig sties. They would not stay buried for long,

Matthieu promised me, and sweetened the threat of the noose with a kiss, for he had contacts in France and they would be glad to take these prizes and hold them in coin for him. His plan was to amass a great fortune, independent of his father, and escape to the continent where he would live out his days as a free and rich man.

I did not dare ask him where I lay in this great plan of his.

Since that time in the woods, against the tree, we disappeared into the forest as often as we dared to enjoy the pleasures of the flesh. Sometimes Matthieu would be quite rough with me and I would be bruised and sore for days, yet at other times he was as tender as a young lover should be, and I would float through the trees at the gentleness of it, sighing my happiness into his broad shoulder.

The gossip-mongers were still trading on rumours of acts of witchery within our small village. Tales came across the water from Guernsey of good men and women arrested on charges of sorcery, with some banished and others burned at the stake. Here on Jersey, folk claimed to have seen the Devil dancing with his whore witches on the beach at Devil's Rock, before he changed into a cat or a goat or a big, black dog, depending on who was telling the story. A young healthy baby died in his crib and his mother swears she saw her neighbour, a woman she has ever been bitter towards, casting spells through the window at the babe as he lay sleeping. The woman was taken up and she was here, in this oubliette, before me. She died before they could try her and went to her grave with her name forever stained by the word 'witch'.

Matthieu brought me tales from the big house, where the maids and farm workers were clucking like hens over a tabby cat that gave birth to five pure black kittens, and then proceeded to eat them all one by one. They drowned the cat in a bucket. *At church, the sermons warned folk to be on their guard against the devilment that plagued our town. The priest encouraged people to find the Devil in their neighbours, their servants and in their own families, and many endured the holy trinity trials before either being sent away or released back into the care of their own kin on a promise not to gad about the island. The villagers went about their daily business eyeing each other with suspicion and seeing malice where there was once only good purpose. Ma Le Brun was put into the stocks at the castle for giving herbs to a woman with her eleventh babe growing inside of her. The herbs were to make the child come away and the woman would claim a miscarriage, however the charm did not work and the woman cried loud and false against Ma Le Brun for selling her useless weeds and promising her the child would not survive to be born. She was lucky, Ma Le Brun, not to have been taken up for a witch. Instead, after a day or two in the stocks, she was released on her solemn promise before God not to meddle in cures and simples again, and to only provide those services to which she was required, namely attending births and laying out the dead.*

Matthieu was desperate to leave and took many chances in his quest for valuables to steal. He wanted to sail before the month was out, before his father had set him to learning the skills of his new occupation. There was talk of a marriage too, to a milksop girl of twelve years old, whose dowry and lands would increase the Chevalier coffers and Matthieu's father was pleased by this.

'I have to go, and soon,' Matthieu would say, pacing the worn path in front of my home. 'I only need one more good haul and I will have enough to vanish from this cursed island and set myself up as my own man.'

'You mustn't risk getting caught,' I would argue with him, desperately afraid he would end up on the scaffold, and me with him as his accomplice. 'Small things are not missed

for some time, you taught me that, but to take something too large and valuable would be folly.'

But he would not heed me and his next act of thievery would be the undoing of both of us.

CHAPTER TWENTY-ONE

Leah

'So it's true? There really was a witch in this house?' Ben and I looked at each other in disbelief.

'I thought it was just a legend, an old family story that had been exaggerated and added to as the years went on, 'I said. 'I had no idea it might be real. But why would they keep someone who they were convinced was a witch in their family home? And why keep them in that horrible room? It doesn't make any sense.'

Before we could speculate any further, we heard the kitchen door open. We hurriedly rolled the thin parchment up again and pushed it back into the leather case, before hiding it behind the couch.

'Leah?' I heard Jayne call out to me.

'Oh my God, Jayne!' I scrambled to my feet and ran to the kitchen. She was standing there with Gabriel just behind her. 'Are you OK? What are you doing here? I mean, have you come back...?' I gabbled. Gabriel was looking at me with a mocking smile.

'No, I'm not coming back,' Jayne said quietly. 'I've just come to see Noah, and to get some more of my things.'

'Does Matt know you're here?' I asked, thinking he must have heard their car pull up outside. Jayne shook her head.

'No, and I don't want to see him. Hi Ben,' she said over my shoulder. Ben had followed me from the lounge and was standing behind me, his warm hand a comforting pressure on my back. His posture was tense and, as I glanced back at him, I could see his face was set in a grimace, and a small muscle had begun to tick next to his eye. He was staring at Gabriel with acute dislike.

'But, Jayne, what about the kids?' I said to her. 'What's going to happen if you've left Matt?'

'We're seeing a family lawyer this afternoon.' Gabriel put his hand proprietorially on the back of Jayne's neck. 'Once we've lodged a formal request for full custody, it'll only be a matter of days before the children will come to live with us.'

I glared at him.

'Jayne, you can't do that to Matt,' I begged her. 'Think of what it will do to him, those kids mean the world to him.'

'NO, this fucking house means the world to him!' Jayne spat angrily. 'I doubt he'll even notice they're gone.'

'Of course, it means that your services will no longer be required, Leah,' Gabriel interrupted smoothly. 'I would start looking for alternative arrangements, if I were you.'

'Leah has a home with me, whenever she needs one,' Ben put in quietly. 'She won't be put out on the street.' We heard the plastic sheeting in the main hall rustle and then Matt was there, hammer in hand, looking sick and furious at the same time.

'You are not welcome here, Gabriel,' Matt said through gritted teeth. 'Please leave. I would like some time to speak to MY WIFE, alone.'

'I have nothing to say to you,' Jayne said primly. 'Any communication between us will only take place through mine and Gabriel's lawyer.'

'Jayne, please,' I begged her. 'For the sake of your children, please just sit down with Matt and thrash this out.'

'It's none of your business, Leah,' Gabriel reminded me. 'You are just the help. If Jayne doesn't want to speak to her estranged husband...' he put a lot of emphasis on the words,'...then she is perfectly within her rights to refuse.'

'You're loving this, aren't you, you fucking prick!' Matt hissed, raising his hammer and taking a step towards Gabriel. 'Get out! Go on, both of you! Just get out! I'll pack the rest of your stuff and stick it out on the lawn later,' he told Jayne. 'You can pick it up then but you are NOT coming into this house ever again! Keys!' he demanded with his hand out.

'I'm here to see my son,' Jayne said firmly. 'I'm not leaving until I see him.'

'You can make an appointment, through MY lawyer!' Matt roared. 'You wanted this, Jayne. You left so you could shack up with that bastard, so you can just deal with the consequences. You will not see my kids without prior notice and at MY convenience. Believe me Jayne, I'm going to make this as hard for you as I possibly can. KEYS!'

Jayne's face dissolved into tears and she ran out of the open kitchen door and back towards Gabriel's car. Gabriel looked like thunder as he bunched his fists.

'We will be granted full custody, Matt. I can promise you that. We'll be in touch.' He turned and stalked out of the house towards Jayne and the car, and they both left in a spray of gravel.

'Leah, find the phone book. We're going to need a locksmith. I want all the locks changed by tonight,' Matt said calmly. 'And can you look after Noah while I fetch Alice from school early? I have a feeling they'll try and intercept you if you and Noah pick her up at the usual time.'

'Sure,' I promised, my voice high and strained.

'And can you look up law firms while you're at it?' Matt threw over his shoulder as he went down the hallway towards Noah's room. 'I think I'm going to need one.'

Ben left soon after, giving me a big hug and a tender kiss on his way out.

'I'll call you later OK?'

I nodded and smiled tiredly.

'Just another crazy day at the office!' I sighed.

'Are you going to show Matt the house plans?'

'Yes, I think so. He might welcome the distraction,' I said.

I heard Matt on the phone to Alice's school, telling them that he had separated from his wife, and only him or I were authorised to pick her up from now on.

'I don't trust that smooth bastard,' he muttered to me later. 'I don't know what his game plan is, but I get the distinct feeling that Jayne is just a part of it, and not the reason behind it.'

'Do you think it's something to do with you inheriting the house, and not him?' I questioned.

'I don't doubt it,' Matt had replied. 'He was directly in line for this place until Pierre found out about me and changed his will. Gabriel's a property developer, you know. I think he had big plans for developing the land and making a fortune.'

'Matt,' I put a hand tentatively on his arm. 'Are you OK?'
He laughed mirthlessly.

'I dunno, I think so. I mean, it's not how I pictured things but... if she wants to leave then I won't stop her.'

'I'll stay as long as you need me to,' I promised him. 'Seriously, I'll look after both you and the kids.'
He thanked me and gave me a swift hug, but his eyes were clouded with misery and his shoulders slumped as he headed back towards the old wing, and went back to work.

I lay awake that night thinking about the stone room and why its name and purpose had been changed. Surely, if you were going to take someone in, even if that someone was supposed to be a witch - especially if that someone was a witch and could curse your family with all sorts of nasty things - wouldn't you give them a better room? This place was huge; there were any number of bedrooms for guests. Or if he or she wasn't a guest, then the servants quarters in the second, smaller attic wing would have been far more comfortable. Maybe that was the point, I thought. Maybe

241

whoever the witch was who stayed in that damp, cold little room wasn't meant to be comfortable. I shivered as I pictured the cruel iron hooks and loops in the ceiling. The window wasn't large enough to let a lot of light in; it would have been a miserable place to be, even in broad daylight, and especially with the haunches of meat and dead animals hanging alongside you.

I drifted into an uneasy sleep, only to be woken again what felt like a few minutes later by the sound of my wardrobe door creaking open. When Matt had built the cupboards and storage space for me, he used some of the old wood from the other flats he had already ripped out. The wardrobe door had creaked from day one, and no amount of oil could persuade it to open silently. There was a metal toggle on the outside of it that turned and sat flush in the square bracket on the other side, so that the door stayed firmly closed until the toggle was turned the other way to open it. There was no reason for the door to swing open, I thought, but my brain was still muzzy from tiredness. It creaked again and I opened my eyes. The light from my digital clock was enough to make out the wall of cupboards. The wardrobe door was wide open. I froze in my bed, and the hairs on the back of my neck and my arms went up. I could see movement within the dark depths of the cupboard. The wardrobe wasn't very deep, perhaps two foot at the most, but it was deep enough for a child to hide in, I reasoned. A small child, Alice's size.

'Alice? Is that you?' I called softly. No answer.
The movement continued and a dark shadow slid fluidly from inside the cupboard and re-formed on the floor in front of it. It was the size and shape of a young child but moved stiffly and awkwardly. It jerked towards me and I stifled a scream as I heard the soft clink, clink of metal upon metal.

'Alice?' I whispered again, my voice hoarse with fear. The shape paused briefly but then resumed its path towards my bed.

I slowly reached out my right hand, feeling the edge of my bedside table and searching desperately for my phone, which should have been right there on the top of the cabinet. I took my eyes off the shape for a second to find it and when I looked back, the shape was only a few feet away from me. I could make out a wild tangle of hair, and see the rags on its body but its face was still hidden by the darkness. I grabbed my phone, glancing away again as I found the torch app on the screen. I looked up and the shape was right in front of me, just standing there, unearthly still and watching me with big, dark eyes. It leaned even closer and I saw its face clearly for the first time.

She was a girl. She looked maybe twelve or thirteen but she was tiny; short and very slight. She lifted her hand towards me and I heard the metallic clinking again. She looked confused when she saw my face and pointed to my twisted lip, then brought her finger back to her own face. In the dim light of my phone screen I saw how her own features were contorted; her lip was drawn upwards almost exactly like mine. She had big front teeth, strong and white, which pushed through prominently and gave her the look of a startled hare. She pointed at my face again, a question on her expressive face. I nodded at her silently, and pointed at my own lip before gently pointing at hers. I nodded again. She seemed to understand and she gave me a tiny smile, before taking a step backwards. Her legs moved clumsily and she continued to back away with a curiously sideways gait, like a crab. My phone screen went black and I tapped it to bring it back to life. The girl was nearly back at the wardrobe door by now and I watched in awe as she faded into a liquid mist and melted into the blackness inside the cupboard once again. The last thing I saw before my phone screen dimmed again were the brutal iron manacles around her ankles, and the short length of chain in between them. The wardrobe door slammed shut and I heard the toggle slide back into place. I could feel I was alone and that the strange girl had gone. I breathed out, unaware that I had been holding my breath for all this time. So - I had just met Jenny.

CHAPTER TWENTY TWO

'Jenny says she's sorry,' blurted Alice as she sat at the table the next morning.

'What do you mean, sweetie?' I asked her. It was Saturday and we were having a leisurely breakfast after a bit of a lie-in for all of us. I spooned mashed banana into Noah's hungry mouth and watched as Alice toyed with her cereal.

'She said she sees things a lot better now,' Alice went on. 'She didn't know you were like her. She said that before, it was like she was looking through thick glass...'

'And now?'

'And now, because I broke the bottle, she can see true. That's what she told me, that she can see true.'

'I saw her too,' I confided. 'Jenny. She was in my room.'

Alice beamed.

'That means she likes you now!'

'Does she speak to you?' I asked Alice. 'She didn't say anything to me, just pointed, but I knew what she meant.'

'It's hard to 'splain,' Alice frowned in concentration. 'It's like, she's talking but not from her mouth. I can hear her but not with my ears. I hear her in my head.'

Matt came into the kitchen. Alice and I exchanged complicit glances and she made a zipping motion with her fingers over her mouth, and giggled.

'Alice, your mum's coming to see you today,' Matt said brusquely as he reached for the kettle.

'Yay! Mummy!' screamed Alice with joy. She had been asking for Jayne all week, not believing us for a second whenever we used the 'Mummy's at work' excuse. 'Will she take me out?'

'No, you're to stay here, and Leah?' Matt looked at me. 'I want you to stay with them at all times.'

245

I nodded.

'Is Gabe...?'

'No. I told them both he's not to set foot on this property. I don't want him anywhere near my kids and, until a lawyer tells me otherwise, he won't be having anything to do with them,' Matt said firmly. He took his coffee with him as he went back to his building site next door.

'Is Mummy living with Uncle Gabriel now?' Alice asked me.

'No, she's just staying with him for a little while. Your mum and dad have some grown up things to sort out. I think your mum just wants a bit of peace to have a think,' I reassured her. Alice pursed her lips.

'Jenny says not to trust Uncle Gabriel. She says he's a bad man.'

'Hmmm, I'm inclined to believe her,' I said to myself. There was something about this whole Jayne and Gabriel thing that I didn't get. I could see that Jayne was certainly smitten but in Gabe, I only detected a coolness, a certain satisfaction that he had got what he wanted.

I had a quick shower and, as I was drying my hair, my eye fell upon the small round pot that Debbie had given me the other night. I picked it up and twisted open the lid, sniffing distrustfully at the contents, but it smelled gorgeous; herby and lemony, with hints of lavender. I put a tiny bit on my finger and smoothed it over my red, scarred cheek. At once I felt a pleasant tingling, and my skin felt less tight already. It can't hurt, I thought to myself. It's only plants and stuff, so it can't do any further damage.

Jayne was due at ten thirty so I made sure both kids were nicely dressed in clean clothes. I wouldn't be giving her any ammunition to use against Matt in the custody battle. She would see how well we were managing without her. Alice sat patiently waiting for her, looking up expectantly at every noise outside. Finally, fifteen minutes late, I saw Jayne walking up the driveway. She was alone and she looked terrified. I was torn between my loyalty to Matt as the wronged husband, and my friendship with Jayne, the one who had got me through those early dark days after my attack. I opened the kitchen door and gave her a small smile. Alice brushed past me, yelling 'Mummy, Mummy, Mummy!', and Jayne scooped her up in a big hug.

'Oh my darling girl, I've missed you!'

I let Alice have her time with her mother, and then put Noah on my hip and went and joined them in the garden.

'I've put the kettle on. Let's stay out here on the lawn, it's such a nice day for October,' I said companionably to Jayne, passing Noah to her and watching as tears ran down Jayne's face. 'Come on, the kids can play and we can have a good talk while we watch them.'

She reached out wordlessly and squeezed my hand. I asked Alice to fetch us the picnic blanket and we settled happily in the Autumn sunshine. The only awkward moment between us was when I took Alice inside to help me with the drinks. Jayne knew then that I was under Matt's instructions not to leave Jayne alone with the kids. I figured she wouldn't take Noah alone, without Alice, so I made sure Alice was with me at all times.

'It's OK,' Jayne said somewhat flatly as I handed her her tea. 'I don't blame you. If I was in your position I'd do the same thing.'

'I'm really sorry, Jayne, but Matt asked and I...'

'Don't. It's fine,' she cut me off.

We watched Alice trying to coax Noah to walk on the soft grass. She held both his hands and pulled him to his feet. He would take a few wobbly steps then fall back onto his padded bottom, laughing uncontrollably.

'Has anything happened, while I've been away?' Jayne asked me. 'Anything... not right?'

'Apart from finding out you've been having an affair with Gabriel, you mean?' I raised my eyebrows at her. 'That was a shock, I must say.'

247

'It wasn't meant to happen,' Jayne said quickly. 'I was just so sick of Matt's obsession with this bloody house, and we weren't getting on well, as you know. Gabriel noticed I wasn't happy, that day at the beach. He called me a few times, asking if I was all right, offering me a shoulder to cry on.'

'So how did that turn into a full-blown affair?'

'We met, one day, before my hospital shift. Just for a coffee, in town. He was so easy to talk to, totally understood where I was coming from about Matt and about how much I was beginning to hate the house. It's happened before, he said. Someone inherits The Grange and the next thing you know, their marriage has broken up and families are separated. He said it's a very unhappy house. That's the true curse, I think.'

'That doesn't explain why you started sleeping with him,' I said archly. Jayne blushed.

'He just... I don't know, wooed me, I suppose,' she said lamely.

'Wooed you?' I repeated in disbelief.

'Yes, you know... Flowers, nice dinners out, romantic walks along the beach at sunset. He didn't make the first move, I did,' she said defensively. 'I was so horribly lonely here, Leah. Matt hadn't touched me since we moved here, you were happy looking after my kids all day. I'm the new girl at the hospital and they're all so cliquey, they barely speak to me.' She turned to me with fresh tears in her eyes. 'Gabriel was the first person to take an interest in me. Me. Not the house, not my kids, not me as a nurse but me, Jayne the person. Jayne the lonely, abandoned wife, pissed-off and surplus to requirements.'

We were both silent for a minute.

'So, is it serious?' I asked her. 'Are you going to stay with Gabriel?'

'I... I don't know,' she faltered. 'It's an escape, at the moment. What I really want is to go back to London, all of us. Me, Matt, you and the children. When Matt told me he sold our London house I was so angry. That was always the plan B, if things didn't work out here.' She pushed her hair back from her face and took a deep, wobbly breath. 'Anyway, now that's ruined. Matt's made it so we can't go back. And I hate him for it, Leah. Really, really hate him.'

'That doesn't mean you have to jump into bed with the first man who pays you some attention! And Matt's cousin, for God's sake!' I fired. 'And what about the kids? Is Gabriel really interested in having custody, or is this just another way to make Matt pay for getting the house over him?'

'I'll be the one who gets custody,' Jayne promised. 'Not Matt and not Gabriel. My children will be with their mother, where they belong.'

'Mummy, look at me!' Alice cried as she attempted a cartwheel.

'That's wonderful, sweetheart!' Jayne called over to her. 'Anyway,' she said, changing the subject. 'Tell me what's been happening in the house.'

'Jenny's real!' I told her, and brought her up to date on the crying baby in the stone room, the kitchen being trashed seconds after Matt and I had left it looking perfectly normal, and the nocturnal visit from Jenny last night. 'Alice said something this morning about Jenny being able to see better now after the bottle was broken. It must have been when Alice smashed the witch bottle. I think it's let Jenny come through much stronger than before. Even Noah's seeing her now!'

Jayne grimaced.

'And what does Matt think?' she asked.

'Matt... is burying his head in the sand. He won't believe a word of it, not even when he saw all the things in the kitchen, or when he heard the crying. He's convinced it's air in the pipes, or whatever.'

Jayne snorted.

'Typical,' she said. 'He never did have much belief in any of that paranormal stuff. No creativity, that's his problem.'

We fell silent and watched the children again. Noah crawled over to Jayne and plonked himself down on her lap.

'Oof, you're a bruiser, you are!' She tickled him playfully. She inspected his birthmark carefully. 'You know, I think this has shrunk a little bit. Gabe tells me he arranged an appointment with a surgeon friend of his father's for you?' She said, changing the subject back to Gabriel yet again.

'Yeah, it's on Monday actually,' I smiled. 'I'm hoping he'll be able to give me some good news.'

'That's brilliant, Leah,' Jayne said warmly. 'And tell me, how are things going with the delicious Ben?'

We spent the next hour chatting like the old friends we were, and things were nearly, almost, like old times. Matt came out of the house's main front door once and made a big show of looking at his watch.

'Oops, looks like my time's up,' Jayne said sarcastically. 'Thanks, Leah. It's been great to see my babies, and to have a chance to catch up with you again, of course.'

'When are you coming to see them again?'

'I'm working on it,' Jayne sighed. 'The only way I can get Matt to agree to a visit is to promise Gabe won't be with me, and for you to be a chaperone.'

Alice cried a little when Jayne said she had to go.

'Mummy, when are you coming home?' she wailed. Jayne swallowed hard and put on a brave face.

I'll see you very soon, my darling. I promise.'

She walked back down the drive without a backwards glance. Alice whimpered by my side and clutched my hand.

'Leah, tell Mummy to come back,' she cried. 'I don't like Uncle Gabriel. He looks at me like he's the big, bad wolf!'

'You'll see her again soon,' I said to her, echoing Jayne's words, but I wondered how this was all going to play out, and where it would leave me. Jobless, homeless, friendless? I did not have a good feeling about the future.

'Leah? Am I intruding?' Debbie's strident voice boomed down the phone.

'No, Debbie. Of course not. It's lovely to hear from you.' I told her.

'I've found something that might be of interest to you. Shall I send Ben to pick you up? You can come for Sunday lunch, if you like.'

'Oh. Well, yes, thank you. That would be great.'

'Lunch is at one. I'll send him down at half twelve. Bye for now.' She had hung up.

'I'm going out for lunch. Will you be OK with the kids?' I asked Matt. I saw a swift flash of annoyance in his eyes.

'Well, I was hoping to make a start on the main stairs today,' he moaned.

'Matt, I don't work for you twenty four-seven,' I huffed. 'I am entitled to some time off, you know.'

'Yeah, I know. I'm sorry,' Matt conceded. 'Of course we'll be alright.' He smiled crookedly at me. 'Off to see Ben?'

'Going to his Aunt's for Sunday lunch,' I told him. 'She's found out some more about this house. Oh, I completely forgot!' I exclaimed, and ran to the lounge, pulling out the leather canister from behind the couch. I hurried back to Matt. 'We found this! In the attics.'
Matt took the case from me and studied it with interest.

'What is it?' he asked, perplexed. I took it back and twisted off the lid, sliding the thin parchment out.

'It's an early floorplan of the house!' I told him excitedly. 'Look! The whole thing.'

251

Matt unravelled a small part of the paper and his face lit up. 'This is brilliant!' he gasped. 'Wow! Thanks, Leah. I can have a good study of these when I'm watching Alice and Noah this afternoon.'

'Tell me if you notice anything weird about that horrible blocked-off room,' I said. 'It's on the plans.'

'I will, I will', Matt replied, staring at the parchment in wonder.

Ben arrived on time and greeted me with a swift kiss as I climbed into his car.

'All good?' he asked. 'Any more spooky goings on?'

'Jenny came into my room last night! I finally saw her, and guess what?' I demanded.

'What?' Ben laughed.

'She looks just like me. Her face, I mean. Debbie was right. She had a hare-lip.'

'Weren't you freaked out?' Ben made a mock frightened face.

'No,' I said, surprising us both. 'I mean, it was quite scary when she just kind of poured herself out of the wardrobe in the middle of the night, but when she was looking at me, I didn't get the impression she wanted to do me any harm. Just the opposite, really. I felt like once she'd seen my face was like hers, that she understood, she knows what it's like to be an outcast.'

'So, the crazy knife in the toaster, scissors in the table thing was... what? Just to get your attention?

'I think it's Matt she's angry with. And Gabriel. Alice told me Jenny REALLY doesn't like Gabriel.'

'The Chevalier men, then,' Ben said thoughtfully. 'You aren't in the family she hated so you're not her target.'

'That's one way of looking at it,' I agreed. 'I'm interested to see what Debbie makes of it all. And to find out what she's found for me.'

Debbie's house was full of the delicious smell of roasting lamb. Gracie was waiting at the door to meet us and she grabbed my hand, turning her sweet face up to me with a beaming smile. Debbie greeted me with a warm hug and she inspected my face carefully.

'Have you been using that cream I gave you?'

'I just started to this morning,' I admitted. 'It feels really nice, thank you Debbie.'

'Hmm. Twice a day, remember,' Debbie reminded me pointedly. 'You'll see it will look better very quickly. When is your appointment with that consultant?'

'Tomorrow,' I assured her. 'Fingers crossed!'

Lunch was dished up and, once again, Debbie had outdone herself. Tender lamb fell from the bone, potatoes were done three different ways, and a plethora of fresh vegetables from her garden steamed lusciously in white china bowls. Homemade mint sauce, a thick red wine gravy and an assortment of extra treats were dotted around the table. As Gracie was with us, we put off talking about Jenny until after lunch, and our conversation was a lively mix of gentle banter and more of Debbie's wonderful stories. After pudding, a perfect apple crumble -'Just something from the freezer, my darlings!' - Ben disappeared to clean up in the kitchen again, taking Gracie with him.

'So, bring me up to date!' Debbie leaned towards me in excitement. 'I take it from Ben that you've had quite an eventful few days!'

'Oh God, where do I start?' I held up my hands. 'Right, well, on the night I was here for dinner...'

I filled her in on everything. From the crying baby, to Jayne storming out after learning Matt had sold their London house, to the kitchen being destroyed, to the way the leather case with the floor plans of the house had, quite literally, been thrown at Ben. I told her about seeing Jenny, about seeing the disfigurement on her face and feeling a kind of solidarity with her. I was in the middle of describing how Jayne and Gabriel had threatened Matt with a custody battle when I saw Debbie flinch, at the mention of Gabriel's name.

'You did that last time I was talking about Gabriel,' I pointed out to her. 'You know him, don't you?'

Debbie looked troubled.

'Yes. I know him all right. But I don't really think it's my place to say...' She fidgeted with the spoon in her coffee.

'Has Ben not said anything to you? About Gracie's mother...?'

'He's told me a little, yes. Adele, that's her name, isn't it?'

Yes. Adele.' Debbie's voice was full of contempt. 'But has he told you about why she left?'

'She ran off with the carpet-fitter? That's the story Ben gave me.'

Debbie sighed.

'That's not the full story,' she said bitterly. 'Yes, Adele did eventually run off with the Portuguese carpet-fitter but before that..,' she took a deep breath before continuing. 'Before that, Adele was cheating on Ben with Gabriel Chevalier.'

I was stunned.

'She had been seeing him even before her and Ben got married, and it continued all throughout their short-lived marriage apparently,' Debbie bit her lip, distressed. 'Leah, Gracie might not even be Ben's daughter.'

'What?' I nearly choked on my coffee. 'Doesn't he know? Why didn't he get a paternity test, if there was any doubt?'

'Ben loves Gracie,' Debbie said firmly. 'It wouldn't make any difference to him whether she is his true daughter or not. He just doesn't want to know.'

'Why did he lie to me?' I asked, feeling a bit betrayed. I had trusted Ben with everything about me and in return, he had skimmed over the true story of his marriage to Adele.

'Ben lies to himself,' Debbie consoled me. 'It's not that he deliberately set out to misinform you; it's more like he prefers to obliterate any memory of that time in his life, and of Gabriel Chevalier. It must have been a bitter blow for him to find out that you are tangled up with the Chevalier family.'

She shook her head.

'Now that you mention it, there was a bit of a strange atmosphere when Ben saw Gabriel with Jayne yesterday. Ben seemed to tense up but I thought it was down to feeling awkward at being caught up in a family drama.'

'Well, now you know why I despise the man, that Gabriel,' she spat. 'You want to warn your friend, Jayne. She's not the first woman to fall for his pretty words. Gabriel Chevalier will only ever look out for himself. I don't know what he wants with your friend but you can be sure it will be for his benefit only.' She clammed up as Ben came back into the room. 'Anyway, let me show you what I've found.'

Debbie led me to a small room adjoining the dining room. In here, a large and rather ornate walnut desk dominated the space. The rest of the room was crowded with books. Books lined the walls, books lay on every available surface and books were also propping open the door and propping up one of the legs of the desk.

'My library,' she announced, rather grandly. 'Watch out for the desk, It's a bit wobbly.'

'She won't let me fix the dodgy leg,' Ben put in quickly.

'You'll spoil the authenticity of it,' Debbie responded mock-dramatically. I got the feeling this was an old joke/argument they'd had many times before. There was a sheaf of A4 papers on the surface of the desk. I glanced at them and saw they were photocopies of old documents. The writing was swirly and elaborate and very hard to read.

'Now, these are copies I made of some court papers we have in the archives,' Debbie explained. 'And I think I may have found your Jenny!'

'Debbie! This must have taken you hours!' I exclaimed, looking at all the papers.

'Oh, don't worry. I enjoyed it,' Debbie laughed. 'It was fascinating, really. Once I knew what I was looking for, one name kept cropping up over and over, and realised that this must be the woman we're looking for. See, this is from the records they kept at Mont Orgueil whenever they admitted a new prisoner. I started from when Harewich House was built in 1544 and carried on from there. I looked at the records for any woman arrested for witchcraft and cross-referenced the dates, and any mention of a hare-witch or the Chevalier name and bingo! I got to 1603 and there she was.'

I studied the sheet of paper in front of me. On it, the names of the poor souls who had been committed to the gaol at Mont Orgueil castle were neatly laid out.

Symon Vaudlin   Aged 32 of St Martin   Arrested on suspicion of theft of one hen
Margaret Le Four   Aged 18 of Grouville   Arrested on suspicion of lewd behaviour
Marion Corbel   Aged 48 of St Helier   Arrested on suspicion of false-speaking
Frances Le Cornu   Aged 11 of Grouville   Arrested on suspicion of theft of ale

I ran my finger down the pages, looking for a Jenny in the column of names. Several women were arrested for suspected witchcraft but none had the name I was looking for until, at the bottom of one page I found her.

Jennet Pyke   Aged 14 of Grouville   Arrested on suspicion of witchcraft and theft

'Here! Jennet Pyke!' I cried. 'She's the right age. The girl I saw last night couldn't have been more than fourteen, and the name - Jennet, that could easily be mixed up with Jenny, couldn't it? We've only got Alice's word for it that the ghost's name is Jenny. Jenny sounds more friendly, or maybe the way Jennet spoke, with her hare-lip, made her name sound more like Jenny!' I babbled.

'That's EXACTLY what I thought!' crowed Debbie, punching the air. 'So I kept looking for her, for Jennet Pyke, and I found a mention of her in the Bailiff's court assizes in the same year of her imprisonment.'
Debbie laid another sheaf of papers on top of the gaol records.

'People were often kept in the oubliette at Mont Orgueil for months. The assizes only took place once a quarter so you had to wait until the next one to get your trial. Until then, you were only held on suspicion of your crime, not convicted of it. After conviction you would probably been returned to the prison to wait until your sentence was carried out, if you lived that long.'
I scanned the new pages. The over-the-top swirls and embellishments became easier to decipher as I read on. I learned that a capital 'S' looked like a lower case 'f', and that there was often the letter 'y' where there, in modern times, would be an 'i'. The letter 'e' was added to many words unnecessarily, rendering them confusing in context. For example, soul became soule, do became doe and so on. Once I began to make sense of this, the words of the old court document started to flow and I eagerly searched for mention of Jennet's name.

'Found her!' I shouted, pointing to one of the pages. 'Look! It says " Jennet Pyke, aged 14, arrested for witchcraft" and goes on to list the charges against her. "Bewitching the son of the manor..." - I wonder if by the manor, they mean our house? "...Theft of holy items from the parish church at Grouville for diabolic uses", "Causing the death of Mme Roche's pig by the casting of spells",

257

"signing the Devil's book and dancing with the same", - Christ! The list of things she's supposed to have done goes on and on.'

Debbie and I read through the rest of the list together. All in all, Jennet Pyke, a fourteen year old girl, had a total of fifty-one charges laid against her, and more than thirty-seven people testified against her, claiming that she did indeed "cast many diabolic spells and caused people to fall into a decline, their cattle to die and many signs of the Devil to appear".

'Oh my God, that poor, poor girl,' I breathed. 'She was fourteen. Just fourteen.'

'And look here,' said Debbie. 'After the charges were read out, they go on to commit her to trial. They needed first the Constable and six sermentès - those are sworn witnesses - to be convinced of her guilt, then the Crown Officers have to agree to prosecute. Look, it says "...being a hare-witch and accused of many crimes of witchcraft against the good people of Grouville, she is to undergo the Judgement of God and the Holy Trinity trials in which she may either prove or disprove her guilt in all charges".

'What does that mean? The Judgement of God and the Holy Trinity trials?' I wondered. Debbie rustled through the pile of photocopies on the desk.

'A-ha! Knew I had it somewhere,' she said victoriously, pointing to a paragraph on the page and reading from it. 'The Judgement of God was a set of three different tasks, or trials, set out by the court - hence the name the Holy Trinity. The first was the trial by the holy cross, the next the trial by water and the third the trial by fire. Each one was horrific in its own right but to have to undergo all three together, and one after the other, well - our Jennet didn't stand a chance. In the first trial, the trial by the holy cross, the accused was made to stand upright with their arms out wide in a cross shape. If they could maintain this position for "one full day and one hour", it says here, so that's twenty-five hours non-stop, then they were judged to have God on their side and the charges laid against them would be dropped.'

I stepped to the rug in the middle of the room and stretched my arms wide in the pose described. My arms ached after only a minute.

'There's no way anyone could do that!' I protested. 'They set them up to fail!'

'And bear in mind that these poor wretches had been brought from the dungeons where they might have been for many months, chained to the floor and unable to stand, with little or no food. To even stand upright again would have been incredibly painful!'

'So after she failed that one, what did she have to do next?' I asked.

'Um, the trial by water,' Debbie read on. 'A deep cauldron of water was held over a fire and brought to boiling point, whereon the accused was forced to reach into the water to retrieve a heavy lead weight in the bottom of the cauldron, and carry it for a distance of nine feet. The scalded arm was then wrapped in bandages for three days. At the end of the three days the arm was unwrapped. If the arm was perfect and showed no signs of scalding the accused was deemed innocent, however if there were signs of burning or infection then their guilt was undeniable.'

'Bloody hell!'

'And likewise the trial by fire was similar, except the accused was required to lift a red hot iron from the middle of a burning fire and carry it for nine feet before their hand was wrapped up for three days. Again, if when the hand was unwrapped it was found perfect and whole then the charges were dropped. If there were signs of burning they were found guilty.'

'But, how can that even happen?' I cried. 'To suffer serious burns on both arms, but be found guilty and sentenced to death anyway because you hadn't healed within three days? It's barbaric!'

'They would have been taken back to Mont Orgueil after their trials as well, and left to fester in the oubliette. After three days they would have had signs of a serious infection.'

'So, they had no chance,' I stated. 'Any one of those trials would have seen them found guilty, but to put someone, a child, through all of them...'

'I know,' Debbie agreed. 'Seems they had it in for Jennet from the off.'

'So she was found guilty and then what? Sentenced to death?' I asked. Debbie skimmed through the rest of the court papers.

'Yes. Found guilty of witchcraft - they would have got her on the charges of theft and hanged her anyway, if by some miracle she passed the Holy Trinity trials - and sentenced to be strangled to death and then her body burned to ashes.'

'And did they? Go through with the sentence?'

'Ah, here's where things start to get weird,' grinned Debbie.

'As if they weren't weird enough,' I grumbled.

'Quite,' agreed Debbie. 'But it says here she was transported back to Mont Orgueil but then later it says she was..., where was it?' She flicked through page after page, searching for the castle records again. 'Oh, here! She was "released into the charge of Monsieur Chevalier of Le Manoir".'

'What? What does that mean?' I asked, completely baffled.

'All the other castle records state that when the prisoners were taken to the market square in St Helier for the carrying out of their sentences, but Jennet wasn't ever listed. Her sentence was never carried out. At least, not the one the court decided on anyway. She was taken out of the dungeon by Monsieur Chevalier, the man who lived at Harewich House at the time. He took her there and she then just disappears from the records.'

'I'm beginning to see why the name of the house changed to Harewich House now. So he took her home with him? Did she live there, I mean, were the charges against her dropped?'

'That we don't know,' Debbie concluded. 'But from what you've told me about the meat pantry being re-named the Witch's Room, I think it's safe to say Jennet was held in that room, probably against her will.'

'Shit, this just gets worse and worse for Jennet.' I rubbed my eyes and face tiredly. 'Where do we go from here?'

'I think that the charges she was accused of, the one about bewitching the lord's son, is key here. If Monsieur Chevalier is "the Lord", then she was up to something with one of his sons. We really need to find a family tree from this time. It might give us some clues about the Chevalier family. It might even give us some clues about what happened to poor Jennet!'

'There must be one somewhere,' I said. 'They seem to be a pretty pretentious lot, the Chevaliers, so they must have charted their illustrious family history.'

'If you found something as precious as the original floor plans for the house in the attics, my guess is that there's more up there to find,' Debbie suggested.

'You haven't seen the size of the attics!' I said seriously. 'I haven't got a clue where to start.'

'Jenny helped you last time, she threw the case with the plans at you and Ben,' Debbie pointed out. 'Maybe you could ask her for her help again.'

Jennet's Story

Jersey 1603

The first I became aware of the charges laid against me was when I was taken up in the middle of the night. I lay asleep in my lean-to shack, dreaming strange dreams of men with the heads of dogs who barked at me as if I could understand what they were saying. Slowly I came awake and realised that the barking was real and outside and coming closer to me. There was barely time to sit up in my bed before two soldiers burst through my open doorway and grabbed me roughly by the ankles, pulling me along the hard-packed floor and dumping me in a heap in front of my home. Their dogs strained on their leashes and their teeth snapped at me, the soldiers letting them get close enough for me to smell and feel their rancid meaty breath hot on my face.

'Here's the hare-witch!' one man cried in triumph.

'Christ's bones, she's an ugly bitch!' sneered another man, who jerked my head towards him so as to see the twist of my lip.

'She should have been taken up long ago,' said the first man, spitting at my feet.

'She should have been drowned at birth,' corrected the second.

They tied my wrists and ankles with rope and then tied these ropes together, so as my hands and feet were bound as one and held awkwardly in front of me. It was a most uncomfortable position to lie in, Sister, and they did jolt me deliberately many times in the cart on the way to the castle. I did not know what I was supposed to have done. Not then, Sister. I was certain Matthieu had been caught stealing and had named me in his crimes as well. I lay awkwardly in the cart on the way to the castle, looking up at the grim outline on top of the cliff with cold fear. To be arrested and taken to Mont Orgueil was the thing people feared the most. It meant no return; for when you left there you were either already dead, or soon would be.

I was hauled in front of a tired-looking clerk who made me stammer out my name thrice over, before he made his mark in the great ledger before him.

'Jennet Pyke, you are hereby accused of theft, witchcraft and other charges, too numerous to name, and will be brought before the assizes in due course. Until then, you are to be held at His Majesty's pleasure, here at Mont Orgueil castle until such time as your hearing. Take her away,' he barked to a soldier standing by. 'Clap her in irons, hands and feet! We don't want her casting spells and turning herself into an owl or a bat and flying away free.'

The rope tying my limbs together was undone, allowing me to stand unsteadily, and I was bundled down some steep stone steps, damp and growing green with algae, and slippery on both sides. I slipped many times, and the soldier jerked the ropes around my wrists upwards which did pain me greatly, Sister, and I wept with the pain and the fear. I had no thought on what charges of witchcraft could be brought against me, for I had done no one any harm. It was the reason I kept to myself, in the woods, and did not seek out the company of others. To be with other people was to be always in their suspicion, for their country ways and superstitions were ever a danger to me, all of my life. A slatted metal trap door was opened in the floor, and a wooden ladder was lowered down into the dark and fetid pit below.

Truly, you must have noticed it yourself, Sister, upon your first visit to me? The smell? Oh, I know you have grown used to it now, Sister, for you have been coming here for many days now.

The smell coming from the rank hole caused my stomach to empty itself and I retched bile onto the flagged stones. The *soldier next to me cursed as some of it splashed his fine leather boots.*

'Ye dirty devil's whore!' he shouted at me, and brought his fist to my face. The blow felled me and I sank to my knees as blood dripped from my split lip and onto the floor below to mingle with the juices from my stomach. The soldier wiped his boot on my dress casually, then lifted his foot to kick me into the hole. Down, and down I tumbled. No luxury of a ladder for the likes of me, Sister. I fell in a heap onto the straw below. I was lucky; the filthy straw was full of old meat bones and human waste, but it broke my fall and perhaps saved me from even worse injury.

I lay there, Sister, winded and stunned. I thought that this was the worst of it. That being locked inside this damp, rotting pit that had been scraped out from the side of the old castle walls, and which let in the winds, the rain and the scavenging beasts, was the worst it could get for me.

I was so very wrong, Sister, wasn't I?

First came the chains; iron manacles that were fastened around both wrists and both ankles, before a thick iron nail was hammered through the loops which lined up together, and bent double so that I was sealed inside the cuffs. Chains were then looped through a ring in the oubliette walls and my irons were attached to these so I was able to hobble a few feet in either direction but not so far as to give me the freedom of the whole pit. As my eyes became used to the gloom, I could make out other shapes in here with me. Pitiful lumps of human flesh they were, Sister, with hollow eyes and running sores. They sat slumped against the cold, damp walls or leaned forward with their hands covering their faces, rocking in their madness. A few looked up as I tumbled down to join them - and this is what broke my heart the most, Sister - they saw my face in the pool of light cast by the open trap door, and they crossed themselves, Sister. They made the sign of the cross against me and spat on the straw to ward off the Devil.

Don't you see, Sister? They were already in the bowels of hell and yet they were still afraid of me. They still had fear of me as a witch even though they too were chained up and condemned to die anyway.

I do not know how long I sat slumped in my irons, unaware of how many days and nights passed. More poor wretches were thrown down from the trap door, only for their limp bodies to be dragged out days or weeks later. I barely noticed. I was so sure of Matthieu's love for me. I was so certain he would come for me, that he would tell the soldiers that they had made a terrible mistake and to release me or face the consequences. I imagined him raging at the clerk with the ledger, tearing it from his hand and ripping out the pages in that great book that claimed me a witch and a thief. I simply could not understand why I had been accused of theft; I had taken nothing. I had hidden the things Matthieu stole but he moved these on quickly, so quickly that often the goods were already in France by the time the owner had noticed them gone.

Frances, that poor boy - he's dead now Sister, did I tell you? He shuffled over to me after I had been here a few days. I do not know why he took it upon himself to talk to me, to tell me that the thin shaft of golden light on the left wall meant it was daylight - it is the only way to tell night from day in here - or to nudge me out of my trance each morning when the trap was opened and the hard bread and water were thrown down. He became a sort of self-appointed guardian to me. Mayhap he was thinking that it would be better to be on the side of a witch than to incur her wrath by being against her.

Hey-la, it does not matter now he is dead but I wish I had told him thank you. He told me what to expect in here , you see. He talked of how it was to go before the Bailiff and the court, and how folk you had never even seen before would swear on the Holy Bible of your crimes against them. He told me of the Holy Trinity trials, and how it was likely I would be forced to endure one to prove my guilt. There was little chance I would be proclaimed innocent, the trials did not allow for that.

More time passed and one day my name was called for the assizes. I had been in here long enough by then, Sister, to know that calling just one name was unusual. The previous call for the assizes had taken half of the people in this pit but, this time around, it was only my name that was shouted. One of the soldiers tread heavily down the ladder and shouted for me again.

'Here,' I whispered weakly, and moved my chains so they clinked against the iron loops. 'I am here.'
The soldier undid the large padlock which held my chains to the wall and hauled me upright. I was unable to stand on my legs so he lifted me bodily back up the ladder until I lay blinking on the stone floor. The light, Sister. I could not get used to the light after being in the darkness for so long. I could see myself too, Sister. My once-green dress was faded to grey rags and stained brown and black in places where the mould had caught it. My skin was almost the same shade of grey as the ragged cloth and great sores had opened up underneath my cuffs. They ran wet with foulness and I felt such shame, Sister.
'Get up!' The soldier scorned, kicking me in the side for good measure. I half-walked, half-crawled back along the corridor, the heavy chains linking my hands and feet making hard work of it. The air had never smelled so sweet and I took greedy gasps of the herb and pine-scented goodness of it. I stumbled up the steep stairs, heading away from the

oubliette and towards the clerk's room where daylight and freedom lay just on the other side of the wall.

'Jennet Pyke?' The same clerk who had entered my name in the ledger upon my arrival sat at his desk. I nodded and he made a mark against my name. 'You are to be taken to Market Square in St Helier where the Bailiff has assembled his court and will hear the crimes of which you stand accused.' He jerked his head at the soldier and I was pushed towards the great open doorway and I was free, Sister! Sky and clouds, trees and birds, I was never so happy to see them all!

My joy grew even further when I was dragged to where a two-bullock cart was standing. I stood dumbly, not understanding what I was supposed to do, when the smith was called and he struck the twisted nail from the cuffs encircling my ankles, removing the hated things from me. Oh, the relief, Sister! I felt so light I was certain I would float away on the sea breeze and leave them all on the ground gaping after me. I moved my feet from side to side, relishing the freedom to stand in a normal stance. The soles of my feet caught at the sharp stones on the track; after so long in the damp, stinking straw of the oubliette they had lost that hardness I had had since early childhood, and they were soft and black with filth.

My giddy joy was short-lived though as I was led to the back of the cart. I waited, expecting to feel rough hands hoist me up and onto the boards, but none came. Instead, the chains around my wrists were looped through a hook in the wooded slats.

'Witches don't ride, witches walk!' a harsh male voice said.

A bark of laughter from the soldiers as I felt someone grab the neck of my dress and pull down hard. I felt a brief moment of panic as the material held fast and tightened around my throat. Is this the noose, I wondered hazily. Is this the noose they will hang me with? The rotted fabric gave way and ripped open. I gasped for breath as the noose slackened. The soldier pawing at my dress ripped it all the way down to my waist and pulled it away so that my back was bare and, almost at once, I felt the burn of a switch as it was lashed against my skin. I jerked, as much in surprise as with pain, and the switch came down again, harder this time.

'Walk, witch!' The soldier commanded. 'Walk! And if you be slower than the oxen you will feel the switch all the more!'

And so I walked, chained to the back of a cart, my back bare and bloody, with the people of my village all out to witness my shame, and jeer and throw rotten things at me as I passed them. I walked all the way to Market Square in St Helier, which is many miles, on legs that had not held me up for many weeks. My mouthed burned with thirst and my bare feet dripped blood with every agonising step.

Do you think Jesus felt that way, Sister, when he was bid to carry his own cross through the towns and out to the place of his crucifixion? No, Sister, of course I do not compare myself to our beloved Lord, but I feel I know a little of his suffering.

All that long way, I looked for Matthieu. I looked for him in the jeering, disgusted faces of the townspeople. I looked for him as we passed the iron gates to his father's house, and beyond, my own home. I looked for him at every corner, at every communal well, where I prayed to see him rushing toward me with a cup of cold water for me to drink. I looked for him as we neared the town, and the dusty roads turned to cobbles upon which my bloody feet slipped and slid.

And I saw him, Sister.

He was standing at the top of the hill, his face turned away from me but I knew it was him, my Matthieu. I screamed his name over and over as we went by.

'Matthieu! MATTHIEU! MATTHIEU!'

He would not look at me, Sister. I passed within a few feet of him and still he would not turn his face to look at me. He was wearing his splendid red jacket, the one he was so proud of, even when I teased him for being a peacock and a popinjay, the one with the yellow underfelt that showed through the slashes in his scarlet tunic. I shouted myself hoarse, Sister. Even when I was level with him and I was screaming at him, he still did not move to meet my eyes. It was only after I had moved past him, and I twisted myself around as far as my chains would allow to look behind me, that I saw the glint of the dagger sticking out from his eye. His left eye, the one I could not see until I looked back, was gone. In its place was the handle of the knife, its blade buried deep inside Matthieu's skull. I took in the pallor of his skin, the way his hair laid flat and wet on his head, and I knew. In my mind I saw him floating face down in a foreign harbour, the brilliant gleam of his jacket dulling with the dirty water, and I knew.

He had run, Matthieu had. I was not to find out until my trial that he had been seen leaving the nave end of the church with a bulging bag full of silver candlesticks and gilt plates. The priest's own special silver cup, set with rubies and precious stones, had been swiped directly from his table and was buried deep within the bag as well. A suspicious soldier out for a walk followed him as Matthieu hauled the church's treasures back towards his own house, and had reported him to his superior officer at once. A full brigade of soldiers were summoned from the garrison and sent to the Chevalier farm in haste. They found Matthieu on his way to my shack. He was still carrying the bag and, when tipped up, out tumbled the silver and gilt, although the priests silver cup was missing.

I learned then the extent of my lover's deceit. I learned then just how far Matthieu was prepared to go to save his own skin.

When he was arrested, Matthieu swayed on his feet and shook his head as if coming out of a great daze.
    'Why am I here?' he groaned. 'What am I doing here? The last thing I remember was going to sleep last night.' He moaned and retched, and stumbled into the soldiers holding him by the arms. 'Please, tell me. Where am I? I do not know how I came to be here. What is happening?'
He put on such a show of pretence of being confused and bewildered that the officer in charge allowed him to sit down on the ground.
    'You were seen, Sir, taking valuables from the church,' the officer prompted, nudging the half-empty hessian sack at his foot.
Matthieu managed to look both surprised and horrified.
    'No! I would not steal! I have never taken anything in my life, I swear it! And from a holy house, good God, but it is not possible.'
He did much more moaning and groaning as if his head pained him so, then looked up at the officer sharply.
    'The hare-witch!' Matthieu cried. 'She has bewitched me! She has put a spell on me and bid me take the church's silver for her own devious uses and devilment! The hare-witch! It is her, I tell you. Here, she lives on this farm! I'll show you.'
And thus was the tale that Matthieu told, that I had witched him into stealing, and he told it so convincingly that he was released at once and the order made for me to be taken up and arrested. The cook, on hearing the commotion and coming out of the back door to see what was amiss, heard him accuse me so, and jumped in with her own tale of black cats and hare-witched hens. The dairy-maid, in the yard,

270

overheard her tale and ran to tell the housemaids, who in turn ran to tell their neighbours and families and, by the time I was dragged from my sleep by the soldiers and their dogs, a further forty accusations had been thrown at me. Every ill child, every unexpected death, every strange occurrence - all were blamed on me, the hare-witch.

And Matthieu ran.

He dallied long enough to dig up the corner of a pig sty to retrieve the stolen goods there and then he ran for the harbour, catching the first ship bound for the French coast. The foreign sailors took in his fine, embroidered tunic and his puffed sleeves and took him for a gentleman, one with plenty of coin hidden about his person. By the time the ship reached port Matthieu was dead, a dagger in his eye and the stolen wares stripped from his baggage. His body was tossed overboard and floated calmly on the gentle tide, face-down, as I had seen.

And I was glad.

CHAPTER TWENTY-THREE

Leah

With the gruesome details of Jennet's trial and imprisonment running through my head, I headed back to The Grange.

'Mum and Dad are going to come over for half-term, instead of waiting until Christmas,' Matt told me when I came in through the kitchen door. He was leaning back against the fridge drinking milk straight from the carton. I frowned at him.

'Don't do that, it's disgusting. Half-term's the week after next but Alice's class has their Halloween party on the Friday before. Why don't they come over for that? I'm sure they'd love to see her all dressed up,' I added.

'Good plan,' Matt nodded. 'What's she going as again?'

'Well, at first she said she wanted to be a witch but then she found out most of the girls in her class were going for the same thing,' I rolled my eyes. 'You know Alice, always wants to be the one who stands out, so she's now informed me she wants to be a pirate princess ghost.'

'What the hell does a pirate princess ghost wear?' Matt laughed.

'No idea,' I shrugged. 'But it involves a tiara, an eye-patch and a white sheet!'

Matt covered his face with his palm.

Brilliant!' he chuckled. 'That's just brilliant.'

'Er, do your parents know... about Jayne, I mean?' I asked him hesitantly.

'They know she's moved out,' he said flatly. 'They don't know she's shacked up with my cousin though.'

'And are they still OK with me being here, you know, helping out and stuff?'

'Yeah, they're fine. They know I need the help, although I think you'll find my mum a bit overbearing. She'll probably ask you to take a week's holiday while they're here, so she can have the kids to herself,' Matt warned me.

'I don't mind,' I assured him. 'With Alice off school and the good weather holding out, it'll be great for your folks to take them places. Most of the visitor attractions are closing in the first week of November and we haven't been to many of them yet! I've got plenty to do anyway. I want to keep looking in the attic and I have my doctor's appointment tomorrow,' I added shyly. 'Here's hoping he can work miracles.'

'Good, good,' Matt commented absently. 'Hey, I had a good look at those house plans! Aren't they just amazing? They've got the original room measurements and proportions and everything - they're going to be such a help for the restoration.'

'Did you look at the hidden room?' I asked.

'Yeah,' Matt frowned. 'I thought that was a bit weird. What's with the name - the Witch's Room, when it was the meat pantry?'

'Not sure,' I murmured. 'We found a whole lot of stuff out about our ghost today.'

I launched into the story of Jennet Pyke and her arrest for witchcraft, and the trials they made her go through. Matt looked at me like I'd lost my mind.

'And you think this Jennet person is why things have been a little bit odd here, now and again?'

He shook his head in despair. 'I keep telling you, there's no such thing as ghosts.'

'Yes there are, Daddy!' Alice came skipping into the kitchen. 'I'm going to be one for Halloween! I'm going to have a crown and wear a sheet and go like this - Wooooooooooooo!' She opened her eyes wide and lifted her hands to her head, crunching them both into claws and waving them around. We laughed and the tension that had been beginning to build between me and Matt dissipated.

'Well, I'm going to have another poke around upstairs,' I told them. 'I'll be back down in time to make a start on dinner.'

I left them making silly ghost noises at each other and cautiously climbed the stairs to the attics. It felt different, being up here on my own without Ben's comforting presence. The air felt flat and stale with dust. I looked around the vast room, nothing moved.

'Um, hello? Jennet?' I cleared my throat, feeling very self-conscious. 'Um... I just wanted to... um ... well, we were reading today about you, about when you were sent to Mont Orgueil, and I just wanted to... um,' I bit my lip. 'I just wanted to tell you that we know. We know what they did to you, the things they accused you of and the trials they made you do. It wasn't fair. You were just a girl.'

I looked around again but the attic stayed dead and lifeless.

'You were just a girl, who looked a bit different,' I repeated. 'And, believe me, I know all about that,' I said, touching my fingertip to my lip. I strained my eyes to the far left corner, the one that had seemed alive with shadows yesterday, but this time it was tinged with a sepia light. Jenny was not playing today.

'Um, OK, well... thank you for helping us find the house plans. There's one more thing I need your help with though.' I waited in the silence. Was it my imagination or did I feel a subtle change in the air, a slight charge? I took a deep breath and ploughed on.

'I'm looking for the family tree. The Chevalier family tree. We know you were brought here, to this house, but we don't know why. Could you help us again, please? If you know where there might be, oh I don't know, a scroll of paper or a family book, could you show me? Do what you did the other day and make a sound or push something over. Anything, just show me where to start looking.' I stayed perfectly still, ears pricked for any sound or movement, but after a long minute there had been nothing. I let out a long breath, not sure whether to be relieved or disappointed. Grabbing the closest wooden crate of random things, I huffed it out of the attic door and back down the stairs. If Jenny wasn't willing to show herself to me today, I may as well carry on with sorting out Pierre's junk.

I woke up the next morning feeling out of sorts. It wasn't that I'd had another night visit from Jenny, in fact I'd had a good night of unbroken sleep for once, it was something I just couldn't put my finger on. I lay dozing in my warm bed until my phone blipped with a reminder. It was Monday morning, the day of my appointment with the facial injury consultant. The appointment was for half past nine, so I would need to walk into town after dropping Alice off at school.

'Any chance you could look after Noah until I get back from my appointment?' I asked Matt at breakfast time. 'I shouldn't be too long, back by eleven anyhow.'
Matt scowled into his mug of coffee.
'Not really, Leah,' he began. 'It's a week day. That means we both go to work. I work on the house, and you look after the kids. That was the deal.'
'I know. I mean, I just thought…,' I trailed off. 'Oh, forget it. You're right. I'll just have to take Noah with me.'
I wasn't sure if I should have been more annoyed with Matt. On the one hand he was right, it was a week day and it was my job to have the kids on weekdays but, surely he could have helped me out, just this once. It was a fairly big deal for me, after all.

I found myself relaying the conversation to Ben when we met up at the top of the road like we did every school day.

'It does sound like he's taking the piss a wee bit,' Ben agreed. 'But I can take Noah today, if that helps?'

'Are you sure?' I replied, once more surprised at how sweet and thoughtful Ben could be. 'I won't be long.'

'We could meet you in town afterwards, go for a sticky cake somewhere?' Ben suggested. 'I'll take Noah to the playground in Howard Davis park first and you can text me when you're done.'

'That sounds like a brilliant idea!' I beamed. 'Thank you so much. Noah will love that too. He doesn't get to do much fun stuff on his own.'

I walked with them to the entrance of the park, then Ben swung Noah's stroller around and they went off-roading in the park on the way to the playground. I heard them both chuckling loudly as I carried on towards the town on my own. I had directions to the doctor's offices and it meant walking right down the main shopping precinct and down towards the harbour. I held my scarf over my face tightly and dropped my eyes to the ground, avoiding eye contact with everyone who was walking in the opposite direction, towards me. I could feel their curious looks. Openly staring at other pedestrians is the height of rudeness in London; it seemed to be a favourite past-time on Jersey.

The office building was sleek and modern, with a shiny glass frontage. Walking into the marble reception area, I saw a brass plaque that told me that M Harlow, FRCS (Plast), had rooms on the second floor. I looked around for the lift but saw that there was a group of suited businessmen waiting in front of it so I ducked out of a side door and went up the stairs instead, meaning that I was red-faced and sweaty by the time I pushed open the frosted glass door to the doctor's offices. An immaculately dressed blonde woman greeted me with a wintry smile.

'Yes? Do you have an appointment?' She enquired, looking me up and down and obviously finding me not groomed enough for her perfectly styled reception area.

'Y... yes,' I stammered, pulling the scarf even closer to my face. 'Leah Harrop.'

The blonde consulted her computer screen.

'Ah, yes. Miss Harrop, lovely. Take a seat. Mr Harlow will be with you shortly.'

I perched awkwardly on the edge of the low white couch that made up the client seating area, and picked up one of the magazines from the glass coffee table. I wasn't interested in the glossy photos of Jersey's priciest mansions on the cover; I just wanted something to hide my face in. The clock on the wall above me ticked loudly and my heart beat set up its own rhythm in time with it. What if the doctor couldn't help me? Or worse, what if he laughed at me for thinking he would? I sat there nervously, palms sweating, until I heard a door opening further down the corridor.

'Miss Harrop?' enquired a soft, polite voice. I looked up into the kind face of a short, balding man. 'Michael Harlow, pleased to meet you,' he said, holding out a hand for me to shake. 'Please, come this way.'

He led me to a small but elegant room. He had a desk in front of the window but also a separate seating area, furnished with three damask covered chairs and a highly polished low table.

'Sit down, sit down!' he urged me in a jolly tone, pulling out one of the chairs. He sat in the one opposite me, doing that man thing of tugging his trouser legs up before he lowered himself down. 'Now, I hope you don't think me rude but... would you mind taking off your scarf so I can see what we're dealing with?'

His eyes held nothing but kindness, sincerity and a spark of interest. Slowly, hesitantly, I unwound the paisley cotton, baring my entire face in all its hideousness.

'Oh yes,' he murmured softly, almost as if to himself. 'Oh yes. I can definitely do something about that.'

It took a second for his words to sink in. These words, ones which I had not even dared to hope he would say to me, these very words unleashed the floodgates and I burst into noisy, happy tears.

He let me cry for as long as I wanted. He moved to the seat beside me and patted my hand tenderly, occasionally passing me tissues from the box on the table. I sniffed and gulped, hiccupping out apologies which he waved away immediately.

'Not at all, you've every right to cry. I imagine you've been keeping everything bottled up for quite some time now?'

'I just never thought there might be hope,' I blew my nose. 'The hospital in London told me they'd be in touch about arranging some surgery for me, but I've not heard from them. I thought it was because nothing could be done. I half-expected you to tell me to stop being so vain and that I was wasting your time.'

He grinned at me.

'Then I'm pleased to be able to tell you the good news! I'm afraid the waiting times for plastic surgery on the NHS can run into years sometimes. That's why it's better to see someone like me, who has a private practice. Now, to work!' He stood up and moved over to where a small whiteboard was fixed to the wall, picking up a marker and swiftly drawing a remarkably good likeness of my face. 'Most of the damage is limited to your upper lip, although your ear lobe is also somewhat affected. The scarring on your cheek will fade down to almost nothing over time. I know you think it looks bad now, and there are things we could try to speed up the process - lasering, that sort of thing - but I can promise you that the redness will reduce gradually and become more like your normal skin tone. There may always be a slight difference in texture, it might feel smoother than your other cheek for example, but it's not something that will be immediately noticeable. In fact, you'd have to get up quite close to be able to see the scarring once it's healed.'

He made some quick arrows over the face on the whiteboard, then came over to me. Gently, very gently, he pulled at the skin above my mouth, turning it up and inwards to inspect the damage.

'Marvellous things, lips!' he enthused. 'They have the ability to re-generate and heal much faster than other areas of the body. Now, what I propose is a small incision here...,' he moved back to the whiteboard and drew a small line. '...we would graft in a small bit here, move this here, it looks like you've retained most of the muscle under here...' he made more arrows and slashes on the diagram, '... and we'll bring this back in line with the rest of the lip line, the skin cells should heal quite naturally...' He went on, talking about philtrums and tubercles and labiums. I got lost in the medical terminology as he got more and more excited.

'Now, it will take more than one bout of surgery to put things right, we're talking maybe three or four, with ample time in between to heal of course. But, overall, I'd say there's a good chance you will end up with nothing more than just a faint white scar, just here.' He gently touched the side of my mouth. 'Other than that, no one will ever be able to tell you had such terrible injuries. They'll be hard pressed to even notice anything different about your face, unless they look very, very closely indeed.' He went to his desk and started scrolling through the screen on his computer. 'When should we book you in?'

My head was spinning. He was promising me a miracle. He could make me look normal again.

'What about money?' I suddenly thought, a cold, sick feeling in my stomach. 'How much is this going to cost?'

He looked at me silently for a moment.

'Regrettably, there will be a fee, of course. I should think we're looking in the region of fifteen thousand pounds.'

'Fifteen thousand...' I gasped. I had a bit of cash left from the crowdfunding money, but nothing like fifteen thousand pounds. Mum didn't have that kind of money either, not that I'd dream of asking her for a loan, and if I wanted to bring a civil case against Liam's wife, the woman who caused all this, I was looking at months and months of legal wrangling without any promise of compensation at the end of it. 'I don't have... I mean, I can't afford...'

'There is an alternative,' the doctor put in, tapping a pen against his knee. 'It might not be something you'd be interested in though...'

'What is it?' I asked warily. He looked at me shyly.

'I teach at a London hospital. I also write for various medical journals.'

He paused and I looked at him in confusion, not seeing the connection between his teaching and me not being able to afford his fees. 'Your case... is a very interesting one. Unfortunately, this type of thing - acid attacks - are on the increase. It would be a great help to me in my research, and as a consultant practitioner and teacher, if you would consider becoming a case study for my students.' He sat back in his chair, studying me intently. 'Of course, it would mean a huge reduction in what I would charge you. The only thing is that any surgery would have to take place in London, and in front of a small group of medical students. How would you feel about that?'

My heart soared. He was offering me a lifeline for the second time in less than half an hour.

'Great! I mean, I'm in!' I cried. 'When do we leave?'

'...and then he laughed and said he'd make all the arrangements soon,' I said joyfully to Ben an hour later. We were in a cafe in the central food market. Noah was fast asleep in his stroller having been thoroughly tired out at the park with Ben.

'That's amazing news!' Ben said warmly, taking my hand in his.

'I know it will take some time, things won't change overnight,' I went on, bubbling over with excitement. 'But he said that I should see a big difference, even after the first operation. You won't be able to see my teeth under my lip anymore. I'll still have a scar but at least I won't be so rabbity.'

'I can already see the difference,' Ben told me. 'Even just getting such good news has given you the boost you needed. Soon you won't need to hide that beautiful face at all.'

We smiled at each other and I thanked my lucky stars for whatever had brought such a good, kind man into my life.

'So, what's next for Jenny?' Ben picked up his cup and swallowed the last of his coffee. 'Between you and Debbie, you've worked out who she was, when she lived and how she came to end up in the dungeons at Mont Orgueil.'

'The next thing is to find out where she went from there,' I mused. 'We got to when she was released from the prison into the care of a Monsieur Chevalier, who we believed lived at Matt's house back in the early seventeenth century. It was around the same time that the house started being referred to as Harewich House rather than its proper name, so we're assuming that Jennet was taken there, and perhaps kept there for a while, but we don't know what happened to her after that. It's so frustrating! It's like I've been given a huge jigsaw puzzle to do and have gotten so far with it only to discover that it has pieces missing.'

'I'm sure you'll find out more. I agree with you that there must be more family history up in the attics. I can always find some time to help you, you know.'

'Ben, she threw a big chunk of leather at you. Has that not scared you off?' I teased.

'Nope. It's only made me more curious. And anyway, I'm willing to risk more heavy things being thrown at me if it means I get to spend more time with you.'

I ducked my head shyly, still not used to the way Ben openly admitted to liking me.

'Well, I should have a lot more free time over half-term,' I said. 'Matt's parents are coming over for a week.

They'll want to spend all their time with Alice and Noah so I'll make myself scarce, give the family some space.'

'Do you want to come and stay with me and Gracie for a few days?' Ben put in seriously. 'You know you're always welcome.'

'Thanks,' I smiled. 'But I'll be fine. I've got my own little flat so I shouldn't be in their way.'

CHAPTER TWENTY-FOUR

Alice was getting so excited about the Halloween party on the last day of school before half-term. She changed her mind a dozen times about what a pirate princess ghost wore exactly, but eventually settled on an old bedsheet, which I hand-stitched into shape for her. It went over her head in the traditional ghost costume way, but I sewed in proper sleeves and used the excess material and some elastic to create a full, swishy skirt. The effect was homely and patchwork but she loved it. She insisted on wearing the gold plastic tiara she had received for her fifth birthday and teamed it with a black eyepatch, complete with skull and crossbones, covering her eye.

'I'm a pirate, princess ghost!' she squealed happily, looking at her reflection in the mirror.

'Are you sure you're comfortable in there?' I asked her. 'Can you see OK?'

'No, I can only see from one eye,' she told me, as if it were the most obvious thing in the world. 'But it's OK, I can see from my other one.'

'Do you want me to cut the eye holes bigger?'
She shook her head.

'No, it's perfect!' she giggled. 'And no one will know that it's me! I can run up to people and scare them and they won't be able to say 'Oh, that Alice!', they'll say 'who was that pirate princess ghost?' instead.'

I looked at her swishing the folds of her costume happily. She no longer asked for Jayne each morning, just occasionally mentioned her in passing. She appeared to have accepted the new situation as normal now.

'Sweetie, you know Nana and Poppa are coming to see you this week?' I unwrapped the ghost costume from her head.

'Yes! I can't wait!' she burst out. 'Nana always brings me a present when she comes to see me and Poppa lets me eat his special toffees. They haven't come to see me since we came to Jersey, so do you think my present will be extra special and big?'

'Probably!' I laughed. 'They'll be here late on Thursday so they can take you to the party on Friday, OK?'

'Are you coming too?'

'I'll be there too, yes. But Nana and Poppa will help you get dressed in your costume and take you there; I'll be there at the hall already because I'm going with Gracie and Ben.'

'Do you like Gracie more than me now?' she asked me quietly, lower lip wobbling. I caught her up in a fierce hug.

'Never! You're my special girl, my little bunny, remember!'

'Aunty Rabbit, when you get your face fixed I won't be able to call you that anymore.'

'Alice, sweetheart, you can always call me that. I won't ever mind being called Aunty Rabbit by you.' She stepped away from me and looked sadly towards the open lounge door.

'I wish Jenny had been to the doctor like you. Then she could have gotten her face fixed too, and the bad man wouldn't have been so mean to her.'

'Do you know what he did to her, the bad man?' I pressed her gently.

'Not really. She doesn't like to say. But I think she had a baby and he took it away from her so she has to look for it.'

Curious and curiouser.

As if by speaking about it had conjured it up, we heard the crying baby again that night. I lay in my room, hearing the pitiful wailing on the other side of the wall. I heard Matt get up and open his door, before pausing, shutting it closed again and going back to bed. Neither of us wanted another excursion into that horrible dank, stone room so we both turned over in our beds, and tried to ignore the cries. They stopped eventually but I couldn't shake the feeling of guilt, that I should have got up and gone looking for the baby, all the while knowing that there would be no baby to find.

Matt was already at work early the next morning when I went to make breakfast. I took him a cup of coffee before I went to get the kids up and he grunted his thanks.

'Rough night?' I asked, willing him to mention the crying in the night.

'Woke up in the middle of the night, couldn't get back to sleep so I thought I'd be better off getting an early start.' He refused to meet my eye. I let the subject drop.

'I'll see you at lunchtime. I'm going up into the attics again as soon as I get back from the school run,' I told him.

'Let me know if you find a double bed frame up there,' Matt requested. 'Mum and Dad can go in your old room but I doubt Dad's bad back will thank me if I put them on a mattress on the floor!' He smiled crookedly.

'Sure,' I said coolly, 'I'll keep an eye out.'

I was pulling the remains of a motheaten rug off a pile of old suitcases when I heard the yell. I paused, yanked the baby monitor from my pocket and listened carefully. The sound of Noah's sleepy snores filled the air reassuringly. Not Noah then, so who was shouting? I heard another surprised bellow followed by a yelp of pain.

'Matt?' I stood at the open attic door and called down. 'Matt, are you OK?' There was no answer so I abandoned my rummaging and descended the main stairs down to the large entrance hall. Matt came running out from the great hall where he had been working. He was white-faced and a trickle of blood dripped down his face from a graze near his hairline.

'OK, I bloody believe you now!' he shouted, coming to a stop at the bottom of the staircase. 'You and your ghost, I've just bloody seen her! She threw a fucking screwdriver at my head!'

'What?' I said, confused. 'You've just seen Jenny?'

'Yes! Ah God, my head hurts!'

I led Matt back to the kitchen, making him a cup of tea with three sugars for the shock. He sat at the table, shaking and swearing under his breath. I peered at the wound on his head.

It wasn't large and the bleeding was already slowing down so I cleaned it up as best I could.

'Don't think it needs stitches,' I murmured. A circular bruise, the outline of a large screwdriver handle, was already blooming red and blue but it didn't look too serious. 'Tell me what happened.'

'I was just working away, like always, and I heard someone call my name. I thought it was you at first but then I realised they were calling "Matthew", not Matt; and it was in a weird accent, like a French accent.' Matt brought his hand up to his head and winced. 'I looked around but couldn't see anyone, so I just cranked up the volume on the radio and got back to work. A second later my big Phillips screwdriver hit me square on the head. It was on the other side of the room, I know it was, I saw it there five minutes before. I think I shouted out and I turned around and she was standing there, just looking at me.'

'What did she look like?' I butted in, wrenching his hand away from where he was poking at his bruise. 'Leave your head alone, idiot, your hands are all mucky.'

Matt took a deep, shaky breath.

'She was small, really tiny like a child. She had black hair, all messy and knotted up, and she had on a filthy grey dress. Oh, and she had these big chains on her.'

'Yep, that's our Jenny, all right,' I concurred.

'It was the look on her face that really got me though,' Matt continued. 'She was really glaring at me, like she hated me. And she just kept saying "Matthew, Matthew" over and over again. I thought she was going to attack me, or throw more stuff at me, so I just got the hell out of there!' Matt put his hand on my arm. 'I'm so sorry I didn't believe you, Leah. I think I did know there were weird things happening in this house but, I just love this place so much, I didn't want to believe it. I thought that if I didn't acknowledge them, they would just stop and go away.'

'I don't think that's going to happen,' I said softly. 'I think Jenny really needs our help. Alice says that Jenny was hurt by a bad man here, an early Chevalier.'

'And what? You think she's mad at me because I'm a Chevalier man too?' Matt scoffed.

'It's possible,' I said, treading carefully. 'She does seem to hate men, but from what I'm finding out about what happened to her when she was alive, she's got every right to.'

Matt groaned.

'I don't think I want to know. But do me a favour, Leah?' he begged. 'One, tell your ghost to lay off throwing tools at my head, and two, please don't say anything to my Mum and Dad!'

When Matt left on Thursday evening to collect his parents from the airport, I sat Alice down for a serious chat.

'Sweetheart,' I began. 'You know our friend, Jenny...?' Alice nodded, more interested in playing with the fringe on my scarf. 'Well, I don't think we should talk about her when Nana and Poppa are here.'

'Why not?' Alice asked innocently. 'I talk about her to you.'

'Yes, I know but...' I hesitated, picking my way carefully. I didn't want Alice to think I was asking her to keep secrets but at the same time, I didn't want Matt's folks to think I was encouraging her to believe in ghosts either.

'It's just that maybe your Nana and Poppa might not be able to see Jenny, like we can, and they might be a bit frightened if we talk about someone they can't see.'

'Jenny gets angry when people are afraid of her. Gracie got scared and tried to run away and that's why Jenny scratched her face.' Alice ran her fingers through the golden threads of the scarf abstractedly.

'Yes, well, that's another thing...' I persevered. 'Sometimes Jenny does things that aren't very nice, like hurting Gracie or messing up our kitchen, and we don't want Nana and Poppa to be scratched like Gracie, do we?' Alice shook her head vehemently.

'But she won't,' Alice promised. 'I know she won't.

'She might, Alice,' I said gently. 'She hasn't hurt you or me, or God forbid, Noah, but she did hurt Gracie and Gracie's only a little girl. She hurt your Dad today too; she threw his big screwdriver at him and it hit him on the head - really hard!' Alice let out an involuntary chuckle before she could stop herself. 'It's not funny!' I chided. 'He was really hurt!'

'She doesn't like Daddy because of his name, like she doesn't like Gabriel because of his name either.'

'Alice, that doesn't make any sense. Why would Jenny not like people because of their names?' I asked, thoroughly confused.

'Because they are Chev... Chev... Chevlers.'
She struggled to pronounce the old French surname.

'You mean Chevaliers?' I asked and she nodded.

'Matthieu Chevalier and Gabriel Chevalier,' she recited the names with a credible French accent. 'They are the bad men, the ones who hurt Jenny, so she doesn't like that Daddy and Uncle Gabriel have the same names.'
Oh God, I really needed to find that family tree! If there was any truth in what Alice was saying, I now had both the names of the men who had been instrumental in her death

and the dates of when she ended up in this house. More pieces of the puzzle.

'Hello! Hello, my little lambkins!' Matt's mother, Linda, burst into the lounge where we were all sitting in high anticipation. Alice gave an excited shriek and ran into her grandmother's outstretched arms. Noah crowed at the top of his voice and bounced heavily on my lap. Matt's father, Ian, followed just behind his wife and he scooped Noah up and held him high in the air.

'My boy! Look at my big boy!' he beamed, holding Noah firmly around the middle and making swooping, flying movements, complete with sound effects. Noah screamed with laughter. Ian passed the baby to Linda who settled him onto her well-padded hip and cuddled him close, while Alice ran to her Poppa to be swooped up into the air too. 'Well, well, look at this big grown-up girl!'

He gave her a smacking kiss on the cheek and we all laughed when Alice cried 'Yuk! Scratchy, Poppa, too scratchy!'

'Hello, nice to meet you,' I stood up and held my hand out politely. 'I'm Leah. I help Matt out with these two monsters.'

There was a slightly awkward pause and Ian and Linda exchanged a quick glance.

'Of course! Lovely to meet you at last, Leah,' Ian recovered first and shook my outstretched hand warmly. 'Linda and I can't thank you enough for all you've done for Matt lately. He'd be lost without you, he says.'

Linda gave me a quick, limp handshake but she wasn't quite as effusive in her greeting.

'Hello,' she said, with a touch of frost, barely detectable but still there, in her voice. 'I hope Matt's given you some time off while we're here. You've been with the children day and night for a few months now, you must be looking forward to a break.'

It was a clear warning - back off, we're family and you're not. I smiled serenely.

'Yes I am. Matt's told me your plans to take the kids round all the visitor sites in Jersey before they close for the winter. What a great idea! I'm sure they'll both love that. I've got plenty to do, you won't see much of me. I'll use the other door in the main hall to come and go, that way I won't be intruding on your space in the flat. Let me show you to your room.'

I indicated the door opposite the lounge and walked past them to open it. It was actually Matt's bedroom. We hadn't found a suitable bedframe apart from one old single wire one that looked like a mediaeval torture device, so we put fresh bed linen on Matt's bed for his Mum and Dad, and Matt would bunk down on the mattress in my old room.

Ian and Linda loosened up considerably after a late dinner of shepherd's pie - a recipe I had borrowed from Debbie - and a few glasses of wine. Alice and Noah had been allowed to stay up late in honour of their grandparents arrival and both were now sound asleep, Noah still on Linda's lap and Alice curled up in a ball on the mat in Noah's playpen. I excused myself as soon as I had cleared the table.

'I'm off to bed, unless you need anything?' I directed my question at Linda.

'No, love, you're all right. Thank you for such a lovely meal.'

'I'll be up to get the children's breakfast if you want a bit of a lie-in. It's the Halloween party tomorrow so I'll get Alice's costume all ready for you. You can walk her to school, she knows the way,' I suggested.

'Thanks, love. That'll be grand. I'm so looking forward to seeing all her little friends,' Linda gushed. 'And thank you for looking after them so well. You enjoy your time off. Matt tells us you have a boyfriend?' She arched her eyebrows.

'More of a friend than a boyfriend,' I admitted. 'You might meet him tomorrow. His daughter Gracie is Alice's best friend.'

Escaping to my little bedsit I let out a sigh of relief. I hoped I had handled things well. I didn't want to step on Linda and Ian's toes in any way; I was more than happy to have some time to myself that didn't revolve around school runs and Noah's nap times.

In spite of the wine, sleep was a long time coming. I kept trying to connect the dots around what I knew about Jennet's life, and coming to the same conclusion, no matter which way I looked at it. She was kept here in this house, in that horrible little room, by a man Alice referred to as the "bad man", possibly named Matthieu or Gabriel. But why? Why would a high-standing lord remove a convicted witch from her prison cell and take her into his home? And what was the purpose of keeping her in that room? And more to the point, what HAPPENED to her in there? The questions went round and round in my head until finally I dozed off, the clanking of the water pipes in the flat's only bathroom singing me to sleep.

WHUMP!

I sat up in shock. My heart was beating hard and fast and I was panting like I'd just run a marathon.

WHUMP!

The noise came again. It sounded like a door slamming several flats away. I wondered if Matt, in his shock at seeing Jennet and being hit by a screwdriver, had neglected to close a door or a window when he finished his work on the great hall for the day.

WHUMP!

I couldn't ignore it. If it was a door or window banging, the sound would go on all night and drive me crazy. I groaned and tossed off the bedcovers. For a moment, I contemplated waking Matt and asking him to go and find out what was making the noise, but the thought of sneaking down the hallway in the middle of the night into Matt's room, and the possibility of Ian and Linda hearing me and jumping to the completely wrong conclusion, put a swift halt to that idea. I was on my own. Whimpering at the thought of creeping around the old part of the house in the dark, I pulled a sweatshirt over my pyjamas and pushed my feet into my comfy slipper boots. The autumn night was chilly and I shivered, although only partly from cold, as I turned the key to the door on the opposite side of the room and opened it to reveal the old clay floor tiles of the hallway. I knew that I would need to walk towards the main front door, before turning left into the large room Matt was trying to take back to the original proportions of the great hall. I only had the torch app on my phone and the blue-tinged light cast an eerie glow over the dark panelled hallway.

WHUMP!

The sound was definitely coming from my left but not in the room I had thought, the one that Matt was working in. It was coming from higher up, in another of the old flats on the next floor. Strange, I thought, I didn't think that Matt had got that far yet, although I knew he was hoping to remove part of the first floor over the great hall, as the room would have been of double height originally. The wide curving staircases loomed above my head and ascended into the black void of the upper floor. Taking a deep breath to steady myself, I put my foot on the first step. Really, what's the worst that could happen, I chided myself, I've already seen the ghost and she didn't seem to want to harm me so just get on with it, scaredy-cat! I trod carefully, feeling the wood under my feet creak and shift with my weight. The old carpet was littered with scraps of wood, flakes of plaster and hidden screws and nails. I moved upwards slowly, keeping the torch beam of my phone on the step just in front of me, afraid of what I might see if I moved it any further up.

WHUMP!

It was closer, the noise, and definitely on my left. I rounded the gentle curve of the stairs and saw the level floor above me. The hall up here was narrow; the cowboy builders who converted the house into flats in the seventies squeezed as much space as they could from the once grand proportions of the original layout. I counted two closed doors on my left, and two closed doors mirrored them on the opposite side. A few more steps and I was on the first floor, wondering which door I should try first.

WHUMP!

This time the noise sounded like it was right next to me. I jumped and spun around to my left, catching sight of a dark shadow lurking at the first left-hand door. It was faint and barely perceptible amongst the peeling wallpaper and painted door, but as I continued to look, my breath a mere squeak in my throat, the shape rippled fluidly and formed into a small woman. Her grey eyes glinted at me in the reflection of the torchlight.

'Jennet!' I breathed, frozen in fascination and fear. She looked at me scornfully, as if my cowardice amused her, and drifted backwards, back through the closed wooden door. I waited, unsure whether she wanted me to follow her or if I should try all the doors randomly.
WHUMP!

The door to my left swung open with a long, slow creak.

CHAPTER TWENTY-FIVE

The room was unremarkable. Faded pink carpet with beige wood-chip wallpaper, and dull white painted cupboards. The bright moon outside gave enough light to see the space quite clearly. I crept through the open door, holding my breath, unsure what it was I was meant to be doing in here.

WHUMP!

The source of the strange thumping noise became immediately clear.

While this room was almost identical to all the other empty rooms in the old flats, it had one discernible difference. The flat was built along the back wall of the house and the builders had kept the small casement windows set deep into the two-foot thick walls. Underneath such a window in this particular room, a wooden bench had been constructed and fitted snugly into the space. Built as extra storage, it had a tatty, padded top upholstered in what had once been a cheap pink velvet and this created a cosy place to sit and look out at the fields beyond the house. It was this wooden planked lid that was creating the noise I had heard all the way downstairs in my own room. Even as I watched, the lid raised itself up a few inches, enough for me to see the hinges inside attaching it to the boxy frame beneath, before dropping down again with some force and letting out the loud WHUMP.

'Jenny?' I spoke to the empty air. 'Jennet, are you there?'

The lid rose up almost fully and crashed down again, but Jenny did not materialise.

'Is there something in the box, something I need to find?' I asked, feeling somewhat stupid. Of course there was what she wanted me to do, of course there was

294

something in there, why would she be showing me an empty storage chest? As if answering my question, the box lid flipped up, crashed against the back of the wall and stayed open. A musty smell of mould and damp wood drifted over to me. I took a few steps further into the room, but apart from the built-in cupboards, it was empty. The box looked empty too. Feeling an almost crushing sense of disappointment, I moved to the edge of the wooden frame, leaning one hand on the top of the lid to keep it locked in place. I certainly did not want to put my hands inside, only to have the heavy top come crashing down on top of them.

There was nothing.

The chest was completely empty. The rough wooden boards at the bottom held only a thin layer of dust. I huffed in annoyance.

'There's nothing in there!' I said to the room, and turned to walk grumpily back to the door, intending to go straight back to bed. The bedroom door slammed closed in front of me with such a bang that I could feel the vibrations in the floorboards under my feet. 'OK,' I said warily, taking a step backwards. 'Jennet, if you're there...'
The lid of the chest slammed down hard too. I swallowed nervously, my mouth and throat bone dry.

'Jennet, if you're there, can you show me what it is I should be looking at?'
Before I had even finished the sentence, the lid swung up again and once more, stayed open. I knelt down gingerly and peeked over the edge of the frame. The box was still empty. Yet as I was kneeling there, wondering if I could make a run for the now closed door, the wooden planks at the bottom of the chest began to hum. They quivered and shook, before jumping up an inch or so. It was like watching popcorn in a hot pan. The boards continued to rise and fall for a minute, before one popped out completely and was hurtled up and out of the chest, coming to lay beside me on

295

the floor. The other boards took their cue from the first and, one by one, they propelled themselves out of the frame and lay strewn around the dusty carpet. At once, the mouldy, mildewy smell intensified and I gagged on the mushroomy aroma.

In the space beneath where the boards had been lay a large book. Old, so very, very old. Even I could tell that. It was black with age and dirt but the dark brown cover was solid and square. Dull gold lettering shone through in patches and I wiped my hand carelessly over the top of the book, hoping to be able to read the title.

Holy Byble

I felt around the book, trying to lift it out of the chest. It resisted initially having been glued fast with damp, but then the back cover gave way with a soft sucking noise and the rest of the bible came away, leaving the back pages behind. I thought: oh shit, I've wrecked it already! It was incredibly heavy, even without its back cover, and large. I figured it had to be at least two feet long, a foot and a half wide, and around six inches deep. It moved insecurely in my hands and I could feel more pages already coming loose. Carefully, I lay it next to me on the floor, front cover face down and turned back to the chest. Using my fingernails, I tried to prise up the back cover but it just crumbled around my fingers. I needed something long and slim to try and lever under it and I remembered the slivers of wood that littered the stairs. I could try and use something like that, the only problem was the closed bedroom door... I looked behind me, the door had now mysteriously and silently opened again of its own accord and I was free to leave.

Padding on quiet feet, I looked around the landing just outside the door and spotted the perfect tool. An old louvre window blind lay in a tangle along the other wall and I was able to wrench one of its hideous plastic slats from the cord binding. I used the sharp edges to burrow under the fragile paper and damp-riddled backing, loosened the grip caused by years of mould and damp conditions, and soon the last few pages of the bible were reunited with the rest of the book. I had nothing to wrap it up in, and I definitely wouldn't be able to carry it back to my room in one piece so, shivering in the cold night air, I took off my sweatshirt and laid the bible gently inside it, using the sleeves to tie around it in a protective knot. Holding it close to my chest, I slipped down the stairs and turned back towards the hallway towards my own bedroom door.

Jennet was standing there in a pool of moonlight.

She gave me a nod, and a small, serious smile, then disappeared.

Back in the warm sanctuary of my room, I turned on the light and unbound my precious parcel. Even in the relative softness of its protective jumper wrapping, the great book was looking extremely sorry for itself. The spine had long since disintegrated into nothing and I grimaced in disgust as the electric light brought out a family of silverfish. They scurried from the depths of the bible and I brushed them away frantically before any decided that my bed would be a good place to relocate. The front cover, now without the reinforcing strength of its back partner, hung at a skewed angle and I could see that any further investigations tonight would only serve to damage the book even further. I needed professional help, a conservator, a specialist in damp-ravaged centuries-old books, or else I would be risking making a complete hash of things and end up with a pile of mushy, unreadable pulp. There was nothing else I could do for now. I would speak to Debbie in the morning, she'd know what to do.

Linda commented on the dark shadows under my eyes at breakfast.

Couldn't sleep,' I said truthfully. 'I stayed up reading for a while.' Almost truthfully.

Alice's Halloween costume was ready to go, folded up into a carrier bag. The children were to attend lessons as normal during the morning but parents and grandparents were invited to come back at twelve o'clock to help the kids into their costumes. The party would start at twelve-thirty sharp. I waved them all off with relief, aching to crawl back into bed, but the mystery of the hidden bible intrigued me. I gave Debbie a call on her mobile.

'Leah, darling girl, I'm afraid I can't talk at the moment. I'm at work at the archives.' Debbie's strident tones echoed down the line.

'Oh, OK,' I faltered. 'Only it's probably archive stuff I need to talk to you about anyway. I've found something you definitely need to see.'

Debbie was silent for a second, then she spoke again sounding as excited as a young girl.

'Ooh, goody! I was hoping you would! Why don't you bring it here to me, you know where the Jersey Archives are, don't you?'

I didn't, but she gave me comprehensive directions, right down to what number bus I needed to get from outside our driveway, and what instructions I needed to give to the driver of said bus. Half an hour later I was standing in front of a modern white cube. I expected the archive building, its purpose being to house the island's most precious written history, to be ancient - dark and fusty - but this sleek glass and brick building was light and light-hearted. I swung through the revolving doors, clutching the bible - now wrapped in a spare bed sheet and housed in a large shopping bag - as close to me as I could without squeezing it too hard and warping its ancient shape even further. It was quiet inside and felt like a public library. The receptionist gave me a warm, friendly smile and looked at me inquisitively.

'Hi, I'm here to meet one of your volunteers. Debbie ...umm'

'Debbie Miller?' she asked brightly. I nodded.

'Oh, she's just lovely, our Debbie! I'll call up to the reading room for you.' The receptionist picked up the handset and punched in a number. 'Stuart, can you tell Debbie there's someone at reception for her please? Thanks.' She put the phone down. 'She won't be long.'

In fact, Debbie was already galloping down a glass staircase.

'Hello!' she cried, giving me a squeeze. 'And what in the name of Dickens do you have there?' She eyed the plastic package in my arms with glee.

'I found it, last night. I had some help.'

Debbie and I exchanged conspiratorial glances.

'She showed herself to you again?' Debbie breathed.

'More like she frog-marched me up some stairs, locked me in a room and smashed a wooden chest to pieces in order for me to find it,' I corrected.

'Well! What a lark! Whatever it is, it must be important. Let's have a look, I've booked a meeting room for some privacy.' Debbie led me down a short corridor.

'I think you might need some gloves, and do you use those pillow things to prop up delicate books?' I asked her, my knowledge limited to what I had seen on BBC Four history programmes by Lucy Worsley.

'Will we need all that?' Debbie replied, looking at me curiously.

'All that, and then some.'

Debbie gasped in awe as we unwrapped the bible together.

'Oh my goodness!' She breathed. 'Oh dear, it's in a right state, isn't it?'

'I found it under a cupboard in the floor,' I told her. 'It wasn't wrapped up or anything, and it was horribly damp.'

'Yes, I can see.' Debbie murmured, carefully lifting the loose front cover up. A clump of foxed pages stuck to it. 'Damn, I was hoping to be able to read the inscription inside. That way we'll know when it dates from.'

'But it's old, right?' I said.

'As old as the house in all probability,' Debbie replied. 'If the house was built in the mid sixteenth century there's a chance this could be what they call a Geneva bible, one of the first bibles to be translated into English. If it's a bit later then it could be a very early version of the King James bible, the one we're more familiar with today. I'll have to call Lisa about this.' Debbie walked to the door and asked the receptionist to find Lisa, the archive's expert paper conservator. Minutes later a lively woman with very short hair had joined us in the meeting room. She didn't bat an eyelid at the scarf covering my face, all her attention was on the broken book in front of us.

'Wow! What a find!' she exclaimed, pulling on a fresh pair of latex gloves and coming over to where the bible lay on the table in the middle of the room. 'Geneva? Early King James?

'That's what I thought,' conceded Debbie. 'But I wasn't going to try and find out, it being in this state.'

'Too bloody right,' Lisa agreed. 'I'll get my kit.' She bustled out of the room and returned with a set of tiny tweezers and scalpel blades. With perfectly steady hands, she separated the front binding from the pages sticking to it and turned the cover over to reveal the first page.

The Holy Byble. Publisher: Imprinted at London : By Christopher Barker, printer to the Queenes Majestie, 1580. The Newe Testament Of Ovr Lord Iesus Christ Publisher: London: Imprinted by Christopher Barker, 1580.

'Geneva!' both Debbie and Lisa said at the same time.

'Bloody hell! Fifteen-eighty?' I said disbelievingly.

Lisa used her tweezers to turn over another page.

Byble de la Famille Chevalier

'The Chevalier Family Bible!' we all spoke in a rush.

'Important families, and by that I mean rich important families, used to record their family histories in these bibles,' Lisa told us.

'The family tree!' Debbie and I looked at each other in excitement. 'It's got to be written in here somewhere.'

'Is that what you're after? You need the Chevalier family tree?' Lisa asked, and we both nodded.

'Leave it with me. If there is a family tree in here I'll find it for you,' she promised. 'But in the meantime, I need to get this to the scanner, pronto!' She scooped up the bible, bed sheet and all, and transferred it to a trolley lying empty in the corner of the room.

'Scanner?' I questioned. 'How the hell is she going to get that wreck through a scanner?'

'Oh, we have some fancy-schmancy, super-duper scanners here,' Debbie assured me. 'Digital. It means we can take copies of each page without having to move the book around too much. Not sure how it works, but it does.' she mused. 'And Lisa will want to make a start on conserving the binding and cover. Most covers in those days were made of calfskin leather and saving them can be quite tricky. Especially ones in that bad a state. Come on,' she held open the door of the meeting room for me. 'I'll get you a cup of what they have the cheek to call coffee in this place. We'll need it before we face the hell that is a Halloween party for five-year-olds!'

301

On the bus back I felt strangely bereft without my bed sheet and carrier bag parcel. I knew the bible was in the best possible hands, and that if there was a record of the Chevalier family hidden somewhere inside, then it was definitely of the right age to cover when Jennet had been released into Monsieur Chevalier's charge. I just hoped Lisa had some news for me soon. I was worried Jenny would make an appearance, or do something sinister, while Ian and Linda were staying at the house. I hopped off the bus at the top of the school road, pushing all thoughts of Jennet and the ruined bible firmly to the back of my mind. I was looking forward to seeing Ben, and Gracie in her black cat costume that Debbie had lovingly run up for her.

I found them both in the school hall, Ben looking bemused at being surrounded by a hundred overexcited ghosts, vampires and monsters, amongst others.

'They haven't even started on the food yet,' he warned, nodding over towards two groaning trestle tables full of sugary treats. 'And look at them!'

I spotted Alice in her costume, running around as excited as the next child.

'Wooooooooooooooooo!' she wailed, holding up her arms in true cartoon ghost fashion. There were nudges and smiles from the other parents, who didn't know quite what to make of the plastic tiara and the pirate eye patch. Gracie, looking adorable in a black leotard with a long black tail, felt pink and black ears and drawn on whiskers, followed behind her shouting 'Meow, meow, meow, meow, meow!' at the top of her voice.

'Don't they all look simply marvellous?' laughed Debbie, joining us after her shift at the archives.

Traditional Halloween games were scattered about the hall. The children could bob for apples, pin the tie on the scarecrow or dig for buried pirate treasure in the specially constructed indoor sand pit, but most of them were content to run about with their friends, comparing costumes and waving at their mums and dads.

'Oh yes, marvellous,' agreed Ben. 'How long before we can leave?'

Debbie gave him a hard poke in the ribs.

'Behave yourself, lad. It wasn't all that long ago that it was you in one of those costumes making a nuisance of yourself!'

'Yes, but I was only interested in the biscuits.'

'Yes, you were certainly a chunky little thing!' Debbie laughed. 'Did Leah tell you about her find today?' she asked, changing the subject.

'No, I haven't had a chance yet. I was just about to.' I said, but before I could elaborate we were distracted by a commotion on the other side of the hall. Alice had ripped off her ghost costume and stood there, arms crossed and with a huge scowl on her face, shouting at someone we couldn't yet see behind the other parents who had grouped in to watch the entertainment.

'NO! No, I don't want you here!' Alice yelled, stamping her feet.

Oh no, here we go again, I thought, remembering the showdown at the zoo back before school started. Someone must have replied to her because she clenched her fists tightly and bared her teeth.

'GO AWAY! Daddy, tell him to go away!' she cried. I saw Matt for the first time then. He too was standing with his fists clenched and his face was a white mask of anger. Ian and Linda were standing helplessly to the side with Noah, their confusion evident. There was a shift in the audience and it was then that I saw Jayne, with Gabriel beside her. I broke away from Debbie and Ben and rushed to Matt's side.

'Jayne, what are you doing here?' I asked her.

'I just wanted to see my little girl in her costume,' she croaked, embarrassed at all the attention.

'You should have asked me,' Matt said through his gritted teeth. 'And you shouldn't have brought him.'

Gabriel smiled his smooth, oily smile and moved closer to Jayne, putting his hand possessively on her shoulder.

'I'm afraid we come as a package deal these days, Matthew old chum,' he smirked.

'GO AWAY!' shouted Alice again, directing her fury at Gabriel. 'I don't WANT you here!'

'That's not the way we speak to grown-ups, Alice,' chided Jayne softly.

'I don't CARE!' roared Alice. 'I hate him! And I hate you!' She started to cry.

'Alice, baby...,' Jayne put out her hand to her daughter but Alice batted her away. Turning to Gabriel, Alice narrowed her eyes and looked directly into his.

'You're going to be dead soon anyway,' she told him. 'Why can't you hurry up and be dead and then my Mummy will come back to live with us again.'

'Whoa, little bunny,' I eased myself forward through the crowd. 'Rein it in. You can't go around telling people they're going to die!' I whispered furiously to her. Already I could hear the scandalised rumblings and murmurs from the group of parents who were witness to this debacle.

'Yes I can!' she said defiantly. 'Anyway, it's true. Jenny told me.'

'Jenny told you what?' I asked.

Alice continued staring Gabriel in the eye.

'Jenny told me that Gabriel will die, his head's going to be cut off.'

There was a shocked collective intake of breath from everyone around us. I watched as Gabriel attempted to look unconcerned, but I could see him pale slightly underneath his tan.

'Well, that wouldn't be very convenient now, would it?' He looked around at the group. 'Not now that I'm going to be a daddy myself,' he went on smugly. 'Jayne and I are expecting a baby!'

The room burst into excited chatter, no one was even bothering to try and pretend they weren't hanging on to every word anymore.

'Jayne, is this true?' demanded Linda. 'Are you pregnant?' Jayne at least had the grace to look ashamed and she nodded miserably.

'This isn't how I wanted you to find out,' she implored, turning to face Matt. At the mention of Jayne's pregnancy his face had closed off completely, and he stood stock still.

'Aren't you going to congratulate us?' Gabriel mocked lightly. At that, Matt sprung at him like a wounded bear, knocking Gabriel off his feet and sending them both sprawling to the ground. Several of the male teachers, who had been quite happily watching the drama up until then, rushed forward to separate the two brawling men. Ian put a restraining arm on his son's wrist.

'Now's not the time, son,' he suggested. 'We'll talk about it at home, eh?' Matt shrugged off his father's grip without a word and stalked out of the hall. I knelt down beside Alice, expecting more tears but instead saw that she had a small satisfied smile on her face.

'Did you see that?' she crowed. 'Daddy knocked him down!'

Gabriel was standing up again by this point and he made a big show of shooting his cuffs and patting down his hair, before putting his hand on Jayne's back to usher her out of the hall. Alice broke away from me and marched up to him. She pointed at his head.

'Dead, dead, dead ,dead,' she chanted. 'You're going to be dead.' She made a big chopping motion with her hand and laughed cruelly. 'Chop, chop, chop, chop, chop off your big fat head!'

'Alice, that's enough!' I admonished. She smiled that disturbing smile again and I suddenly realised where I had seen it before. It was the same spiteful twist I had seen on

305

Jenny's face last night. 'Come on,' I took her hand, 'I think the party's over.'
Debbie and Ben came rushing up to us.

'Are you OK?' Ben looked at me with concern.

'Eeeeeeeee! That was better than Coronation Street!' squealed Debbie. 'You don't half have some drama in your life, Leah my girl!'

CHAPTER TWENTY-SIX

At home, the atmosphere was strained. Only Alice and Noah carried on oblivious to the tension between Matt and his parents.

'Come and look at my laptop,' I cajoled Linda. 'I've got the Jersey Heritage website up. You can have a look at where you want to take the kids tomorrow.'

She looked at me sharply.

'Did you know?' she lowered her voice and hissed at me. 'Did you know that little madam was pregnant with another man's baby?

'Linda, I swear I didn't. It was as much of a shock for me as it was for you. I've only just found out about the affair. Matt kept it to himself for ages.'

'I don't blame him! Being made a fool of like that, you can tell it's damaged the children already. What was Alice going on about today - talking about chopping people's heads off?' she snorted derisively. 'Not that I would be sorry to see that happen to that nasty little prick!' She caught my look of surprise. 'Oh, I know he's my cousin and all that, but he always was a self-satisfied little arsehole!'

'Well, it's certainly been a hard time for Matt,' I said diplomatically. 'He must be glad you're both here.'

Linda softened a fraction.

'He's never really opened up to us about what went wrong,' she said sadly. 'They seemed so happy when they were living in London, even though they almost never saw each other and had no money between them.'

'Matt sold the London house. Without Jayne knowing,' I admitted. 'She hated it here, in this house. She was desperate to go back but Matt's obsessed with this place, and wouldn't hear a word of it.'

'Sold the London ...!' Linda gasped. 'Well, I never! He hasn't told us that yet.' She sat down heavily.

'Sometimes I wish he'd never inherited this place. I tried to talk Pierre out of it, but he was that set on it. Oh, he was a nutcase too, was Pierre! Kept going on about how it had to be Matthew who inherited, how the so-called Chevalier curse was still killing off the family. That's how he put it! Killing off the family.'

I chewed my lip, debating internally whether to open up to Linda and tell her about Jenny, about what we had found out so far, but she took a deep breath and stood up again, grabbing the cloth from the kitchen sink and swiping furiously at the taps.

'It's all nonsense, of course. I grew up with tales of that bloody family curse.' She battered the cloth angrily over the windowsill. 'Even when my brother died, they blamed that ridiculous curse. They couldn't just accept that Matthieu died of leukaemia...'

'Matthew?' My head shot up at the mention of Matt's name.

'Yes, my brother Matthieu. Died when he was fifteen. Matt's named after him.'

'Oh,' I said. 'I'm sorry to hear that.'

'It was a long time ago,' she sighed.

Alice came bounding into the kitchen, wearing her Halloween costume again.

'Take that thing off!' Linda flapped her hand at Alice. 'And come and tell me what all that fuss was about at the party.'

'What fuss?' Alice asked, grabbing her juice pouch from the table and taking a big, theatrical slurp.

'All that shouting at Uncle Gabriel and telling him he was going to get his head chopped off!' admonished Linda. 'Where on earth did you get such an idea?'

I crossed my fingers and prayed for Alice not to bring up Jenny's name.

'I don't like Uncle Gabriel. He took my Mummy away,' pouted Alice.

'I know it must seem like that,' I told her gently. 'But it's not that simple. There's a lot of grown-up stuff going on that Mummy and Daddy are trying to work through OK? And Nana's right - it wasn't nice to tell Gabriel that he was going to get his head chopped off.'

'But it's in the book!' protested Alice.

'What book?'

'The book Nana gave me yesterday. The queen doesn't like people and she says "off with his head!" and they get their heads chopped off.' Alice made the chopping motion with her hands. Linda tapped her palm to her forehead.

'Of course!' she muttered. 'Alice's Adventures in Wonderland. I gave her the picture book yesterday. That's where she got the idea from.'

'Well, I'm glad we cleared that up,' I said, relieved.

'Did you like my song? I made dead and head rhyme,' Alice chattered happily. 'And did you see Daddy knock Uncle Gabriel to the floor? That was BRILLIANT! And anyway, he WILL be dead soon, Jenny told me.'

'That's enough, Alice,' Linda warned. 'Now, come and see on Leah's computer where you want us to go tomorrow.'

The weekend was mercifully quiet. Ian and Linda would bundle up both children early in the morning and take them off in the car they'd hired for the week, bringing them both back tired, fractious and clutching a new toy or game each day. Matt disappeared into the other wing almost as soon as he'd finished breakfast. He had hardly spoken since the incident at the party and his face was grey with stress and fatigue. Thankfully, Jenny had been quiet, and there had been no ghostly crying in the night. Everything remained where it was supposed to be in the flat, nothing was moved or broken and Matt had no more screwdrivers thrown at him.

That's not to say she wasn't there.

I could still feel her presence at night, hear the swish of her skirt or the metallic clunk of her chains. When I had to get up in the night to go to the bathroom, I would catch a glimpse of her reflected in my bathroom mirror. Just a flash and then she was gone, but I felt that she was waiting for something and her patience was wearing thin.

I had to be patient too, and I knew I would not hear from Lisa at the archives about the bible until the working week began again, so I took advantage of having time to myself and spent my days with Ben and Gracie. Together we roamed the island, climbing the vast concrete fortifications left behind by the German Occupation and exploring the many woodlands and cliff paths. The raw beauty of the Jersey coastline took my breath away and I never tired of walking along the golden sands of St Ouen's bay, Gracie swinging on one hand and Ben firmly holding the other. Even as October turned into November, the good weather held and we would finish each walk with an ice cream, sitting on the sand dunes and looking out to sea, comfortable in each other's company. These days out put a fresh glow on my cheeks and a sparkle in my eyes that had been missing for a long, long time.

'Your scar's definitely fading already,' Ben told me, smoothing away a lock of stray hair from my cheek. 'It's not as pink as it was.'

'It must be Debbie's magic potion,' I laughed. I had been using the homemade remedy faithfully, rubbing it on my scar twice a day and enjoying the pleasant tingle it left on my skin. 'Maybe I won't need the laser treatment after all.'

'Aw, I'm going to miss that cute little bunny!' he teased and I swatted his arm.

'Hmmm, I definitely won't!'

When I got home on Sunday evening, the chill of the autumn air was just beginning to make me feel cold, and I was looking forward to a hot shower and some Netflix. I let myself in the main door and stepped over a new pile of planks that had appeared on the floor.

'Trip hazard!' I yelled in Matt's direction. He was still working and I could hear him whistling along to a song on the radio. The wood had been placed across the hall and blocked the way to my flat door. 'Oh, bollocks,' I grumbled. I would have to go through into the flat and get to my room that way. As I swished through the plastic sheeting, I heard a low keening sound, and found Linda crouched on the lounge floor with Noah in her arms.

'Linda, what's wrong?' I knelt down beside her, looking Noah over for any obvious injuries. Apart from being red-faced and grumpy, he looked fine. Linda was still moaning and clutching Noah far too tightly, rocking him in time with her cries. I held her shoulders and tried to make her sit up. Noah was wriggling to be set free and, as he twisted in her arms, I saw the livid red line marking his throat. 'Oh my God, what happened to him?' I demanded.

'I... I ... I..,' Linda stuttered.

'Take a deep breath,' I instructed her. 'Calm down and tell me what's going on.'

'I put him down for his nap, like usual,' Linda whispered. 'Then I went to the kitchen to get something organised for dinner. I had the baby monitor with me, and Noah looked like he was going to go straight to sleep.' She looked at me, her face ravaged by horror and she looked like she'd aged ten years. 'The baby monitor, I heard a noise. It was unholy, like nothing I'd ever heard in my life before. A kind of a growling, gibbering babble that got louder and louder, and then I thought I heard the word "baby".' She shook her head as if hearing it again. 'I ran to his room as fast as I could. I was thinking all sorts of things, like maybe a wild dog had got in and was attacking him, but when I got to him ...,' she broke off, unable to speak again.

I rubbed her arm sympathetically as she choked the rest of the story out. 'When I got to him, he was... hanging. He was all tangled up in the cords of the blind on the window and he had managed to get it stuck around his neck and he was being strangled! Oh, Leah, I've never moved so fast in my life! He was struggling and turning blue and I just lifted him up and pulled the cord away from his neck. He went all floppy and I thought he was dead!' She burst into sobs again. I let her cry, passing her the box of tissues from the coffee table.

'But he's not dead,' I soothed. 'Look, he's perfectly fine.'

'That's not all.' Linda blew her nose. 'I was there, in the room holding Noah over my shoulder and jiggling him up and down and trying to get him to breathe... and I saw her.'

'Who?' I went cold, knowing what she was about to say.

'The witch. The ghost, or whatever. She was standing in the corner of the room looking at me, and I knew it was her I had heard on the monitor.' Linda shivered. 'It was only for a second, and then she disappeared.'
My skin crawled in fear.

'You think... you think it was her?' I said. 'You think she tried to kill Noah?'
Linda shook her head emphatically.

'No, no, that's just the thing,' she stressed. 'She didn't try to hurt Noah, she saved him! Look, come with me and I'll show you.'
We stood up shakily and Noah lifted his arms for me to pick him up. I tried not to see the hurt on Linda's face that he wanted me, and not her. Linda led the way to Noah's room.

'The cot's been moved!' I said. 'It's all the way over by the window now.'
Linda looked shamefaced.

'That was me,' she admitted. 'I moved his cot over so he could be nearer to the fresh air. I never gave a thought about the blind.' She took Noah from me and put him in his cot. He immediately pulled himself up by the bars so that he was standing and then we watched in disbelief as he hauled himself up even further, using the side of the cot to climb as high as the windowsill. He leant over and made a grab for the cord of the window blind where it dangled freely, pulling it towards him and looking back at us with pride at his own cleverness.

'He did it himself,' I realised. 'He climbed up and grabbed the cord and probably fell, with the cord around his neck.'

'Yes,' agreed Linda. 'And it's my fault, entirely my fault. If I hadn't moved his cot he wouldn't have been able to reach it.' She rescued Noah from repeating the accident again and he howled, kicking his legs unhappily. 'And if she hadn't made such a racket over the baby monitor it would have been too late. She didn't try to hurt him, she saved him!' Linda said again and met my eyes. 'When she looked at me, she had such pity on her face. Oh, her poor, poor face. You know, I never believed in the stories about a witch haunting this house; but I think I may have to now.'

Jennet's Story

Jersey 1603

Hey-la, but I run ahead of myself. You want to know about the trials, Sister.

As I say, I did not know of the depth of Matthieu's betrayal then. I just knew that he was dead and my own heart stopped beating then anyway. His father came to see me after I was returned to the oubliette, Sister, did I tell you?

I was here, cradling my poor scalded arms as best I could and trying to drift away from the pain, when they came for me again. I knew that they had condemned me to death but I did not realise the sentence would be carried out so quickly, and when they called my name I thought that I was going to be taken out and burnt, then and there.

Instead I was taken to a room here in the castle, a fine room with warm rugs and a roaring fire. There was wine on the table and the remains of a good meal on the pewter plates. I stared at them hungrily and did not notice the man sat in the studded leather chair at first. The guard escorting me threw me down on the floor and I gasped when my damaged hands hit the flagstones. The man stood up and slowly walked towards me, putting his foot on my shoulder to stop me from getting up.
'Is this her, the witch?' I heard him ask.
The guard must have agreed for I heard the man grunt in disgust.
'Where is my son?' he asked me, pronouncing his words loudly and slowly, as if I were a simpleton. I was so dazed from the fire in my arms that I did not realise it was me he was speaking to at first, and therefore said nothing.

'Where is my son?' he asked again, louder this time. I looked up at him fearfully.

'I do not know,' I whispered.

He bent closer to me, wrinkling his nose at the stench of me. He clutched my face in one huge hand and squeezed it painfully.

'I will ask you once more,' he said patiently. 'Where is my son?' And he hooked his finger under my top lip and pulled hard.

Oh, the pain of it, Sister! The room went white and I was near to faint. He pulled and twisted so my lip was stretched to far beyond its natural shape. I squirmed and screamed but he held me fast with his other hand. All I could do was to try not to pull away and make the pain worse. He let his finger drop and I could see blood on it. More blood pooled in my mouth and I swallowed it down, along with my salty tears.

I was condemned to death anyway. There was nothing more they could do to me.

'Your son is dead,' I told him, looking him in the eye and holding his gaze.

'Nay, he is alive!' Gabriel Chevalier roared in anger. 'He boarded a ship to France, the same day you were taken up. We know that much.' He slapped me around the face hard. 'Where is he? What were his plans? Was he coming back for you or were you to join him later?'

'Your son is dead,' I repeated. 'He took a dagger to the eye and he lies rotting at the bottom of the channel.'

He gave a mighty bellow and hit me again.

'You say wrong!' he shouted.

'I say true!' I insisted. 'You have had me convicted as a witch and I tell you, this is what my witch's eyes show me. I saw your son, on my way to my trial. I saw him standing at the crossroads when I was being dragged past behind the cart. He would not look at me, but I saw the blade in his eye and knew him to be dead, I knew him for a spirit. He would not look at me because he is as much a coward in death as he was in life!' I spat.

He clenched his hand into a fist and punched me hard on the side of my head. The room went dark.

Oh, I know, Sister. I digress again, I am sorry.

The trials, yes. You may have noticed, Sister, how reluctant I am to talk about them but I am at this part in my story now and I must describe the torments they put me through.

When the cart finally stopped, I was on my knees, being dragged behind it. My feet were worn through and the guard had long given up on whipping me as it no longer encouraged me to stand up and walk. They took me to the market square, in the centre of St Helier, and struck my chains free from the cart, at once shackling the heavy iron manacles around my feet again. The crowds had followed me from the roadsides and stood, five deep, jeering me and waiting for the Bailiff to open the court. They had taken rooms above the inn, the Bailiff and his chosen men who were to hear the evidence against me, and I was escorted there without so much as a drink of water to clear my parched throat. The favoured few, the fine lords and ladies who were there for the entertainment, and the village folk who had a claim to make against me, shrank back in exaggerated fear and horror as I was dragged into the room. I was not allowed a stool to sit on, instead I had to endure tall tale after tall tale of my witchery and devilment whilst standing on my torn and ragged feet. In truth, I did not listen to most of it. The tales were all similar in their damning of me. I was too thirsty and too lost in the misery of knowing Matthieu was dead, to take much notice of the villager's accounts. The fog only lifted when I heard Matthieu's name mentioned, and it was then that I learned the true depth of his betrayal. He decried me as a witch to save his own skin and left me behind without so much as another thought.

The Bailiff banged his hammer on the table in front of him and the court fell silent.

'Jennet Pyke, you have been brought here today to answer to these accusations of theft, witchcraft and diabolical doings. They number so greatly that there is no sense in continuing with this trial. However, I am obliged by the laws of this island to bring a fair judgement and, as such, I am committing you to the Holy Trinity trials. You will be tried by holy cross, by water and by fire, in that order, one after the other and before the good people of this town.'

There was an outcry in the courtroom, clapping and cheering and excited whispers. No one had ever been committed to all three trials before, and certainly not all at the same time, to be carried out in succession. This was unheard of. Any one of the trials would have been sufficient to secure a judgement of guilty; to have me undergo all three was unnecessary and unduly cruel.

They began straight away. The trial by cross, Sister, is considered the most gentle of trials, usually reserved for neighbourly disputes and arguments between husbands and wives. My hands were unchained and I was bid to stand in the centre of the room, arms up and outstretched and my feet together, in the shape of the holy cross on which our Lord Jesus died. I was not allowed to move my feet, my shoulders nor shift my weight from one foot to the other. I was to stand perfectly still. If I could hold this position for one full day and one hour, I would be judged to have God on my side. They set an old crone to watch me carefully while the court went in to dine. She was armed with a long pointed stick, and told to poke me if I should so much as slump a little. This she did with great vigour. I stood in that position for what felt like hours. I could feel the lice in my hair moving *about, and flies had come to feast on the bloody gashes on my back.*

That was my downfall, Sister. The itching. I tried so hard, Sister. I prayed and prayed as I was standing there, beseeching God to give me the strength and patience to endure, but I failed after less than two hours. I could not take the feel of flies on my flesh, their legs crawling over me and the tickling of their wings. I moaned and dropped my arms, surrendering to the itching and reaching behind me to swat at the horrid creatures. The old crone screeched and almost fell off her stool in her hurry to tell the Bailiff, and I was dragged out of the room and into the brightness of the market square to the second trial.

The trial by water, it sounds so innocent, does it not? You may be forgiven for thinking this trial is similar to the pool dunkings given to other women accused of witchcraft, Sister, but you would be gravely mistaken.

My skin shrivelled in fear as soon as I saw the fire. I knew it would soon be me on those flames, but for this time they brought out a large iron kettle and hoisted it above the centre of the blaze. The kettle was filled to the brim with water and it steamed gently as they brought it to the boil. A cast iron weight, borrowed from the weighbridge and used to weigh sacks of grain I believe, was lowered in to the bottom of the kettle. It weighed nine pounds, they whispered amongst themselves, the correct weight for such a trial as this. I knew I would struggle to lift a nine pound weight with one hand, let alone retrieve it from the bottom of a boiling pot of water. I think I was crying by now, in fear at the pain to come, but even if I had thrown myself on the ground and confessed to all the charges against me, they still would have me endure this trial. It was a show now, an entertainment for the townsfolk, and a warning to other women, women who walked a different path to others and who, in consequence, found themselves outcast from society.

The water was boiling rapidly now and the Bailiff gave the signal for me to begin. Once more I prayed to the God who had failed me so many times before. Taking a deep breath and turning my face from the spitting, rolling water, I plunged my hand in deep.

The pain did not strike me at first. I stretched my fingers wide, searching for the loop on top on the iron weight. I had to stand up on my broken toes to reach the bottom of the kettle and they were perilous close to the burning wood.

'This is just a taste of things to come, eh witch?' a man yelled at me harshly. 'So you will know what it feels like to burn!' The crowd laughed at his wit.

All at once my hand and arm caught fire. I howled at the agony of it and scrabbled in the water, my fingers just brushing the top of the weight but never grabbing hold of it. In desperation, I stepped into the fire to be closer to the kettle. The crowd roared its appreciation at the sight of my bloodied foot beginning to smoke, but the baying soon turned to groans of disappointment as I hooked two fingers around the iron loop and heaved with all of my strength. The weight came up out of the water more easily than I thought and I hauled it free of the kettle, dropping it on the ground in front of me. My arm and hand had turned dark red and I could see the skin beginning to split in places. The cooler air outside of the water made the pain even more torturous and I still had to lift the weight back up again and carry it a length of nine feet in order to complete the trial.

How I managed it, Sister, I will never know. I was still in ankle chains, remember, and they swung heavily and slowed me down greatly. No, Sister, I do not believe it was God who gave me the strength. It was at those trials that I stopped believing in God.

I crumpled, exhausted and in unimaginable pain, just across the line chalked on the cobbled ground of the market, the line that marked the nine feet distance. The Bailiff lifted his hand and gave the order that my hand and arm were to be bound tightly. It would be unbound in three days' time to look for the signs of corruption that would mean I was in league with the Devil. They wrapped my arm in a filthy piece of cloth, making sure to give it a good, hard squeeze as they did so, and the crowd relished the screams that I gave.

But my ordeal was not yet over, Sister.

The last trial, the trial by fire, was exactly the same as the trial by water except this time I had to lift the weight from the centre of the fire. The blaze had been left to burn down until it was white-hot, and the iron weight was glowing red by the time the Bailiff gave the order to begin. Using my other hand, and my other foot to step into the fire, I did pluck the weight from the fire quickly, and hobbled as fast as I could towards the nine-foot line. My hand seared and the smell of roasting flesh coiled up from my smoking body.

'Roast rabbit! Roast rabbit!' the crowd chanted, and one small boy was dared by his friends to run forward and stick out his leg to trip me up. I stumbled, and dropped the weight a mere foot from the line, and thus failed the trial.

I lay on my back on the cold cobblestones, barely breathing, staring up at the sky. My arms no longer felt like a part of my body. Someone rushed forward and bound my other arm tightly, too tightly. Someone else threw a bucket of cold water over me to revive me. I opened my mouth to take in as much of the gloriously cold liquid as I could. I felt myself rising up. I was floating away, above the heads of the jeering, jostling hordes. A woman screamed. I could see myself lying there far below and wondered why she had screamed. Another bucket of water was thrown over me and the shocked mutterings from the crowd grew louder.

Someone pointed at me and I fell back into my body with a jolt. They knew. They could see it clearly now and they were sickened at the sin that they had collectively committed. The water had drenched what was left of my dress and it clung wetly to my stomach. Without the material to hide it, the bump was pronounced and it stood out clear and proud from my starving frame.

It is against the law to put a woman with child through the trials, Sister. This is the secret I have tried for so long to keep hidden, Sister. The one you still have not seen and guessed for yourself.

I am carrying Matthieu's baby.

CHAPTER TWENTY-SEVEN

Leah

'Leah, we've got something!' Debbie's eager voice greeted me as I answered my phone.

'Oh my God, has Lisa called?'

Debbie was not working at the archives this week as she was taking care of Gracie for the half-term holiday while Ben was at work, but she had elicited a promise from Lisa to phone her the minute she found anything of interest in the bible.

'Yes, and it's something all right! Do you want to meet me at the archives again? I'll have to bring Gracie but she'll be fine with Toni on reception - she likes to help.'

'Yes, of course! I'll be there as soon as I can catch the bus,' I promised. I danced around my room in excitement and got ready in record time.

'I'm just out to meet Debbie for a while,' I said to Matt. He was working on deconstructing a nasty seventies' kitchen, having finally knocked through the last dividing wall in the great hall.

'Watch out!' he warned, as I skirted past a tower of wood-veneered cabinets. 'There's a lot of broken glass panels in there. Why anyone ever thought that a combination of fake mahogany and glass shelving made a nice feature, I don't know. Where are you off too then?' he asked me. It was good to see him more cheerful. He was making real progress on the ground floor of this wing of the house, and the hard work took his mind off Jayne, and her pregnancy with Gabriel.

'The archives. We've found some more records on Jennet,' I lied. I hadn't told him about finding the bible in the empty flat upstairs. In theory, the book belonged to Matt, and I didn't want to show him until we'd discovered everything we could about the history of the Chevalier family. Matt had every right to refuse to let us examine the bible and, after his brush with Jennet, he just might. By unspoken agreement, Linda and I had not mentioned the real reason for the bruising on Noah's throat to Matt. Linda simply brushed it off as an accident, a jumper that was too tight and got caught up around the boy's neck, but she had dealt with it quickly and thrown the too-small jumper away, she assured him.

I met Debbie and Gracie in the car park at the archives and we walked into the reception area, bursting with curiosity and in a fever of anticipation.

'Is it what I think it is?' I said.

'Lisa said as much on the phone,' Debbie confirmed. 'She said she'd never seen anything like it before.'

Lisa came through from her conservation lab as soon as she heard we were there.

'Ladies, be prepared to be blown away!' She led us into the humidity and temperature controlled room. The great bible was on a stainless steel table, propped up on a wedge of varnished wood, with acid-free tissue paper separating each fragile page. 'It was a few pages in,' Lisa explained. 'That's why it looked like a lump of pages stuck together.'

'Is it the family tree?' I held my breath, taken aback by the beauty of the delicately painted frieze of flowers and leaves that decorated the edge of the bible's interior pages.

'Yes, but not like one I've ever seen.' Lisa slowly peeled away the tissue covering the centre of the page.

'Is that it?' I asked with disappointment. It looked like a badly folded piece of brown paper, the kind you might see covering a parcel.

'Wait and see,' instructed Lisa, as she took up a tiny pair of tweezers and levered the first layer of paper open. It unfolded like a flower. Then she moved on to the sheet underneath and it did the same. She continued tweezering

323

and carefully unfolding until we were left with the final piece, the original page in the bible. Piece upon piece of parchment, so thin I could see through it, had been laid on top of each other so cleverly that when they were folded out they formed a large map, like a patchwork quilt. It was like a huge, elaborate origami sculpture.

'You can see where the later pieces were added,' Lisa said. 'The paper is thicker, of a better quality. The ones at the bottom of the pile are of a very fine parchment but they've been protected by the layers of newer paper on top of them.'

'It's beautiful,' said Debbie reverently.

'The sheets are gummed together, probably using some kind of animal glue. Some of the edges are quite damaged where the glue has dried out and degraded the composition of the paper,' Lisa went on. 'This is one of the most comprehensive family trees I've ever worked on. They went to great trouble to detail every single branch of the tree, and when they ran out of room, they simply glued another piece of paper onto the side and carried on.'

'Can we see where it begins?' I asked, and Lisa nodded.

'The first entries were written directly into the bible itself. It was common practice at this time for a family bible to have a page or two dedicated to recording the births and deaths in the family.' Lisa laid tissue over the unfolded sections so that they were protected as we leaned over to read the earliest page.

Henri Leonidas Louis de Chevalier   *b.1531 d.1585*
M.   Marguerite Marie Barteau   *b.1545 d.1581*

'Wow, it's so old!' I breathed and Lisa laughed.

'We have older examples here at the archive, but I suppose it does make you think - people were writing in this book almost five hundred years ago.'

We traced the branches, not daring to touch the brittle parchment.

'We know Jennet was fourteen when she was in Mont Orgueil in 1603,' Debbie said. 'We need to look for the Chevaliers who could have conceivably been the sons of the lord of the manor at that time, and similar in age to Jennet.'

We didn't have far to look.

The first Chevaliers, Henri and Marguerite, had had four sons and three daughters, two of which died in infancy. The eldest son lived to inherit the house and title from his father. Gabriel Chevalier - I flinched at reading that name - was born in 1552 and married an Agathé Dussault in 1571. They had two sons and a daughter in quick succession, followed by another son some twelve years later. Tragically, Agathé had died the same year as her youngest son was born in 1587, and Gabriel Chevalier had not married again.

'Look at this,' Debbie exclaimed in wonder. 'This Gabriel Chevalier lived until 1611 so he must be the man that was mentioned in the prison records, the one Jennet was released into the care of.'

'Unless it was one of his sons,' I suggested. We bent over to read the tiny writing.

'No, it couldn't have been. See, his sons all died before Jennet was taken from Mont Orgueil. Guillaume in 1602, Jeanne in 1602 as well...' I paused, reading the name of the last son and feeling a cold sickness in my stomach. '... and Matthieu, in 1603.'

'Matthieu!' Debbie looked up at me in shock, 'Do you think ...?'
Lisa wasn't aware of the significance of the name or our loaded silence, and she continued to decipher the line of succession.

'They all died without issue,' she said. 'Agnes, the daughter, was married off at fourteen so she would have

325

taken another family name. If all of his sons died without having children, there would have been no one to inherit.'

'But there's another branch here, look, underneath Matthieu's name.' I pointed to where a line had been drawn from below Matthieu's date of birth and death. 'He had a son, in 1603, the same year he died!'

'Who with?' Debbie frowned. 'There's no record of marriage next to him.'

'There might be.' Lisa had her trusty tweezers out again and she gently drew them across the sepia-coloured parchment next to where Matthieu was listed, barely touching the page. A tiny scrap of paper, completely unnoticeable up until now, fluttered open and folded out. It was no bigger than a ten pence piece and was glued fast to the bible page. On it, another line had been marked next to Matthieu's name indicating, if not a marriage, then a relationship which had resulted in a child. The paper joined up with the line underneath, to Matthieu's' son, Edouard.

'What else does it say?' I demanded impatiently. 'Who was Edouard's mother?' I couldn't see the whole scrap of paper under Lisa's careful hands.

'Nothing,' Lisa said in surprise. 'It has nothing on it. Just a question mark.'

'It HAS to be her.'
Debbie and I had collected Gracie and were watching her play on the swings at the nearby park. 'It makes perfect sense. If Jennet is the mother of Matthieu's baby, and Gabriel Chevalier lost all of his own sons, then that baby would be his only heir.'
'You think he took Jennet out of prison to the house so she could have the baby safely?' I asked. 'If so, why was she put in the same room as a bunch of dead meat? And what happened to her afterwards?'
'You've told me you've all heard a new-born crying in the night, and Alice said Jenny is still looking for her baby. Don't

forget she was still a convicted witch and under a sentence of death. Maybe Gabriel Chevalier sent her back to Mont Orgueil as soon as she'd given birth and kept the baby for himself; as his grandson it would have been the only way to carry on the family line.'

Debbie's mobile rang and she excused herself to answer it. I went over to Gracie.

'Fancy a go on the slide?'

She grinned and jumped off her swing, running across the grass to where the yellow and red animal-themed slides waited for her.

'Watch me, Leah!' She climbed the dozen steps to the top of the metal chute and swung her legs into a sitting position. 'Wheeeeeeeee!' She slid all the way down and landed with a bump on the padded mat at the bottom.

'Watch me again!' she commanded, as she ran around to the steps again.

'I'm watching.'

Debbie walked towards us, a thoughtful look on her face.

'Do you mind going back to see Lisa again? She's discovered something else, something very strange indeed.'

Gracie was delighted to be heading back to the archives.

'I'm a good helper, Toni said I was. She lets me put the stamps on the envelopes and I'm allowed to say hello to the people coming in.'

'It's not too boring for you?' I asked her.

'No way! This is the best day ever! I like it when I'm with you and Aunty Debbie, Leah.'

I squeezed her hand and smiled down at her, unbelievably touched at her easy acceptance of me.

'I like being with you too, Gracie.'

'What is it? What have you found?' Debbie and I were being escorted back to Lisa's lab.

'This is the gift that keeps on giving!' joked Lisa. 'Honestly, I know I asked you to come back and take a look at something, but since then another mystery has come to light as well.' She led us back to the brightly lit table. 'I was working on the covers, checking out the damage to the bindings and the spine. And I found this.'

A sheet of parchment lay unfolded on its own dedicated tray. A rough beige colour, it had darker brown creases across its centre where it had been folded a number of times. The writing, in ink which must have once been black but now faded to a burnt umber, was almost illegible and in a language I didn't recognise.

'What is it?'

'As far as I can tell, it's a letter of some sort,' Lisa explained. 'It's written in an unusual mix of Latin and old French. something we usually only see in ecclesiastical writings.'

'Like from a church?'

'Sometimes. Or from an abbey or a monastery. Well-educated sons and daughters of good families who went into the church would have used this particular style of language in their correspondence.'

'Can you read what it says?'

'Not really. I've taken a digital copy and I've got someone trying to enhance it now. It's in pretty bad shape, I don't think we'll be able to read all of it. I've sent it to be translated as well.' Lisa paused, gazing at the letter with an indecipherable look on her face. 'I could make out the odd word though, just from having a quick look. There's a name mentioned several times.' Lisa put on her glasses. 'Look, here. And here again. Jennet Pyke.'

We'd barely recovered from that bombshell when Lisa told us about the other mystery that was bothering her.

'I was following the family tree, trying to see when the last entry was. It was in the mid eighteen-hundreds by the way, then it just stops.'

I thought back to when I was leafing through Pierre's handwritten notes on the writing pad I found in one of the stored boxes. He had attempted to chart the Chevalier family tree, starting with his own birth and tracking backwards. He'd stopped during the 1880's. Was he trying to continue the records, to join it up at the place where the bible had stopped?

'That was at the same time the name of the house was changed to The Grange,' Debbie noted. 'I wonder if that was when this bible was hidden away?'

'It could definitely be possible, given the poor condition it's in,' remarked Lisa. 'Anyway, I noticed something weird about the lines of succession. I know it's hard keeping up with all the family names, this family liked to use the same names for their children and grandchildren, so I made some notes to make it easier - and to be sure of what I was seeing.'

She showed us her findings, written in pencil on a wire-bound notebook. 'OK, taken from where we were looking before, late sixteenth/early seventeenth century, every Chevalier who was descended from that direct line and who was named Matthieu, has died young, and without an heir. And every single Gabriel Chevalier has had a son who either died in infancy or childhood.'

I froze in horror, remembering Linda telling me about the curse, the one that killed off the family as she put it. Remembering how she told me about her brother dying of leukaemia at fifteen, her brother called Matthieu.

'That's bizarre!' burst out Debbie. Lisa shrugged.

'I know, but we're trained to look for patterns, Debbie. You know that. And, well, this pattern jumped out at me almost instantaneously.'

We followed the generations of Chevaliers through the centuries. Lisa was right, and her written notes were impeccable.

Matthieu Chevalier   b.1625 d.1635, died aged 10
Matthieu Chevalier   b.1644 d.1660, died aged 16
Matthieu Chevalier   b.1661 d.1661, Stillborn?
Matthieu Chevalier   b. 1669 d.1672, died aged 3

The list went on and on. On the opposite side of the notepad, Lisa had documented the Gabriel's of the family.

Gabriel Chevalier - son - b.1623 d.1623, Stillborn?
Gabriel Chevalier - son - b.1652 d.1652, Stillborn?
Gabriel Chevalier - son - b.1677 d. 1678, died aged 1
Gabriel Chevalier - son - b.1701 d. 1704, died aged 3

Lisa had followed the direct line of succession from the first Gabriel Chevalier, the one who we suspected of holding Jennet prisoner in the Witch Room, and traced it right up to where the records ended. Not a single Chevalier bearing the name of Matthieu had lived past thirty years of age, and not a single Gabriel Chevalier had escaped the tragedy of losing a son, sometimes two, in the entire family tree.

'But what does this mean?' puzzled Debbie.
'It means the curse is real,' I said grimly. 'But Matt, our Matt, is thirty-two and he's OK, he isn't dead and he's got two children.'
Debbie didn't need to voice the rest of what I was thinking.
Matt wasn't dead – not yet.

Jennet's Story

Jersey 1603

Sister, you have come back!

In truth, I did not think you would, after I confessed my secret to you on your last visit.

But what is this? Why do the guards call my name?

What is happening, Sister?

I am to go with these guards, they tell me to stand up so they can unlock my chains from the rings in the walls. But I do not understand why they are taking me.

Is it to be now? Is it today I am to be burned? Oh, Sister, I am so frightened! I am not ready! But what about the babe inside me? They cannot put me to death with the babe still inside me, for it is an innocent life, and they would be committing murder if they put us both on the pyre.

Sister, pray for me in the hour of my death and say a special prayer for the life inside me, the life who will now never be born. The chains! You will remember your promise, Sister, about the chains? They must take them off me before I die. These manacles must be struck off too, or else I will not be able to go to my rest. You will see to it, Sister? You will honour your promise to me?

Thank you Sister, and God bless you for your company these past few weeks. It has been a great comfort to me to be able to unburden myself of my life's story.

God bless you, Sister. God bless you.

CHAPTER TWENTY-EIGHT

Leah

The family tree had shaken me more than I could have thought. I was torn between confessing all to Matt, showing him Lisa's findings and begging him to take more care, or keeping quiet. It was all too ridiculously unbelievable that a four hundred year old curse was still picking off members of the Chevalier family, one by one, here in the twenty-first century. But the proof was all there. No Gabriel had ever lived without losing a son, and no Matthieu had ever lived without losing his life too young.

I reasoned that there was nothing I could do with Linda and Ian still in residence. Matt would think I'd finally given in to madness if I told him he was destined to die young; he was still trying to get his head around the fact we had a real ghost in the house. Linda had commented on me being a bit quiet but thankfully, nothing untoward happened at The Grange for the rest of the week and on Friday we waved Matt's parents off at the airport, breathing a sigh of relief at getting back to our normal routine. For Alice that meant school, and for me and Noah, more sorting through the endless boxes of junk left by Matt's great-uncle Pierre.

Debbie phoned with some disappointing news. While the digital scans of the mysterious letter found in the bible had come out well, the team at the archives was having trouble with the translation, and Lisa had emailed a copy over to a colleague in Paris in the hope that he might be able to help. The colleague was on annual leave, and not due back until the middle of next week, so the translation would have to wait. It was a frustrating delay to finding out why Jennet's name had been written in the letter. Who wrote it, to whom and why? I had a strong feeling it was the key to finding out what had happened to Jennet in this house so long ago, and why she was haunting us with such venom now.

Jayne called me every evening, so I could pass the phone to Alice so she could say goodnight. She hadn't tried to see the children again but I knew she had tried calling Matt regularly to arrange another visit. He refused to even pick up the phone to her, so I was surprised one night when I heard a car coming up the driveway. It wasn't Ben - we had just spoken a few minutes ago and arranged to meet the following day. We didn't really know anyone else in Jersey, not well enough to receive a surprise evening visit anyway. I waited to hear a knock at the kitchen door, but it didn't come, so I looked out of the window to see if I recognised the car. It was a sleek, silver Audi - Gabriel's' Audi. There was no one near the car, or on the lawn. If it was Jayne, surely she would have come in through the kitchen, but she couldn't be so stupid to turn up again with Gabriel. Matt was going to go mental.

They must have gone to the big front door, I thought. They probably saw the lights on and realised Matt was still working so they went that way to confront him. I crept to the connecting door, expecting to hear Matt and Jayne's raised voices, but what I heard chilled me to the bone.

'Put that down,' Matt said quietly. 'I don't know where she is but she's not here, so get out of my house.'

'It should never have been YOUR house!' Gabriel roared, his voice full of rage and spite. 'It should have been MINE! If it hadn't been for Pierre losing his marbles and changing his will, I would have inherited and I'd be sitting on a fortune by now.'

'But you didn't, I did,' Matt replied calmly. 'Now, I won't ask you again. Get out of my house.'

I pushed through the plastic sheeting. Matt might need reinforcements and I wanted the pleasure of seeing Gabriel thrown out of the place. They were both in the great hall, squaring up to each other. They barely noticed me as I crept into the room.

'Where is she?' Gabriel asked again. 'I got home tonight and she's packed her stuff and left. I should have known she'd come crawling back to you.'

'Matt's telling the truth,' I stepped forward. 'Jayne's not here. We haven't seen her.'

'Shut up, you fucking freak!' he spat at me. 'You know, I can't believe I once thought you would be my way in. I took one look at your disgusting face and thought 'Now there's a girl who'll be an easy lay, grateful for my attention and close to the family.' That's until I realised Jayne was ripe for the plucking.' He grinned viciously. 'Oh yes, once I saw how unhappy she was , how much she hated lugging around her porky body - well, let's just say I figured out real quickly which one of you two mutants was my ticket to finally owning this house. Her getting up the duff was just the icing on the cake! I'd have the house, and the next heir.'

Matt took a threatening step towards Gabriel, his fists up.

'You shut up about Jayne!' he warned. 'If she's left you it's because she's finally realised what a nasty piece of shit you are! I'm going nowhere, mate. This house will never be yours. It's mine, will always be mine and it will be Noah's after me.'

'We'll see about that.'

Gabriel reached to his right and picked up the long handled lump hammer that was resting against the wall under the window. He lifted it high, like a baseball bat, and ran at Matt. I screamed as he swung wildly and the heavy metal bar connected with the side of Matt's head with a sickening thump.

Jennet's Story

Jersey 1603

I had not thought to ever see you again, dear Sister. Not here, not in this great house, not in this room of dead, stinking meat.

Monsieur Chevalier has taken great pleasure in telling me that you are the reason I am here. That you went to him and told him of my baby, of how it is Matthieu's child. He did not believe you at first, Sister, for he could not fathom how his son would ever rut with the likes of me.

'Why couldn't he have practised on the kitchen maids, like other boys of his standing?' he mused. 'Instead, he dallies with a witch. The same witch who told me my son is now dead and lost in French waters.'

You went to him in secret, Sister, and asked if I might be spared my burning until after the birth of my baby. His grandson, you reminded him, and with all his sons gone, all dead within a year of each other, he had no heirs. I know about Guillaume of course, I told you of how I encountered his ghost in the forest after he was felled by his horse. I know about Matthieu. But I did not know that Jeanne, the middle brother, is also dead. A skirmish with thieves, a sword slash to his hand that went putrid and he was in his grave within the week.

Hey-la, so the great man has no heirs and now he wants the baby in my womb.

I must tell you, Sister, of what has occurred since my removal from the oubliette.

Once more I was taken through the cold stone hallways and into the same room where Gabriel Chevalier had beaten me senseless. I expected to be taken to the cart again, Sister, to be brought to the market square, only this time I would see the stake with its faggots of wood and barrels of pitch to make the flames burn hotter. Instead I stood in dumb confusion as Gabriel Chevalier eyed me from his leather chair again. He nodded to the guard and the remainder of my dress, by now just filthy, pitiful rags, was torn from my body so that I stood naked and shamed in front of him. He looked at my big belly, sticking out from my stick-like arms and legs, and grunted.

'Take her to Le Manoir,' he ordered, and I was dragged by my chains to the wagon waiting outside. This time I rode inside, on a bed of fresh straw, and I dared to begin to hope my sentence had been overturned and that I was going home.

The looks on the faces of the servants as I was brought into the man's great house told me I was not welcome here. They crossed themselves and gave each other grimaces of sympathy as they were instructed to take me to the laundry. The housekeeper ordered a bath, with warm water, Sister! And soap to wash the stink of prison from my body. My arms caused the laundrymaid to cluck and fuss, for they are both still mottled with red and purple lines and I cannot stop my fingers from curling up into claws. The bathwater was changed many times before it ran clear and then they started on the lice in my hair. They could have just hacked it all off, so matted and dirty it was, but they poured oil into it and worked it and worked it until the worst of the knots came free and a comb could be tugged through the length of it. It was hard, dirty work but they treated me fairly, if not kindly, in their brusque way.

Oh, the feeling of being clean again!

336

They gave me a dress to wear. It was grey and shapeless, soft with many washings. Patched so many times it was hard to see the dress it had once been, but it was clean. They fed me too, Sister. Soft gruel and a plain soup, as my teeth had loosened during my time in Mont Orgueil, and my stomach did rebel against it the first time, as it was not used to feeling full. Finally, washed and dressed and feeling respectable, I found my tongue and began to ask why I had been brought here and treated so well. Maybe, I thought, maybe Monsieur Chevalier knew about the baby and, after the tragic death of his youngest son, wanted to keep me close. He would care for me and treat me like a daughter, and Matthieu's son or daughter would be raised here, in this fine house with servants and pretty clothes and plenty of food and we would want for nothing.

I could laugh when I think of it now, Sister. After all I had endured, I still had faith in the man.

Instead they brought me here, to the hanging room. They hang meat here to cure and because it keeps longer in the cold. A straw pallet had been laid in this corner, and they bid me to lie on it. I did as they asked. I was so grateful for all they had done for me. I did not realise my arms would be chained to the wall above my head, while my legs would be fastened to the iron loops on the floor. I did not realise I was to be kept here, on this bed, in these chains, until my baby comes and then Monsieur Chevalier will take him away whilst I am sent back to the castle for the court to carry out my sentence of death.

And so I lie here, with my companions, the dead animals brought in here to bleed out. A maid, the most lowly one I should think, is sent to me hourly with a pot for me to piss in and a cup of water for me to drink. She feeds me, the same thin gruel, three times a day and patiently wipes my mouth when I dribble it back out through my hare-cursed lips. She is not allowed to speak to me and she dares not meet my gaze.

He sends a woman in to me, now and again. She presses hard upon my belly and pushes at the baby within.

'Not long now,' she tells him. 'The babe has moved down and lies in the right place. The woman is small though. She may not survive the birth.'

'It matters not,' he laughs. 'Tis the contents I need, not the vessel.'

Did you know, Sister? When you gave up my secret to Gabriel Chevalier, did you know what he would do to me? Did you know I would spend my last days chained to this wall in a cold, stone room, waiting to see if death will claim me by hell's flames, or if I will die from a gush of blood between my legs?

I curse him, Sister. I curse Gabriel Chevalier and all that follow him. May he know the loss of a son in every lifetime. May he sire a brood of sons and call them all Matthieu, and may they all die, one by one, by foul and painful means before they are old enough to sire sons themselves. May he never know another moment's peace and may his sleep be broken each night by the heavy weight of what he has done. May his line falter and shrivel up and die out. It will be of his own doing.

I curse them all, the Chevalier family. I curse them all! I curse them all! I curse them all!

CHAPTER TWENTY-NINE

Strangely, it put me in mind of summer days in the park; the crack of leather on willow as the local cricket club played out their weekend matches, or those old coconut shy games at the fair. It was an incongruous noise, a dull hollow thud, and Matt crumpled and fell without a sound. The head of the hammer had left a shallow crater, just behind his ear, and Matt's skull had shifted somehow; warped into something misshapen and misaligned. I knew he could not survive such a devastating injury. His legs jumped and twitched and his feet drummed against the wooden floorboards. He was making a low, moaning sound in his throat, the same single pitched tone over and over again, like when he played cars with Noah and pretended to be the rumbling engines.

Gabriel stood above him, his arms still holding the hammer and he raised it above his head again as if to deal Matt a second blow.

'Stop! You've killed him!' I wailed, scrambling over the pile of discarded cabinets, desperate to get to Matt.

'Call an ambulance, NOW!' I reached Matt and knelt beside him, knowing I shouldn't try to touch him but aching to cradle his poor, broken head in my lap.

'I don't think so,' Gabriel panted. 'I'm going to finish him off.' He twisted to look at me. 'Or maybe I should deal with you first.'

I recoiled from the maniacal glint in his bloodshot eyes. He was enjoying himself; he had relished killing Matt and now looked to kill me too. He took a step towards me and I looked frantically for a way to escape. There was only solid wall behind me, and Gabriel stood between me and the only door.

'Gabriel,' I begged. 'Please, just think about what you're doing. If we get help for Matt now, there's still a chance he might make it. I'll tell them it was an accident, say he tripped and fell. You don't even have to admit you were here!' I gabbled, inching backwards and feeling only the stone fireplace   at my back. Gabriel took another purposeful step towards me, raising the bloodstained hammer up in readiness for another strike.

'Nice try,' he grinned, his eyes wild. 'But I rather think he's done for. And you, well ... let's just say I'm doing you a favour. With a face like that you're better off dead.'

He swung the hammer high and I whimpered, ducking my head and squeezing my eyes shut. I waited interminably for the feel of cold metal hitting home, splitting skin, splintering bone and crushing the life from me.

But it didn't come.

Instead, I heard an unearthly screech and I opened my eyes to see Gabriel staring in horror at the wall above the fireplace behind us. He still had the hammer in his hands, raised in a frozen tableau. I looked up, sensing a shift in the already charged room.

Jennet was crouched above the fireplace lintel, clinging impossibly to the wall like a malevolent spider. She hissed and bared her teeth.

'Gabriel...' she drawled, hatred filling her face.

'What the fuck ...?' Gabriel looked at her in utter disbelief, then his face changed again and the rage I saw earlier returned. He bellowed in anger and ran at her, smashing the hammer into where she was squatting. Jennet vanished and the hammer head hit the granite wall and disappeared into a black void behind it. Gabriel tugged the weapon free in a fall of stones and dust, and whirled around, brandishing it like a sword.

'Where are you? Where are you, you loathsome bitch? Come out! Come out and let me send you to hell where you belong!'

He stood in a fighter's stance, his face screwed up with fear and fury. He was sweating profusely and kept having to toss his hair out of his eyes as the sweat dripped down and momentarily blinded him. He lunged this way and that, hammer ready to strike, but his enemy remained invisible. Gabriel's breathing gradually slowed as he scanned all four corners of the room. There was no sign of Jennet and he physically relaxed, turning back to me with a jaunty step.

'Looks like I got that witch good,' he bragged. 'Now, your turn.'

He screamed as three vertical slashes opened up his face, one directly across his right eye, and he clutched at it with his free hand to stem the flow of blood already streaming down his cheek.

'Ah, fuck! She got my eye! The bitch got my fucking eye!'

He moved his hand back to the handle of the hammer and I saw that his eye was curiously flattened. His eyeball was pierced and it leaked its gelatinous contents like a punctured grape. Jennet was back in her spot above the fireplace wall and she laughed delightedly at her handiwork. Her hands were twisted into claws and her black fingernails curved wickedly sharp, the right hand stained with Gabriel's blood. He brought the hammer up again to deliver the fatal blow to her and only succeeded in hitting the wall again. Bits of plaster and shards of granite rained down on Matt and me. Jennet flew across the room and roosted on the frame above the door. She swiped her hand across, almost lazily, and more gashes appeared on Gabriel, this time across his stomach. His designer shirt bloomed bright blossoms of blood.

A small, anxious face peeked around the doorway, underneath Jennet.

'Alice! Alice, run, sweetheart, RUN!' I yelled at her.

Alice looked fearfully at the blood-soaked Gabriel, and then beyond him, to where her father lay in a motionless heap.

'Daddy!' she screamed. 'Daddy, Daddy!'

Gabriel, who had been looking down at the ripped skin of his belly, brought his head up sharply and lost interest in

Jennet, instead focusing his deranged features on Alice's terrified stare. He snarled, and hefted the hammer high.

'Alice, RUN!' I yelled again. 'GO!'

'Alice...' The word was a mere whisper next to me. Matt's lips moved almost soundlessly but he mouthed Alice's name again. 'Alice ...'

With the very last of his strength, Matt stretched out his arm slowly. He was shaking violently, but that familiar look of stubborn determination I loved so well was etched on his face. With a trembling hand he clutched at Gabriel's ankle and clung on as tightly as he could. As Gabriel raised his hands and coiled his body to run at Alice, Matt's grip on his leg forced him off balance and the hammer flew backwards into the wall and stuck fast. Without the counterweight of the heavy metal hammer head, Gabriel fell forward, arms spiralling almost comically. He took one faltering step, then another, but couldn't regain his control and his own body weight propelled him forward. He crashed heavily into the stack of glass-shelved cabinets, turning slightly at the last second so that he lay on his side amongst the splintered wood and smashed glass panels.

I watched, holding my breath, expecting to see him push himself up and go after Alice again, but he lay still. I crawled slowly on my hands and knees towards him warily. A pool of blood crept towards me and met me halfway. So much blood, a thick, viscous tidal wave of blood. Gabriel had landed on top of the razor-sharp glass shelving units and they had sliced into his body like a hot knife through butter. One had cut into his thigh, another through his side just above his hip bone, and the last - the last and most devastating - had entered his neck, just underneath his chin, and guillotined his head from his body. Gabriel's face held a look of surprise and indignation, as if he was furious to find that his head was a good foot away from the rest of him. Chop, chop, chop off your head, I thought darkly.

Jennet was still perched above the door. She looked at the fallen men with grim satisfaction. Like a big black crow, she dived forward and flew across to the fireplace, evaporating into the granite blocks of the wall and leaving no trace of her. The silence was deep and overwhelming.

I ached all over but forced myself to stand and shuffle over the sea of broken glass and blood toward the door. I needed to find Alice. In the confusion, she had finally heard my pleas to run and bolted down the hallway to hide in my room.

'Alice? It's me, Leah. It's Aunty Rabbit.' I limped to my bed. I could hear her noisy sobs coming from underneath. 'You're safe now, little bunny. It's all right, you're safe.' I crouched down painfully and peeked under my bed. Alice was curled into a ball and I held my hand out to her. She crawled out and onto my lap and we held each other, crying and rocking gently.

I breathed a sigh of relief at the distant wail of sirens. Alice, clever little Alice, had found my phone and pushed and swiped at it randomly until she managed to redial the last called number. Ben had answered and, upon hearing Alice's terrified cries, had promptly hung up and called the police. He arrived less than five minutes after they did.

Three police cars and two ambulances crowded the driveway, their blue lights flashing. Alice, Noah and I were led out to a waiting car and wrapped in warm blankets. The house was now a murder scene and we would not be allowed back in until the scene of crime officers, or SOCO's, had done their job. Matt was still clinging on to life and one of the ambulances whisked him away, but from the looks exchanged between the paramedics, I knew that his injuries were catastrophic and it would only be a matter of time before he gave up his fight for life.

The duty coroner was called out to certify Gabriel's death and the police photographers captured every splash of blood, and every broken sheet of glass. We sat in the back of the squad car until both children fell asleep, Ben keeping a silent vigil beside us. A constable was dispatched to find me a hot drink and he kindly kept me informed of the progress of the SOCO team.

'Looks like we'll have to call the coroner back,' he said cheerfully, handing me a Styrofoam cup full of tea. 'That won't make him happy.'

'Why? I thought he was finished doing what he needed to do.'

'Found another body, haven't they?' he informed me. 'The SOCO's were moving the lump hammer from above the fireplace; it's the weapon used to assault Mr Cooper so they were taking it down for bagging. They pulled it out, and look!' He showed me the screen of his phone. I stared at the photo on the screen, barely able to believe what I was looking at. The hammer had caused a hole in the wall about six inches wide. When the officer in charge of bagging it for evidence had pulled the head free, it had pulled out a large chunk of granite along with it.

A delicate skeletal hand protruded from the hole and rested languidly in mid-air, the dull metal manacle around its wrist just visible.

CHAPTER THIRTY

Translation of the letter found in the 1580 Geneva Bible, identified as belonging to the Chevalier family, and dated November 1603 - Archive document No. - 11/02659/14
Language - Old French/Latin

'... It is my fervent prayer that this letter finds its way into sympathetic hands and the name of Jennet Pyke is not lost...(illegible)... forgive me my most divine Father for I have committed a grievous sin and I fear I am guilty of such an error of judgement that I cannot bear the consequences of mine own actions. ...(illegible)... in my holy work of counselling those under sentence of death and hearing their confessions, I encountered a convicted witch by the name of Jennet Pyke. Her tale, as told to me by her, and shall remain in my confidence... (illegible)... such a tale of a woeful life, more sinned against than sinner... (illegible)... is my responsibility and duty to think first of the unborn child, a most innocent soul despite the nature of its parentage.

Forgive me Lord, for I am a meddling old fool.

I did make the witch, Jennet Pyke, a solemn promise that I would see her chains struck off as she went to her death, as she was of the belief that the iron would hold her immortal soul to this earthly realm and she would not be granted her eternal rest in the house of our Lord Jesus Christ... (illegible)...

When she did confess to me of her condition and of the man who had fathered the babe, I at once went to the named father's own sire and informed him of her dire circumstances. The man had lost all of his sons in the year previous, the youngest most recently and in a most suspicious state of affairs...(illegible)... came to him that, if the unborn child was a boy, he would be the only blood relation for the continuance of his great family's line.

I must confess that I was of the thinking that I could both provide Monsieur Chevalier with a much-wanted heir and give Jennet some comfort in her last days. The sin of pride, I know, thinking I could interfere and earn the gratitude of Lord Chevalier and have the witch think of me kindly as her harsh life was cushioned with easements, food and warmth all the while she waited for the birth. Even as she knew she must give her son up, and she must be returned to the castle to await her legal and just sentence.

I did not know he would treat her with such cruelty.

....(illegible)... was shocked and sickened upon entering that dank room with its stench of old blood and the dead eyes of the game meat following me. Jennet was laid on a pallet in the far corner, her hands chained fast to the wall above her head so that she could not rest her arms by her sides, which I believe to be a most painful position to lay in day and night.

Similarly, her ankles were fixed to a loop in the flags on the floor, with only a short length of chain between them, and then only enough for her to lift her haunches so as the servant could slide in the pot beneath her for her to relieve herself. She was unable to turn over on the pallet and did suffer the most horrendous running sores on her back and legs...(illegible)... near her time, her face and extremities did swell so, she was quite unrecognisable as the pitifully thin wraith I had encountered in the oubliette of Mont Orgueil.

When she did first see me she gave me such a look of betrayal it was all I could do not to turn and flee...(illegible)... bid sit next to her and read to her from the great bible belonging to the Chevalier family, the same one I now hide this letter in. She ranted and raved. I believe her swelling sickness moved into her brain and she was quite mad in the head by the time she went into labour. ...(illegible)... did curse the Chevalier family and all its descendants with much anger.

A woman from the village was summoned as Jennet sweated and heaved on the straw bed. I went out and pleaded with Monsieur Chevalier for her shackles to be removed while she laboured, but he was steadfast in his refusal. Her toil went on for many hours.....(Illegible)... at one point did consider cutting the babe from her belly for, as Monsieur Chevalier did say, Jennet was condemned to die and whether she died by rope, by fire or travail in childbirth, it did not matter to him.

At last the boy was pulled from her body, thin and small, but alive and with no sign of the infliction that had marked his poor mother. The midwife wrapped him in cloth and sent him up to a chamber where a wet-nurse awaited him. His mother did not even get to see him...(illegible)... white with loss of blood but of sufficient strength to call out for her child. I bid her to lay still, that her boy was safe and well and would have every richness in life, as the heir of a great lord with lands and coin aplenty.

...(illegible)...room was quiet with just Jennet and myself in residence when she began to shift upon the bed in great pain again. The midwife did not return to see to the delivery of the afterbirth and, with my healing experience in the nunnery, it fell to me to see Jennet be made comfortable and clean. I bent over her on the bed and lifted her skirts to attend to her when, Lord God strengthen me, another baby

was in the course of being born! *The head was crowning and with a gentle tug from me, a second babe slipped from her womb and lay silent on the straw. It was a little girl, Jennet. You had a beautiful, little girl - perfect in every way. Except that she did not live to draw breath but instead lay like a sleeping angel, her cherubic face forever known only to our Lord.*

'Sister,' Jennet called to me quietly. 'Sister, where is my baby?' ...(illegible)...

I lay the still bundle on her chest but she could not lower her arms to cradle it. I wept bitter tears at the howl of grief and rage that came from inside Jennet's very soul. I wrapped the babe in the old sheets the servants had provided in readiness for the birth, and tucked it into Jennet's side and she quietened. She slept, and after a while, she stirred again.

'Sister, can you see him?' she whispered. 'There is a fine young man, come here to me.'
... (illegible)... looked around the small storeroom but I could only see the hanging carcasses of the butchered animals.
'He is such a handsome boy,' she said in wonder. 'So kind and loving.'
'Is it Matthieu, child?' I asked of her, thinking in her delirium she had brought her lover back to her.
'No,' she breathed. 'No, tis my brother, my twin. Oh, look upon his face, Sister, and declare you have never seen such a handsome man in all your time.'

She was staring at the corner in rapture. I looked but there was nothing there.

'He has come for me. My twin, my brother. He has so much love for me and he will take me from this wretched place and we shall be together forever. We will dance

among the trees and dine from golden platters, and I shall never be alone again. He does not mind my face, he looks upon it with such tender love.' Jennet strained against her shackles. 'Sister, I am going now. He is waiting for me. Remember your promise, Sister, remember.'

And Jennet did lay down again peacefully and died.

I was forced to inform Monsieur Chevalier of Jennet's death, and of the second babe, born dead. He grunted and told me it had saved the parish the job of putting her to death. He ordered two manservants into the hanging room to remove her and the unfortunate baby. They snipped a lock of hair from her head before rolling her hastily in the soiled bedsheets...(illegible)...

...did ask why, they informed me of the witch bottle the master had employed the midwife to make, a precaution against Jennet the witch coming back from the grave to persecute the family. ...(illegible)... if he would see her decently buried. I did request he have her chains removed, as it was her last dying wish, but he laughed without mirth and said he would dispose of her as befitted a convicted witch and her dead brat.

I knew then that I had failed her.

I was not present when she was taken from the house and I could not be sure if she was laid to rest ...(illegible)... without the shackles of this life weighing her down.

I repeat my hope that this letter be found and that Jennet Pyke be remembered for what she truly was, a young girl, abandoned at a tender age, subject to suspicion and ill-use her whole life and who met her untimely end at the unyielding cruelty of a brutal and callous man.

May God have mercy on her soul, and may He grant me forgiveness for my part in this, the story of the hare-witch.

I remain , sirs, your most devoted servant.

Sister Marie-Therése de la Sacre Cœur

CHAPTER THIRTY-ONE

I wept when I read the translation of the letter. All the pent up emotions and horror of the previous months were finally released in a torrent of tears as we read Sister Marie-Thérèse's account of Jennet's final hours.

She had twins,' Debbie said sadly. 'That's why the family line continued. The baby boy was Edouard.'

The days following the deaths of Matt and Gabriel were a blur of bland hotel rooms and police interview suites, as our statements were taken and sense was made of what had occurred on that fateful night. The Grange was still off limits, but none of us wanted to return there anyway, so I took up Debbie's kind offer of a spare room while we waited for the Jersey police to conclude the case.

The coroner had declared the bones found behind the wall above the fireplace as "bones of antiquity" and had removed them, manacles and all, to the mortuary at the hospital where they awaited examination by a local archaeologist. The space inside the chimney breast had been cleverly hollowed out and then covered over by thin veneers of granite; so carefully done that it was impossible to tell the false blocks from the solid ones. Jennet's remains had been crammed inside a gap the size of a narrow chest, and then bricked up again so as to stay hidden for more than four hundred years. She had been bent over at the middle, her chains still secured around her wrists and ankles. The fragile and badly decomposed bones of a new-born infant had also been found with her, tucked into the corner at her feet.

Matt had lost his brave battle for life and had passed away in the early hours of the following morning. Gabriel was declared dead at the scene, obviously.

Jayne, the reason for the fight between the two men in the first place, had checked into a B&B that night, as it later turned out. After seriously regretting her involvement with Gabriel, she had moved out of his house, wanting only a quiet space on her own for a few days to reflect on what she was going to do.

'It's all my fault,' she wept, burying her face in my shoulder. 'If only Gabe hadn't rushed things. He was so thrilled about the baby, Leah. He lost a son last year with his ex-girlfriend. He was only a few months old – cot death – and Gabe was so cut up about it. But I had so many doubts, I knew Gabe wasn't long-term partner material but the baby made me make up my mind. If I hadn't left Gabriel he wouldn't have gone looking for Matt, and Matt would be still alive.

'Shhhhh, you couldn't have known,' I soothed her. So, Gabriel had known the painful loss of a son after all. The curse had come for him too. 'I think Gabriel would have attacked Matt at some point anyway. It was all to do with the line of inheritance of the house, and not really about you at all.'

'That BLOODY house!' Jayne angrily wiped the tears away from her face.

We were invited to see Jennet's skeleton, laid out on the steel gurney as the archaeologist went about her investigations. I was struck by how tiny she really was, and how the wide cuffs of the iron manacles swamped her bones. Because of where she was hidden above the fireplace, her body was partially mummified due to the dry conditions. Fine strands of black hair still clung to her skull, and strips of leathery skin stretched over her bones.

'She was quite malnourished in childhood, we can reasonably assume,' said Georgia, the archaeologist. Georgia was a bundle of energy. Small-framed herself, with a tumble of dark hair, she looked very much like Jennet might have done had she been born into modern times. I couldn't help wondering that if Jennet had been born perfect, without a cleft lip, she might have had a normal life. She would have grown up as part of a community, got married to a man who loved her, and had a brood of children, instead of being an outcast, unwanted girl who was reviled and despised as a witch.

'We've sent away a sample of bone for carbon dating, but from what you've told me and from the records you've shown me, we can safely say that these are definitely from the early seventeenth century.'

When I first met Georgia, she sat me down and asked me to tell her the entire story, from the very beginning, and not to leave anything out. To her credit, she didn't laugh or scoff at me at any point, interrupting only to clarify a name or date.

'What will happen to her?' I asked. 'When you've finished with her, I mean.'

'Well, usually she would be passed on to the relevant authorities and probably cremated. Sometimes, the owners of the property where the bones were found can petition to have the remains released to them, especially if they can prove a family connection.'

'We do have a family connection,' I promised. 'We want to give her a decent burial, Jennet and her baby, but there's one more thing we need to do...'

Georgia waited expectantly.

'Can you please take those damn chains off her?'

The story of the double murder and the body in the fireplace made national news, and The Grange became a magnet for curious onlookers and ghouls wanting to see where a man had been decapitated and where a real skeleton in chains had been discovered. Jayne refused to set foot in the place ever again. She moved out of the police house she had been allocated and into a rented apartment with the children. As she was still Matt's next of kin, the money he had made from selling the house in London was transferred to her, along with a small life insurance pay-out. They had taken the policy out when they were granted the mortgage for the London house, and then promptly forgot about it. The premiums had been paid by direct debit from Matt's account and so the policy was still valid at the time of his death.

Jayne planned to leave Jersey as soon as possible, and was talking about buying a small place near Matt's parents so they could see the children often. Gabriel's parents had offered to adopt Jayne's baby when it was born, but Jayne was adamant he or she was welcome in their little family.

'Promise me you won't name it Matthieu or Gabriel,' I begged her, seeing how she stroked her burgeoning bump with such love.

'I won't, I promise,' she assured me. 'I'm thinking Lilly for a girl, or Levi if it's a boy. I'm going to put The Grange into a trust for Noah, for when he's old enough,' she decided. 'Gabriel's father will oversee the administration until Noah reaches twenty-five, then it's up to Noah to decide what he wants to do with the place.'

Linda and Ian flew back to Jersey to take Matt's body back to the small Devon town he'd grown up in. They wanted him to be buried somewhere he'd been happy, and far away from the Chevalier family plot in the Grouville churchyard, where Gabriel had been laid to rest.

'I thought I'd kept him safe,' Linda wept mournfully. 'I thought by taking him away from Jersey as a baby, the curse couldn't reach him.'

Jayne did not go to either funeral.

An amateur metal detectorist, making the most of the opportunity of the empty house, unearthed a battered, silver cup from the ground inside the old piggeries, exactly where I had seen Alice digging that day. It was identified from church records as being the silver chalice stolen from Jean Pinel, the rector of the church, back in 1603. Most of the precious stones had been lost or levered off but the engraved rim was still intact. No one can say for sure whether this was the item of church property that Jennet had been accused of stealing, but the dates fit, and there seems no other explanation for how the chalice got there. Both the cup, and the iron manacles found on Jennet's skeleton are now on display at the Jersey Museum.

'But why now?' I asked Debbie. We were negotiating the steep cliff path at Noirmont Point on a cold, windy day and both looking forward to meeting Ben and Gracie at the Portelet Inn for Sunday lunch later. 'Why did it all happen now, after so many years?'

'My guess is that everything fell into place,' she said. 'Think about it, both a Matthew, albeit spelt differently, and a Gabriel Chevalier in the house at the same time; there was you, with your face similar to hers; a baby in the house too - it all mirrored what had happened all those years ago. And then there was the witch bottle. It wasn't until Alice smashed it that you actually began to see Jennet.'

'The bottle was hidden so close to her, in the fireplace,' I remembered. 'But it was just an old bottle full of pins and hair and old wine. It wasn't magic, it couldn't have kept her imprisoned.'

'They were a superstitious lot in those days,' Debbie reminded me. 'What people believe in can be a very powerful thing, and Jennet believed that the bottle was a spell to keep her from harming the family.'

'Alice was the first one to see her, in the garden. Do you think that's because Alice has Chevalier blood? She's a direct descendent of Jennet's son, when you trace back through the family tree.'

'Alice was the catalyst, I believe,' said Debbie. 'She was like a doorway into the house. Jennet attached herself to Alice, manipulated Alice into doing things she wouldn't normally do or say.'

'She doesn't remember any of it, Alice. Just sits and draws horrible pictures of men with smashed heads or with their heads chopped off,' I confided. 'Sometimes she'll look up from her picture with such a confused look on her face and ask why we don't live in London anymore. Jayne's got her going to a child therapist though.'

'She's young, she'll be fine. Leaving Jersey is probably the best thing for her.'

We interred Jennet's remains, and the remains of her baby girl with her, near the tiny fisherman's chapel in the larger, more modern graveyard down the road from the church of Grouville. It was a sunny place, and quiet, and I hoped Jennet would finally find some peace. Everyone who had been involved in the investigations turned up to pay their respects; Lisa, Georgia, the other archive staff. We lowered Jennet and her baby girl into their final resting place, and were glad that she would be remembered.

We tried not to notice when Alice waved to the empty air across the grave. Nor did we comment when Noah shouted 'Da-da!' and tried to run towards the gates, to where there was no one standing. In the car on the way back to the apartment, we passed the driveway to The Grange and Alice spun around in her car seat.

'Look!' Alice cried. 'Look, it's Jenny! And she's dancing!'

Jayne pursed her lips and said nothing. I did not admit to seeing the young, slim figure twirling and skipping, her arms and legs free at last from their iron bindings, as she whirled among the trees.

CHAPTER THIRTY-TWO

I'm enjoying my life now. Debbie and I rub along together well enough, although Ben teases me about getting fat on all her good cooking. I have found a job with a small marketing company, only part time for the time being, and I spend my days there designing flyers and magazine advertisements for real estate agents. It's not much but the staff are great, and they don't mind that my face is a little bit different.

Mr Harlow has arranged for the first of my surgeries to go ahead in a few weeks' time. Ben and Gracie are flying to London with me, much to Gracie's delight at going on an airplane for the first time. They will do the tourist thing, go to London Zoo and on the London Eye, while I'm in theatre, and then they'll be my dedicated visit team, along with my mother, while I recuperate.

Ben and I visited The Grange for the last time, collecting the last few bits of my belongings. I walked through the empty rooms, feeling the stillness of the house, as if it too was at peace.

'Do you think it's really over?' I asked Ben, locking the heavy wooden door.

'Yeah, I think it is,' he smiled, and took my hand.

As we drove away down the driveway, I made the mistake of looking back. Matt's pale, sad face stared at me from the window in the great hall. He raised his hand in a farewell salute, and then the sunlight flashed on the glass and he was gone.

THE END

Acknowledgements

Huge thanks go to everyone who loved my first spooky novel, *The Crowlands*, and left such amazing reviews on Amazon and Goodreads. The encouragement of complete strangers has inspired me to keep on writing ghost stories.

Thanks to Debbie, and Harry the cat of course, for allowing me to pinch pieces of her life, making her one of the most lovable characters in this book. Thanks also to Georgia, for her unwavering support. Georgia pops up in this story too, and is exactly as I've described her.

Thank you to my family, some of whom I've borrowed names from for various characters. My 92-year-old Grandad is one of my biggest fans and I hope he enjoys *Hare-Cursed* as much as he did my other books.

Thank you to Deborah Shead, for the cover design.

Finally, thank you to Ant, for letting me use the VW campervan as a mobile office, for bringing me endless cups of tea and for cajoling me to take regular breaks for windy walks along St Catherine's breakwater. And for suggesting I use the Scooby-Doo ending – *"I would have gotten away with it if it weren't for you meddling kids!"* Sorry, love, but it didn't quite work for this one!

Dear Reader,

Thank you for reading *Hare-Cursed*! I would love to know what you thought of it so, if you have a spare minute, please post a review on any of the following sites:

- Amazon.co.uk
- Amazon.com
- Amazon.com.au
- Goodreads

Reviews help us budding authors tremendously. Not only do they help us find out where we could improve in our writing, but they highlight our work to other readers looking for their next great read.

For a sneak preview at what I'm writing next, follow me on Instagram -   @tmcreedy.author

Best wishes,
T M Creedy

Printed in Great Britain
by Amazon

43178638R00213